# The Memory Palace
# Of
# Giuseppe Arcimboldo

## by
## Bruce Killingsworth

2016

killingsworthbruce@gmail.com

*This book is dedicated to:*

*Samantha Steele,*

*Marco Beasley,*

*Monserrat Figueras,*

*and, of course, Giuseppe Arcimboldo*

Illustrations courtesy of: THE ATHENAEUM

# The Memory Palace Of Giuseppe Arcimboldo

-Night-

The painter is sitting in a room that has grown too dark and too cold to be comfortable. It is too dark to see colors properly, the painting on the large easel next to him, lit by a number of flickering candle ends stuck to the easel's frame, appears to be done in murky shades of grey and brown. The sputtering and sighing chunks of oak in the dying fire do very little to illuminate the sheets of drawings scattered on the floor at his feet, and even less to warm the drafty tower chamber. The air in the room is heavy and acrid with the smell of wood smoke, naphtha and walnut oil. A rat sweeps several day's worth of spider webs from the dark corners of the room, making soft swishing and scratching sounds. It pauses to clean its whiskers and study the papers spread on the floor. The rat sees a small fragment of cake resting on one of the drawings, a sketch of a lion being leashed and led away by a group of naked children. After much deliberation and several false starts, the rat darts forward into the weak light and claims its prize. In recompense, before it scurries back into the shadows, it leaves a tiny black grain of excrement on the drawing. Yet the painter continues to sit motionless, staring at the papers at his feet, or beyond them, his gaze focused on something infinitely further away, further than this room in this cold castle in Prague, further than this January in the year of Our Lord 1587, further than the confines of his own experience. The painter ponders the Universe, the World, the Work of the Creator, the never to be underestimated hubris of Mankind.

Giuseppe Arcimboldo is a tall, thin, and distinguished looking man of sixty who is usually quite lively, in spite of the advancing aches in his bones and joints, phlegmatic humors, and irritatingly unreliable bladder. These frigid Czech winters have become increasingly uncomfortable for him, and he has often begged the Emperor to allow him to permanently return to his native Milan. The painter and inventor has astonished his peers with a new fusion of art and philosophy. His paintings, done in a new and provocative manner, are famous, and his work is endlessly discussed and debated in every Court in Europe among the cultured elite, those educated in the new Humanist values. His most popular pictures are bizarre, elaborate, and unique. They're so unique that the artist has been asked to make multiple copies of his masterpieces to be distributed as highly valuable and sophisticated gifts from the Emperor to other heads of state.
Arcimboldo is widely known as a man of rare intelligence and vision, in this castle and in Prague he

is popular and well respected. His official title is Master of Court Festivals and Masquerades, or simply Master of Entertainments, and this carries with it a status as high as a counselor of state. In fact, since Arcimboldo is supremely skillful and knowledgeable in those things most important to the Emperor, his access to Rudolf II and his influence at Court is *higher* than any counselor; he is one of the Emperor's closest confidantes.

Rudolf II, Emperor of the Holy Roman Empire, is the greatest collector and patron of the arts in Europe; Rudolf's Court is crowded with artists and craftsmen of all kinds, jostling for the Emperor's attention, but Arcimboldo has been preeminent for many years. Courtiers and aristocrats alike admire the Italian's wide learning, refined culture, and polished, courtly manners. Arcimboldo has a modest and engaging personality. He is self-taught and widely read in the latest Humanist philosophy, and it's reflected in how he presents himself: he can quote and refer to authors and great thinkers both antique and modern, his sentences tumble fluidly from one language to another, spontaneously and instinctively he chooses the most elegant sounding phrases, the perfect idiom, metaphor, or verbal accent to accompany his thought. His speech is lively and musical without being foolish, and, while the Italian's words race along, his large and expressive blue eyes add a separate commentary, sparkling with excitement, tensing with irony, widening with awe, darting about as though they seek ideas flying around in the air. He's a man who embodies what is known as the 'New Knowledge'.

It would be a rare thing for the inhabitants of this castle in Prague to see Arcimboldo as he is now, eyes unfocused and staring in blank introspection, his hands and body immobile, his mouth tightly closed.

But this moment, this evening, as he sits here alone in his workroom, he contemplates tomorrow's extraordinary experiment – a bold attempt to penetrate the barrier between the realm of the World and the realm of Heaven. Arcimboldo is frightened. He is excited. He is frozen with uncertainty. He is on the brink of an event that will change his life.

Certainly he has never had to test his physical courage to this degree before, he has been an artist and courtier in exclusive service to the Emperor; he has never killed a man, never been a soldier or swaggering bully, never an adventurer, never a jealous and enraged lover. In his younger days he never had occasion to use sword or dagger, his conflicts were intellectual disputes, his weapons were words, images, ideas. As a member of the Emperor's household, Arcimboldo has been as secure as a mortal man can be from the dangers of plague and riot – a constant threat in the crowded, tumultuous, ever unpredictable streets of Prague. However, on this particular evening, he assesses his life and whether he is prepared to leave it.

He admits to himself that he is *hesitatingly* willing to participate in an unprecedented experiment in alchemy, an attempt to cross the line of safety between the world of Man and the divine realm of the Creator, a dangerous transgression. Arcimboldo is fearful that he is actually in peril of losing his life, but his concern runs deeper than for his physical welfare, he fears for his eternal soul. He fears that his deep love of knowledge and his deep love of God will not be sufficient to excuse him and protect him in the face of his transgression. And, he is frightened not just for his own body and soul, but for that of his patron and friend, Rudolf II Habsburg, King of Bohemia and Hungary, Archduke of Austria, Emperor of the Holy Roman Empire.

Arcimboldo is twenty-five years older than Rudolf, and he is well aware that Rudolf's desire to surpass his uncle, the King of Spain, is monumental, passionate, and dangerously delusional; nevertheless, the artist shares the Emperor's passion to go beyond the natural limitations of human experience and knowledge. Arcimboldo is one of very few people who can understand Rudolf's most private inner philosophy and motivation. The Emperor believes that he is *uomo universalis*, unique among men, and uniquely placed by circumstance and God's will to look behind the veil of Nature's most powerful and secret mysteries. In addition to being eminently well educated, serious, observant, and thoughtful, Rudolf is jealous and envious by nature; he learned this in his youth from his fanatically self-righteous relatives in Madrid, where he was raised, taught, and molded to be a senior member of the most Christian, civilized, and superior family on Earth; he has been taught how to be a Habsburg.

How can Rudolf present himself as superior to the World? The pressures of being a Habsburg are daunting. The citizens of his Empire, the World, and his Habsburg relatives all have expectations; how can he impress and outdo this frighteningly critical audience? For a start, how can Rudolf compete with the wealth flowing into Spain? The gold and silver of the New World are being soaked up by Spain as quickly as her ships can bring it east, wealth that allows those that rule to pursue their most extravagant desires and the most sanctimonious hypocrisies. Besides allowing them to control millions of people with their armies and navies, the wealth of the New World allows Spanish royalty to commission the production of luxury goods of unparalleled complexity, craftsmanship, and beauty.

Ruling distant territories and commanding vast fleets of ships isn't the kind of power that Rudolf is passionate about, he does not seek to dominate, he is not a conqueror, a killer and enslaver of men. It's the luxury goods that Rudolf's after; beautiful and original objects made from other beautiful and original objects, displayed within a beautiful and original space. The Emperor employs agents throughout Europe with lists of particular artists, works, and genres, if he can afford the purchase, the precious object is brought to Hradcany Castle in Prague.

Most often, the Emperor prefers to have his art crafted under his eyes, he is fascinated by the tools used by painters, sculptors, goldsmiths, gem cutters, engravers, clockmakers, bookmakers, taxidermists, and without a doubt – alchemists. He wants to know the nuances of the crafting, and he needs to know what philosophical world view dominates the intellect of the craftsman and the design of the crafted object. He studies the symbolic powers of the completed object, and how its energy and symbolic messages harmonize with other objects in the Natural World. The Emperor will sit in front of a favorite object or painting for half a day without speaking or moving, particularly if the object or painting holds detailed and realistic images, or unique and unnatural characteristics.

This goal of understanding the complex and detailed messages contained in the Natural World, God's message to Man, is the most worthwhile and rewarding ambition a Prince or a man may have (and in this the artist is in wholehearted agreement with his patron). Three Holy Roman Emperors in succession have employed Giuseppe Arcimboldo over the past twenty-four years, all the time with the same objectives: to discover new powers and virtues at the crossroads of science and art, and to glorify the House of Habsburg.

Arcimboldo's art and invention allows the House of Habsburg to communicate to the World.

What exactly is the private dream shared by artist and Emperor alike? Being able to understand the complexity of cause and effect, and the true relationships of all things in the Natural World, the Stars and Heavens. This knowledge would settle the chaotic debate and discord among Religions, it would bring peace and prosperity to the World, and fame and glory for all time to the House of Habsburg.

In pursuit of fame and glory, Rudolf seeks to discover the secrets behind the Natural World by means of science, magic, or accident – he is not particular. Successfully decoding these secrets will undoubtedly allow him access to unimaginably vast resources of wealth and power. Thusly, Rudolf looks for wisdom in the most arcane places, and, as one might say, to leave no stone unturned, he has engaged the services of the English alchemists, Doctor John Dee and Edward Kelly. These two very peculiar men are prepared to lead the Emperor into the presence of the Divine Light.

Arcimboldo and Emperor Rudolf will engage in tomorrow's experiment accompanied by a small group of like-minded philosophers, artists, and noblemen who have been sworn to secrecy. They have been planning and working toward this goal for over a year. However, they have had to be very careful to keep their intent a secret.

The city of Prague, and especially Hradcany precinct around the castle, is infested with spies and informers. Catholic and Protestant factions coexist in a very uneasy balance, maneuvering against each other, and misleading Rudolf as often as possible. There are foreign spies working for Rudolf's uncle, the King of

Spain. Naturally, more spies serve the Pope and his Prague Nuncio, Germanico Malaspina. The Venetians have spies. There's concern that fanatical French Catholics, known as the Holy League, have spies in Prague. Certainly, there is no doubt that the Sultan of the Ottoman Empire has informers infiltrated throughout the Empire. Informers are even employed by Rudolf's mother, Maria, who, disgusted with anti-Catholic sentiment in Vienna and Prague, and disappointed with Rudolf's tepid support of Counter-Reformation initiatives, stormed off to Madrid in 1581, and has not returned since. And if all these spies and informers were to be combined and totaled, that figure would be eclipsed by the number employed by Rudolf himself. Keeping a secret in the capital city of the Holy Roman Empire is a difficult affair. And yet, in a city teeming with alchemists, a city at war with the Turk, a city whose religious factions are at war with each other, secrets are as common as sin. Should word of the Emperor's experiment become public knowledge, disaster will follow. Some of those invited to participate in tomorrow's affair are, it must be admitted, beyond the pale, notorious; and the experiment itself would be viewed by the Church and citizenry with much disfavor.

As the room grows darker around him, the painter sits without moving, with eyes closed, deeply in thought. This experiment will be the ultimate test of his own personal philosophy, a culmination to his years of studying the historic and scientific power of art and visual symbols. He believes what has been explained to him by other artists and men of learning, that there is a power to art beyond beauty and realism; images convey Symbols to the Mind, those Symbols harmonize and create thought. Arcimboldo explores the juxtaposition of images and Symbols. He aims to open up new directions of thought in a human mind (the Emperor's mind) by presenting imaginative groupings of objects found in the Natural World. His paintings show unexpected, tricky, virtually impossible groupings, presenting hitherto unseen combinations of visual Symbols, stimulating hitherto unknown thoughts in the Mind.

The most enlightened and divinely inspired thinkers of the last hundred years, Leonardo da Vinci, Nicholas Copernicus, Paracelsus, Marsilio Ficino, and many others, have been graced and rewarded with knowledge; these men have begun to understand the language of Symbols, known so well to the ancients but forgotten for many generations in Europe. Symbols, whether mathematical, artistic, architectural, or philosophical, are helping thinkers understand the great complexity of the World we live in.

Like many others, Arcimboldo's imagination has been fired by the promise of what the philosopher, Giordano Bruno, describes in his book, the *Cena*, *'behold now, standing before you, the man who has pierced the air and penetrated the sky, wended his way among the stars and overpassed the margins of the World. By the light of sense and reason, with the key of most diligent enquiry, he has thrown wide those doors of truth which it is within our power to open and stripped the veils and coverings from the face of Nature. He has given eyes to blind moles, and illuminated those who could not see their own image in the innumerable mirrors of reality which surround them on every side'.*

Yet at this moment, on the very brink of possible revelation, Arcimboldo hesitates, he doubts, he is troubled and afraid. The artist wonders if he has made some mistake in his work for the coming experiment. Is there a part of his mind trying to tell him something is not as it should be, something he has done wrong, perhaps one small detail amidst the stupendous mountain of images he has created? As with all kinds of experimentation, a single detail can make all the difference.

Arcimboldo now does a mental exercise he has become extremely adept at, he imagines that he enters the Memory Palace he has built in his mind, an enormous place filled with rooms and corridors, windows and doors, constructed by exhausting mental labor and discipline. He has filled each room with things he wishes to remember, going from room to room in his mental palace he can store away and then relocate large amounts of information, sequences and associations; he only has to think of a particular room and by automatic association its complete contents flow forth into his conscious mind.

Since the ancient Egyptians, intelligent and curious people, thinkers and philosophers, have tried to find ways to hold on to the overwhelming amount of information the World offers to those who will open their eyes to it. Many different memory systems are popular, his friend Giordano Bruno advocates a system too mathematical and geometric for Arcimboldo's taste; the artist prefers a very visual system; and now, to calm his anxiety, he wanders the rooms and corridors in his Memory Palace. He imagines each spacious room is open to the night sky above, the radiance of the Stars and Celestial Bodies casts a soft but sufficient light. Arcimboldo can move backward in time to his youth and the stained glass windows he helped his father create for the Cathedral in Milan, simple designs and colors, simple and gentle symbols of Christ; and he can move forward through his galleries of knowledge, memories, and experiences, to the present moment. This wing of the Memory Palace holds his memories of the paintings, drawings, and objects he has made for the Emperor's experiment, they hang on the walls of his mental image and they are surrounded by visualizations of their Symbols, Virtues, and Powers. They are detailed, they are correct, they resonate with potential.

Arcimboldo feels comforted by this analysis, and his resolve has returned. He has been waiting here in this quiet and secluded place for Giordano Bruno, due to arrive that afternoon from Wittenberg. He's been waiting hours, and although Bruno is often late and forgetful of appointments, it is now obvious that he is not coming at all. When Arcimboldo opens his eyes, the only thing he can see is the glowing constellation of orange embers in the fireplace. The fire is out, his easel candles are out, and the tall window behind him is a rectangle of black within a wall of darkness, nothing in the room is discernible. Fortunately, this is a small room, one among several workspaces the artist has throughout the castle and the city, he knows it is only several steps to the door.

Arcimboldo is annoyed, he has much to do, he is cold, and he has to urinate. He wipes his hands on a scrap of rag he finds in his lap and stands to pull off the voluminous smock he wears for painting, but because he is shivering with cold he decides to leave it on and shuffles toward the door, feeling the way with hands outstretched. He encounters the wall, then his heavy velvet cloak which is hanging on the door. With a sigh of relief he wraps the cloak around himself and opens the door. There is not a glimmer of light or a whisper of sound on the twisting stairway down from his tower room... but there is an unusual, unexpected smell.

As he steps through the doorway he hears the sound of something whistling through the air, he feels a breeze on his face, and then the sharp whack of wood smashing against the stone door frame. Arcimboldo gasps loudly with surprise and recoils from the door, his painting smock becomes tangled between his legs, and, arms flying out, he falls over backward. As he is falling he hears a grunt, and he feels the breeze again as something swings through the space his head had occupied a second earlier, there is a splintering crash as it strikes the stone door frame once again.

A bulls-eye lantern clanks opens and Arcimboldo is hit directly with its glaring illumination. A hoarse voice exclaims in French, *"merde, il est le vieil Italien!"* Another voice asks with irritation, "where's that heretical bastard?" The light scans the small room.

Lying on his back, Arcimboldo is blinded by the glare from the lantern, he stammers, "what is it you want?"

Apparently it is not Arcimboldo they want to murder since there is no answer, the two figures canter off down the stairs cursing. He has not been able to see their faces, nor does he want to right at the moment. Even before his hands have a chance to stop shaking there is something that must be done... immediately. Arcimboldo discontentedly pisses in the stairwell.

The sounds of his attackers running from the tower quickly fade away, the silence and darkness return so rapidly and completely he might almost think he had dreamt the whole thing, were it not for the aching bruise on his tail bone and a bump on the back of his head. Remembering that his young servant, Silvius, had been commanded to wait for him at the tower's entrance, he begins descending the stairs as quickly as possible, stumbling, left hand feeling for the wall next to him. Anxiously he calls out, "Silvius! Silvius, are you there my boy?" There is no answer from below, nor does any sound or light issue from the two locked doors he passes on the way down. When he does begin to see a dim light on the stairs he slows, and then cautiously, holding his breath, makes his way down the few remaining steps to the tower entry-chamber. Dead silence. There's a flickering, dim light from a bronze oil lamp on a small table, the fireplace contains ashes and embers. At first glance the low-ceilinged chamber seems empty, then, to his enormous relief, he spies his servant, curled up asleep under the table.

"Wake up my boy... Silvius!" Arcimboldo gently pokes the back of the curled up figure with his foot. He starts to become alarmed, and pokes again and again until he hears a sleepy groan. Arcimboldo pokes several more times, less gently, and growls impatiently, "a nice nap you've been having. You'll tell me that you haven't heard a thing, haven't seen a thing, won't you? Get up!"

The very image of innocence, Silvius rolls over, rubbing his eyes. "Why no, Master, nothing happened, absolutely nothing... I've just been... resting a few moments. All is well." The boy's eyes slip nervously and guiltily toward the cold fire and flickering lamp.

"All is well!" Arcimboldo repeats with some degree of sarcasm. He cuffs the boy on the side of the head, but then also lightly tousles his hair. "Come along. Take the lamp."

"Has Master Bruno come, sir?"

"He has not. Come along." Arcimboldo steps to the window but can see nothing of the outside, he puts his hand on the boy's shoulder, stopping him, and steps to the door himself, opening it a crack. Prudently, he listens for a moment, then pulls the heavy door open and cautiously steps out of the tower.

This bastion containing Arcimboldo's workshop also contains workshops for a goldsmith and clockmaker, it is a gun tower built into the northern ramparts of Hradcany Castle, overlooking the Stag Moat and castle gardens. On this cloudy and moonless night the tower and the area around it are deserted. From the south side of the tower, Arcimboldo and Silvius exit onto a small platform adjoining the castle wall, and once satisfied that there are no lurking assailants, they slowly descend the staircase along the wall to the narrow street below. There is a heavy mist in the air, and an occasional swirl of light rain causes the flames in the bracketed torches along the wall to sizzle and gyrate in protest. Arcimboldo pulls up the hood on his cloak and wipes his nose. He says to Silvius, "I want you to do this, listen closely, run to the Chancellor and tell him that there are assassins in the castle. Then find the Emperor, if you can, and tell his servants I am coming to him as quickly as I can. It is a matter of great importance. Now, go! Go!" Silvius trots away across the courtyard, crunching and sloshing through the melting crust of dirty snow and ice.

Arcimboldo steps carefully, and although the chopines he wears have two inch cork soles, he knows in advance his feet will be soaked and numb within five minutes. He wipes moisture from his face and beard with a scented silk handkerchief, then blows his nose, he notices that his heart is still hammering; admittedly he is shocked and worried, yes, but also strangely energized, almost vibrating with alertness.

As he moves further away from the castle ramparts, the darkness and silence of the night are chased away by the sights and sounds of lively activity; looking ahead toward the immense Gothic bulk of St. Vitus Cathedral, he sees the tall, narrow, stained glass windows of the apse are brightly lit from within, Epiphany Eve mass is over and the Church is being decorated and prepared on the inside for tomorrow's celebration. As he passes around the eastern apse of the Cathedral, he notices the tall windows cast a shimmering reflection of azure, rose, and pale gold onto the watery channels and puddles in the ice and snow, the quivering patterns create the kind of transient splendor the artist is powerless to ignore; in the midst of his many anxieties he is distracted... he is considering what materials and techniques he might use to create an artifice of this Natural beauty.

On tomorrow, January 6, the Feast of the Epiphany will be celebrated throughout the city. As is customary, the adoration of the infant Jesus by the Three Wise Men will be reenacted here in this large courtyard square by the goldsmith's guild, to be followed by a pageant and feast for the favored citizens of Prague. Already, barrels of bockbier are stacked in a pyramid twelve feet high near the Golden Portal. Next to the Cathedral, stages, booths, and stalls are being hastily constructed and decorated, many of them tented in expectation of even poorer weather the next day.

Arcimboldo walks west toward the Palace along the southern flank of St. Vitus, he hears the babble of Czech carpenters, Italian painters, and German goldsmiths as he passes around and between them; loud, scandalous gossip – but he is not listening, his mind is elsewhere, engaged on the meaning of the murder attempt on Giordano Bruno, for that is surely obvious, the Frenchmen had come expecting to find Bruno there, at Arcimboldo's workshop. As far as he knows, other than Rudolf and the court painter Bartolomeus Spranger, the only other person who was aware that Arcimboldo had been waiting for Bruno in the Powder Tower is the utterly trustworthy Ottavio Strada. Well... to be exact, it is Ottavio's father, Jacopo, who is utterly trustworthy, Arcimboldo reminds himself, Ottavio is the *son* of an utterly trustworthy man.

Arcimboldo wants to speak with Ottavio first, before he speaks with Rudolf. It is unimaginable that Ottavio, an experienced man of the world, would do anything thoughtlessly or intentionally to endanger the Emperor's experiment. But can he be certain of this?

As Arcimboldo ages, he finds it more and more difficult to assess younger men, to feel that he understands them, to know and share their motivations instinctively, man to man, human to human; all too often he finds that he is more likely to feel understanding and eternal kinship with the plants and animals he diligently studies and paints.

So, absorbed in thought and eager to get out of the night air, he enters the Palace from the second courtyard. There is so much activity around the palaces and castle churches on this night that there are still two soldiers of the Imperial Guard with halberds standing at attention at the south-eastern portal, and, greatly diminishing the elegance of the entry hall, several more Imperial soldiers playing dice on the floor inside. They don't even pause to glance at Arcimboldo as he passes through on his way to the staircase.

Jacopo Strada, an antiquarian from Mantua, has been one of Arcimboldo's dearest friends for more than thirty years. Like many other Italian artists and craftsmen, including Arcimboldo himself, Strada had been lured north to work for the art loving and image conscious Humanists ruling the Holy Roman Empire. Also like Arcimboldo, Strada had been employed by the last three Emperors, Rudolf, Maximilian, and Ferdinand. Many times the two men worked together on Imperial and public entertainments, the decoration of the castle's palaces, and the cataloging of Habsburg art. Now, Jacopo has retired to his magnificent home in Vienna, an elegant Florentine style mansion, Palazzetto

Strada, with a title of nobility, Count Palatine of the Holy Roman Empire (this is a title of nobility Rudolf has been promising for years to bestow on Arcimboldo as well). Jacopo and his son Ottavio have become immensely rich as art dealers and agents for the three Emperors, scouring Europe for precious objects, art, and curiosities, and bringing them back to the galleries and Wunderkabinets in Vienna and Prague. If possible, Ottavio may even be cannier in the business than his father; but Arcimboldo knows that their love of knowledge and beauty is as genuine as their love of money, and their taste and accomplishments are much to be admired. Lately however, Ottavio has only had bad news to tell about his father's health, and since Jacopo does not answer Arcimboldo's letters, he vows to himself that he will make the journey to Vienna in the spring to visit the old man. Arcimboldo misses his old friend, he misses their long discussions about mythology, numismatics, and hylozoism, he wishes Jacopo were in Prague and a part of the Emperor's experiment.

This evening, Ottavio Strada himself answers the door when Arcimboldo knocks. The Emperor has given Ottavio rooms on the Royal Palace's second floor, directly below the Wunderkabinet on the floor above. Ottavio has inherited his father's role as chief antiquarian and curator of Rudolf's coins, books and statuary. It is late, and Arcimboldo begins with an apology, "Master Ottavio, forgive me for bothering you at this hour. Are your wife and daughters here?"

"Maestro Arcimboldus, good evening to you, sir. Please come in, come in." The antiquarian is a handsome man in the prime of life; well dressed as always in blue and brown velvet.

"I have no desire to wake your family, please forgive me. If I may have just a moment of your time…"

"Come in, sir, come in. My wife and daughters are at my house in the New Town, I'm just gathering some illustrations to present to the Emperor tomorrow. A cup of wine?"

"I thank you. Perhaps with some water. May I sit?"

"Please. All is well for tomorrow? Have you seen the Nolan?"

"Ottavio, that's why I'm here. Two Frenchman were waiting outside my workshop. They attacked me thinking I was Bruno. Who would know Bruno was coming to Prague, and coming to see me today?"

Strada has paused in the act of pouring, genuinely surprised. "Sancta Madonna! What's that you say? Attacked? Are you hurt? When did this happen?"

"Not more than a quarter of an hour ago, just outside my chamber in the Powder Tower. I'm actually lucky to be sitting here talking with you. They ran away when they realized I was not who they were looking for, it was Bruno they wanted, *no* doubt. Unfortunately, I'd never recognize them if I saw them again."

"And the Nolan never came?"

"He never came. Saint Christopher protect the man!"

"And *you're* not hurt?"

"By the grace of God, no." Arcimboldo gently touches the bump on the back of his head.

Ottavio opens his mouth to speak, and then closes it. He sits across from Arcimboldo and refills his own cup. He is thinking. His face begins to redden slightly and he looks down at his wine. As he lifts it to his mouth to drink he says, "Frenchmen, eh?"

"Yes. They spoke French."

Ottavio pauses as though seeking difficult words, "and you ask *me*, sir, if I know who told them

Bruno would be there?" He looks intently into Arcimboldo's eyes.

Arcimboldo quickly replies, "now Ottavio, do not take offense, for God's sake. I'm only asking if you perhaps have some idea, any possibility how they could have known. Perhaps you mentioned it to Katharina…"

"Perhaps Rudolf mentioned it to Katharina! By heavens, Arcimboldus, this isn't *my* fault!" He slaps the table; Ottavio's face is fully red now.

Ottavio's eldest daughter, Katharina, had caught the eye of Rudolf and become the Emperor's mistress. Jacopo Strada had been shocked and displeased with his granddaughter, and he blamed Ottavio for allowing it to happen. It had caused a serious rift between father and son and Jacopo had even disinherited Ottavio temporarily. Since Katharina had announced her pregnancy with the Emperor's child, Jacopo had withdrawn his objections; he had also withdrawn himself to his palazzetto in Vienna, where age and illness now had him in an embrace that would not last much longer.

Ottavio knows that now he must show the calmness and aplomb that mark him as a cultured man and privileged courtier. "Please forgive my passion. When someone mentions Katharina… it is not an easy thing for me speak about. Or think about." He swallows all that's left in his cup and makes an elaborate show of setting it down on the table.

Smiling with forgiving compassion, Arcimboldo says, "my friend, forgive *me*, I will see the Emperor, I will speak with Katharina myself. But you understand, Bruno must be protected, he is integral to the Emperor's plans, it is not too much to say there would be no plan at all without the Nolan. There is so much at stake, we must treat these next hours with care, we must have everything ready and perfect for the Epiphany."

Ottavio says softly, "yes, yes. And do you? Have everything ready?" He strokes the porphyry statuette on the table, a rendering of Venus and Eros as a beautiful woman and a small child. It is done by Pier Maria Serbaldi da Pescia, whose is known as *Il Tagliacarne*, which means 'meat carver' in Italian. The name does not come from a clumsiness of work, but because of the nature of the stone he prefers to work in, porphyry, which has the purple-red color of raw meat and is flecked with small white spots. It is also difficult to carve because the stone is so hard. For these reasons porphyry is a valuable and admired material for sculpture.

Thinking about the experiment's state of readiness, Arcimboldo squints and looks troubled, "but you see, this is why we need the Nolan... and the Englishmen. They will know when everything is ready." Arcimboldo now looks earnestly at Ottavio, but really he is looking within himself as he says with fervor, "what we have is beyond describing, and I'm sorry I can't show you," he leans forward for emphasis, "we have recreated the Macrocosm, the entire Cosmos, Ottavio, it is beyond imagining! I cannot say more."

Ottavio, of course, is trying hard to imagine what Arcimboldo is not describing. He stares, rapt, at the old Italian, he knows dozens, no hundreds, of drawings, paintings, and object d'art of all kinds have been disappearing into the Emperor's private space for many months. On this subject of disappearing art: speculation and rumor in the castle among the many artists and craftsmen is wild and intense; that Rudolf is bankrupt and selling all his art; that the Turk is coming in the spring with an invincible army and Rudolf is fleeing the city; that Rudolf has decided to allow the Holy League into his domain, and is preparing for the riots, looting, and civil war that will follow.

Arcimboldo is brushing invisible lint off his cloak and examining his finger nails, a clear signal that the subject has been concluded for the moment and he will say no more. Ottavio is an accomplished courtier, he composes himself, and pretends to have entirely forgotten the Epiphany experiment, he rises, "Maestro Arcimboldus, I have something to show you. A moment."

On the walls of Ottavio's study it is difficult to determine what is real and what is illusion, the four walls have been paneled in intarsia, a jig-saw-like fitting together of polished wooden pieces of different colors, shades, and shapes. In this room, sycamore, box-wood, and ebony were used for light and dark contrast in the intarsia. The paneling presents the illusion of depth and realism; the walls of Ottavio's study appear to extend into a larger space, with a receding tile floor, bookcases, tables, columns, and cabinets – all portrayed with meticulous detail and perfect use of perspective. The wall nearest Ottavio is crafted to look like a large, elaborately carved wooden cabinet with one door partially open (a geometric marvel). Inside the apparently open cabinet can be seen a shelf with two lutes, a shell, and a stack of books, all in perfect perspective. The door of the cabinet that is closed appears to be intarsia as well, however when Ottavio presses on a certain place the door swings open, revealing a genuine cabinet space inside the wall. He removes a calfskin portfolio and lays it on the table. He begins to unwrap it, "these have finally arrived, from Augsburg, the Emperor will be delighted. What he paid for them – I'd hate to tell you. Look."

Arcimboldo stands, saying, "I will take a quick look, but really, I must go, you understand…"

Ottavio reveals the small parchment paintings inside the calfskin. He peers up at Arcimboldo with an experienced dealer's look of amused expectation. Arcimboldo does not disappoint, his eyes locked on the painting Ottavio has revealed, Arcimboldo slowly sinks back down into his chair. "Durer."

Arcimboldo is looking at a watercolor painting of a bird's wing. It is not a European bird; it is a blue-bellied roller, found in Africa. Other than the wing, date, 1517, and Durer's initials, the page is blank, all the better to allow the eye to concentrate on the astonishing realism of the single wing. He is arrested by the color blue, a royal blue, as it shades and blends into the areas of creamy white and sea-green feathers. The stubby but elegant little wing is bordered on the body side by a fringe of soft, burnt-orange feathers. Arcimboldo leans forward to look closer at the feathers, the details and textures are painted so realistically he wants to touch them; he can tell that Durer has over-painted the edges of the feathers with an opaque gouache to make them look jagged and overlapped. The harmony of the colors is soothing, the rhythms and patterns within the several rows of feathers are restful and reassuring. At times, the contemplation of a single, humble, fragment of Nature can provide the highest aesthetic experience. However, in addition, what Durer communicates to Arcimboldo in this simple Nature painting is how the Microcosm reflects the Macrocosm: the beauty in the feather reflects and is part of the beauty in the wing; the beauty in the wing reflects and is part of the beauty in the bird. And further, the beauty of the bird reflects and is part of the beauty of the Natural World. The Microcosm is a small part and reflection of the Macrocosm; a Symbol and reminder of Man's place in the Universe – there is always something larger that we are but a small piece of. The Emperor is very fond of the work of Albrecht Durer; he shares Durer's Humanist world views.

Arcimboldo exhales with admiration, "ah, such blue! This painting is everything I've heard it to be." He carefully points with his little finger to an area where the white feathers are shadowed by the blue feathers, "cangiantismo, yes? And here. And here. Look at the colors." He looks up at Ottavio, who is smiling and holding another parchment to show him.

Ottavio says, "I thought you would like that blue, not a grain of azurite in it as far as I can tell, pure lapis lazuli, the lapis alone must have cost as much as a house in Mala Strana!"

"Yes, and the texture is so fine, how did he grind it to dust? What a beautiful blue, pure ultramarine!"

"Here's one more Durer, a very handsome piece, don't you think?" Ottavio places a yellowed and crinkled parchment on the table. On it, in brown and black ink, is a detailed profile drawing of a rhinoceros. Above, the date, 1515, and the word 'rhinoceros', below, four lines of small and uneven writing, also in black ink.

Arcimboldo says, "yes, of course, the Emperor will like this. The picture will be very welcome. I doubt the Emperor's rhinoceros will last till spring. When the taxidermists are finished I think we will have a new display in the Wunderkabinet. Durer's drawing will be a very harmonious addition. What's this writing? Durer didn't do this. It isn't Latin, is it? I can't make it out."

Ottavio lifts another piece of paper to read off of, "it's Portuguese, I have the translation, it says *'On the first of May in the year 1513 AD, the powerful King of Portugal, Manuel of Lisbon, brought such a living animal from India, called the rhinoceros. This is an accurate representation. It is the color of a speckled tortoise, and is almost entirely covered with thick scales. It is the size of an elephant but has shorter legs and is almost invulnerable. It has a strong pointed horn on the tip of its nose, which it sharpens on stones. It is the mortal enemy of the elephant. The elephant is afraid of the rhinoceros, for, when they meet, the rhinoceros charges with its head between its front legs and rips open the elephant's stomach, against which the elephant is unable to defend itself. The rhinoceros is so well armed that the elephant cannot harm it. It is said that the rhinoceros is fast, impetuous and cunning."*

"Indeed," Arcimboldo says thoughtfully, "fast, impetuous and cunning. I'm thinking of the poor creature in the Emperor's zoo, apparently it hates Prague winters as much as I do, poor creature. Fearless of the elephant... yet ending its days shivering in a muddy horse stall. When do you present these to the Emperor?"

"Tomorrow... actually..." Ottavio consults an old silver water clock on his writing desk, "I will give it to him today. It is past midnight."

"Ottavio, I must go. I thank you for the wine, and, Ottavio, do not be offended, but please promise me, not a word to anyone about Bruno, not a breath." The two men briefly embrace. Arcimboldo looks over Ottavio's shoulder and sees on the wall the portrait painted by Tintorreto when Ottavio was a youth, twenty years ago.

Ottavio's father, Jacopo, had taken the sixteen year old to Venice for the first time that year, 1567, and engaged the most popular painter in that expensive city, Tintoretto, to paint his son with the emblems of his future career: antique coins and statues. This story is told in an allegorical style: the innocent and sober looking young man receives a cornucopia filled with coins from the goddess Fortuna, while turning away from a newly made statue of Venus. In this painting, the gold and silver antique coins are meant to signify his future occupation (following in his father's footsteps) as antiquarian, as do the classical ruins seen in the distance. But skillfully, subtly, and amusingly, Tintoretto chose to paint the statue of Venus turning away in apparent embarrassment from the boy who is reaching greedily for the coins (but truly this is prophetic, the Stradas have never turned away from an opportunity to make money). Ottavio is not sensitive to this interpretation, and has proudly hung Tintoretto's painting in his dwelling ever since receiving it.

Ottavio says to Arcimboldo, "you're certain you're not hurt, Maestro?"

"No, no, I've quite recovered actually, and I thank you for that. I hope to see you tomorrow... today, send to me if you have any news of the Nolan. Sleep well, Ottavio."

"God be with you, sir." And the door closes behind Arcimboldo.

The painter begins a long walk down a structure that has been under construction since 1585, it's the most direct route to Rudolf's current private apartments. It is a part of the Palace the Court has begun to call the 'Long Corridor'. He is thinking about Tintoretto's allegorical portrait of Ottavio Strada; Tintoretto's ability to tell more than one story with a single set of images, and Tintoretto's ability to make subtle comments about human personality and humors. He cannot help being reminded of the inspired painting the greatest Venetian artist, Titian Vecellio, made of Jacopo Strada, Ottavio's father. Jacopo in the prime of his life. Arcimboldo cannot help but smile as he walks alone through the darkened, wood paneled hallways of the Palace. Titian's painting is intended to be a portrait of a successful and newly ennobled man and his interests, and in that it is impeccably done, but again a painter has given the Stradas more than they asked for. The painting also shows us that the subject of the painting, Jacopo, cannot really tear himself away from business long enough to sit for Titian's portraiture: Jacopo turns away from the viewer and is energetically addressing someone off to the side; alarmingly, he swings a valuable antique statue around with both hands, with a flourish, while looking in the opposite direction! Above his head are books of numismatics and catalogues of ancient coins (and perhaps account books), appropriate to symbolize Jacopo's erudition and business passion, but placed as they are on a shelf directly above his head, one might assume they are blocking the man's thoughts about Heavenly matters and God. He is richly dressed, but his magnificent ermine cloak is falling off his shoulders as he vigorously pursues a sale. Jacopo loves this picture. He is sensitive enough to appreciate Titan's skillful design and execution; he is intelligent enough to admit those things Titian shows us are true; and self-confident enough not to care. And, Arcimboldo soberly reminds himself, the sick old man is all too soon going to be eternally *beyond* caring what the world thinks. Ah, Jacopo, you will live forever in Titian's masterpiece.

Arcimboldo passes several servants sleeping in the hallway, and an officer of the Imperial Horse Guard staggering out of a room, attempting drunkenly to readjust his uniform. Otherwise, the hallways of this western wing of the Royal Palace are empty and silent on this early morning of January 6, 1587.

As Arcimboldo approaches the Imperial chambers, he stops from force of habit to check his appearance and attire. He realizes that he is still wearing his old black painting smock under his dark green velvet cloak. He removes the smock, folds it up, and turns about in the hallway looking for a place to leave it. There is a handsome Florentine cassone standing against the wall near the door to Rudolf's outer chambers. It is too dim in the hallway to tell what landscape scenes are painted on the sides of the massive chest but the cassone's carved and gilded edges gleam softly. Arcimboldo lifts the lid, intending to tuck away his smock, and he is shocked to find a body curled up inside. He recognizes it is one of the Emperor's young valets. He is comforted to realize the body is snoring. "Wake up, Nelle, you blockhead! What are you sleeping here for?" Arcimboldo's sharp, irritated voice reverberates around inside the cassone like thunder. The valet convulses awake, looking up and around wildly and guiltily. When he sees it is Arcimboldo and not the Chamberlain his look of guilt changes to one of resentment, and it appears he is going to go back to sleep without speaking. Arcimboldo reaches into the cabinet, grabs the boy's ear and pulls him out, scolding him briskly in Czech and Italian. Eventually, Arcimboldo manages to learn from the rascal that Rudolf is not here, he is with the court painter Bartolomeus Spranger.

Bartolomeus Spranger is the Emperor's favorite court painter. Yes, Arcimboldo admits this, the Emperor spends more time with the rough but agreeable Dutchman than anyone else. And of course, why not? Spranger is convivial, he is widely traveled, he is often painting enormous mythological scenes with the prerequisite cavorting nude figures; naturally he paints and composes with live models, and Katharina Strada is Spranger's and (more importantly) Rudolf's favorite model. Portraying Venus, Circe, Antiope, Omphale, Salmacis, even Eve, the golden haired, milky skinned Katharina contorts her limbs into serpentine poses dreamed up by Spranger and Rudolf together; the results are magnificent, a harmonious tangle of pink and white flesh glowing with health, sensuality, and a spectacularly unrestrained eroticism. Rudolf hangs these beautiful and colorful canvases in carefully chosen places throughout the Palace. It may be said: all the Stradas are well known, but Katharina is the most admired.

Arcimboldo sees Rudolf's personal bodyguard in the hallway outside Spranger's rooms on the Palace's third floor. The six and a half foot tall Ethiopian leans against the wall, dozing perhaps. Rudolf calls him Atlas, but that is surely not his real name, and no one knows the story of his birth and youth. Atlas is mute. He had been a galley slave, a chained oarsman, freed from a captured Turkish galley after the glorious battle of Lepanto, fifteen years earlier, when Don Juan of Austria and the Venetian fleet crushed Turkish power in the Mediterranean. Atlas had been freed from his filthy, splintered bench on a Turkish galley, and gifted to the Emperor who everyone knows is so fond of novelties; his shackles and chains now are the red, yellow, black, and white livery he wears, Rudolf's Imperial colors, worn by all his servants. Although the Ethiope is grey of hair and beard he is still the strongest man Arcimboldo knows; he has seen him lift a fully grown horse off the ground on a drunken dare. As Arcimboldo approaches, Atlas straightens and turns gracefully, menacingly lithesome, like one of Rudolf's lions. He bows to Arcimboldo. He jerks his head towards the door to Spranger's apartments, indicating that Arcimboldo can enter. Arcimboldo smoothes his moustache and straightens his posture, the Ethiopian knocks, Arcimboldo opens the door and enters.

Bartolomeus Spranger is cleaning brushes with an extremely dirty rag. Arcimboldo sees green paint on the Dutchman's homely but hearty face and wispy rust colored beard. He is dressed in a coarse brown shirt and shapeless brown felt hat. At forty-two, Spranger is six years older than the Emperor. He is surprised to see Arcimboldo enter; as he looks up he unsuccessfully tries to stifle a yawn. "Arcimboldus. No one seems to be able to sleep tonight. But... shouldn't you be with the Nolan?"

Arcimboldo shrugs, he glances at the brushes in Spranger's hands, "have you finished?"

Spranger motions with his head toward his painting chamber and rolls his eyes, "I have, the Emperor has not."

"I haven't seen Bruno yet, he never came, and worse, two Frenchmen came to my chamber in the Powder Tower, armed, looking for him. They nearly killed me by mistake."

"They nearly killed you! " He looks Arcimboldo up and down.

"I swear to you, Fortuna and Saint Christopher had me by either hand!" Arcimboldo crosses himself and touches the carved and incised ruby in his pocket. "My servant went to fetch the Chancellor, the Emperor must know immediately."

Spranger stretches out his hand toward the door of the room where Rudolf and Katarina are – as if to say, go right ahead, better you than me. As Arcimboldo walks past him, Spranger touches his arm to stop him, saying, "what about the Summer Palace, the art?"

"It's guarded, of course, but... without Bruno..."

"Go tell him."

Arcimboldo knocks lightly on the door before gently opening it and stepping inside. Rudolf and Katharina have their backs to the door, Rudolf is sitting on the floor and Katharina is kneeling behind him, in the act of tying a black blindfold around Rudolf's head. This chamber has large leaded windows to the north which are being buffeted by rain and hail. The couple on the floor has apparently not heard him enter because they continue their conversation. Arcimboldo winces to hear the Emperor's voice begging childishly in German. "Oh, no don't! Not again, I'm not ready!"

Katharina answers "yes, come on. Once more, my Lord. One more time, and I know you will do it this time." She kisses Rudolf on the top of the head and shakes his shoulders playfully. "Come on now, come on, what's first, what's first?"

"Give me one more minute, I'm not ready!"

"No, once more right now, now or never...what's first?"

Rudolf's manliness begins to return, he clears his throat, "very well then. First will be the Massacre of the Innocents."

Katharina yawns and says, "Massacre of the Innocents, of course, but what comes after that?"

Arcimboldo opens the door behind him and closes it more forcefully, he clears his throat. "Your Imperial Majesty, are you here? Pardon me for intruding." He steps across the floor to Rudolf and Katharina. He speaks in German, "I have important news that cannot wait."

Katharina does not rush to cover herself, she is deliberate and self confident in gathering her clothes around her. She looks at Arcimboldo with curiosity and amusement. She smiles at the artist, a man she used to call Uncle Giuseppe. Politely, she gives the briefest of curtsies, "My Lord."

Rudolf has taken the blindfold from his eyes, he grunts "Arcimboldus. What news?" He waves Katharina further away.

In a lowered voice Arcimboldo says "Bruno, my Lord, never came to the tower today. Instead I was visited by two assassins speaking French. I fear for the Nolan. Have you any news?"

Rudolf looks Arcimboldo over appraisingly, finally commenting quietly, "undamaged I see."

"Well, it was a very close thing... Your Majesty... but about the Nolan-"

"Pooh!" Rudolf puffs out his cheeks and frowns, as if put out, "we can't have him seen, you understand that very well, Arcimboldus, don't you?"

"Of course, but-"

"Bruno visits here in secret; the Englishmen, from now on, they come in secret. It's not what I want... but it's what will be."

This answer tells Arcimboldo that Rudolf knows significantly more about Bruno's location than the painter himself does. Arcimboldo is not sure if this is going to be a good thing or a bad thing. The Emperor does not seem panicked, but Arcimboldo feels confused; Rudolf knows that there are many things that need to be set in motion, and many more things already in motion that need attending to, things dependent on Giordano Bruno. Nevertheless, the Emperor cannot be pressed. Arcimboldo gently probes for more information, "his safety is of course what concerns me, My Lord, and the success of our endeavor. We have worked so diligently, the timing is crucial now. As Saint Augustine says about time-"

"You say these Frenchmen attacked you, sir?"

It is disconcerting to be standing in front of the Emperor while he's sitting on the floor. "Very nearly, very nearly...I can tell you, it must have been the hand of Providence that buffered me from harm, another few inches and...well, perhaps our daily exposure to the Mysteries of the Natural World has already begun to work upon us. Of course, the Nolan would know, were he here to ask – can the energy from-"

"I think you will see him soon, help me up, sir."

Arcimboldo extends a hand to help Rudolf to rise. The Emperor is stocky and florid with pale brown hair and beard. Middle age has chased away all youthful traces in his appearance. His prominent Habsburg jaw and bulging eyes could not be said to be handsome, but Rudolf is not an ugly man. He has the same red color to his face that his father had, that his uncle has, that all Habsburgs seem to have, Arcimboldo thinks of it as Habsburg crimson. When he is impassioned, the red rises from the lower part of his face higher and higher, when the whites of the Emperor's eyes become red he is beyond furious, extremely dangerous, and afterwards ill and uncommunicative for weeks. He stands now, face to face with Arcimboldo, half in and half out of his black doublet and white ruffled collar. The man's normally heavy lidded eyes are puffy and bloodshot with fatigue; dark circles below show he has been having trouble sleeping. His breath is scented with honeyed clove wine. The Emperor says "go to the Summer Palace and I will meet you in an hour, tell Bartolomeus he will go with you."

Arcimboldo thinks: perfectly typical Rudolf, an answer clear and ambiguous at the same time. He bows, "pardon me for disturbing you, Your Majesty." He sees Rudolf has been sitting on the floor, surrounded by a collection of curios and small medallions. The Emperor has been playing the same memory game over and over for days now. He will stare at an array of objects for one minute, then blindfold himself, and repeat from memory the order of the arrangement. Arcimboldo notices that the first object on the left is a miniature painting in enamel of the Massacre of the Innocents. Arcimboldo bows to Katharina, again to the Emperor, and backs out the door.

The two artists intend to exit the Palace through the Imperial stables; it is the most direct route to the bridge over the moat. As they walk, they discuss Katharina Strada and her pregnancy. It will be the Emperor's first child. Spranger tells Arcimboldo that he has heard Rudolf promise Katharina that if the child is a boy he will name him Julius Caesar. Julius Caesar Habsburg! Rudolf is obviously and genuinely captivated by the young woman.
    Shaking his head, Arcimboldo repeats, "Julius Caesar…he'll name his illegitimate child Julius Caesar. Honestly, I don't know whether to laugh or cry."
    "You remember what Alberti said about laughing and crying?"
    "Ha! I do. Very appropriate, my friend."
    Spranger refers to Leon Battista Alberti, a multi-talented Italian philosopher, artist, architect, Humanist, linguist, and poet; dead now for a century, but whose wisdom lives on. Alberti wrote that only an artist who has tried to draw a person laughing next to a person crying realizes how difficult it is to tell the difference between the two.

    The men momentarily pause to stand in the rich, earthy aroma of the Emperor's stables, which hold one-hundred-fifty Spanish stallions, magnificent animals, gently shuffling and snorting as they sleep through the early hours of the morning. Arcimboldo watches one horse, one godlike beast, black as pitch in the colorless lantern light; steam subtly rises from the slumbering equine's nostrils, the massive body is as motionless as a statue. Arcimboldo softly whispers, "*humano capiti cervicem pictor equinam iungere si velit.*"
    Spranger says "Leonardo? Alberti?"
    Arcimboldo laughs lightly, "no, no. It's Horace."

"Horace? If you put a man's head on a horse's body...that was Horace? You surprise me. I thought he would be-"

"Yes, exactly, he disapproves. Ultimately, he says, 'such pictures would be like a book whose idle fancies are shaped like a sick man's dreams'. *Uelut aegri somnia.*"

Spranger repeats slowly and thoughtfully in German, "fancies shaped like a sick man's dreams."

They walk stride for stride from the stable in silence, in thought. Spranger laughs, a short bark, "a man's head on a horse's body? You've gone way beyond that, my friend! What makes you think of Horace now?" Arcimboldo does not answer. Spranger looks sideways at him, "do you doubt our work?"

"No, no, certainly not. Our work has beauty, harmony and wisdom, in and of itself it has value. And the promise of what may come, what we may be able to do, to learn..."

"There you are."

Arcimboldo sighs, "it's strange that the closer we get to our goal the more uneasy I become."

"That's strange indeed."

"I wouldn't have you think me a coward, and it's difficult to explain... even to myself. Perhaps I can say... I love art more than alchemy."

Spranger can see that his complicated friend is in earnest by the look of intense hesitancy on his face. "No one would doubt that, Arcimboldus." He is searching his mind for something positive and comforting. "I can tell you that the Emperor values your work mightily. In his own way, he is in awe. And not just him... what you've constructed is impressive beyond belief."

Arcimboldo forces a smile of gratitude, "thank you, Bartolomeus. But, just between us, I think my uneasiness lies there – when I think of the Emperor."

Spranger nods, "idle fancies shaped like a sick man's dreams?"

Arcimboldo shrugs and acknowledges with a small flourish of his hand. Spranger nods again, and they walk in silence for several minutes. Arcimboldo is the first to speak, "Strada showed me new purchases from Augsburg for the Emperor, have you seen them?"

"What does he have?"

"Durers, two of them, but the blue roller wing... it is magic. Do you know the work?"

"I have heard it was coming, I long to see it."

"That blue, it's like something alive, Bartolomeus, you will think that color blue could never have been manufactured by artifice...it has the startling purity of Nature itself. I cannot think of a blue to compare, unless it be Giorgione, yes, Giorgione in San Rocco. Ah, my friend, do you know his Holy Family, at the Church of San Rocco in Venice? A blue that rivals Nature itself."

Spranger shakes his head indicating he does not know that work. "I have seen Maestro Titian's self portrait in Venice...with his gigantic blue sleeve, that is a glorious blue, to be sure, marvelous, but I can't help feeling, mmm... it's a bit of a show-off. No? Who can afford that much blue on a self-portrait?"

"A Venetian."

"Of course. Those lucky bastards!"

Arcimboldo laughs, "true, true, they're lucky to have first access to all those wonderful pigments coming from the East on Venetian galleys; the rarest colors are as cheap in Venice as umber and orpiment! Let me tell you a story Giovanni Busi told me in 1545, no it was '46 because the plague was everywhere and no one could travel. Busi, of course, was a pupil of Giorgione, and the Holy Family was the first painting he worked on in Giorgione's studio in Venice, this was way back in 1500, 1505...thereabout. Busi saw that

Giorgione's sketches for Mary's robe were blue, grand sweeps of deep blue; but the Venetian had him grinding red. Busi wondered, where is the Maestro going to use all this red? Giorgione told him 'not enough Giovanni, more red, more red', and he grinds and grinds...you follow? Giorgione started painting the robe, quickly, thin coats...red paint! Ah ha, so the blue robe will have an undercoat of red. The Maestro looked at the red...he didn't even try one dab of blue paint, he fumed, he told Busi 'not bright enough! Where is the light, the sparkle of the stars in the firmament? The stars of the firmament must be in Mary's robe, Giovanni. Where is the sparkle that will shine through ultramarine blue? Go get glass, Giovanni; grind it up, not too fine, not to powder. We leave little bits, little stars. And we mix with the red.' More red! Another coat of red the inventive Maestro painted on, this time with ground glass mixed in it. Then, when it was dry, he painted one more coat on top of the shimmering red, one coat only: very finely prepared ultramarine blue. Can you imagine it? Giorgione's brush moved like lightning, he knew exactly where to place pigment and how much to put on. Busi said the blue was glowing, radiating, it was superb... the sparkling stars of Heaven shining through Mary's robe. The Maestro loved that color so much he used the same red under blue, without the glass, for the landscape behind the Holy Family. I saw it often when I lived in Venice. Bartolomeus, the blues in that painting surpass Nature, they are divine."

Spranger nods appreciatively. After a short silence Spranger says, "surpass Nature, you just said 'surpass Nature'... Arcimboldus, do you really think it can be done? Do you think *we'll* do it? What will it look like? To surpass nature..."

Arcimboldo opens his mouth to speak "I..." he closes his mouth, and shakes his head from side to side, as if to indicate that it's quite beyond his imagination.

Spranger grabs Arcimboldo's shoulder and shakes it in a comradely manner, with a grin he says, "well, old man, whether it works or not, where would you rather be? By Jupiter, it's going to be exciting! As for myself, I fairly drool with anticipation."

Arcimboldo has to laugh. "So... the possible consequences don't trouble you then?"

"The possible consequences of getting out of bed in the morning can be troubling! If you allow it to. The calculation is: what's to be gained, will there be rewards worth the effort. Listen to me, I've been around, and as strange as they can be in Paris and Rome, our Emperor takes the cake, no really, you know this... he is my patron and liege Lord and I kiss his feet and anything else he fancies... but if there's a man alive who can bluff his way into the next world, it's him. Of that I am certain. He is one of a kind!"

After a pause, Arcimboldo replies, "we all are, Master Bartolomeus."

Fortunately for these two late night strollers, workmen have built a covered walkway from the bridge over the Stag Moat to the Summer Palace anticipating the comfort of the many important people who will be walking from the castle later this day to the Emperor's Epiphany feast. At the moment, Stag Moat itself is stygian and silent. The deep and narrow ravine lies in the shadow of the northern walls of the castle, and it separates the hunting preserve and the gardens from Hradcany Castle and St. Vitus Cathedral. From this point, at the end of the bridge, the covered walkway stretches almost a quarter mile through the gardens to the Summer Palace, and at the moment, since the weather has become colder and the rain has turned to snow, it is a most welcome and necessary haven. The torches on the castle side of the bridge now appear to be gently bobbing balls of orange cotton in the murky night. The inside of the walkway smells strongly from a recent coat of paint, and the artists' footsteps echo loudly off the freshly cut planks of green linden under their feet. The marvels of the Imperial gardens are invisible to their left and right. The Lion Court, the zoo, the aviary, the pheasant garden, the botanical garden, the singing fountain, Maximilian's Garden of Paradise, the Florentine ball-games court, these beautiful and famous sights are hidden by a double cloak of snow and darkness, Arcimboldo hurries past them. He is tightly wrapped in his cloak and hood but still cold, walking as quickly as he can, following Spranger's swinging iron lantern several feet in front of him. Arcimboldo's hood is tightly wrapped around his ears, so it's Spranger who hears the shout and turns to scan the dark gardens.

Arcimboldo bumps into the Dutchman's back and stops. Spranger is looking off to the right, but there is nothing that can be seen, the shrubbery and geometrical flower plantings they know are there might as well be a thousand miles away, they are completely invisible in the darkness. "Did you hear that?"

"No, what did you hear?"

"A shout, someone is out there. There!" They hear a vigorous rustling of vegetation, but not close by, it comes from far out into the night.

"Yes, I hear it!"

"That's beyond the gardens, it's near the moat."

"An animal, a deer."

"No, not an animal, I heard a shout."

"Who would be out there now?"

The rustling stops. Spranger and Arcimboldo turn to look at each other wonderingly, they continue to walk, trying to step lightly and quietly so they can hear what's happening out in the gardens, and after a moment they both hear a man's angry shout. It is distant and inarticulate, and followed again by a furious thrashing sound, like someone running blindly through bushes and vines hidden under snow. Eventually, there's a sharp cry, then silence, and for ten seconds Arcimboldo and Spranger hold their breath, listening. Then they hear a chilling scream that rises to a shriek and then abruptly chokes off. Arcimboldo gasps, he feels as though his cloak has been stripped from his back, the hairs stand on the back of his neck. Dogs inside the castle begin to bark. There is the sound of running, several pair of heavy feet thundering along the linden planking of the walkway, and several indistinct but urgent voices. Arcimboldo, of course, is unarmed, but Spranger fumbles a paint smeared poniard out of his belt. They turn to face the approaching sounds.

The torches held by two of the three running soldiers are bouncing wildly, throwing swirling patterns of light and shadow on the low ceiling of the walkway. These men are arquebusiers from the Imperial Tercio quartered in Prague, and they must come from the nearby Summer Palace; they would be part of the company guarding the site of Rudolf's Epiphany experiment. An officer leads them and his sword is drawn.

Arcimboldo calls out in Spanish, "Capitano, we are of the Household, we are artists, I am Arcimboldus." He whispers to Spranger "put that away!"

The man wearing the sash of a Spanish officer over his mail shirt halts and looks them up and down without speaking. He turns to his men and motions out to the gardens, commanding them in very bad Spanish, "search that place up and down." In fractured German, he says to Arcimboldo and Spranger "late it is this night." The man is neither Spanish nor German, unusual; most of the captains in the Prague Tercio are retired or cashiered Spanish veterans from the war in the Netherlands.

Arcimboldo asks him in Czech, "Capitan, do you know what that sound was?"

The Captain holds one of the torches above his head and watches his men stumble slowly out into the snow, without answering. (He doesn't speak Czech; so he isn't from here in Bohemia either!) Arcimboldo repeats his question in German.

The officer answers "that was man dying. Where do you go?"

"We are going to the Summer Palace; the Emperor is meeting us there shortly."

This gets the Captain's close attention. He points out into the darkness and says, "do you know who, what happens?"

"No, no, Capitan. We do not know." Arcimboldo speaks very distinctly. "We will go inside now. You understand the Emperor will come soon, he will come this way. Yes? We trust you, Capitan, you will find out what is happening in the gardens." Arcimboldo cannot place the man's accent, he's not Italian, Spanish, German or Bohemian, he doesn't sound Hungarian, French, Dutch or Polish. "Capitano, tell me... what is your name?"

The Captain makes a gentlemanly bow, but regrettably chooses to continue speaking in German, "M'Lord, pleased to be happy here meeting you, my name has always been a service for you, Padraich Noel O'Reilly, Capitano of arquebusiers. Inside will you go. Yes?"

O'Reilly! Arcimboldo is thinking he would never have guessed, a Hibernian... just like that appalling fellow, Dee's creature, Edward Kelly!

The company of arquebusiers that has been camped around the Summer Palace for more than a month is stirring, preparing to move back into the Tercio's barracks in the Old Town at first light. Many have been awakened by the scream in the gardens. The soldiers grumble and swear in a babble of European languages, but predominantly Spanish.

With the dawn, the Summer Palace will no longer look like a military camp, but show itself as the finest example of modern architecture north of Italy. Although the building has been under construction for years under a number of different architects, it has now reached a unified perfection, a perfect and harmonious blend of the current architectural styles of Florence, Venice, and Rome. This is the Emperor's favorite building, there are many detailed plans for its use, much time has been spent in preparation and decoration, and it will be a very busy place as this day progresses.

Underneath the splendid arches that surround the Summer Palace on all sides is a deep loggia, or porch, well lit even now by many torches and lanterns. As the two artists stiffly climb the few steps up to this loggia their breath comes streaming out in great clouds, and they might seem to an observer to be machines, steam driven automata, created by an ingenious toymaker, clockmaker, or alchemist. They are being observed, not by any of the soldiers packing and carrying, but by something all but smothered under a pile of rugs, a small head protrudes from the top of this pile and calls out, "Master Arcimboldus, I am here!"

Silvius struggles out from under the rugs and runs to Arcimboldo and Spranger. "The Chancellor told me to wait here for you, My Lord."

Arcimboldo speaks with him in Czech, "Silvius, my boy, you must be freezing. Where is the Chancellor, is he here?"

"He is here, upstairs in your special room. He awaits the Emperor. He told me to wait for you. My Lord, I did not have a chance to look for the-"

"Yes, yes, Silvius, that is all right. Off with you, lad, you must be exhausted as well."

Silvius bows, yawning. Arcimboldo adds, "one thing only, my boy, do this for me quickly. Go to my room and bring back a pair of black silk stockings... and Venetian felt shoes. Go. No, wait. I'll need a set of black small clothes, another black cap, no design, no embroidery, just black. Black gloves, again plain, no decoration. I expect that I'll spend the rest of the night here." The boy starts to back away nodding. Arcimboldo motions him to wait, "oh yes, Silvius, bring tooth powder and a hairbrush... and another thing, bring me my logbook, my master logbook, for tomorrow's entertainments." The boy had been backing away, now as Arcimboldo pauses, he turns and sprints off into the darkness before his master can think of anything else. Arcimboldo cups his hands around his mouth and shouts after the boy who has already disappeared, "and for God's sake, be careful! There are strange things happening tonight!"

Arcimboldo says to Spranger, "Curtius is here, let us go inside." The old Italian is frozen to the bone and walks with his hand pressed against the small of his back. They advance toward the bronze double door entry to the ground floor of the Summer Palace. These doors open inwards as the artists approach them, and they stand aside for a column of arquebusiers exiting the building. Irritated at being awakened before dawn, the Tercio soldiers give Arcimboldo and Spranger insolent and hostile looks as they pass by. Inside,

Trabante Imperial Guard troops with their red, yellow, black, and white livery, seven foot halberds, and gold-painted morions, are taking over security of the elegant building.

This ground floor has been divided up into just two very large spaces; a thin but elaborately carved and stuccoed wall punctured by three wide doors provides the separation. This design is intended to facilitate large parties, dances, ceremonies, presentations, and feasts. Both spaces are empty now, but very soon these rooms will be prepared for the festivities Rudolf has planned for Epiphany. Tables will be set up for a sumptuous meal, and also a stage that will be used for a play. There will be musical entertainment and dancing. Two elegantly dressed men stand on a staircase at the far northern end of the spacious interior. They are in conversation, but break off when they see Arcimboldo and Spranger; they descend and come toward the artists. Colonel Franz Choma is commander of the Imperial Hartschire Horse Guard, Adam Dietrichstein is the Imperial High Steward; these men are responsible for the security of the Emperor, Hradcany Castle, and the city of Prague.

"Where is the Emperor, is he not coming? Am I to have no sleep tonight? Arcimboldus, what's this I hear? Assassins inside the castle? By the Mass, how can that be? Are you well, sir? I believe you are not, I see you are limping."

"I'm not injured, my Lord High Steward, I am old. The problem is not my health, although I thank you for the thought. The problem is..." and with this Arcimboldo looks around him to see who else is nearby. He lowers his voice. "The problem is the Nolan. I don't know where he is! I can't tell you, Lord Dietrichstein, how important it is we begin our work at once. If we cannot find the man soon-"

"He is here."

"What?"

"He is here."

Arcimboldo is momentarily caught off guard. "He's here? Bruno? Where?"

"Upstairs, with the Chancellor and the sculptor, Mont."

"I must see him." Arcimboldo begins walking toward the stairs. The three other men join him.

The High Steward says, "My Lord Arcimboldus, can you spare one moment? Are arrangements complete for the pageant and procession from the Old Town Square to St. Vitus?" He plucks at Arcimboldo's sleeve to get his attention. "The decorations on the New Tower Gate are splendid. Splendid! It reminds me of what you did in '84."

"I can't tell you if they're finished, High Steward, and I can't take credit for those decorations either, Master Bardi is doing the decoration of town and castle for this Epiphany. You'll need to ask him. Fortunately for me, I've been able to focus my invention here on the Summer Palace. This is my sole responsibility today. You've met Bardi, haven't you? I promise you, he's a creative genius, very experienced, and his team of carpenters and painters are the same we have used here for years. I don't think you need to worry." Arcimboldo gestures to the empty space around them, "and as for this Summer Palace, rest assured, we will have it ready in time for the banquet, everything is laid out and carefully planned. We are well practiced, as you know."

There is a murmur of agreement from his listeners; Arcimboldo refers to Rudolf's fondness for presentation and performance. Ceremonies and entertainments are a common occurrence in this castle and city. These things are expected in a Habsburg prince. Lately however, Arcimboldo has noticed a peculiar trend in Rudolf's behavior: more and more often, Rudolf will organize a Court event, but then chooses to conceal himself to watch the festivities secretly, rather than taking part along with his guests. Also, the Emperor has employed a man who is a very close likeness, almost a double. Rudolf will have the man sit at a desk in a poorly lit room and conduct interviews with new or unwanted visitors, pretending to be the Emperor, while Rudolf watches through a secret panel. This disturbing trend seems to coincide with the stresses Rudolf feels from political, diplomatic, and military reversals. Getting back to the business at hand, Arcimboldo reminds himself, this 'second Rudolf' will have an important role to play in this evening's unfolding of events.

Since the men continue to follow him to the stairs, Arcimboldo must politely remind them, "of course, as you know, by orders of the Emperor I can't allow you inside our space up on the next floor, and I beg your pardons."

The High Steward must accept this, but he can't help himself, he looks put out, he is not at all used to being left out of things. Colonel Choma merely nods. He says to Arcimboldo, "my apologies, Arcimboldus, for not catching those Frenchmen sooner. I am overjoyed that you are not hurt, My Lord."

"About that... Colonel, how comes it that French assassins are roaming about Hradcany Castle?"

"Well, sir, rest assured, they are no longer 'roaming' about... anywhere... if that is a consolation to you."

"Ah. Am I correct in guessing that you refer to the violent sounds in the garden? You have caught them?"

"I do. We have."

"But Colonel, the Tercio Captain was ignorant of-"

"It was our own assassins that were chasing the Frenchmen, *not* the Tercio soldiers. You are right," Colonel Choma allows himself a wry smile and lowers his voice conspiratorially, "the Tercio Captain will know nothing about who the dead men are or who killed them."

"Why do you play this game? And why are the Frenchmen here... now? How could they have known about the Nolan?"

The Colonel steps closer and speaks quite seriously, "the Emperor's informers reported to him that men with the French delegation are spies and assassins, they track Giordano Bruno by the order of the Holy League and the Duc du Guise. The Tercio's officers are Spanish, they cannot be trusted."

"Spies and assassins! And they have come with the delegation!"

"This is what the Emperor has told me: they work for certain men within the delegation, and these men are in the service of the Holy League. They have been searching for Bruno in every Catholic city in Europe. They have been waiting for him to leave the protection of the Protestant Princes. Now they are hunting him in Prague. Naturally, he must stay hidden until he returns to Wittenberg."

High Steward Dietrichstein petulantly mutters, "am I *always* the last to be told of these things? After all, I am High Steward."

Arcimboldo knows that Giordano Bruno makes new enemies everywhere he goes, however he believes he already knows the answer to the question he is about to ask, "Colonel, what is the name of this man who is hunting the Nolan?"

"I believe his name is Fabrizio Mordente."

Arcimboldo is caught in a moment of indecision; he wants to ask Colonel Choma more about Mordente and the French delegation, and equally, he wishes to rush into the room at the top of the stairs and speak with the Nolan himself. Arcimboldo's brain, needing sleep, is working furiously to make this small decision. In this momentary pause, the ground floor doors begin to swing open and loud voices are heard.

Neither of the two warmly dressed figures coming through the doors is Rudolf. These men brushing snow from their shoulders are two more members of the Emperor's secret cabal, Austrian nobleman Reichard Strein von Schwartzenau, the Emperor's close friend, and Doctor Thaddeus Hagecius, the Emperor's physician and astronomer. Both of these reliable and intelligent noblemen are close confidants of the Emperor and will be present during the experiment. Arcimboldo has known them quite well for many years. Thaddeus Hagecius is two years older than Arcimboldo, looking more ancient than that, the old astronomer has a permanent squint and a peculiar posture from studying the stars night after night. His companion, Baron Schwartzenau has been a close personal friend to both Rudolf and his father, Maximilan II. He has held several positions at Court for the two Emperors, both in Vienna and Prague, but for the past several years has been living in his castle of Freideck in northern Austria; Castle Freideck has a reputation of being a miniature Hradcany, or a copy of the magic castle, Schloss Ambras. The fifty-one year old Baron and his eighteen year old son are eager associates of occultists and alchemists, patrons of book, map and manuscript sellers, amateur scientists and antiquarians, and fervent believers in Rudolf's version of Humanist philosophy and the Natural World. These newcomers to the Summer Palace are eager to report news they have just heard from a Tercio captain. Sensational news about two recently murdered men found in the Stag Moat. Shocking! On Epiphany Day!

Arcimboldo is impatient and does not allow himself to be distracted by the news the men carry, he excuses himself, "My Lords, we have only just arrived here ourselves, indeed Bartolomeus and I heard the screams of the murdered men." He looks toward the stairway, "however, I have not spoken to the Nolan yet, and I must. As you know, this is a day like no other, we must move forward and not lose sight of our goal. Pardon me, I will go upstairs to speak with Bruno immediately, before the Emperor arrives. Master Bartolomeus, will you accompany me?"

With a sigh of exhaustion, Hagecius says, "My Lord Arcimboldus, do as you say, by all means. I will wait here for the Emperor and catch my breath. Will you wait with me, Baron?" Colonel Choma excuses himself and exits, he is eager to see what has developed out by the moat. The High Steward chooses to accompany Arcimboldo and Spranger. Huffing and puffing with irritation he mounts the stairs once again.

The High Steward is heard mumbling under his breath, "complication and confusion! By Sisyphus! Have I been condemned to spend the rest of my life going up and down these blasted stairs!"

Arcimboldo chuckles and answers soothingly, "as Tullius Cicero would say, my Lord Dietrichstein, *'nihil est enim simul et inventum perfectum'*. Nothing was ever invented and perfected at the same time. We are bound to have confusions and anxieties. It is to test our mettle. Ultimately, what we do may seem foolish and unnecessary one moment and indispensible the next."

"Do I seem foolish, My Lord?"

"No, not at all. That's not what I mean, I talk about contradiction and interpretation. You do not *want* to walk these stairs again, and yet you feel you must. I cannot help wondering why."

"I'm too tired to appreciate your depth of thought, sir. But there *is* a reason I accompany you. There's something I've been meaning to ask you." The High Steward steps close to Arcimboldo, puts his hand on Arcimboldo's shoulder, he speaks softly and rapidly in his ear, "do you think I might come in, just for a moment?"

Arcimboldo looks at him and shakes his head.

"No? Well... I wonder if I might have a look, a single peek... perhaps if you just open the door widely as you enter I can look over your shoulder. After all, you know, I am a Humanist too, devoted to the sciences... and High Steward as well, by God. Can I not be trusted to keep a secret? I won't breathe a word to anyone... just between you and me, eh? The Emperor will never know... eh?"

Arcimboldo does not respond.

Dietrichstein blusters "well... who knows what may happen, as Steward I may have to enter suddenly during the experiment, something may require the Emperor's attention, I really should be allowed to go inside, there may be an unanticipated necessity..."

Silence. They climb two, three, four steps.

Dietrichstein speaks again "I wonder if I might-"

"You may not. My Lord."

"Well, after all, who are you to say so, I may just as well ask Rudolf himself!"

"My Lord High Steward, it is the Emperor's decision, and I think you know how earnest he is about it. This room must be kept private and secret." Arcimboldo shakes his head with a look of wonderment. "Of course you may ask him, I'm only trying to save you an unpleasant rebuff; but should you be so misguided as to try to enter during the experiment, the Emperor's reaction would be... incalculable... I would not even venture to guess at the degree of vexation this would cause him, therefore, I'm sure you will carefully consider – how many years have you known the Emperor? – you will carefully consider what you do." Seeking to say something ameliorating to the red faced and frowning High Steward, Arcimboldo continues, "I will open the door as widely as it will go, you will not be disappointed."

They stand before a large door with no keyhole or doorknob. The thickened and strengthened wooden door stands within a substantial stone door frame. Carved with wonderful skill, the stone frame gives the impression of being an enormous elongated mouth topped with a grotesquely flattened nose, eyes and brow. It is an exact copy of the street door to the Palazzetto Zuccari in Rome. Naturally, when walking through the door one has the sensation of being swallowed by the space within. For his temporary purposes, and for absolute security, the Emperor has had this room constructed so that there's only this one door, and it can only be opened from the inside; this effectively means that (short of breaking in) someone must always be inside to open the door. And so it has been for almost six months, Bartolomeus Spranger's friend and assistant, the Swiss sculptor Hans Mont, has practically been a prisoner inside the first floor of Hradcany's Summer Palace.

When Arcimboldo knocks it is Mont who opens the door a crack to peer out. As soon as it opens, Arcimboldo asks, "is Giordano Bruno in there?"

Mont answers, "yes, Maestro Arcimboldus, should I wake him?"

"No, we will come in." And Arcimboldo pushes on the door to open it. He pushes it fully open, and nods with his head for Spranger to go inside. Spranger and Mont soon disappear into the glitter and shadows within the large chamber. Arcimboldo turns and bows to the High Steward. "My Lord, will you be waiting downstairs to meet with the Emperor, or will I see you later at the pageant?" As he straightens up he sees there will be no answer forthcoming from the High Steward; the man stands as if struck, unblinking and mouth open, hand halfway raised in a forgotten gesture, he stares in disbelief. The halberdier that stands guard next to the door has half turned upon seeing the High Steward's face, unable to resist temptation, he also looks in, and he also stares, slack jawed and saucer eyed in uncomprehending fascination. Arcimboldo feels like Medusa; he releases these men from their spells by firmly shutting the door.

The Summer Palace stands on the verge of dense, ancient forest. This particular location near Prague's Hradcany Castle had always been forest, a part of the Royal hunting preserve, until 1538, when architect Paolo della Stella began to build a mansion surrounded by gardens for the much beloved wife of Archduke Ferdinand, Anna Jagellonska. Stella spared nothing in creating the beautiful stone reliefs on the gallery arcades and beneath the arches, carving the fine sandstone with his own hands alongside his crew of masons; thirty-six slender Ionic columns and an incredible one-hundred-fourteen panels in relief, illustrating mythological scenes, hunting parties, and wars. The most delicate and beautiful relief, carved by Stella himself, is of the Archduke in full Imperial regalia giving a fig flower to his ever beloved Anna. The unfinished building was severely damaged in the terrible castle fire of 1541, and still not repaired when

Queen Anna died in 1547, in the course of giving birth to her fifteenth child. Ferdinand had moved his Court out of Prague after the devastating fire, but to commemorate his wife Ferdinand named the structure after her, Queen Anna's Palace. Over time, people have begun to call it simply the Summer Palace. A new architect, Baron Boniface Wohlmut, was engaged by Rudolf's father, Maximilian, to complete and expand the building in 1573. Wohlmut added another floor above the ground floor arcades, creating a splendid balcony over the arches, he also gave the building its most unique and eye catching feature: the copper plated roof in the shape of an inverted ship's hull; the roof's graceful surfaces majestically rise, curve and pinch inward to meet and form the long horizontal ridge of the 'keel'. The uniquely shaped surface is painted with vertical red and white stripes and decorated with symbols of the Habsburg Empire.

On this early morning of January 6, 1587, it is up underneath the Palace's snow covered roof, inside this extraordinary Italianate structure, where the controversial philosopher and mathematician, the former Dominican friar known across Europe simply as 'the Nolan', dreams of transmutating shapes, geometric abstractions, and serpentine mathematical equations. Giordano Bruno was born the son of a soldier in Nola, a village on the slopes of the Vesuvius volcano. He became a Dominican friar at the same convent where the great theologian Thomas Aquinas is buried. During those years in Naples, Bruno's intelligence and skill in the art of memory became so famous that Pius V called him to Rome to demonstrate his ingenuity. Inevitably, Bruno had to flee Naples and the Dominican Order when accused of heresy, his crime was to have annotated a copy of Erasmus and then hidden the banned book in the convent urinal. The Church of

Rome could not hold the attention of this man whose genius penetrates and transcends all conventional knowledge. He wanders Europe, London, Paris, Munich, now Wittenberg. As great as his genuine intelligence is, Bruno's inflated self-estimation manages to make him an outcast wherever he goes: he is adored at first, then disliked, then driven away.

This man, whose given name is actually Felipe but who now prefers to be called Jordanus Brunus Nolanus, dreams of circles within hexagons within circles within squares, hermetic shapes, letters and images, Egyptian symbols, God the Creator and the Creation of God, he sees the boundary of knowledge and he longs to touch it. No, Giordano, be honest! That will not be enough either. Bruno must penetrate the Mystery of the World; he must see what is behind it. Bruno dreams he is soaring past the Stars and Planets, he is among the Constellations, with his finger he can trace a glowing Copernican diagram against the velvet blackness of the Universe. He draws a figure of circles bisected by lines according to Pythagorean theory; in the circles he draws triangles, diamonds and rhomboids, with Greek letters at the intersections of lines. It is a diagram he has invented himself, it is called the Speculum Magorum. Floating here in Space immersed in his mathesis, Bruno hears his name being called.

The dream universe begins to drop away, but puzzlingly, the diagram remains vividly in his vision, Giordano's heart convulses with fear, momentarily he believes he is dead. Awakening more, he sees that indeed his circular diagram, the Speculum Magorum, is there in front of him, and next to it a face that he recognizes. The carefully trimmed gray beard and moustache, large and well modeled aristocratic nose, expressive blue eyes under nobly arched brows... he knows this man who has awakened him. This is Giuseppe Arcimboldo.

"Ah ha, Hermes Trismegistus awakes. *Trismegistus visibilem deum.* Welcome, my friend." Arcimboldo lays his hand on Bruno's arm.
"But of course, *in medio vero omnium residet sol!*" Bruno smiles broadly; it is accentuated by his bushy moustache, and youthful twinkling eyes. He embraces his old friend, "Giuseppe, you have done stupendous work here! My heart races with excitement at the thought of what we are about to do!" Bruno gestures around, "I am inspired! Write this down. Hans Mont! Bring paper, pen, ink. I will write." Mont is nowhere near, and perhaps Bruno's request is rhetorical since he begins to grandly declaim in lightning fast Italian, "no one has such powers as he who has cohabitated with the elements, vanquished nature, mounted higher than the heavens, elevating himself above the angels to the archetype itself, with whom he then becomes co-operator and can do all things!"
Arcimboldo clears his throat, and very deliberately says "Fabrizio Mordente is in Prague."
"You jest."
"I do not. And how is it I discover you here, when I expected you at the Powder Tower?"
"I did not know about Mordente, but now I see the connection; I was kidnapped by Rudolf's Polish assassins, not half a mile out of Wittenberg. By Apollo I was terrified! I thought they were the Holy League at first. They brought me here, when it was still light, what time is it now? But Giuseppe, I must tell you, I can't imagine how you accomplished this... this..." Bruno stands and turns around to view that part of the room he can see, waving his hands in the air. "I don't

think I intend to *ever* leave this room. I will live here." Bruno places his hands over his breast, bows his head, and sighs as if overcome. Then he raises his head toward Arcimboldo and says, "why is that execrable turd in Prague?"

"Who's this Mordente, and what's this about the Holy League? I understood the Emperor kidnapped you because of his promise to the Pope and the King of Spain?" The speaker is Chancellor Jacob Kurtz von Senftenau, who, as is the fashion, Romanizes his name to Jacobus Curtius. This is, obviously, also the case with Josephus Arcimboldus for Giuseppe Arcimboldo; Doctor Thaddeaus Hagecius, whose real Czech name is Tadeas Hajek; Copernicus whose birth name is Mikołaj Kopernik; Paracelsus for Philippus von Hohenheim; Vesalius for Andries van Wesel; Zacharias Ursinus for Zacharias Baer; and many others. Certain types of well educated people have changed their names in this manner. They wish to advertise their learning and their respect for re-discovered Humanist values by renaming themselves in the Latin style of that pinnacle of Civilization, Intellect and Industry, the Roman Empire. Now, sweating profusely, this warmly, and very uncomfortably dressed Chancellor, Jacobus Curtius, sits gingerly on a bench made from a ladder set across two barrels. "Is the Holy League after you? Surely not here in Prague! Unless... is it the French?"

Bruno turns to Arcimboldo with a questioning look, "*is* it the French?"

"It does look like it, the assassins who came looking for you were French; by the way, Rudolf saved your life by bringing you here. *Mordente* is with the French delegation from Lorraine. And, according to Colonel Choma, Rudolf's spies have discovered that the Holy League has infiltrated the French delegation, and they are *hunting the Nolan*. That was the exact word he used 'hunting'." Arcimboldo looks meaningfully at Bruno "hunting... you."

"Oh... ballocks."

"Who is this Mordente, I've never heard of him... have I? Perhaps the name is familiar..." The corpulent Chancellor Curtius wipes perspiration from his brow and upper lip with a large handkerchief, the gold embroidery glints in the subtle candlelight that surrounds them.

"Giordano, can you do this quickly? Tell the Chancellor about Balaam's ass."

Bruno composes his face as though he is hiding a secret smile. This is the thing he enjoys most in the world, speaking to an audience about himself. "Fabrizio Mordente! It is the fault of that *cowardly* sycophant, that *mincing* buggerando, that I had to leave Paris! Not *my* fault at all, rather, I should be *praised* that I strove so hard, against constant criticism and calumny, to bring illumination to the dim and musty chambers of their closed Gallic minds. Perhaps I scolded Aristotle overmuch at the Ecole, but that is a small thing compared to-"

"Giordano!"

"My Lord, do you know what a proportional compass is? Used for surveying, navigation, gunnery-"

"A gunner's quadrant!"

"Correct. A most useful tool, however, mystifyingly invented by that most unworthy man, Fabrizio Mordente. Initially, I befriended the man and called him the God of geometricians, I praised his invention up to the sky. Immediately upon seeing Mordente's compass I realized I had the jawbone of an ass, so to speak, that I needed to bring down Aristotle's hypothesis of incommensurability of infinitesimals." A warning look from Arcimboldo keeps Bruno on track. "Out of the infinite reservoir of kindness in my soul I offered to translate the gentleman's work into Latin, since naturally he is deficient in that language. I persuaded him it would be the best way to share his wondrous discovery with the erudite and aristocratic circles where it would be most applauded. And yet, strangely, the *ingrate* objected to my finished translation, flying into a brutal passion when he heard of those additions I had made for his *own* good, and not appreciating the necessity of my niggling criticisms... for example my demonstration that he, the inventor, did not properly understand the true significance of his own work, nor was this to be expected from a pedestrian intellect such as his, but reserved for those with deeper insight. How people hate to hear the truth!"

"Didn't you follow that up by publishing a pamphlet called the *Triumphant Idiot,* comparing the man to Balaam's ass?"

"Indeed, *Idiota Triumphans* is an important examination of that Principle where inspiration can come to simple people, who then speak in an inspired way without fully understanding what they are saying. Balaam's ass carried the sacrament without knowing the significance of what it was carrying, just the same way Mordente carries this divine message of superior mathematical calculation without understanding its amazing uses and potential, things even unknown to the curious Egyptians, grandiloquent Greeks, and subtle Persians-"

"Did you not consider this treatment might, perhaps, excite the man's passions beyond the rational?"

"The ungrateful rapscallion! Should I care? All Europe knows, the Nolan is the most *reasonable* man in the world when it comes to civilized debate and honorable discourse, am I not? However, what does he do? The vile dog runs to the Duc du Guise, the slanderous tongue of that man set the Duc against me."

The Chancellor mops the back of his neck and under his several chins with his handkerchief. Absentmindedly he says, "while you're here the Emperor will protect you... probably. Can't say there's much love for Guiscards here, His Majesty hates them as much as he does Henry's mignons. But these metaphysics are beyond me."

"Pshaw! Metaphysics! I assure you, what others boast of as metaphysics is only a part of logic-"

"Can we open a window? By Hades, I'm being stewed!"

Arcimboldo has just begun to lose his chill, so he does not regret having to tell the Chancellor that all the windows have been covered and sealed. Now that the enormous fireplaces have been lit in anticipation of the coming event the room is beginning to warm. Arcimboldo says, "you will want to wear less clothing this evening, My Lord. With the alchemists' furnace lit it will be even warmer in here." Grumbling, Curtius struggles to his feet, "I will go downstairs then, to wait for the Emperor. When will all be ready? Will you test it?"

"As soon as Rudolf and the Nolan approve our final arrangement we will be ready. We want all to be perfect by the time Count Rozmberk brings the Englishmen."

As the Chancellor slowly moves toward the door Arcimboldo calls out to caution him, "carefully, My Lord Chancellor, carefully. Watch you do not trip on the wheels." To Bruno he says, "you may mock Mordente as you like, but the Holy League is another matter, another matter entirely." Bruno tries to speak but Arcimboldo speaks over him, "you have Rome against you now, the Roman Inquisition may not be what the Spanish was, but you best be very careful my friend, you're running out of places that will hide you." Arcimboldo watches Bruno to see if the man will react with reason or with petulance. Bruno says nothing, he looks down, he is thinking. Arcimboldo continues, "this place right here is safe, it doesn't matter who is in Prague, or even in the castle, here you are safe. The Emperor will protect you until you return."

"Return where?"

"To Wittenberg!"

"Return to Wittenberg? You assume we will fail?"

"No... I..."

"Oh, then you assume everything will return to the same familiar, comfortable patterns. All of this for one quick peek at the Infinite, and then back under the secure cover of blind ignorance, eh? What do you imagine will happen?"

"What do you mean?"

"Will Nature be indifferent that we have stripped her bare? Do not think all things will be the same and continue on in the same way if we master the elemental forces of Nature. Can you grasp that? But the Nolan... *I* contemplate success, what it will mean for me. And what will that be, Giuseppe, hmm? Should I go back to Wittenberg to teach mathematics and history? Once we discover the correct methods and processes... what can we *not* do! What will be in Wittenberg for me when Prague becomes the center of the World?"

Arcimboldo rubs his forehead. The pleasant sensation of returning warmth has made him realize he has had no sleep and most likely will have none this night, he yawns. He feels tired and disoriented, and the monumental day's work has not even begun. He says, "Giordano, my old friend, Light of the World, unmatched genius, I will not dispute with you. I become lost in this argument, and I feel I may wander in it indefinitely if I allow myself. Let us imagine that we are men of action, we will think only of what must be done next, and next and next, until we've laid down enough *causes* to anticipate an *effect*." He searches Bruno's face, hoping the man will look him in the eyes. "Unlike you, Nolan, my mind is more comfortable following the twisting and thorny path of science than wandering in the arid desert of undiscovered philosophies-"

"Wrong!"

"Let me finish. I am here to provide art, my skill, my eyes and hands. You are here to provide direction, a plan, an organization, a reasonable design to our mighty efforts. We each have our place, our role in the entirety," the image of Durer's blue bird wing flits across Arcimboldo's consciousness, "Rudolf has his indispensible and unique role, as do Rozmberk, Dee and Kelly, all of us are pieces of a whole."

Bruno has his arms crossed but is nodding, expectantly. "Yes, of a surety. And?"

"I'm saying that right now you and I have an important role to play, to wit, we must assess our work: our correctness, our completeness, our harmony, our perfection. And I trust we can do it with good spirits and without a cloud of unnecessary confusion and distraction." Arcimboldo rises from where he had been sitting, on the edge of the cot Bruno had been lying on. He grasps Bruno's circular diagram, the Speculum Magorum, he says, "let us review the images."

Shortly thereafter, there is a knock on the door. Arcimboldo sighs, he constructs a smile of calm confidence and sophistication for the Nolan, a courtier's smile, he says, "the Emperor. We begin." On their way to the door, Arcimboldo and Bruno must nimbly pick their way through the maze of objects in this lofty and dimly lit chamber. There are strange twisting shapes that resemble giant candelabra, huge wheels that stand on end and reach almost to the ceiling, various metal platforms and racks that stand, lean and even hang from chains of iron and bronze. Bizarre shapes and silhouettes extend into the distant shadows of the enormous room. However, it is the objects that these bizarre metal structures support, display, and illuminate that provide the most marvelous and powerful impressions; there are so many objects, of so varied and extraordinary an appearance, that the eye of the observer finds it impossible to alight and rest on any single thing. Even, as it is at the moment, unready, dimly lit and motionless, this assembly attracts the beholder with irresistible force; it is astir with the vitality of living ideas, infused with the energy of the World Spirit. In this room, secretly, these artistic, well educated, and brilliantly inventive men have recreated the Cosmos.

It is not Emperor Rudolf at the door; it is Bartolomeus Spranger and Hans Mont. They inform Arcimboldo that the Emperor is in the gardens, on his way, he has paused to inspect the bodies of the two men fished out of the Stag Moat. Mont hands Arcimboldo a bundle wrapped in a cloth, "your servant gave these to me for you, My Lord."

"I thank you. Um, Master Mont, where have you left the urinal? And is there water?"

"Both are where the Nolan was sleeping, sir, look under the cot for a jug."

Arcimboldo turns to Bruno and Spranger, "Masters, excuse me, I will take a moment to myself. Bartolomeus, I think you and Hans can begin lighting all the wicks." Arcimboldo pauses in the act of walking away, in Italian he says, "Giordano, a moment please."

He puts his arm around the Nolan's shoulder and maneuvers him away from earshot of the others, "Giordano, look at me, I'm serious. You need to hear this now. Do not be frivolous with the Emperor. Do not mistake his silence and reserve for ignorance or timidity. Do not think you can read his mind or predict what he will say or think. Do not correct him. Do not think you can amuse him. Never laugh, and smile as infrequently as possible in his presence. Above all, Giordano, above all, do not think you will know when you have gone too far..." Arcimboldo holds up his hand to halt Bruno's indignant protest, "just a minute... you will not know when you have gone too far, by the time you do it will be far too late, too late. I tell you this because I cannot help you if you do something foolish... you understand? There is nothing I'll be able to do." Bruno is glaring at him. Arcimboldo pats the side of his face in a brotherly and affectionate way. "Don't be angry, Giordano." Bruno does not answer.

It is still dark and still snowing as the Emperor sweeps up the steps to the Summer Palace. He wears a huge black bear skin cloak trimmed in white rabbit fur – the contrasts in color and animal attributes create a powerful and all-encompassing Symbol. Rudolf is accompanied by Georg Erasmus Schwartzenau, Baron Schwartzenau's young son, Jan Sixt Trautson, the Marshall of the Imperial Curia, Atlas, four servants, and four personal bodyguards; these bodyguards, all handpicked elite soldiers, known as Trabante, show their dedicated allegiance to the Empire by fastening their ermine cloaks with a Habsburg emblem: a triple chain with a pendant golden medallion of an eagle clutching an arrow in its talons. Rudolf pauses to remove his brimmed flat cap, shaking and brushing the snow from it, the shivering halberdiers standing guard either side of the doors hasten to open them for the

Imperial entourage, and the interior of the Summer Palace is revealed. The ground floor is brightly lit and bustling. Half a dozen old women scrub the floors, clean and light the fireplaces; a dozen men are setting planks on trestles and assembling scaffolds; a score of boys race about carrying buckets, vases, bundles of faggots, rolls of cloth, chairs, platters; and one youth drags an intruding dog out by a side door.

In the midst of this maelstrom, five men stand in conversation: Chancellor Curtius, High Steward Dietrichstein, Baron Schwartzenau, Doctor Hagecius, and Cesare Ripa, who is Arcimboldo's lieutenant in charge of decoration and the setting up of the feast and entertainments. All of these men turn and bow to Rudolf as he enters. They are copied by all the others in the room, who then pause and watch expectantly. There is a chorus of "Your Majesty"s in German as the four aristocrats approach the Emperor. One would think he did not answer, but if you had been standing right next to him you would have heard him say "mmmm." Cesare Ripa is now exhorting his workers to return to their jobs, in unintelligibly fast Italian and very poor Czech (perhaps this is why the old women continue to move at such a very slow pace!)

"The artists are upstairs, my Lord."

"Mm hmm."

Georg Erasmus and his father exchange greetings, and a lively description of the wounds on the dead men he has just viewed with the Emperor.

"Shall we go upstairs now, my Lord?" The High Steward has extended his arm toward the stairs as an invitation to the Emperor. As Rudolf continues to stand there without speaking or moving the High Steward begins to slowly, awkwardly lower his arm, as it finally falls to his side, Emperor Rudolf steps forward and marches toward the stairway.

Arcimboldo tucks the wire rim of his short ruff collar underneath the edge of his black doublet. As he does he smells the pleasant odor left on his fingers from the tooth powder he has just used. Doctor Hagecius had recommended this most excellent recipe: half a gram of white coral, a gram of seed pearls, a gram and a half of meerschaum, all ground to powder with one clove and a pinch of sugar, applied with the finger or a strip of clean linen soaked in tepid white wine. Since Arcimboldo has begun using this powder he finds his breath is sweeter, his mouth feels cleaner, and foods taste better, also, he is glad not to be continually sipping spiced and sweetened wine to freshen his breath, it leaves him drowsy, the heat of the wine does not agree with his humors and gives him headache, gas, and sour stomach. It is a pity more Germans at the Court do not do likewise and follow this latest Italian fashion. Arcimboldo brushes his hair, beard and moustache, and puts a black, tight fitting felt cap on his head. He does not need his cloak or gloves; he leaves them on the cot. He takes his logbook under his arm, reaches into a pocket and gently squeezes the engraved ruby he always carries there for good fortune, straightens his clothing, breathes in deeply, lets the breath out slowly, then marches toward the door.

The large group of men has gathered at the top of the stairs, in front of the door, the only door, to the first floor interior of the Summer Palace. The expression on the huge, grotesque stone face surrounding the door appears to flicker and change, to wink and leer, in the inconstant light from the surrounding torches. Doctor Hagecius is wheezing from the climb and leans on the arm of young Georg Erasmus to recover his breath. The High Steward steps forward confidently and raps on the thick wooden door.

Rudolf clears his throat and says, "a pleasant night to you, My Lords, we will go on from here." Marshall Trautson immediately takes the very clear message and bows to the Emperor, turns and descends the stairs. The High Steward has paused, looking hopefully at Rudolf, who looks balefully back at the man. Finally Rudolf says, "Lord High Steward…" in a tone the High Steward clearly knows; he cringes, bows with a mumbled, "Your Majesty", and dejectedly follows Trautson down the staircase. Rudolf steps forward and knocks again on the door. It is opened almost immediately by Giuseppe Arcimboldo, who bows and fully opens the door while stepping to one side, giving Rudolf a clear view of the Cosmos he has created.

Rudolf stumbles slightly as he walks over the threshold because he is looking up. Arcimboldo reaches out and steadies him by grabbing his arm; he releases the Emperor immediately. Unexpectedly, as he is doing so, Rudolf reaches out and quickly squeezes Arcimboldo's wrist, looks him in the eye and holds contact, and smiles. Extraordinary! Arcimboldo cannot remember the last time he saw the Emperor smile in public. He is honored, he courteously returns a half bow to the Emperor, who says, "Arcimboldus, what have we done here? This is beyond all my expectations. Your work is *sprezzatura artficiosa*, We honor you."

Rudolf has just told Arcimboldo that his work is *sprezzatura* – a kind of charismatic talent whose performance is without defect of any kind. He combines this with *artificiosa*, which means unnatural, crafty, simulated or manufactured. The Emperor's message is subtle and complicated; work done so artfully, so skillfully, that it appears perfectly Natural and not contrived. Arcimboldo understands quite well, and is honored once again. He bows and replies to the Emperor, "this room contains all the chains of causation in this World, everything that is and was. May it serve your purpose and glorify God and the Empire."

The group of aristocrats and artists wander about the large space in admiration of the detail and marvelous variety. The full effect of the lamps and candles is truly magical: the crystals, pearls, gemstones and finely wrought silver and gold sparkle, gleam and scintillate; the life-like colors in the hundreds of small paintings of animals and plants harmonize, resonate, and compete with the brilliant gems for the attention of the beholder. The portraits of living creatures are displayed high up or low down according to their position in the Natural World: fish and creatures that live within the earth are lowest down, birds and creatures of the sky on the highest supports. And when one looks up towards the birds and the curving vaulted ceiling painted deep blue, what twinkles above? Hundreds of tiny pieces of mirror, mortared to the vaulted ceiling, placed to simulate the Stars and Constellations, reflecting the dance of light from the candles and lamps below. In the exact center of the room, forming a central point of focus (as if that were possible in such a space), is the alchemist's oven. A copper hood over the brick oven attaches to a narrow duct which snakes up through the shadows and Constellations, exiting unseen through the roof twenty feet above.

Arcimboldo has been showing the Emperor and his comrades examples of the illustrations of animals and plants that are on display. They stand in front of the large array of watercolors done from Pliny's *Naturalis Historia* that grace an iron wheel twelve feet high. On either side of the wheel are scores of small animal and plant portraits done by Joris Hoefnagel and

Hans Hoffman, two of Rudolf's favorite nature painters (Rudolf pays Hoffman to send him exact copies of Durer paintings that he is not able to buy). Each picture in this room, in fact, each object, is secured in a niche or rack with its own small light source: a small lamp, or candles in a glass bowl. The artists who have created this room have not had everything in its place and fully lit like this before, the effect is tremendously impressive, even to Arcimboldo, Spranger, and Mont, who have spent so much time here; often these men will stop in what they are doing and stare, captivated, having found some new or unexpected detail or perspective. Arcimboldo notices Bruno, he says to Rudolf, "Your Imperial Majesty, may I present to you, the Nolan, Jordanus Brunus Nolanus, mathematician, historian, philosopher, and scholar, vital to our enterprise, and your devoted servant." Arcimboldo gracefully leans toward Bruno and motions for him to approach.

Rudolf removes his bear skin cloak and hands it to Arcimboldo. The inside of the cloak has been lined with deep red silk embroidered in black and gold thread. The embroidery depicts the Habsburg double-headed eagle surmounted by a crown. Arcimboldo works to fold this bulky piece of clothing as Bruno approaches modestly. He is still wearing the Dominican friar's cassock he left Wittenberg in. He is almost of an age with the Emperor, but appears much younger due to his unusual and unfashionable choice of wearing a moustache but no beard; his clean shaven chin and cheeks do much to increase his natural handsomeness, dark eyes, and youthful appearance. Bruno makes an adequate bow to the Emperor who says, "Nolanus, you do us honor." Rudolf expansively waves his arm in the air, "this is superb, extraordinary, it is beyond my vocabulary! You have guided us to this moment of

Jubilation, sir, We are grateful. You must be very proud."

Arcimboldo is again surprised at the graciousness of Rudolf's speech. He closely watches Bruno to see what his response will be, ready to jump in immediately if necessary. The Nolan, having heard about Rudolf's aloofness, expected a gruff question about mathematics, philosophy, or history; he is put slightly off track by the polite complement. He makes a long and expressive bow to the Emperor that would do credit to the most accomplished courtier, and Arcimboldo raises an eyebrow in surprise. Bruno rises and smiles mildly and modestly at the Emperor, but says nothing. Not a word. The Emperor grunts and nods in approval of Bruno's modesty and reserve, qualities he had been told the man did not possess. Schwartzenau exclaims in delight at a marvel he has discovered, and the Emperor moves away to speak with the Baron. Arcimboldo beams at the Nolan, he is surprised, delighted, and relieved.

The most well informed Humanists, the most widely read, those with an intuitive understanding of the wisdom passed along from the ancient world, appreciate nothing more than a multilevel message; a message that communicates the complexity, diversity and interdependency of all God's creations. Rudolf, even more than his father did, believes that understanding these Humanist messages are critical, vital to understanding how the World will change, and therefore vital to his responsibilities as ruler of the Empire. Rudolf attempts to collect the Wisdom of the World in order to understand the World.

An example of the type of message Rudolf collects and is sensitive to is embodied in a complex object from the workshop of Cornelius Gross in

Augsburg. An extremely rare tortoiseshell has been polished and crafted in the shape of a buffalo's horn, creating an object with attributes of both land and sea. This horn, about twenty inches long, has a hinged cover on its large end which extends into a startling life-likeness of a serpent's head. This cover is made of the most exquisitely worked gold, the hammered arcs simulating the snake's scales are perfection itself, it seems one can almost sense movement beneath the skin. The twisting and knotted serpent's tail, on the small end of the tortoiseshell horn, is just as carefully and skillfully created, and the form is so realistically designed that one can imagine the golden tail is actually twisting and writhing. This serpent-like horn rests on two golden legs, the legs of a cock, and golden cock's wings are attached to the sides of the horn, so cunningly modeled that one feels the feathers are fluttering. The legs of the serpent-cock stand firmly on the back of a golden tortoise whose legs are splayed out, the tortoise appears to be pinned down by the animal on its back, and its head is raised in an effort to snap at its tormentor with sharp teeth. On the back of the serpent-cock rides a golden man, a Triton with billowing cloak, ragged beard, and scowling expression. The Triton brandishes a miniature golden shield with the emblem of the House of Habsburg painted upon it. This work is astonishing in its beauty, detail, and complexity. Is this a work of art? Not entirely. It is a tool, a utensil. It is a drinking cup (although, to be honest, it has rarely been used as such); the hinged serpent-headed cover folds back allowing the vessel to be filled with wine and then drunk from. Of course, it is much more than a simple cup, and yet more than just art, more than a crafted object (it has been part of a living creature), more than a living creature (it has been changed and added to by Man, enhanced into a Symbol for a much larger, Universal, Natural Truth). It is an object symbolic of the Earth, Air and Water. It is a Symbol and example of transformation and transmutation.

This object now rests on a bronze shelf within the first floor of Prague's Summer Palace among other similar marvels made of gold, silver, gems, and the rarest of naturally found organic objects such as pearls, corals, bezoar stones, ostrich eggs and elaborate shells. The transformed tortoiseshell-horn-animal is bathed in the warm glow of the hundreds of lamps and candles that now light the room. The detailed, intricate carving and molding of the gold shimmers in the soft light, the amber and umber tones of the tortoiseshell look liquid, like honey. Giordano Bruno lightly touches the horn with that thought in mind, can it be as soft and liquid as it looks?

Not far from the alchemist's oven is a part of the room used for exhibiting World Systems. Among them are diagrams from Giordano Bruno's *Liber De Umbris Idearum*, one-hundred-fifty images of great personalities and inventors, and the emblems that symbolize their ideas. The genius behind *De Umbris Idearum* is that the whole sum of human knowledge accumulated through the centuries can be represented by the works of these one-hundred-fifty people. Many of the images Bruno has developed rely on a mysterious iconography of Egyptian or Cabbalistic figures, some are almost entirely geometric. The Speculum Magorum is among the diagrams of *De Umbris Idearum*. Next to Bruno's work are a set of celestial images from Marsilio Ficino's *De Vita Coelitus Comparanda*. Pico della Mirandola is represented by a map of Europe on which is superimposed circular and oval medallions inscribed with signs of the zodiac, the planets and the months, all parts of the human body, the gifts of the Holy Spirit and the corresponding sins; these are surrounded with illustrations of the seven Ages of Life. Nearby are many other images illustrating the World views of Aristotle, Plato, Lucretius, Agricola, Petrarch, Copernicus, and others.

Hans Mont and Georg Erasmus have been relighting candles and lamps blown out accidently by the group of men as they walk around. The blundering, sweating Chancellor Curtius bumps into a stand, causing a carved and polished coconut mounted in gold, pierced with crystal, and surmounted by a golden monkey reading a book, to fall, bounce, and roll across the floor. Arcimboldo is retrieving it when there is a knock on the door.

The Emperor's servants, who have remained outside, inform him that a message has just come from Count Rozmberk, he is on his way, and although his coach may be delayed by snow he will have the English alchemists at the castle by mid-day. Rudolf is pleased. Although there is no more smiling or complementing, the Emperor is conversing in a relaxed and cordial way. He is preparing to leave, he will next return this evening at the important moment of transformation – his transformation. With this thought, Rudolf feels an unaccustomed swirl of trepidation in his bowels, his jaw tightens and he becomes silent. He wishes to see Katharina and contemplate his unborn child.

Arcimboldo watches Rudolf. He watches the expression subtly change on his face and thinks how unreadable the man has become. He cannot begin to guess what thoughts haunt the Emperor's melancholy Mind. It's become almost impossible to discover the once youthful features (features he could read like a book) in the Emperor's fixed, maturity-padded countenance. Arcimboldo remembers the pencil sketches he did of Rudolf trying on his crowns for the first time, many years ago, fifteen at least. They were done without any attempt to flatter or enhance reality; one of them showed the crown of the Holy Roman Empire falling down comically on the young man's forehead and ears, two fingers too large at least. That drawing presented a smooth, beardless face, with wide open, earnest, naïve eyes. A childhood spent at the solemnly religious, soberly refined, humorless Court of the King of Spain had not quite extinguished visible expressions of humanity, such as hope, humor, and a desire to trust the World around him. Nowadays, such expressions have been replaced by a determined emptiness. The saturnine expression of a man who feels himself unequal to the grace bestowed upon him; a man who, in spite of sincere spiritual contrition and great personal authority, remains undelivered of the fear of his loneliness and smallness. Arcimboldo wonders: has this room, this experiment, revived a flicker of hope within Rudolf's breast? Or has Katharina and his unborn child done this? Or both? Perhaps Arcimboldo has flattered himself thinking the Emperor was smiling at him earlier, perhaps what he saw was a brief flicker of hope being reborn in the man.

The Emperor and his entourage prepare to leave this wonderful, artificial Cosmos. Arcimboldo gives Mont instructions to put out the lights, refresh the candles, cotton wicks and lamp oil, and rest for a few hours. It is decided that Giordano Bruno will stay in the room as well.

As the group of men begins to pass out of the room, Bruno asks, "where is the portal image?" Arcimboldo feels a shard of ice in his stomach. He says, "you mean the St. John?"

"I mean the Bacchus. It should be right here near the entry, it is our portal."

Rudolf has stopped in the doorway to listen. Arcimboldo says, "yes, of course, it's here, we've moved it out of the way for convenience, everyone passing in and out; it will be in place tonight."

"I want to see it."

"Of course, it's right there, next to that fireplace behind you."

The room has enormous fireplaces in its east and west walls. Bruno walks closer and bends down to inspect the painting, he immediately says, "it's not Bacchus, you haven't changed it!"

In 1518 Leonardo da Vinci painted a version of St. John the Baptist that is simple and very mysterious at the same time. Very simply, it is a naked man sitting in a grotto, pointing over his shoulder, and holding a tall, thin cross; an atmospheric landscape recedes in the distance. This man holds a cross, he points over his shoulder – therefore the simple meaning is: he is St. John witnessing the coming of Jesus. But if one examines the details more closely, mysterious questions arise: why does John have the body of a finely muscled man but the face and hair of a woman? Why is John's face shadowed and sad? Is John about to speak, to grimace, or about to smile? Why is John completely naked? Why is the grotto so dark, what else is hidden there, is John really pointing to the inside of the grotto? Rudolf and the favored guests who have seen the picture have often debated the content and meaning. Arcimboldo, knowing Leonardo's Humanist philosophy and symbolism as well as anyone, believes there is a deeper meaning to the painting, he claims that the artist shows us Christianity, in the form of John, pointing back nostalgically to the pagan philosophers of the past. Rudolf accepts this, he likes this interpretation, and had agreed that this picture represents a type of transformation that should be included in their Cosmos... until the picture was described to the Nolan.

Giordano Bruno felt the symbolism was wrong; he wrote to Prague advising that the image should be changed. His interpretation was that St. John was burying the past not inviting it forward. He wanted the naked St. John to be transformed into Bacchus, a figure from pre-Christian mythology. That would be a powerful transformation; more effective than if it had been painted that way to begin with. Arcimboldo had been asked to make the changes.

Now, Bruno complains, "Christianity is burying the past, not inviting it forward. This cannot be our portal." Rudolf approaches, frowning.

Arcimboldo could not bring himself to paint over Leonardo's picture. He had hoped he could argue his way out of this, he sees it will be very difficult. He says, "Master Bruno, Nolanus, let us consider the Heavenly energy contained in the work of that divine Maestro, Leonardo. Should we dilute that pure inspiration, the product of that faultless mind that could see to the center of all things? The virtue of the Maestro's design is...inviolable-"

"Arcimboldus-"

The Emperor joins the conversation, "I thought we discussed this already."

Bruno is dogged, unshakeable, "Arcimboldus, the painting's design must conform to our design, my design, otherwise it is only a pretty picture, and not a suitable tool for our metamorphosis. And it has little value to us here in its present form."

"Arcimboldus, did we not discuss this?" Rudolf now speaks in harsh German.

"Yes, My Lord. However..."

"What? However what?" Rudolf's face is darkening.

"I felt it would be prudent to think about this again, we may be destroying the power of Leonardo's work. Perhaps we could find another painting, among your many Brueghels-"

"Should I ask Bartolomeus to change this painting?"

Arcimboldo does his best to stifle a sigh. "I will do it, Your Majesty. Since you both feel it's a necessity, I'll do it immediately."

Arcimboldo looks at Bruno. Is that a smirk on the man's face? The dog! The Emperor is waiting impatiently, and Arcimboldo quickly wraps Leonardo's painting to take with him. As he passes by Bruno he whispers, *"brutto cattivo!"*

As the group begins down the stairway, Bruno follows them out onto the landing, he calls out to Rudolf, "Your Majesty, may I say a few words of inspiration and instruction, something that will harmonize in all our minds until we meet again tonight?" The Doctor and Chancellor groan in tired protest, and Rudolf looks reluctant, but he stops to listen to what Bruno has to say, the others wait expectantly as well.

The Nolan stands above them all, on the landing. He steps forward, lifts his chin high, clears his throat, raises his right hand dramatically, palm upward, like orators of old. He speaks in Latin, softly at first, then with greater and greater enthusiasm, "My Lords, think on this and prepare your minds properly. Unless you make yourselves equal to God, you cannot understand God, for the like is not intelligible save to the like. Believe that nothing is impossible for you...think yourselves immortal and capable of understanding all...all arts, all sciences, the nature of every living being. Mount higher than the highest height, descend lower than the lowest depth, draw into yourself all sensations of everything ever created, fire and water, dry and moist, imagining that you are everywhere, on earth, in the sea, in the sky, that you are not yet born, in the maternal womb, adolescent, old, dead, beyond death. If you embrace in your thoughts all things at once – times, places, substances, qualities, quantities, if you do all these things, then you may understand God. I will meditate on this and prepare myself. I urge you all to do likewise." Bruno drops his head on his chest dramatically, turns and reenters the room, and slowly closes the door behind him, without once looking at his audience. After a silent pause of several seconds the group begins slowly descending the stairs again, not a word is spoken.

As he descends from the first floor to the ground floor of the Summer Palace, Arcimboldo imagines that the wrapped painting beneath his arm fairly vibrates with protest and alarm. The Emperor quickly exits the Palace without a backward glance, and a string of tired nobles and servants follow him. Baron Schwartzenau's son, Georg Erasmus, comes to Arcimboldo and asks if there is anything he can do to help out, he is far too excited to be able to sleep. With an understanding and indulgent smile, Arcimboldo asks him to take Leonardo's painting to his room in the Royal Palace; he thanks the richly dressed young man, and thoughtfully watches George Erasmus, Leonardo da Vinci, and St. John the Baptist leave the building. Arcimboldo asks Bartolomeus Spranger, who is standing near him, "will you try to sleep?"

Spranger yawns and says "I *am* tired, I'm not sure I'll be able to sleep, but I'm going to try. Will you walk back to the castle now?"

"I can't just yet, I must speak with Cesare. Do you intend to go to your house to see your wife?"

"No, I'll stay here. I'll go into town to see her later... yes, I really should." He yawns again. "But right now... sleep."

Arcimboldo hesitantly asks, "Bartolomeus... so... will I find you in your rooms if I'm in need of conversation... and perhaps... advise?"

Spranger looks closely at Arcimboldo. "*You* need advise? You must mean the Leonardo."

"Would *you* do it?"

"I would. Of course. You know I would. But I understand what you're feeling, I understand your nervousness about covering his invention, oh yes! Covering Leonardo's God sent inspiration." He shakes his head as if to clear away an unpleasant thought. "By St. Luke, it makes me shiver when I think about it like that. But think of it like *this*: Leonardo's invention is still there, you are cloaking it, not destroying it. You're creating a new message for a greater purpose, an important purpose, a purpose Leonardo would fully endorse; you are *combining* with Leonardo's invention to create a more powerful Symbol and a deeper Mystery." Spranger laughs lightly, "I learned these things from you. You know there's truth in what I say. I hope..."

Arcimboldo nods in agreement, he looks in Spranger's eyes, "I thank you, Bartolomeus, I thank you. I needed to hear that, I *do* believe in what you say, I'm marvelously cheered by your sound counsel."

The two friends pause, look at one another openly, frankly and honestly, but each man's private thoughts wander away along his own rutted highways of hope and fear.

"By the way... you never introduced me to the Nolan."

"I did not. I apologize. He is…" Arcimboldo waves his hand vaguely in the air.

"Yes. He is. Without a doubt." Spranger winks and smiles. Then, his homely face expands, stretches and distorts in an enormous yawn. "Good night, or is it good morning? Come to my rooms if you wish to talk. But knock loudly."

Of the two large rooms that comprise the ground floor of the Summer Palace, the front room, facing the Imperial gardens, is intended for the play, music, and dancing; the adjoining room further to the east is being set up for dining. In the banquet room trestle tables have been set up in a large squared off U-shape and covered in thick gray felt. Women and boys are spreading Flemish white lace tablecloths across them. The elegant window sills and white stucco carvings along the walls are being decorated with festoons of freshly gathered ivy and holly, much of it still icy and wet. Alongside the walls, every ten feet, are tall and elaborate bronze pedestals resting on blackened bronze lion's paws. The pedestals support delicate vases, cleverly carved masks, artificial fruit, taxidermy birds, both real and carved garlands, and numerous candle holders.

In the front room, the stage is being constructed, at the moment the flyloft is being assembled – the web of beams over the stage which support winches, curtains, and scenery. The stage itself is fifteen feet wide and twelve feet deep, but only three feet high. A half-dozen workers stand on and around the stage with their hands on their hips staring into the open trap door. Issuing from down in this dark and cramped place Arcimboldo hears the irritated, bird-like voice of his assistant, Cesare Ripa. Cesare's rapid Roman dialect is hard for Arcimboldo's northern ears to follow at the best of times, but it seems to be that there is not enough room under the stage for the lifting device that will dramatically raise the cradle holding baby Jesus. While Arcimboldo is waiting for his voluble assistant, he opens his logbook and begins to review the production schedule for the day's entertainments.

Today's events are hastily arranged things compared to the usual castle pageants, tournaments and theatrical productions, which customarily allow six months or a year for preparation. It was a little over a month ago that the Emperor was *'invited'* to host an Epiphany dinner for Ferdinando de Medici, Grand Duke of Tuscany. The Tuscan prince is interested in marrying now that he has come to the title of Grand Duke. He is interested in a closer relationship with France; therefore he is exploring the possibility of a marriage with Christina of Lorraine, a Valois princess, granddaughter of Queen Catherine de'Medici. Ferdinando is very particular, he does not trust the ability of artists to portray Christina accurately (imagine a Florentine Duke not trusting an artist!). He desires to meet his potential Grand Duchess in person before he begins the elaborate and lengthy engagement process. To be discrete he will meet Christina in Prague as if by chance. It will be announced that Ferdinando is traveling from Florence to Cracow, and that Christina is traveling from Paris to Venice, by apparent accident they will both find themselves in Prague for Epiphany. Rudolf has been enlisted as a matchmaker, he has been persuasively asked to host an occasion that allows these two regal and cosmopolitan aristocrats to meet publically in a manner befitting their wealth and breeding. It is a favor asked by France and the Grand Duchy that the Emperor cannot diplomatically refuse (although it is maddeningly inconvenient), he has no reason to refuse (that he can advertise) – the insult and embarrassment would be serious indeed.

So, the visiting High Royalty cannot be turned away, that much is clear. However, it's also clear that the Emperor's experiment cannot be delayed; astrological experts, Giordano Bruno, Doctor Hagecius, and Doctor John Dee have all independently cast horoscopes that indicate Epiphany is the optimal moment; indeed, Rudolf and his advisors have been planning the momentous but secret event for well over a year. The coincident timing has become an unfortunate complication, but what can be done? The two functions will have to take place simultaneously. As Rudolf and Arcimboldo planned the coordinated events, they decided the best approach, in order to maintain control over all things, would be to have both events happen simultaneously in the Summer Palace. The cream of European Royalty will be having a civilized feast, chatting pleasantly, laughing, enjoying delightful music and delicious drink; while unbeknownst to them, over their heads, literally, Emperor Rudolf will be mastering the secrets of the alchemy and changing the course of the World.

Cesare Ripa has mastered the secrets required of him, and crawls free of the stage. He confers with his chief and mentor, Giuseppe Arcimboldo. "Jesu, Maestro, if it were possible to find a crew of thicker blockheads we would not be in Prague! I'll never use Master Havel again, his idea of-"

Arcimboldo looks up from his accounts ledger and interrupts, "yes, yes, and on that subject, Cesare, have you paid them yet?"

"No!"

Arcimboldo murmurs, "good, good" as he runs his finger down a ledger list in his logbook. "Who else hasn't been paid yet?"

Cesare looks wary, "Maestro, they'll *all* expect to be paid today, you know."

Arcimboldo closely refers to his ledger sheet once again, as though he might have missed something, "well, Cesare, let's see. Hmm. Hmm. That may not be possible, no, no, I don't think that'll be possible. Hmm." Cesare is shifting from foot to foot nervously. Arcimboldo look up decisively "this is what you will do, pay the chandler-"

"But-"

"Pay the chandler and do it handsomely, make sure you do it in front of as many tradesmen as possible, then instruct the man that we will need another hundred, no, two-hundred spiral and two-hundred straight candles delivered to you here... by dusk, absolutely by dusk, not a second later."

"What about all the other bills, my Lord?"

"Tell them the... High Steward will be happy to oblige them... the day after tomorrow." Arcimboldo cannot repress a smile at the image this forms in his mind.

"The High Steward?"

"Yes."

"The day after tomorrow?"

"Exactly."

The snow has stopped, the clouds have parted, a half moon brightly lights the city of Prague in anticipation of Epiphany dawn, which must be very near, perhaps it is hidden by the storm clouds in the east. As Arcimboldo leaves the Summer Palace he believes it is dawn because there is so much light on the snow in the gardens, but looking up he sees the sky is still black. A black, star filled sky, and to the east: black cloud. But the half moon shines brilliantly on the snow covering the Imperial gardens, it illuminates the patches of snow clinging to the lofty spires atop St.

Vitus Cathedral, and sets the edges of some feathery, scudding clouds glistening, they become so pale as to be almost white against the dark sky. These ghostly, silent, metamorphosing shapes rush to the west as if fleeing the approaching sun.

Before Arcimboldo gets to the walkway he pauses to wrap himself securely in his cloak, it is not snowing but it is very cold. He claps his hands to warm them and thinks of his gloves, left upstairs. He debates to himself whether it will be worth the effort to go back and get them, however, clapping his hands has given him a sudden thought that *does* require him to go back up the steps and into the Palace. Arcimboldo calls out, "Cesare!"

A head pops up from the stage trap door, "Yes, Maestro!"

"Do you have the musicians?"

"Master Phillipus wasn't happy, but yes we have them."

"Where?"

"They're locked in Captain Wroclaw's guard room in the castle."

"And my instructions?"

"No beer, no wine, no drink but water, my Lord."

"Perfetto, Cesare."

No matter the cold, Arcimboldo must stop quickly by the side of the walkway to urinate, as he stands there waiting, shivering, he thinks: he has been inventing, designing, and producing stage plays, tournaments, coronations, weddings, royal events of all kinds for more than thirty years, he has learned his lesson many times over, so now he knows how to prepare properly, he has no intention of letting drunken musicians spoil his carefully planned events ever again.

Giordano Bruno's exhortation to 'think like God' has left an unpleasant uneasiness in his stomach. Rather than explore that thought, Arcimboldo concentrates on concrete details of the day ahead as he hurries back to the Palace. He passes quite a few hunched and serious castle workers on the long walkway to the bridge over the moat. They are beginning their busy day, rushing to complete chores that must be done at first light. Some will be going to the zoo, menageries, and aviaries to feed the animals. Arcimboldo recognizes several gardeners on their way to the orangeries and greenhouses, with very grim looks on their faces. Some of these people passing him will be reporting to Cesare at the Summer Palace. Imperial sentries are already posted at the entry to the bridge over the moat; it is still black as Hades down in that ragged, snowy chasm, Stag Moat, but Arcimboldo notices the sky in the east beginning to lighten over the threatening cloud mass on the horizon.

The northern portal is bustling with activity and the brightness of the massed torches makes Arcimboldo squint his eyes. The ground floor of the castle is swarming with workers preparing for a very busy Epiphany Day. However, upstairs, the hallways of Hradcany Castle are silent, cold and dark. Most of the lamps and torches lit at the beginning of the evening have now burned out and Arcimboldo travels part of the way in total darkness, relying on his memory of these familiar pathways. Arcimboldo's rooms, on the third floor, are reached by a low-ceilinged hallway paneled in dark wood, padded burgundy-red leather panels, and faded tapestries.

There is a small table and a wooden chair against the wall next to his door. The bronze lamp on this table is cleverly made to look like the leg and talons of a bird of prey, and upon this base rests the neck and head of a laughing, bearded man. The head is thrown back wildly, the mouth is stretched open to its fullest, inside the mouth flickers a wick in the last moments of its life. The large life-like talons are sharply pointed and fiercely extended, but they provide a secure footing for the lamp. This startling but marvelously crafted object comes from Padua, from the workshop of Severo de Ravenna, a very imaginative genius. Arcimboldo firmly grasps the heavy bronze lamp above its talons, lifts it as high as his head, and enters his chambers. As he had expected, the room is dark, he had told Silvius he would not be returning. He sets his logbook and the bronze lamp down on a handsomely carved oak chest as the light flickers for the last time and dies. Arcimboldo carefully crosses over to the door of his painting studio. Inside the studio, the large leaded windows have lightened with the sullen hue of a reluctant dawn, but there is not enough light to illuminate the room, so the artist must fumble in the dark for a flint and stub of candle.

When Arcimboldo has lit several lamps and candles in his rooms he notices the wrapped up painting just next to the door to the hallway, it's the Leonardo, left by the Baron's son. What can he do to avoid touching it? He turns his back on the painting, thinking...a cup of watered wine if he can locate some, perhaps a crust of stale bread to soak in it, yes, just the thing. He busily searches his room for water, wine, and bread. He finds bread and nibbles, he finds wine and sips. He drifts over to his logbook, opens it, leafs through it, tapping absentmindedly on the table, he hums a Bohemian folk song, he straightens items on his desk, he stands gazing blindly out the windows. Now, finally, he must stop procrastinating and force himself to get to work. He stares at the wrapped painting as though he had found a scorpion in his room. He rushes toward it, unwraps the cloth, rushes to an easel in his studio, positions painting and candelabra, drops himself into a chair in front of the easel, and, with difficulty, forces himself to come eye to eye with John the Baptist.

Arcimboldo's first thought, as his first thought always is when studying a Leonardo da Vinci, is: *'why can't I paint like that?'* Arcimboldo crowds his paintings with life, in all its varied and splendid forms, perfectly detailed, harmonious, symbolically correct expressions of the Natural World. What he strives to express – the complexity and beauty of the Natural World, and the mysterious promise that there is more to be discovered, all of that and much more is in the eyes of St. John as painted by Leonardo. The eyes alone. There is a living intelligence and human soul behind those gentle eyes and enigmatical expression. *'Why can I not paint like that, why can I not give my creations that kind of life force?'*

There is a dark grotto behind the luminous figure of St. John; the colors of the grotto are black, umber, and very dark earth green – *terre verte*. Arcimboldo intends to transform John's Christian cross into Bacchus' thyrsus, a slender staff of giant fennel, wound with ivy, topped with a pinecone, an attribute always carried by the God of wine, ecstasy and merriment. John's hair, which is very shadowed, is also shades of umber, and Arcimboldo intends to paint an ivy wreath on the saint's head to further his transmutation into the pagan God. He must also paint a cheetah or leopard skin somewhere on the naked body to characterize Bacchus' African origins.

Causing the identity of the figure in this painting to metamorph is a kind of magic Arcimboldo *can* perform, although in this case he takes no pleasure in it whatsoever. Arcimboldo knows that all the painters in Europe, in the World, desire to copy Leonardo's mystery and beauty – seeking to copy that which is uncopyable; instead they copy technique, *maniera*.

Leonardo produced such subtle and marvelous compositions in everything he set his hands to, yet Arcimboldo knows that in Leonardo's opinion, what he achieved was always insufficient. The Florentine's creative genius was never satisfied, his Mind was always able to find a more subtle or complex improvement. Leonardo was tortured by this: his hands and eyes were unequal to his Mind. Arcimboldo very deeply feels that is true for himself as well, his eyes and hands are unequal to his Mind. No matter how perfectly he executes his conception – on viewing the completed work, his Mind immediately goes beyond what he has done. And often Arcimboldo wonders: are his conceptions imperfect to begin with, flawed in some way, or is there something about the creative process, a lesson learned during the process that inevitably, mysteriously, invalidates or diminishes the conception? With a melancholy sigh the artist rises to grind and mix the paint he will need to change the St. John, a substantial amount of brown umber.

Arcimboldo looks up from his workbench, at the magnificent silver, copper, and brass wall clock given him by Rudolf. It shows just past the seventh hour. It was fabricated in Prague by a clockmaker according to Rudolf's very specific design, under his direct supervision; it is meant to show the phases of the moon and the locations of certain planets, but to the everlasting regret of the clockmaker (who has since moved back to Breslau), the only thing this clock will do is mark the twenty-four hours and chime once a day. Of course, Rudolf rejected the clock (and the clockmaker), but Arcimboldo saw a mastery in the metal work; the eye of an artist combined the colors of the metals, silver, copper, and brass in the design of the mechanism. The inspired hand of a sculptor decorated the surrounding areas with gilded scroll work and colored enamel astrological figures. Rudolf gave Arcimboldo the clock as a present when he noticed his interest; Arcimboldo finds it beautiful, and useful enough for his needs. He yawns, blinks several times, and decides he will lie down on his bed until half past seven to rest and fix the images of this night's events in his Memory Palace.

He closes his eyes and enters the softly lit galleries within his Mind, the Memory Palace of Giuseppe Arcimboldo. Each room is anchored with an image that can be easily remembered for its vividness or uniqueness. Arcimboldo will create a new room – a new gallery in his Palace for tonight's events, and he will fix all of tonight's events in place by the image St John. St. John will mark the Eve of Epiphany, 1587. Starting with St. John, he naturally recalls his experiences with Leonardo's painting; the painting brings to mind Giordano Bruno, and Arcimboldo records his image of the Nolan, in the cassock of a Dominican friar, with his hand raised, speaking in front of the grotesque mouth of the door frame. He records the exceptional wonders behind that door, the strange smile from Rudolf, the illumination of all those beautiful paintings and objects; it is easy to fix *that* sight forever in his memory. The thought of the artwork in that room portraying the living creatures of the

Natural World takes his memory to the delightful, unexpected viewing of Durer's blue bird wing, with Ottavio Strada. *Now* that blue wing is fixed in his mind until the end of time. Through Ottavio, Arcimboldo thinks of the man's daughter, Katharina, and he records in his memory the image of her blonde hair, bare shoulders and alabaster back as, giggling, she tied the blindfold around the Emperor's eyes. What's left? The French assassins and Fabrizio Mordente.

Arcimboldo remembers the moment he was attacked; he remembers falling backwards in the doorway of his chamber in the Powder Tower. He can feel the giddiness now in the pit of his stomach as he remembers flying backward. Strangely, the feeling persists, but instead of flying backward it seems he is flying upward. He opens his eyes, and instead of seeing the ceiling of his bed chamber he sees the Stars, the Moon, the racing, wispy clouds. He turns and looks down, he sees the castle, the Lesser Town, the Vltava river, the Old Town, the New Town... still he flies higher and higher, he sees all of these places come together as the city of Prague... the city of Prague, he never imagined, it looks like the head of the Emperor, look there – Hradcany makes a noble forehead. Arcimboldo would never have imagined, but you see, one just needs a different perspective. He is no longer in his Memory Palace, of course, he is dreaming. Arcimboldo may not realize it, but he has fallen asleep.

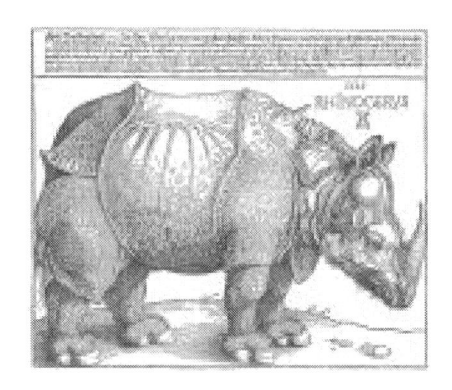

-Day-

Ting-ting! Ting-ting! Arcimboldo stretches comfortably; his first sensation is *'I am hungry'*. He opens his eyes to see two ripe figs, a large white raspberry, and a black olive on a long stem...alas, painted images, part of the portrait he is working on for Rudolf; the Emperor portrayed as Vertumnus, the God of Nature. From the shadows of his bed chamber, Arcimboldo looks beyond the half finished Vertumnus, through the doorway to his studio, and he sees a flood of brilliant sunlight illuminating a painting on an easel. Daylight, delightful! A magnificent morning! His delight at the cheerful sunlight fades as he recognizes the painting he is looking at, the unfinished St. John. Then the following thought: this is the morning of Epiphany Day! He has slept, and the painting is unfinished – unstarted! Nine already! Arcimboldo's beautiful clock can be relied on to chime at the ninth hour, whether one wants it to or not, but rarely is it an irritation to him; usually, Arcimboldo is up long before the ninth hour, shuffling about, as he is now, searching for the urinal.

Cold and shivering yet again (how tired he has become of Bohemian winters), he pulls the green velvet counterpane off his bed and wraps himself in it. He crosses to his studio window and looks out over the snow covered castle courtyard, and beyond to the north, the snow shrouded forests of the Royal hunting preserve. The world is cloaked in the most wholesome pure white, just like the inside of every church in Christendom; white is the official liturgical color of the Epiphany season.

Although the air in the room is chilled, the warmth of the sun coming through the glass of the window is glorious! It is, in fact, stupefying, an enticement to do nothing at all but stand, basking in the natural warmth sent directly to this place, at this exact time, from Sol, the center of all things. From this height in the castle, Arcimboldo can see over the wall, over the moat, to the Lion Court. The Emperor's animals, those whose cages he can see, are all sheltering in their snow-covered huts; except for a large brown bear who is angrily reaching through his bars, grabbing for a piece of meat a group of foolish pranksters are taunting him with.

There is a sharp rap on the door, and then it is quickly opened, and Silvius enters. A very brief bow, the boy speaks in Czech, "good morning, my Lord." He looks rather tired. "They told me at the Summer Palace you came back here... so I've just run back, you see, that's why I haven't had a chance to-"

In German: "good morning, Silvius. You're well, I hope? Lay out my clothes now, please. But make a fire first."

In Czech: "Nelle gave these to me, sir. This one you have to look at first."

In German: "from the Emperor? Hmm. Give them here." Arcimboldo takes the packet of letters. He sees an envelope bearing the Imperial seal in red wax. Breaking the seal, he sees a quickly written message in

Rudolf's hand, perfunctorily expecting Arcimboldo in the Imperial private apartments an hour before midday. And there are letters from Milan! There is a letter from his most beloved friend, the poet Paolo Lomazzo, and to his amazement, a letter from his son, Benedetto. He will have to read these later.

With Silvius' help, Arcimboldo quickly dresses in doublet, gartered breeches to the knee and hose, all of black velvet, shot with gold thread. He rests his hand on the boy's shoulder to steady himself while he steps into his velvet lined duckbill shoes. His black silk sleeves are tight at the wrist, puffed and padded at the elbow and shoulder, Silvius laces them to the shoulders of his doublet. He prefers to wear a white lace neck whisk instead of a full ruff. Because he is tired of being cold he asks Silvius to find his *zipone*, a padded, buttoned, and collared tunic worn over the doublet, extending down to his knees. It also is black and richly brocaded with gold and silver thread in the Venetian style. He pockets his incised ruby and a Venetian gold lace handkerchief.

Looking critically in a mirror, Arcimboldo scents his beard, hair, wrists, gloves and ruff with orange oil dissolved in aqua mirabilis. He feels thick headed from lack of sleep, and his stomach is growling with hunger. The bump on the back of his head is sore to the touch. The sweet scent of the orange oil is powerful, slightly nauseating. While he has been moving about his rooms, he occasionally steals a glance at Leonardo's St. John, and scowls. From a drawer in his desk Arcimboldo removes a portable drum watch four inches wide and an inch thick, and sets the time against his wall clock. This drum watch has a beautiful chased design of animals leaping through foliage, and a sun dial on the hinged cover. It is the product of a watchmaker here in Prague, Christopf Schissler. It will be an indispensible tool today.

Arcimboldo picks up his logbook and tucks it under his arm. He looks at the St. John, he looks at Silvius, he looks at the St. John, he looks at the door, he looks at the St. John, he sighs, he tells Silvius to cover the painting and to prepare twenty granos of raw umber and ten granos of green earth for him. He instructs his servant to meet him at the Summer Palace later this evening, before the banquet for the Tuscan Duke. Arcimboldo expertly swirls a black cloak over his right shoulder and behind his back, the cloak comes to rest precisely where he intends it to, draped casually yet artistically over his left shoulder. The old Italian twitches and gasps slightly with a twinge of pain from where he was bruised in his fall the evening before. Arcimboldo thinks he can finish the additions to Leonardo's painting in an hour, and he believes he will have more than enough time after the mid-day pageant and ceremony in Old Town, at the entrance to the Stone Bridge.

Now, Arcimboldo stands before the door to the hallway. He squeezes his ruby and asks for Fortune's favor; he crosses himself and prays for the correct guidance from God and the Holy Spirit. He pats his pocket to make sure he has the letter from his son. Arcimboldo resolutely steps into the hallway of Hradcany Castle, and whispers to himself, *'Epiphany is at hand'*.

January 6, Epiphany Day. In the snowy streets of Prague, groups of young people known as *sternsingers* are running from door to door. They are dressed fancifully as the Three Wise Men. In each group there's one young King carrying a long pole with a gold star nailed to the top. The groups are singing songs about the Holy Family, the Three Wise Men, the Three Kings, the Three Magi, the Star of Bethlehem. The proud youth who carries the Star leads the harmony and chooses the songs. On every Epiphany morning the streets of the city are full of laughter and song about how the Magi from the East follow the Star to a place of prophecy, they find the Holy Family there, they offer rich gifts to the Son of God, the Three Magi give the thanks of mortal human beings to the Eternal and Universal. The *sternsingers* visit each Christian home in the city, and they are happily offered food and drink in the homes they visit. As a sign of gratitude, the young people then perform the traditional house blessing, and conclude by marking the year over the doorway with chalk. All the houses in each district and street in the city will be visited. It is a yearly event that both Protestant and Catholic grace with civility and camaraderie. During his years with the Habsburgs, Arcimboldo has learned a German word for this civic good feeling and friendliness, it is *'gemutlichkeit'*.

It's traditional in Bohemia and Germany to bake a cake on Epiphany Day called Three Kings Cake, and it's always baked in a round pan in the shape of a crown. The sticky golden buns are filled with orange and spice, meant to represent the gifts of the three kings: gold, frankincense and myrrh. In Hradcany Castle kitchen, the Three Kings Cakes are baked to suit the Emperor's taste; besides containing orange and spice the golden rolls will hold jam, poppy seeds, and curd. The Emperor will have his served warm with a sauce of vanilla and powdered sugar. Arcimboldo licks his lips as he comes down the Palace stairs because he can smell *ofennudel* baking, the yeasty dough used for Three Kings Cake; the odor has spread from the bakery in the kitchen all throughout the ground floor, and

Arcimboldo intends to forget about Leonardo's painting and follow the aroma to its source.

Arcimboldo is descending the shallow, wide steps down to the castle kitchen. The delicious aroma has become more complicated but no less enticing; now the distinct odor of fried onions and apples with fennel and rosemary, roasted wild boar, and the spicy sweetness of Three Kings Cake mingle in the warm, humid breezes drifting up the stairs from the kitchen below. Although he is greeted with quite a few "good morning, My Lord"s, Arcimboldo is inexorably pushed to the side by the heavy traffic of servants coming and going with every sort of basket, bag, tray, and box imaginable, containing just as varied an assortment of foods and spices. Today this kitchen will provision public banquets outside St. Vitus Cathedral and St. Adalbert's Chapel, an Imperial Epiphany reception in the enormous Vladislav Hall, and, of course, the exclusive and strictly aristocratic entertainment for Ferdinando, Grand Duke of Tuscany and Christina of Lorraine, princess of France, at the Imperial Summer Palace.

A basket covered with a white cloth is carried on a woman's shoulder. As she maneuvers her way up the stairs she finds herself directly in front of Arcimboldo, and as she tries to squeeze around to his left the basket is practically pushed in his face; the steamy smell of freshly baked dough filled with sweet spices is so strong he can taste the flavors. Only his strong sense of decorum prevents him from slipping his hand underneath the cloth and pinching off a large morsel of a hot, sticky bun.

Emerging at last into the din and chaos of the vast hall that serves as the interior kitchen of Prague

Castle, Arcimboldo feels as much a spectator as he would at the scene of a battle. He immediately notices how colorless everything is except for the food, which is spread and hanging over every available surface. The men and women who rush about the kitchen wear dull, colorless clothing, dyed long ago and hastily with pigments made from inexpensive vegetable or earth dyes; clothes and aprons that are now faded to the same hue as the neutral shades of stone, iron and wood that surround them. Therefore, as a contrast, the color in the food stands out... beautifully, artfully, almost Symbolically (as seen by Arcimboldo's finely attuned eyes, and interpreted by his enlightened Mind). The light coming in from the windows far up in the walls makes the natural colors of the foods seem to glow, every combination appears harmonious. Arcimboldo watches a woman who stands at a nearby chopping block, a slab of iron hard wood turned almost black from long, long use in the kitchen; she is chopping a purple vegetable, creating a mound of purple next to two large mounds of similarly chopped onion and parsley. Against the dry darkness of the old wood, the mounds of purple, emerald, and ivory shine and vibrate with perfect harmony. The mound of parsley looks like a volcanic island, and a memory comes bubbling up from his Memory Palace.

Once, years ago, Arcimboldo was on a Venetian galley off the coast of the volcanic island of Stromboli, a green, almost perfect cone, rising from the Mediterranean Sea. Arcimboldo was traveling with Rudolf's father, Maximilian; they had come there to witness the volcano's eruptions, which had begun several days previously. The galley had arrived in the morning, joining scores of other craft circling the small island. Arcimboldo was sketching, the botanist, Carolus Clusius, and Doctor Hagesius were studying the volcanic cone with a glass, Emperor Maximilian, and Don Alvaro de Bazan were testing the Emperor's mother-of-pearl and gold inlaid wheel-lock pistols, called 'puffers'. The volcano had been silently, sullenly smoking all day, until toward evening, as the last light left the sky, a deep sound was heard, if you can imagine: the sound of distant thunder but sustained and increasing as though it were being produced by something that was moving closer and closer – a sound like ten-thousand converging ox carts on cobblestone streets. And so, louder and louder, and at last the mighty explosion, a violent spray of smoke, ash, fire, and sound – deafening, blinding! The subsequent wind and ash had strangely dampened Maximilian's enthusiasm for observing further, and the Emperor had departed shorting after. However, the indelible impression the brief event left in Arcimboldo's mind was immediately fixed within his Memory Palace.

Just as Arcimboldo is aware of the Natural cause and effect concerning the rumbling noise made by volcanoes, he is aware of the cause and effect behind the rumbling noise he hears now, even amidst the general cacophony in the room; it is approaching from the pantry hallway, soon to explode into the kitchen, Master Nikolas Paulus, chief cook for His Imperial Majesty, and chief, no, God of the Imperial kitchens. Like Vulcan, God of volcanoes, Master Paulus is perpetually angry; his penetrating, baritone eruption of disapproval will momentarily stir the kitchen.

"...drop them right in the hot ashes, you can brush the ashes off later, do you understand? And for Christ's sake, I said crushed almonds not sliced! Now look here, *that's* properly done, but, can you not see, *that's* not, no...a disgrace, let me show you!" Paulus is continually surrounded by his lieutenants of the kitchen, they hover around him now, coming and going like a swarm of bees. The Maestro of the kitchen cuffs one worker on the ear, grabs another by the collar and drags him off to a stack of dirty pots and pans – a demotion, scullion work! He now brandishes a long handled spoon, preparing to sample some sauces made from the drippings of the roasted boar. As he bends to taste the sauce his glance happens to fall in Arcimboldo's direction, and he freezes in place. Now he straightens, still holding the spoon over the large pan, untasted; he glares, frowns, and begins shaking his head from side to side, as if to indicate a refusal from the very first moment.

In emphatic German the chef says "no! Impossible! Don't waste your time asking. I don't care what special occasion you've got now, even if you were entertaining Christ and his Apostles I wouldn't be able to give you a thing. Absolutely nothing, not an egg, not a chestnut, not as much flour as would cover my-"

"Master Paulus, delightful to see you this beautiful morning, a joyous Epiphany to you, sir!" Arcimboldo approaches Paulus; he has momentarily become the center of attention. Paulus' staff stares at Arcimboldo with frowns they have copied from their chief. "Do not fear, sir. I do *not* have another request to tax the resources of your renowned kitchen. The entire castle, no, the entire city – the entire Empire, sir, is filled with pride at the sumptuous feasts you prepare, food that is fit for Gods!" Paulus appears slightly mollified, much of the staff drift away and lose interest. Arcimboldo does understand the man's reaction, it is the artist's role to plan and organize grand festivities, events that almost always involve elaborate services of food and drink; Arcimboldo's inventive and unique designs (and frequent change of plans) are rarely welcomed by the volcanic chef or his staff.

"My Lord Arcimboldus. What brings you here to this place of martyrdom today? Our arrangements are agreed upon, are they not?"

"Agreed upon, absolutely, sir, agreed upon. You haven't a thing to worry about. And I assume *I* have nothing to worry about either?"

"I already saw Cesare this morning, he'll send carts throughout the day to pick up food, and he'll leave two of your people here to prepare the next course. As for whatever you're doing upstairs... we will give the baskets to Cesare... nothing to worry about, eh? *Mark* the baskets, yes, understood. Nothing to worry about, eh?"

"Perfetto, perfetto. There is one trivial matter, Maestro, I hesitate to trouble you with it, as busy as you are."

Paulus has an extremely skeptical look on his face; he purses his lips and scowls.

Arcimboldo steps closer as if to confide, and in a lowered voice he says "Maestro, I'm starving! Can you give me some food?"

Paulus responds with a brusque nod of the head, "see Brigitte." Then he vigorously returns to the battle, waving his wooden spoon like a baton, he is just in time to marshal his forces for the spitting of three more wild boars destined for the ovens.

Brigitte is baking. She is surrounded by a half dozen other bakers, middle aged women like herself, they stand at a table in a billowing cloud of white powder, and Arcimboldo, terrified of what this cloud will do to his black clothing, tries to (gracefully) get Brigitte's attention from a distance. Unsuccessful, and feeling foolish now as well as hungry, Arcimboldo stops a running youth and gives him a coin to bring Brigitte to him. There is a loud burst of rude Italian when the boy stops her at her baking, but the boy points to

Arcimboldo, and when Brigitte sees him her plain face opens up in a genuine, joyous smile. "*Maraviglioso! Giuseppe, il mio Milanese!*" Brigitte confidently brushes past the smirks, frowns, and taunts of her fellow bakers as she saunters toward Arcimboldo. "*Porca miseria!*" she contemptuously throws over her shoulder with a toss of her head. In a brave attempt at beautification she uses her powdery fingers to smooth hair from her face and forehead, *and then* she wipes her hands on the apron hanging from her wide hips. This spirited woman is also from Milan, and she adores the tall and aristocratic artist.

She approaches Arcimboldo as if she intends to throw her arms around him and he leaps backward, crying out in Italian, "Brigitte, be careful! By St. Honoratus, what are you doing? Not here!"

Laughing at him, she shows she is joking, "calm, calm, my dove. Would I dirty your beautiful cloak?"

"Joy of Epiphany to you, my dear."

"And to you, My Lord."

"Brigitte, I could not resist the smell of Three Kings Cake, I followed the smell of baking like a sheep returning to the fold."

"Oh... I see."

"Might I persuade you to bring me the merest morsel, the smallest bite, a bit of crust, a crumb? I faint with hunger."

"I can't do that, my poor boy, the last basket of Three Kings Cake just went up the stairs." She laughs at the look of dismay on Arcimboldo's face; she pinches his cheek although he does his best to pull away, "*poverino*. I won't break your heart, more cakes are baking... ten minutes, and you will have one hot from the oven. Yes?"

Arcimboldo looks doubtful; he takes his drum watch from his pocket to know the time. "Brigitte, my angel, ten minutes is all I can spare this morning. You will bring me some cake in ten minutes? Yes?"

"Wait over there, Giuseppe-"

"Arcimboldus, for God's sake!" He interjects in a fierce whisper.

She laughs and tosses her head, "Wait over there, *Giuseppino*." She is pointing to a table with several baskets of bright yellow fruit. "I'll be right back. Then you will help me make some quince pies."

"Ten minutes. Brigitte, ten minutes. I mean what I say! By Job..." Arcimboldo sulkily walks to the table which supports three cheerfully sunny baskets of yellow and orange quinces. Across the table a woman is slicing freshly baked bread to be grilled as toast, the toasted slices will then be ground to powder and used as an ingredient in many of the dishes prepared in this kitchen. Master Paulus still firmly believes in the Humoral Theory of cooking – many foods need to have their natural qualities balanced or countered by special cooking or the addition of other ingredients to avoid ill effect on a person's health; some food, like beef, is boiled to counteract its dry and cold humors; pork is roasted to dry out its wet humor. Fish is, of course, dominated by its cold and wet humors, so frying is an effective way to dry it out and warm it up (in more than one respect). The Bohemian chef Paulus carefully and scientifically plans the Emperor's meals with the Imperial Doctors Crato and Hagecius, using the widely known Latin health handbook, *Tacuinum Sanitatis*.

Arcimboldo is contentedly chewing a slice of freshly baked bread when Brigitte returns with a tray of pie crust and a bowl of eggs. Without a word, she whisks the bread out of his hand, leaving him literally open mouthed in surprise. His indignant expression melts a moment later when she returns with the slice of bread, now soaked in the drippings of the roasted wild boar. For several seconds the world narrows to a single point, the sensations on his tongue and in his mouth. Brigitte smiles and nods knowingly. She points to the baskets on the table, "now, My Lord, find the smoothest quinces you can and put them right there."

Brigitte rapidly cuts a hole the size of a groschen in the end of each cleaned quince and scoops out the seeds. She fills each fruit with equal parts sugar water, cinnamon and butter, and plugs the hole in the top with butter. Arcimboldo holds up a quince as though admiring it, he plays a game with Brigitte that they are both fond of, he points to the fruit and says "what color?"

"Yellow."

"Tsk, tsk. Here, yellow ocher. Here, lead-tin yellow. Here's antimony yellow, Naples yellow. Here's orpiment and here's tawny. What's this?"

"Mmm... straw?"

"Brava! And this?"

"Gooseturd green."

They both laugh. Briggite has Arcimboldo stick a dozen cloves into each finished quince, which he does, in spite of his fine clothing, and ignoring the pointing and staring going on throughout the kitchen. After four of the colorful fruit are prepared this way, Brigitte puts them into a pie crust, and then fills the open spaces between quinces with egg yolk. Arcimboldo looks at his watch again as Brigitte is putting the top on the quince pie. He says "Brigitte, I must go."

"But the Three Kings Cake! Just a minute, just one more minute... I'll go check on them now."

Arcimboldo reaches out to grab her hand, stopping her from running off, and to her great surprise, Arcimboldo bows and kisses her hand, powdery and greasy as it is. "Brigitte, farewell!"

Brigitte isn't the only one in the kitchen that watches in wonderment as Giuseppe Arcimboldo climbs the stairs leading to the courtyard.

The cheerful morning sun is gradually becoming filtered by a thin layer of haze, although the mass of dark cloud in the east still appears to be holding its distance, continuing to flow to the south. The air is brisk and smells strongly of snow. Arcimboldo pulls on his gloves and wraps his cloak about his shoulders. He sneezes. He walks toward Hradcany Castle's western portal, he must visit Rabbi Loew in Prague's Jewish Town, and he has no intention of walking in this snow. Riding, although enjoyable enough on a fine day, is out of the question due to the painful bruise on his tailbone. He will request a Hungarian coach and driver in the Imperial stables.

Arcimboldo allows thoughts of important business matters at hand to replace his lingering memories of rosy, plump, and saucy Brigitte. At the urging of Giordano Bruno and Doctor John Dee, Rudolf has negotiated to buy a rare and expensive book essential to their alchemical experiment. The book is the *Sefer Yetzira*, the Hebrew Book of Formation and Creation. Much older and rarer than the books of the *Zohar*, it can be interpreted in a similar way by those who are sufficiently knowledgeable in mathematical and symbolic arcana. It was thought impossible to obtain, but Mordecai Maisel, by far the richest man in Prague, came to the Emperor's aid once again, brokering the sale of the book from the ancient, eccentric, and mysterious Moravian, Rabbi Loew. The Rabbi is here in Prague with his book, at the yeshivot next to the New Old Synagogue. Arcimboldo must collect this book and authorize Maisel to pay Rabbi Loew the astonishing sum of five-hundred thalers.

Rabbi Loew is infamous among the alchemists, occultists, and credulous of our time as the man who has magically created a homunculus, what the Hebrew call a Golem. Rudolf has begged Maisel to have Loew bring the Golem to Prague, he will buy it at any price. The Rabbi did not deign to respond to the Emperor, and Arcimboldo shivers slightly at the thought of what he may shortly be dealing with.

The artist can hear the commotion issuing from the Imperial stables before he is within sight of it. The grand embassy from Tuscany arrived not long before, and the carriages, horses, and grooms are in a state of complete uproar. Arcimboldo stands to the side and watches the tired horses being uncoupled from the magnificent Tuscan coaches and carriages. The gray Florentine Friesians are graceful and nimble for their size; but now they are sweating, steaming, and snorting impatiently when pulled around by the grooms, exhausted after the steep uphill climb to the castle at the end of their long journey. Arcimboldo hopes to find a coach available. Coaches are considerably more comfortable than carriages that sit directly on top of the axels; a coach is suspended from chains, and, while bouncy, avoids the bone crushing shocks of other, older wheeled vehicles. This new word 'coach' is what all Europe is calling this new invention in transportation, coming as it does from the place where it was first used, Kocs, pronounced 'coach' in Hungarian. Kocs is the midway point from Buda to Vienna, an important stopping place for the carriages and riders coming from the front lines of the Turkish assault. To those in Kocs, the speed of these new lightweight coaches is more important than the comfort they offer; a continuous flow of (mostly bad) military news rushes north and west from the battlefields of ravaged and de-populated Hungary.

Arcimboldo rides downhill in the small carriage he has been able to engage, and this only by claiming he is on the Emperor's business. The driver is in a surly mood, and only agreed to go because the artist insisted that he intends to be back in less than an hour, however the look the man gives him clearly indicates he doesn't believe it.

Arcimboldo sees only a few groups of *sternsingers* racing behind their golden stars; this is surprising because he had expected the early morning sunshine to bring the entire city outdoors to celebrate Epiphany. It certainly seems that there are fewer people than usual in the streets here in Mala Strana, also called the Lesser Town, just below Hradcany Castle. Perhaps the snow over night and the clouds looming in the east promising more snow to come have kept many indoors. The carriage clatters up onto Stone Bridge to cross over the river and there is very little traffic here as well. The dark greenish-gray water of the Vltava River, pinched by ice forming on its banks, flows by very fast. This river is Vltava to the Czech speakers of Prague, and Moldau to the German speakers; both languages derive their names from the Old German words '*wilt ahwa*', meaning wild water.

There is a very cold breeze here over the river and Arcimboldo sits back to find a warmer nook inside the carriage. The grand structures he sees coming up ahead of him have been temporarily decorated according to a design by Master Giovanni de'Bardi; the theme of Epiphany is symbolically and allegorically illustrated on enormous sheets of fabric and attached to the sides of buildings and also around scaffolding specially constructed for this purpose. On a hazy, colorless day, such as today has become, the vivid colors and giant images on the painted facades produce a dramatic effect.

The two-thousand foot long Stone Bridge terminates on the eastern bank of the Vltava in the Knights of the Cross Square, from which Prague's main street, the narrow and winding Karlova Street, continues east through the Old Town. Arcimboldo asks the driver to stop for a moment in the Knights of the Cross Square. Ahead, the steeply gabled roof of the New Tower Gate is impressively draped with snow, seen from below it seems the snow is clinging to nearly vertical surfaces a hundred feet above the ground. To the left, forming the northern boundary of Knights of the Cross Square, is the gigantic conglomeration of interconnecting buildings known as the Clementium, and between the Clementium and the river is the Church of St. Francis. All of these handsome buildings have been decorated for Epiphany by the crews of painters and carpenters working for Master Bardi.

The crowds of citizens that should be wandering about admiring the public art, and complimenting the religious zeal and generous civic munificence of the Habsburgs are nowhere to be seen. There is a smattering of nervous and furtive burghers, merchants, and craftsmen with their families closely gathered around them. What has frightened these people, Arcimboldo wonders? Alarmingly strange. Also strange – there are no common people about, and this is an unexpected and disturbing warning that the Protestant community of Prague has decided to stay at home. There are no beggars, no packs of young pranksters, no surly, loitering, crippled soldiers, no groups of blushing, giggling girls, or noisy, boisterous matrons, no doddering old folk clinging to each other for affection and balance. It is the absence of this large and always present segment of the population that is the most disquieting thing about the Knights of the Cross Square this Epiphany morning.

Arcimboldo sees there is a decorated parade wagon in front of the Clementium. This enormous building serves as the Jesuit headquarters and spearhead for the Roman Catholic assault on Protestant theology in Bohemia. The admirably crafted parade vehicle is no doubt for Christina of Lorraine, who will ride on this wagon through the streets of the city up to the castle, followed by other beautiful wagons decorated for Epiphany. The French princess, along with her traveling companions, has been staying with the Jesuits at the Clementium as many other prominent Catholic visitors to Prague do. It is expected that cheering crowds of citizens will line the route she will soon travel, although that expectation is becoming more doubtful by the moment. As a foreigner and Catholic princess, Christina will represent to the easily perturbed Protestants of Prague: foreign Catholics, Papists, privileged aristocrats, the authoritarian Roman Catholic repression that circumscribes their lives.

Although Arcimboldo would very much like to speak to Master Bardi about the coming procession and parade of decorated wagons, he cannot allow himself to take the time to track the man down. He asks the driver to turn left into the narrow avenue between the Clementium and the Church of St. Francis. When they reach the Jewish Cemetery several minutes later they turn right, and drive alongside the large cemetery; this street is a lovely place in spring, with a canopy of new, bright green leaves on the linden trees that line the street and cemetery walls. After several hundred feet the carriage turns left in front of the Jewish Town Hall. The streets of the Jewish quarter are completely deserted. This, however, does not surprise Arcimboldo. He knows that on days when Christians come together to celebrate, and feel very much at one with their crucified God, it behooves a Jew to stay indoors. Without any particular animosity, as an almost unconscious act of simple prudence, like bringing drying laundry in out of the rain, the Jewish community of Prague chooses to stay quietly indoors with family, away from windows and doors, on Christian holidays. And today, Epiphany Day, is no exception.

The New Old Synagogue is next door to the Jewish Town Hall, and Arcimboldo has his carriage stop there. He instructs the man to wait, and crosses the street to a public urinal he notices, it is built against the wall of a hospital for the old and sick. Except for the driver of his carriage he is absolutely alone on this silent street. As he stands facing the brick wall and waits patiently for relief, he considers the man who built this hospital, as well as the beautiful Town Hall building behind him. Mordecai Maisel has also built a synagogue, schools, and baths for his community. He makes interest free loans to the Jewish poor, supports private scholars, and sends financial aid to suffering Jewish communities elsewhere in Europe, and even beyond Europe. He is known to all as a humble, generous, and fair man. So... how has Mordecai Maisel grown so rich? His most profitable venture, one that shows no signs of slackening, is loaning money to Emperor Rudolf II.

Maisel has been at the heart of Prague, even during the very dark days following the castle fire in 1541. The fire had been blamed on the Jews; a Jewish man had been tortured until he confessed. To the immense delight of the Czech and German burghers and merchants, Emperor Ferdinand punished the Jews by expelling them from the Empire. Some wealthy and well connected Jews, such as Mordecai Maisel, were able to purchase the right to remain in Prague. Maisel made huge loans to finance the rebuilding of the city and castle; one could say that the rebuilding might not have been possible without him. Rudolf's father, Maximilian, upon becoming Emperor, realized how important Jews were to the economy of the Empire; in 1567 he rescinded the expulsion order, and now twenty years later, Prague's Jewish Town flourishes as never before. This year, out of the approximately eighty-thousand people that live here in the capital of the Holy Roman Empire, eight thousand of them have their homes in the Jewish quarter; it is the largest and richest Jewish community in Europe.

The New Old Synagogue, next door to the Jewish Town Hall, is the oldest in Europe, built in 1270. Arcimboldo descends the short flight of steps from the street to the entrance vestibule in the southeast corner. He finds the doors to the Synagogue locked, and he knocks hesitantly. As he waits, he absent-mindedly fondles the ruby in his pocket, and steps back to relish the skill of the stone carver who created the tympanum above the portal. He admires the subtle asymmetry of the vine leaves and their twisting branches, the delicate precision in the clusters of grapes; these superbly executed details make the tympanum a prayer in itself, calming the body and energizing the Mind. The high point of the triangular carving surges upward, lifting the entrant's thoughts upward toward God. Arcimboldo hears faint voices on the other side of the door and he knocks once more. One door is immediately opened by the Mayor of the *Platea Judaeorum*, the richest man in Prague, Mordecai Maisel, wearing his medallion of office around his neck on a thick gold chain.

"Ah, yes. It's you."

Arcimboldo bows. "My Lord Mayor, good morning to you, sir."

"One moment." The door closes and there are muffled voices for several seconds, then the door opens just enough to allow the stout old man to slide out through the opening, it instantly closes behind him. Without hesitation, Maisel waddles to the steps and begins to climb up to the street.

Arcimboldo says a little uncertainly, "have I interrupted you, sir? I sincerely hope not, I thought we had agreed upon the time."

The Mayor breathes heavily while climbing the steps and speaks loudly to Arcimboldo over his back as he continues to move up toward the street. "No interruption at all, my Lord Arcimboldus! You don't have to say that. I am always delighted to be of service to the Emperor. Should he need anything, anytime at all, he will have *all* that I have. Follow me, sir, if you will." Arcimboldo nods and follows the man. He glances back for a last look at the tympanum and he sees the Synagogue doors have opened a crack and several inquisitive faces are peering out watching him, when they notice him looking back the doors are quickly closed with a reverberating thud. Maisel is gesturing grandly with his hands, "should the brave armies of the Empire need succor in their fight against the feckless Turk, the glorious House of Habsburg, be it ever blessed, has only to lift a finger, any finger, the smallest finger, and Mordecai ben Maisel will be there. Follow me, my Lord. The shirt off my back, the last crumb of food from my larder... the shoes off my wife's feet! Nothing is too great a sacrifice for our incomparable Emperor." The Mayor pauses in front of the school house next door to the Synagogue, he looks appraisingly at Arcimboldo while with quick, practiced movements he adjusts his dark velvet robes, blindingly white ruff collar, embroidered kippah, and golden chain of office. "So, Arcimboldus, Rabbi Loew is here, and he has agreed to sell his book to the Emperor. He is an...unusual man. Difficult, yes, difficult at times. Brilliant, of course... of course. But... how shall I say... difficult. You will, perhaps, find it hard to understand him." Arcimboldo nods his head to indicate he understands what the Mayor is telling him. Maisel says "do not be concerned by what he might say. Do not feel he will refuse to sell you the book. He will sell. Leave it to me." Arcimboldo nods his head again. Maisel continues, "and the Emperor agrees that for this small service I'm to have licenses to build on all the empty lots in Zderaz, all the way to Karlov, yes?"

"It is understood, yes, My Lord Mayor."

Maisel cannot resist slightly licking his lips in anticipation. "Very good. Excellent. Everyone will be happy. Is that not God's will?"

Only two of the shuttered windows in the school house, or yeshivot, are allowing light into the dim, unheated room. Mayor Maisel introduces Arcimboldo to Rabbi Chernick, from Prague, the regular teacher here, and to an extraordinarily ancient looking man, with wild white hair and beard, pale, almost translucent, age-spotted skin, and milky, red rimmed eyes behind a pair of looking lenses held in place by thick iron frames. His shapeless black robe is dusty and stained. He is surrounded by stacks of tattered books and manuscripts. His hands shake. His voice is hoarse and inconstant. This is Rabbi Judah Loew ben Bezalel, the infamous old man who everyone believes has created, brought to life, and then enchanted the first and only Golem in Europe.

Arcimboldo is unsure whether a full bow is appropriate for the seated Rabbi, he slightly inclines his head, smiles politely, and makes a graceful gesture with his hand while saying in German, "His Imperial Majesty is extremely grateful to you, Rabbi. Regretfully, he is unable to meet you himself. It is an honor for me to be able to make your acquaintance, sir." Arcimboldo's hand comes to rest over his heart as a testament to his sincerity.

"Hmmff."

"The most esteemed Mayor," a sweeping gesture toward Maisel, "a loyal and patriotic subject of His Imperial Majesty, has assured His Majesty that you possess this rare and valuable book, sir, the *Sefer Yetzira*. I believe I pronounce it correctly, do I not?"

The Rabbi is impassive but Mayor Maisel nods his head in affirmation. He clears his throat and quickly says "Rabbi, perhaps you will show Lord Arcimboldus your *Sefer Yetzira* now?

Ignoring Maisel, Rabbi Loew squints at Arcimboldo through thick circles of glass and iron. In a voice barely louder than a whisper he says, "why do you want this book?"

Arcimboldo looks at Maisel and raises his eyebrows. He says to Rabbi Loew, "Emperor Rudolf is a most learned man. And a man with great responsibilities. He collects knowledge, wishing to have a better understanding of the World."

"Hmmff. What does he do with all this... this... *understanding*?"

"Well... sir, I would have to say, the Emperor is responsible for millions of people, and to their countless ancestors, the sacred trust of the ancient and honorable Roman Empire. These are responsibilities the Emperor takes very seriously. He wishes to make correct decisions. He wishes to be wise and informed."

"Bah! He wants to conjure."

"What?"

The old man cackles hoarsely, and it sounds like paper being crinkled, "he wants to make magic! Magic! Magic!"

Arcimboldo feels embarrassed to have the Emperor accused of this, and guilty because it is essentially true, "the Emperor is scientific, sir! Do not think him a fool because he so earnestly desires your book. Do you mock him because he desires knowledge, *hidden* knowledge, that your religion has possessed since the dawn of Civilization? Why, sir?" Arcimboldo's eyes dart this way and that, in search of the perfect phrasing for his argument. "Now, I will admit, he may have, ah, certain *experimental* practices in mind, if you understand me, great discoveries are not always made in the light of day. I know I can confide in you men as scholars, yes? Your book, Rabbi, would be but a small part in a much larger compendium of knowledge, art, and philosophy."

"A small part you say? Not so important? You have so much else... perhaps you do not need my book at all."

"No, Rabbi, that is not what I mean. I only wish to stress that the Emperor is neither frivolous nor mercantile in his search for lost knowledge, he seeks it for a noble purpose, he seeks it for his own Mind, to benefit the Empire and..." Arcimboldo pauses, feeling he has stepped too near the edge of a cliff.

"And? Yes? To benefit what... who?"

"Well... God."

The old man cackles and sputters with mirth. Arcimboldo feels his lace collar is suddenly far too tight, he longs to loosen it, he surreptitiously wipes a few beads of perspiration from his brow as he pretends to smooth back the hair at his temples. Mayor Maisel, sensing deep water, changes the subject. He sends Rabbi Chernick to fetch the book, and then produces several small glasses and a tall thin bottle. Rabbi Loew refuses refreshment but Maisel pours thick, dark wine into glasses for Arcimboldo and himself. Arcimboldo repeats Maisel's "*mazel tov*" as they touch glasses and drink.

"The Talmud forbids teaching esoteric doctrines. It warns of the dangers when these things are taught publically. You do not want to buy this book." Rabbi Loew lays his wrinkled hand on the calf skin cover of the book that Rabbi Chernick has just placed on the table in front of him; the old man strokes the cover affectionately. "This is not for you, Josephus Arcimboldus, nor for the Emperor. Not for any Emperor, King or Duke. Not for any philosopher, magician or alchemist. This manuscript here, this ancient book, these eternal words, are only for a man of God who is capable of understanding their meaning. Rudolf Habsburg is not that man."

Arcimboldo is thinking: *thank God the Emperor is not here!* He clears his throat and says, "Rabbi, how can one understand the book unless one reads it, and how can one read it unless he possesses it?"

"Hmmff. In the second chapter of the *Hagigah*, rabbis are warned to teach the mystical creation doctrines, the *Sefer Yetzira*, only to one student at a time. This is not something that can be grasped by most people no matter how hard they try. There is an *aggadah* in that chapter, I will tell it to you." The Rabbi removes the looking lenses from his nose and wipes his moist eyes, blows his nose and licks his lips. Arcimboldo sips the very sweet wine and patiently waits for the Rabbi to continue. He is studying the skin on the back of the old man's hand, which again strokes the marbled calf skin cover of the old book. The colors and textures of man and book are almost identical.

Wheezing, Rabbi Loew speaks again "I will tell you this story: four famous rabbis were clever enough to find a way to visit God's Orchard, that is, as you would say, the Garden of Paradise. Of the four learned men who entered: Rabbi Ben Azzai looked and died; Rabbi Ben Zoma looked and went mad; Rabbi Archer destroyed the plants; only Rabbi Akiba entered in peace and departed in peace. You see, only one of those four learned rabbis was fit to see beyond our World. What do *you* expect to achieve? Whatever knowledge you are seeking with this book is more dangerous than you can possibly know."

This was not what Arcimboldo had expected, he was glad of Maisel's warning about Loew's contrariness. The Mayor now speaks, "and yet, Rabbi, you have agreed to sell your book to these men."

"This book is worthless to them. Their money is wasted. I only wish to be sure they understand they will never unlock the secrets of the *Sefer Yetzira*, they are not the men destined to do it." The old man appears to be looking into the far distance, perhaps it is a far distant past he sees, "Isaac Luria gave me this book, long ago... long ago, he was a man to see the Kabbalah in everything, he knew how to understand this book. What a mind!" Sputter, cough, wheeze. "For seven years he meditated in silence, alone, in a small hut by the Nile. He would only visit his parents and wife on the Sabbath, and then he would only speak in single words, only Hebrew. In his meditations he would speak with the Prophet Elijah. A very blessed man. A very learned man. A master of gematria. He knew how to understand this book. That was long, long ago." He lays his hand on the *Sefer Yetzira* as he catches his breath, "this book... I give it to them, what do I care? I am old, who knows how much longer I'll be alive. This book is not for me either. Not anymore." He takes his hand off the book, slowly, reluctantly.

"You will give it to us?"

"Hmmff! What do I care what you'll do with it? What is that to me? This book doesn't belong to me anyway, so...should I sell it? Who am I to take money for a gift from God? It belongs to God." Rabbi Loew thoughtfully taps the table. "I believe Mordecai said... five-hundred thalers?"

"Certainly, Rabbi. Five-hundred."

Mayor Maisel drains his glass with satisfaction. Rabbi Loew pushes the book across the table and Arcimboldo carefully takes it. He would very much like to leave right now, but there is one more thing he promised the Emperor he would do.

"Mayor Maisel, I remember now that we had asked the Rabbi for one more thing. Has he decided?"

Maisel looks uncomfortable, "the Golem?"

"The Emperor is remarkably interested."

Both Arcimboldo and Maisel look at Loew. Arcimboldo says, "Rabbi, is there a Golem?"

Loew is expressionless and does not answer.

Maisel says, "Rabbi Loew, these men think you will sell them your Golem. Do you wish to answer?"

The Rabbi speaks in Hebrew to Maisel and then to Rabbi Chernick. This is not a language Arcimboldo understands. Rabbi Chernick says apologetically in Czech, "the Rabbi is tired. He will rest now." There will be no Golem. Rudolf, Bruno and Dee will be disappointed, but Arcimboldo feels relieved.

The sound of the wind is loud in the empty street outside the yeshivot, and that wind is extremely cold. Besides the wind, he hears angry crows scolding each other in the trees of the Jewish cemetery, and there is another sound, he can just barely make it out during lulls in the wind, it is a rushing, murmuring sound, like the river would make, but he is too far away from the Vltava for that to be it. The driver of his carriage has changed his demeanor now that he returns to the Castle, he is brisk, he chats to his horse in Czech, he even shares his opinion on the weather with Arcimboldo. As they pass through the narrow avenue between the Church of St. Mary and the Church of the Holy Savior they are well sheltered from the wind, but coming out into the Knights of the Cross Square Arcimboldo is skewered by a cold northeastern blast that brings a certainty of snow.

Master Giovanni de'Bardi is on top of the parade wagon in front of the Clementium, and Arcimboldo will stop now and take a moment to speak with the unlucky artist and designer. The square is virtually empty, there is no traffic coming off or going onto the Stone Bridge over the Vltava. Some of the cleverly painted fabric covering the outside walls of the Clementium has come undone; it bulges, struggles, and flaps ferociously in the wind. Tellingly, it has not been repaired. Arcimboldo instructs the carriage driver to pull over next to the tall parade wagon. Bardi looks down, over the edge of the decorative balustrade atop the wagon, and his face tells all, he looks like a man going to execution.

Arcimboldo's voice is sympathetic sounding as he calls up to Bardi in Italian, "Maestro, who can control the forces of Nature?"

"This God damned city!"

"Fortuna has not favored you, to be sure. But next time-"

"*Favored me?* Fortune has shoved a broomstick up my-"

"Yes, yes, the winter is always a challenge for us to-"

"Arcimboldus! Never mind the fucking weather, this town is full of mad men! They are mad men! How can you live here with these mad men?"

"What do you mean?"

"They've ripped my beautiful parade wagons to shreds! Destroyed them. Scattered them all over Old Town Square. And pissed on the paintings! Those heretical Hussite bastards! I'm ruined!"

"What... why?"

"This is the last one left. I've got to save it!" Bardi's head disappears, and Arcimboldo hears him screaming at people inside the wagon, which has been draped on all sides with painted fabric, splendid scenes of Arcadian landscapes, mythological figures, and Habsburg related imagery. "Push! You worthless bastards, push!" The wagon had been designed to move as if by invisible magic: two donkeys and a crew of men are meant to hide beneath the canvas covering and push the vehicle, while in front, a small dog would be leashed and appear to pull the entire wagon, Christina of Lorraine and all. Apparently Bardi had a team of men inside pushing at that very moment. The wagon lurches forward several inches and stops. "What! You women, is that all you've got in you? Lift up your skirts and push again like men you...donkeys! By Jesus, you'd better push because those child devouring Lutheran maniacs will skin you and roast you alive if they catch you! I hear them coming!"

This last admonition was not well chosen by the frantic Italian artist. Its result is immediate. Canvas flaps open in the side of the vehicle and half a dozen men run out; they sprint across the snow and disappear around the corner of the Clementium without once looking back. Bardi waves his fists and screams after them to no effect, "cowards! Bastards! Finocci!"

The Maestro is correct about one thing however, the sound of an angry mob can now be distinctly heard over the rushing wind. What may have been mistaken for a murmuring river in the distance is now clearly a sound made by several thousand loud and angry voices. The sound approaches the unnaturally deserted Knights of the Cross Square from the east, echoing down the narrow streets feeding into the large, empty, open square. Arcimboldo's carriage driver makes as if to drive off and Arcimboldo stops him. He calls to Bardi, "Maestro, come! Come quickly!"

"Arcimboldus, you must help me. Give me your horse, pull my wagon over the bridge. Please, for God's sake, it's all I have left! The Philistines are on my heels, you must help me!"

The driver of Arcimboldo's carriage catches the drift of Bardi's desperate request, and lets fly with a string of oaths in Czech. He says to Bardi in colloquial Czech, "if you touch my horse, Italian, you will return to Italy without testicles!"

Bardi approaches the driver with red face and flaming eyes, he looks every inch a man beside himself with frustration and reversal. He pulls a knife from his belt.

Just at this moment, a mounted soldier gallops into the square from Karlova Street. It is an officer of the Imperial Horse Guard. The horse rears up and wheels about as the officer stops quickly to take in the tableau of figures around the two vehicles in the square. The breathless officer hoarsely shouts, "riot! The Protestants run riot! Get out of here! Run! Now!" Another Imperial horseman gallops into the square, the rider carries a wounded, bleeding soldier behind him. Over his shoulder the officer shouts, "as you value your lives, flee now!" He whips his horse and it leaps into a run; the two horses gallop onto the Stone Bridge and race west, across the Vltava toward the Lesser Town and the Castle.

Arcimboldo's driver snaps the reins he holds and his horse begins to move forward. Bardi curses and grabs hold of the horse's harness to stop it. Simultaneously, there is a volley of gunfire from Karlova Street, and as Bardi turns toward the sound, the driver of the carriage pulls a stout stick from under his seat and clubs the Italian on the head with it. The gunfire brings a sudden silence to the shouts of the advancing, angry crowd, a silence that lasts for several brief seconds, then with a jagged roar it returns twice as loud as before. The roar drowns out several more gun shots, and six or seven militia soldiers come running frantically into the square from Karlova Street, throwing away their weapons and tearing off their uniforms as they go. The carriage driver is beside himself with fury, cursing Arcimboldo, all artists, all Italians, and all Protestants; but to his credit, the man does not flee, he helps Arcimboldo lift the unconscious Giovanni de'Bardi into his carriage.

While the driver returns to his seat, the rioting Protestants burst out of Karlova Street like bees from a disturbed hive. There is confusion as the densely packed throng pours into the open space of the Knights of the Cross Square, ripping down the painted fabrics and false facades put up for Epiphany, shredding them, stamping upon them, then, upon spotting the two vehicles, in particular the beautifully painted parade wagon, they surge forward, "Papists! Italians! Roman bastards! No Holy League in Prague! No! Death to Papists, death to the Holy League!" These impassioned screams are accompanied by a frenzied, inarticulate, lusty hooting, whistling and yelling: anticipation of more highly satisfying acts of destruction. Arcimboldo's driver turns his carriage and, whipping his horse furiously, makes a run for the bridge. A shower of stones rains down on the fleeing vehicle. The rioters are in pursuit, Arcimboldo turns in his seat to watch them coming. He notices the windows are all open along the top floors of the Clementium, full of faces watching the spectacle below; it is a spectacle of a vastly different nature than they had been expecting to be entertained with this Epiphany Day.

As the carriage nears the bridge, the driver pulls back on the reins and pulls his wheel brake. Arcimboldo flies forward in the carriage, winding up on the floor tangled with Signore Bardi. A new sound is heard over the general din, a loud rhythmic thudding sound. When Arcimboldo gets up off the floor he sees why the carriage has stopped. Colonel Choma leads a company of Imperial Hartschire cavalry across the bridge at a thundering gallop. The finely accoutered knights have thrown back their ermine capes which fly out behind them like wings, revealing their glistening hauberks; like their commander they have drawn their swords and point them at the enemy. Those who have experienced battle against the Turk on the Hungarian plains hold the reins in their teeth and gallop with a sword in one hand and pistol in the other. The hooves of their war horses thrash up billows of powdery snow, and the riders appear to emerge from a white cloud; they must appear as a host of avenging angels traveling at the speed of a lightning bolt, bent on divine retribution. It is a chilling sight for those rioters in the front ranks, they freeze, then realizing what is about to happen, they attempt to scatter like cockroaches. The charging column of Imperial knights slices through the mob of poorly armed citizens like a knife through butter. The bravest, drunkest and most foolish among them engage the mounted soldiers, and battle rages in the Knights of the Cross Square. Arcimboldo watches, stupefied with horror, he feels he is Dante, witness to the abominations of Purgatory. To the cheers of the audience watching from the Jesuit Clementium, as well as the groans of rage and pain from scores of Protestant citizens lying wounded in the square, Colonel Choma and his comrades drive the heretical masses back into the maze of streets, avenues, lanes, and courtyards of Old Town Prague. The white blanket of snow left on Knights of the Cross Square the night before is no longer white; it is various shades of red, pink, yellow and brown.

No more sounds from the scene of the conflict can be heard as the carriage rumbles slowly up the steep twisting street toward the castle. Their horse is still wild eyed, frothing, and biting at the bit, and wisely the driver keeps it moving slowly and steadily homeward, talking and even singing to the animal to calm it. There are still some *sternsingers* scampering happily around in the Lesser Town beneath Hradcany Castle. Many here on this side of the river are unaware of the brief pitched battle fought in the center of the city and of the several hundred Protestant dead and dying lying throughout Old Town.

Riots and protest are common events in this divided city, but the sudden extreme violence of today's conflict is surprising to Arcimboldo – and yet perhaps not: this is an acute embarrassment for the Emperor, with distinguished visitors in the city he would have been incensed to hear that this day of all days was being marred by civil disorder, his orders to Colonel Choma would have been to clear away the troublemakers as quickly as possible. The consequences of this horrible event are still developing in Arcimboldo's mind. He feels a tickle on his cheek and discovers a snowflake. It has begun to snow. As more flakes swirl through the carriage, Giovanni de'Bardi begins to wake, groaning.

Bardi spasms and jerks, then he opens his eyes and winces. His hand goes to his head and he stares at Arcimboldo, who is discomfited by the malice in the unfortunate man's look. Arcimboldo is slightly relieved to discover that Bardi does not glare at him, but over his shoulder at the back of the carriage driver. Without speaking or moving his eyes, Bardi's hand drifts down to his belt, he finds his knife is gone.

"Maestro Bardi, my countryman and friend, I can't begin to express my sorrow at your terrible-"

Bardi interrupts with a torrent of oaths, curses, and dire pronouncements. Arcimboldo can't help appreciating the variety of insult and creativity of description; this isn't the best use of a knowledge mythology, history, and several languages, but it does make for an impressive outpouring when angered. Although the driver doesn't speak Italian, Greek, or Latin, he somehow gets the point, and, without a word, removes his stick from under his seat and rests it in his lap.

Bardi concludes with a groan, "Arcimboldus, why didn't you just leave me there with my wagon? I have no future."

"Now, Maestro, it is not the end of the world, come, come. And you should know, were it not for this man you would not be alive now." Arcimboldo gestures over his shoulder to the driver of the carriage.

Bardi looks to be gathering his energy for another impassioned outburst, Arcimboldo forestalls him, "listen to me, Giovanni, look here, you don't realize what's just happened. More is lost than a parade of painted wagons. You don't realize how many hundreds have just died."

Bardi's eyes widen, "what do you say?"

"Hundreds. Without doubt. And that will just be today. This has been a tragic loss, tragic."

"Hundreds? Sancta Madonna! What happened?"

"The Horse Guard drove the Protestants out of the square... with the edge of their sword, literally."

Bardi almost smiles for a moment, and then he shakes his head in awe, "Jesu! If I ever get out of this God forsaken city I will never leave Italy again."

"Do not think the worst of us, in spite of today, Giovanni. Prague is violent and fractious, yes, but for this to happen on a Christian holy day, I just don't understand it... I can't imagine what created this kind of animosity so suddenly, Epiphany has always been a peaceful celebration in Bohemia."

Bardi pulls a dirty, crumpled piece of paper from his disheveled and bloody doublet, he hands it to Arcimboldo, "this is what drove your Protestants mad. If could get my hands on the person who printed these..."

Arcimboldo reads, *'Fellow Citizens of Prague! How long shall the wicked reign over our people...'* he looks at Bardi with astonishment on his face. "Where did you get this?"

"Have you not seen it? They're scattered all over Old Town, I picked that one up on the steps in front of Our Lady of Tyn."

Arcimboldo is frowning "but this is false, this is..."

"False? Too bad for you...and this heretical city."

"Emperor Rudolf is *not* inviting the Holy League into Bohemia, I assure-"

"He should."

"Giovanni, have you been to France at all in the last ten years? Do you know what's been happening there? Haven't you heard of the St. Bartholomew's Day massacre? The siege of La Rochelle?"

"How else can you deal with stubborn fanatics like these damned Lutherans?"

Arcimboldo purses his lips and shakes his head, "well... happily, Rudolf doesn't feel as you do, he believes that people should be allowed to discover their own path to God, within reason. Catholic doctrine should be protected, yes... but to force religion on a person at the point of a sword..."

"We're talking about forcing people to see reason and truth for their own good."

"Truth? Do you think those people have just been taught reason and truth? They've been taught to hate twice as much as before! Giovanni, what is it we seek to do with our art, what is our message? What are we seeking if not the truth... just decoration for the wealthy? Is truth created so easily on the point of a sword? If it is... then we are mere... decorators, daubers, jesters, and all our learning and culture is mere entertainment. I know you, you're a learned man, you understand the past, there is-"

"What is true now was true in the past. God is the truth, and whatever is in His mind is truth, whatever His plan is – *becomes* truth. The Church is a window into God's truth."

"Yes, but how does one know-"

"Are you still a Catholic, Giuseppe?"

"Of course."

"You should come back to Italy before you become like your Emperor, who, if you'll pardon my saying so, wanders with devils in a hermetic fog. Of course, his father died a heretic, so what can one expect? Come back to Italy and leave this cold, pagan and violent place!"

Arcimboldo takes a deep breath, he smiles dryly and says, "my friend, without telling you that you are absolutely wrong, I will say that *I* believe the World is more subtle and complicated than you imagine. Sometimes the truth is elusive, reluctant to be recognized, hidden among contradictions. However," he holds up the false and provocative printed message and waves it, "that this thing exists is undeniably *true*, I hold it in my hand; all those bodies, *Protestant* bodies, lie out there, that is also undeniably *true*, you can go kick the corpses. One has caused the other...and the Emperor will receive all the blame. And without knowing the truth of what is in God's mind, or the truth of what His plan for us might be, Rudolf must clean up this mess, make right what can be made right, and suffer the mockery and criticism of those who do not have his responsibilities."

"I'll admit, Giuseppe, whoever printed those sheets stirred up this destruction, not the Emperor. That is true." Bardi struggles to rise up and look out of the carriage toward the river and Old Town Prague.

Arcimboldo sighs and shakes his head sadly, "by Christ, Giovanni, you are lucky you did not see it. I've never seen a battle before. Jesu, the blood!"

"Allow people to find their own path to God... and there you go." Bardi gestures toward the east and the scene of the recent slaughter, he winces from pain.

"Let me look at your head." Arcimboldo leans forward to gently probe through the congealed blood in Bardi's gray hair and finds his scalp laid bare to the bone. "Mmm. The Doctor will clean this and close it, you must have this done as quickly as possible. I'll take you to Hagecius as soon as we get to the castle. Sit quietly." In case the driver does understand Italian, Arcimboldo says to Bardi in Latin, "this man struck you very hard, I think he tried to kill you, you are a lucky man. Do not provoke him further."

In Italian Bardi snorts, "it would have been a kindness! Now I will be imprisoned in this place, no doubt alongside many of the heretical ruffians who destroyed my work. St. Anthony spare me!" he crosses himself and mumbles a prayer.

"Why should you be imprisoned, Giovanni? None of this was your fault, your work was splendid, everyone saw it."

"Who will pay my crews, my workers, my carpenters, my tailors, my painters? They all look for payment. Who will pay the wool merchant, I owe him for one-thousand braccia of wool cloth? And there's the silk, taffeta, satin, sarsenet, not to mention linen and canvas, four-thousand braccia of canvas!"

"Giovanni, why would *you* owe for all this?" Arcimboldo feels that the disappointment and blow on the head have unmoored the man's senses.

"Won't all of these people expect to be paid for their work?"

"It is the Emperor's expense to be borne, not yours."

"He has paid for nothing, and promised nothing, by contract I have borne on myself all the expenses. I have nothing left, and a mountain of debt."

"Why did you do this?"

Bardi sighs, closes his eyes. He speaks in a defeated manner, as someone who has thought himself clever only to find he has been a fool. "Last year, last spring, I assisted Emilio Cavalieri with the triumph he designed for Pisa. Do you know the man?"

"Certainly."

"*He* paid for the manufacture of all the parade wagons, all the costumes and decorations, naturally he had to borrow from Venetian Jews. We received our fees for the design and organization from the Pisans, all very well. But after the festival, when the city was full of talk of the excellence of our design, and the beauty of our pageant, Cavalieri *sold* the wagons and decorations to the city fathers of Pisa."

"He sold them? Novel…"

"He told the Pisans that the Sienese and Florentines were eager to have the magnificent festival decorations used in Pisa. The jealous Pisans couldn't bear the thought, the town guilds bought all the wagons, chariots, paintings, costumes and sculptures."

"Ha! Clever Cavalieri!"

"He made six-hundred-thousand scudi."

"Jesu! Six-hundred-thousand!"

"Yes. Clever Cavalieri...foolish Giovanni de'Bardi. I had hoped to sell all the parade wagons, paintings and decorations, or better still, get them to Vienna and use them again, then sell them. I had hoped to be rich."

"Perhaps the Emperor will give you something for your splendid work, Giovanni."

"For a pageant that never took place? For parade wagons that carpet Old Town Square in a million pieces? Do you think he will? You know him best. Will he stay the guilds from trying to collect the debt I owe them? Will he protect me from all my creditors? Do not give me false hope, Giuseppe."

Arcimboldo looks out the window without answering, but Bardi is watching him, hoping for an answer, finally he says, "what do you think, Arcimboldus, will he help me? Will Emperor Rudolf pay me *anything*?"

After another several moments of reflection, Arcimboldo looks Bardi in the eye; he tries to hide his embarrassment with a show of extreme sincerity, he puts his hand on Bardi's shoulder and squeezes, "my friend, Giovanni, fellow artist, you are an unlucky man, I will do everything I can to help you... everything I can. So... we will get you to the doctor... and then get you out of Prague."

The southern gate to Hradcany is guarded by Trabante guards, sworn to protect the Emperor, clad in red, yellow, black, and white, with long military cloaks that nearly reach the ground. Although it is only mid-day torches are already burning inside the gate house behind the halberdiers. The ornamental portcullis within the gate is closed and Arcimboldo's carriage waits for it to be raised. Naturally, Hradcany's portcullis is more inventive and symbolic than most. This portcullis is crafted as an optical illusion, a visual trick, instead of a grid of metal bars set in a pattern of right angles, this portcullis is wrought of curved and tapered metal bars, placed in a design to imitate a long hallway with an arched ceiling, stretching away in perspective, and at the vanishing point, where all lines would meet, is a golden Sun emanating graceful, sinuous rays of gold; a gleaming metallic emblem of the rising Sun of mysterious revelation, symbolic of Copernican Natural philosophy, Sol, the center of the Heavens, the center of life. The golden Sun rises as the portcullis is slowly wound upward, lustrous even on a gray and snowy January day.

There are many soldiers in the outer courtyard, and quite a few somber, bearded men in black (the Emperor's shadowy and secretive corps of spies and informers) about to exit the castle and circulate throughout the city. Rather than part with the carriage driver in the Imperial stables, Arcimboldo prefers to have Bardi and the driver part company here, with many people about. Fortunately, Bardi can walk, unsteadily, leaning on Arcimboldo's shoulder. Arcimboldo courteously thanks the driver and apologizes for the trouble and the extraordinary amount of blood on the carriage's back seat; he offers the man several coins, which he takes ungraciously, avoiding Arcimboldo's eyes and drives away without another word.

Arcimboldo hails one of the Emperor's Household Guards that he happens to recognize, and the soldier helps him walk Bardi into the large inner courtyard to the south of St. Vitus Cathedral. Here thought (and probably news) of the morning's massacre does not exist. Fewer in number compared with Epiphany Days in the past, but still joyful and noisy, the Catholic citizens of Prague's Castle district stroll through the snowfall from booth to booth around the Cathedral; bagpipes howl, jugglers caper, n'er-do-wells throw snow balls, drunks bellow with hearty laughs and slap each other on the back, children do their best to escape watchful parents while licking the remains of Three Kings Cake off their fingers, a trained monkey refuses to do anything but shiver – to the increasing rage of its owner, and on stage the glass blowers guild presents a pantomime featuring the Devil, the Sultan, and a figure costumed something akin to a burning bush.

Rather than observing the medical procedure, Arcimboldo's eyes roam around Doctor Thaddeus Hagecius' medical office, two small rooms next to the doctor's living quarters in the Royal Palace. He notices Hagecius' graduation diploma *in artibus* from University in Vienna has a date of 1550.

After cleaning Bardi's hair and head, the learned old man had then set a bowl containing a black, oily resin in front of the injured artist. Hagecius had put a small live coal in with the resinous substance, which did not catch fire but began to smoke gently. The doctor asked Bardi to hold his head over this bowl and breathe deeply. In a minute or less, Bardi staggered and Hagecius caught him expertly and settled him in a chair.

Now, Bardi sleeps deeply, snoring loudly with mouth wide open; the doctor works to clean, close and bandage the wound. "Ah, Arcimboldus, I see you remember the comet of '77! Open that window just a crack, will you?"

Arcimboldo has been studying a woodcut engraving of the Great Comet of 1577, made by Prague engraver Jiri Daschitzky. In the engraving, Daschitsky shows himself standing outside at night, with a portion of Mala Strana visible behind him, a servant holds lantern and drawing board and the artist is sketching the phenomenon sweeping across the skies above. Standing around Daschitzky watching him work and marveling at the Heavenly display are Imperial doctors Hagecius and Crato, the Hungarian intellectual Andreas Dudith and his wife, and Bohemian Count Adam of Hradec with his wife and servants. Arcimboldo unlatches and opens the window; letting festive sounds from the courtyard as well as fresh air enter the room. He says, "that comet was one of the most unforgettable things I've ever seen, of course. Doesn't it seem much longer than a mere ten years, Thaddeus?"

"Indeed it does. 1577... what a year that was... first Rudolf's coronation as Emperor in June, then the comet in the first week of November."

"I have thought many times since that I wish I had tried harder to capture the colors, do you remember how the comet would light the sky and the whole town with that sullen glow...and the shadows it cast were dark carmine, do you remember that? Just that color there." He points to Bardi's discarded and blood soaked doublet.

"Yes, yes, the comet's tail was yellow with soft red borders, improbable but magnificent. Heavenly flames. The fires of creation. Indeed, that astronomical wonder brought me together once again with Tycho Brahe. The genius of the man! He was able to show so clearly that the tail of the comet was flowing *away* from Sol... inspirational deduction! You know that I'm trying to convince Tycho to come to Prague, the Emperor would favor him singularly."

"That will be a triumph for Bohemian astronomy, and the Emperor... and you of course, Doctor. Will Brahe come?"

"Tycho believes there is an advantage to being some distance apart, and you know he is not entirely wrong about that, you remember that's how we were able to triangulate the comet in the sky: my calculated observation of the relative positions of the comet and Moon here in Prague, and Brahe's in Denmark. It was clear that the comet was higher than the Moon, therefore in no danger of striking us."

"How did you triangulate?"

"On the night of November twentieth and at exactly the same time, using the distant stars as a reference grid, we both observed the comet in exactly the same place, but the moon was in different places, therefore the moon was in front of the comet. Tycho calculated the comet's distance as being three times the distance from the Earth to the moon... although, I must tell you, I could never complete that calculation the same way twice in a row, so I cannot corroborate." The Doctor ties off the bandage that wraps Bardi's head like a mummy's. "And... unh! There we go! Another hard headed Italian will live to breed, paint and drink the heady wines of Latium. Oh, how interesting!" Hagecius is now studying a pattern of moles on Bardi's upper arm.

"What do you see?"

"Do you see these moles here around this man's arm and elbow? Clearly he is plagued by a heated and splenetic disposition, and you see how they circle, his anger will cause him much difficulty. And these three here by his armpit... very bad, very bad indeed, this man's unreasonableness will most likely be his demise."

"Doctor, I have never read your book, *Aphorismi Metoposcopici*, and I regret that now, your ability to diagnose illness and even predict the future by the interpretation of moles on the body is amazing, baffling! We must talk of this again."

The doctor gives the most exaggerated and theatrical bow of thanks an old man is capable of. "I cannot say acceptance of *Metoposcopici* is widespread, but I thank you kindly."

"Mmm, may I have that apple, dear sir? I faint from hunger." With apple in hand, Arcimboldo points to the engraving on Hagecius' wall, "that's you, isn't it, Doctor?"

"Yes, that's me! Ten years younger, by God. That there is the artist, Jiri Daschitzky, did you know him?"

"Not well. I believe he died several years ago, did he not? Um... Thaddeus, I have a favor to ask. Is there somewhere you can keep this man safe and hidden for the next several days?"

"Hidden?"

"Just out of sight, but most definitely keep him here in the castle; he is in some trouble with the guilds...it's nothing to trouble yourself with, but I want to get him out of Prague as soon as he can travel."

"How far will he travel?"

"Florence."

"He will need several days rest first, and he can stay in the room next to this one." The astronomer-doctor wiggled and twisted his neck as if trying to loosen something, a frequent habit, no doubt the result of long nights spent looking up at the sky. "Arcimboldus... is this something you need me to keep from Rudolf?"

"No, no, no. In fact I intend to tell His Majesty the first thing after I leave you."

Hagecius looks relieved, he smiles and nods, "good, good. Help me put him on that couch, facedown."

After helping the doctor, Arcimboldo once again picks up the carefully wrapped package he has been carrying under his arm. Hagecius indicates the package with his eyes, "is that from the Hebrews?"

"Yes, My Lord, it is Rabbi Loew's *Sefer Yetzira.*"

"And the Golem?"

"The Rabbi would not discuss the Golem. Rudolf will be disappointed, I know." Arcimboldo fingers the ruby in his pocket.

"So Maisel could not persuade the man?"

Arcimboldo shrugs, "it seems not."

It is Hagecius' turn to shrug, "ah well… disappointing, yes, but it was hardly essential to our purposes." He gestures to the *Sefer Yetzira*, "may I see it?"

Arcimboldo carefully unwraps the ancient book; and taking it from him, Hagecius reverently caresses the worn calf skin cover. The old doctor opens the book to the first page of text. Following the text with his finger, he slowly translates for Arcimboldo, *"by thirty-two mysterious paths of wisdom Jehovah has engraved all things, He who is the Lord of hosts, the God of Israel, the living God, the Almighty God, He that is uplifted and exalted, He that Dwells forever, and whose Name is holy; having created His world*…oh by Jove, Arcimboldus, this is tremendous… and incredible, we actually have it!"

Arcimboldo wants to check the time, but finds his drum watch is missing; he must have lost it in the carriage! A handsome bonus for the surly driver. Arcimboldo gently takes the *Sefer Yetzira* back from the doctor, who is almost reluctant to let it go. Arcimboldo rewraps the precious book of Creation and Formation, saying, "pardon me, My Lord, I must give this to the Nolan shortly."

Hagecius casts a look of longing on it as it disappears beneath folds of black cloth. He clears his throat. "Ah, my friend, this evening... what will happen? I can hardly believe we are on the brink." He shakes his head as if to clear it from unwanted thoughts. "I regret that I cannot go into town today to help the doctors there, they will most likely need assistance."

"Thaddeus, you have no idea how right you are."

"There were many casualties?"

"Hundreds."

"Hundreds!"

"I had never seen a battle before, until today, I know you were doctor to the troops in Austria and Hungary...you must have seen-"

"Four years at the front, and I was at the defense of Pressburg in '67, and my friend, I do not wish to disappoint you, but you still have not seen a battle. Hartschire cavalry against armed civilians is not a battle, do you see any wounded knights here? No. When you see Imperial knights locked in mortal combat with Turkish Janissaries from dawn to dusk, then you'll have seen a battle!"

"The blood! Madonna, it was everywhere!"

"Bloody? At Pressburg I was amputating arms and legs from sunrise to sunset, when I left the tent at dark there was a pile of limbs outside higher than my head." Hagecius shudders at the memory. "Hundreds of citizens you say?"

"No doubt many more in the streets of Old Town... I have not yet heard what conditions are like in Old Town Square, but I understand the riot began there." Arcimboldo removes the printed broadsheet given him by Bardi, now quite gruesomely patterned with bloody fingerprints, he shows this to Hagecius. "This forgery, this vile and malicious lie is what caused this destruction."

"What is this... give that here, sir. By St. Peter, Arcimboldus! Oh, shhh, quietly, we must leave this man to sleep, come with me next door."

Next door, in Thaddeus Hagecius' living quarters, are found the printer Jiri Nigrin of Cerneho Mostu and the doctor's assistants, Igor and Daniel. Hagecius gives instruction to his people as to what should be done with the comatose Giovanni de'Bardi, they bow and exit. Hagecius introduces Nigrin to Arcimboldo, explaining that the printer has just brought him a finished work; it is a collection of 374 motets by the very popular Bohemian composer, Jacobus Gallus. Due to the troubles in town, Nigrin is now unable to get back across the Stone Bridge to return home. Arcimboldo furtively eyes the bloody broadsheet in the doctor's hand, he is eager to hear Hagecius' opinion on it, and he is conscious that he is very late for his appointment with Emperor Rudolf; however, the Italian is also quite interested in music, and extremely fond of Jacobus Gallus. While Hagecius reads, Arcimboldo says, "I'm especially partial to Gallus' use of *coro spezzato*, Master Nigrin. May I see the work?"

*Coro spezzato*, or the polychoral style of music, was invented and popularized in Venice. As far as Arcimboldo knows it is the only case of a musical style arising from a single architectural peculiarity. In the Basilica of San Marco, in Venice, the choir lofts are separated by such a distance that there is a disconcerting sound delay from one choir to the other; the Basilica's *Maestro di cappella* always had a very difficult time getting the two widely separated choirs to sing the same music simultaneously. In 1545, Adrian Willaert, who was *Maestro di cappella* of San Marco at that time, creatively solved this problem by writing music intentionally making use of the delay. Willaert had the opposing choirs sing alternating and contrasting phrases of music, to enchanting effect; the shifting direction of the sound, and those mysterious, transient periods of overlap were haunting, ethereal, beautifully spiritual, and extremely popular with audiences and worshippers in San Marco. Arcimboldo has experienced this auditory effect in the Venetian church, and he has been deeply moved and inspired by the Natural magic revealed. The golden light under the Basilica's magnificent dome, the clouds of rare incense floating through the huge space, and the divinely beautiful music, seem to magically combine into a single mystical and tangible substance. Now, this technique of antiphonal music created by opposing choirs is intentionally copied throughout Europe, and Jacobus Gallus is one of the foremost modern composers in this style.

Nigrin eagerly shows Arcimboldo the newly printed, six part *Opus Musicum* of Jacobus Gallus while Hagecius closely studies the bloody, tattered broadsheet. "Look here, My Lord, 374 motets that cover the liturgical needs of the entire year." He opens the work and Arcimboldo can smell the recently pressed ink coming from the pages. "Here is the motet *O Magnum Mysterium*, this serves the period from the first Sunday of Advent to the Septuagesima, the ninth Sunday before Easter." He puts his finger on the page, "you see, My Lord, Venetian polychoral harmony for eight voices." By this time, the bloody paper in Hagecius' hand has been noticed by the Prague printer, he has trouble taking his eyes off it, and while he believes he is showing Arcimboldo *O Magnum Mysterium* he is in fact pointing to a blank space on the page. He finally points to the broadsheet, "one of those was on my doorstep this morning."

"This?"

"Yes. Is it true, My Lord?"

Hagecius answers firmly, "no. Not a jot. It is a dastardly counterfeit."

"Good Lord!"

"Indeed. This is mischief indeed. A cowardly act, anonymous and provocative."

"It is written by a Frenchman, My Lord."

Arcimboldo and Hagecius look at each other in surprise. Arcimboldo says, "how can you know that, Master Nigrin?"

The printer takes the sheet to a table and smoothes it out, Arcimboldo and Hagecius look over his shoulder. Nigrin explains, "this is printed in Czech, and speaks to fellow citizens. Look at the word 'problem'. There should be an accent *acute* over the 'e', instead it is an accent *grave*."

"A simple mistake."

"In your own language, a common word like 'problem', mistaking the direction of the accent mark? I think not. Which language do you know that spells this word 'problem' exactly the same, but with an accent grave just like we see here?"

Arcimboldo and Hagecius answer together, "French."

"Now, a Frenchman *pretending* to be Czech would be very likely to unconsciously err on the accent mark of a word otherwise identical in both languages, as in the word 'problem'. It is much more likely that this is the *simple mistake* that has happened here."

Eyebrows raised and eyes wide, Arcimboldo says, "that is well reasoned, Master Nigrin, well reasoned. We are most humbly in your debt, sir. I must take this information to the Emperor as soon as I can." Arcimboldo pauses and it appears a thought has crossed his mind. "Um, Doctor, before I go, may I trouble you, is your urinal still behind that screen in the corner?"

The daylight is weak although it is only an hour past mid-day. The snow continues to fall on this city on the Vltava, covering the traces of the morning's brutality in Old Town; while up on the hill above, the spires and towers of Hradcany gather thicker and thicker coats of white. Preparations for the evening's grand entertainment go ahead throughout the castle, and they continue without hesitation or adjustment in spite of the day's other losses. The parade and pageant that had been carefully organized by Giovanni de'Bardi to grandly convey the Emperor's guests through the city and up to the castle have of course been destroyed by the riot. But everything else is still on schedule. The Emperor's guests are currently at a special Mass in the Cathedral. Of those important guests: the Tuscan embassy is lodging in the castle and arrived long before the violence started; the French have been guests of the Jesuits at the redoubtable Clementium in the Knights of the Cross Square. Christina of Lorraine and her party have safely been brought out of the town and up to Hradcany; to the Emperor's embarrassment, this has been done in closed and well guarded coaches rather than open and marvelously decorated parade wagons. And as for locating Rudolf, Arcimboldo is certain that wherever he might be it is not in St. Vitus attending Mass.

Arcimboldo climbs a stairway in the Royal Palace, and at the end of a long hallway stretching away to his right, he sees a group of men looking out of the large leaded glass windows, Bartolomeus Spranger is among them. Arcimboldo approaches them intending to ask Rudolf's whereabouts; they are chattering excitedly in German. When Spranger sees the Italian he excitedly clasps his shoulder, "Arcimboldus! By Apollo! I heard you were down there when it all happened! I am overjoyed to see you here, and in one piece. Tell me what you saw!"

The others turn to appraise Arcimboldo and hear his answer. "I am unhurt, my friend, thank you. What did I see? A thing I wish to God that I had not seen. The battle, the riot, whatever one calls it, was bloody, horrible... violence beyond anything I have *ever* seen before. But now, most urgently, I must speak with the Emperor, do you know where he is?"

"In his apartments, of a surety, I've just left there." Spranger rolls his eyes and shakes his head in an unspoken warning of difficulties ahead. He leans toward Arcimboldo and whispers in his ear, "did you see the Jews? Did you get it?"

Arcimboldo nods and pats the small wrapped package he carries as an answer. He asks quietly, "and your wife, Bartolomeus? Your home in the city? Have you any news?"

Spranger nervously strokes his sparse, rust colored beard, "my wife is secure, I know my brother-in-law will manage, I'm not concerned." The confidence in his voice is not matched by the flicker of uncertainty in his eyes.

The other men assault Arcimboldo with questions about the details of the fight, and Arcimboldo answers as briefly as possible, excusing himself by repeating his urgent need to see the Emperor. Before he rushes away he looks through the window to see what the men have been watching. He sees the eastward view toward the river and distant city is dominated by white and gray, landscape, buildings, and sky. The cloud and snow veil the troubled center of Prague, but not completely, one can clearly see tall columns of gray smoke rising high into the sky in half a dozen places throughout the city. Arcimboldo cannot help but pause, "what? Are those fires?" He asks.

"The Protestants burn Catholic homes and buildings throughout the city."

"Holy Mother of God!"

The others eagerly supply him with details of the rumors they have heard: having routed the rioters and driven them to ground in Old Town, the Hartschire knights have returned to the bridge and hold it secure to protect the west bank of the city and the castle; the enraged and maddened Protestants take vengeance where they will, on Catholic neighbors, shops and buildings; and the worst of all, the Prague Tercio refuses to leave its barracks to restore order!

Arcimboldo bows perfunctorily to the group and bustles away, saying quickly to Spranger, "walk with me a moment, if you will, sir." When out of earshot he says, "and the Emperor?"

"What you would expect."

"How bad is it?"

Spranger shrugs, "I've seen worse. I believe the thought of what we do tonight holds his anger in check. However, the Tercio's *Maestre de Campo* is with Rudolf now. That officer is infuriatingly intractable, grossly provocative. The Spaniard practically taunts the Emperor. I thought Baron Schwartzenau would assault the man. I couldn't bear to watch any longer."

"What can be the issue, for God's sake?"

Spranger sighs, he holds up his hand and rubs his thumb and forefinger together. "The usual issue, their pay."

Arcimboldo's mind races along far faster than his footsteps. "Bartolomeus, this is what you must do. Find Katharina Strada, if she is not already with the Emperor, tell her she must go to him immediately, tell her what has happened, she'll know what to do." He presses the book into Spranger's hands, "also, please, take this book to the Summer Palace and give it to the Nolan, and no one else. Will you do this?"

"I will, Arcimboldus. God speed."

After the two men have walked in opposite directions for several seconds Spranger turns and not too loudly calls out, "Arcimboldus... the other thing?"

Arcimboldo turns briefly, "there will be no Golem." As he turns back he mutters to himself, unheard by the Dutchman, "thanks be to God." He fondles the lucky ruby in his pocket as he walks.

In the corridor outside the Emperor's apartments there must be a score of Rudolf's personal Household Guards. The torches burning in the hallway cast a dancing orange light on the highly polished glaive each soldier holds at his side. The blade of each glaive is engraved with RII, and the Imperial crown, sword, and scepter; the dancing light makes these markings appear to wriggle and leap on the razor sharp crescents of steel.

Arcimboldo's clothing is disheveled and stained with blood in several places. Standing among the imposing group of soldiers, the artist cleans, smoothes and rearranges his clothing and hair as much as is possible. He feels a sudden surge of guilty surprise when he discovers the letter from his son Benedetto. Unopened and forgotten so quickly? For shame, Arcimboldo. It is true that the day has been extraordinarily distracting, and yet as he knocks on the door to the Emperor's apartments the guilty feeling lingers. He has not received word from Benedetto for over a year, nor has Arcimboldo written during that time. What will be the news... and does that even matter? Would another man have paused one second to tear open the letter and eagerly consume the contents? Has Arcimboldo become more of a father to paintings than flesh and blood? This is not the kind of man he envisions himself to be... and yet... perhaps... this is what he has become. As Atlas opens the Emperor's door, Arcimboldo stands straight, raises his chin, and arranges his face into the calm, attentive appearance of an intelligent man, a gracefully competent courtier, a master of *sprezzatura artficiosa*. In his eyes, if one looks very closely, there can be detected the faintest cloud of self doubt – master of *sprezzatura artficiosa*, yes...master of the most basic human emotions of familial love and attentiveness, no. Quite honestly... no.

Arcimboldo has helped to design the room he stands in now, the Emperor's outer chamber. The octagonal room is not a large space; chairs line the walls and a single heavy, beautifully carved table stands in the center. The room is not crowded with furniture, it is crowded with people. Several members of the Privy Council stand together, speaking earnestly among themselves. A wealthy German merchant sits in one of the chairs, his elbows are on his knees and he holds his head in his hands, the merchant's wife sits next to him with tear stained and distraught face, she has her arms around her husband's shoulders attempting to comfort him. The artist, Josef Heintz, and the sculptor, Adrien de Vries, pause in their conversation and nod to Arcimboldo. The *Sargente Mayor*, second in command of the Prague Tercio, sits alone, the others have moved as far as possible from this nervous and uncomfortable looking Spanish officer. As Atlas enters Rudolf's office, he looks back at Arcimboldo and holds up one finger, an indication for him to wait. Loud, angry voices are heard coming from that room before the door closes again.

Four of the walls in the Emperor's octagonal outer room are covered with dark green leather.

Hanging upon those green walls are paintings of riotous and untamed Natural landscapes; cataracts, chasms, rugged mountain views, mysterious, deeply shadowed forest glens. The remaining four walls are covered by grand hunting tapestries also depicting unruly and undisciplined Natural settings. On the table in the center of the room stands a magnificent bronze statue by Giambologna. In smoothly burnished bronze, Hercules conquers the cruel Erymanthian boar, the Hero's fourth Labor. Hercules swings the flailing animal onto his shoulder; the two figures entwine and spiral upward as they rise from the sculpture's base. This spiraling technique has been perfected by the Flemish master; one can view the sculpture from any angle and still feel the dynamic, powerful expression of strength in the Hero, and the desperate, frantic struggles of the massive boar. The sculpture's message echoes that of the room as a whole: exceptional, divinely blessed Man can fearlessly master the Natural World.

Arcimboldo is very pleased with the effect created by the massive chandelier which hangs above the table. This is his invention entirely. The torches which provide the only source of light in the room rest upon a grouping of gigantic stag antlers. The irregular, branchlike shadows that are cast upon the walls and the highly polished parquet floor by this chandelier further enhance the organic and forest-like ambiance of this space. The shadows seem to bob and sway as though they are created by tree boughs stirred by Nature's gentle breezes. The shadows leap as Atlas suddenly opens wide the door to Rudolf's office, he motions for Arcimboldo to enter.

"Not the same argument again!"
"It's not that I don't understand you, gentlemen. You seem not to understand my position."

"Bah! You scoundrel!"

"You would not treat my master with such incivility."

"How dare you compare yourself to your master, you tin soldier!"

"I'm here at the behest His Most Catholic Majesty, Philip, the King of Spain. Without him-"

The Emperor slaps his desk in exasperation. "God's blood! *I* am your master, sir!" Rudolf has interrupted the back and forth argument endlessly raging between his advisors and the Spanish *Maestre de Campo*.

The officer, Hidalgo Manuel Soranzo, *Maestre de Campo* of the Prague Tercio, bows to the Emperor. "Of course, Majesty, *perdoname*. And yet my commission and title are signed and awarded to me by His Most Catholic Majesty, and I am bound to honor the instructions given to me by that-"

"Your instructions are to destroy this city...this capital?"

"Certainly not. Of course not. Just pay us as you have promised and we'll serve you as faithfully as ever."

"We *have* paid you, you Iberian bastard!" Marshall Trautson exclaims. He picks a large bag of coins off Rudolf's desk and flings them down again with a jangling crash.

The Hidalgo's hand jerks unconsciously toward the hilt of his fine sword, he hisses out, "you have not. I may not accept that. I have told you so repeatedly."

"Why should you care where this money comes from, gold is gold."

"I may not accept money borrowed from Jews."

"Why does that matter? You toy with us, sir!"

"The *'why'* is not my concern, Lord Marshall. I'm bound to follow the orders of His Most Catholic-"

"Your Most Catholic King had no trouble taking all the Jews' gold before he kicked them out of Spain!"

The Spanish officer grinds his teeth, he shakes his head, he twirls his mustachios agitatedly. He adjusts the richly embroidered orange sash of rank he wears. The beautiful orange silk is also used in his ruffled sleeves and pantaloons. He carefully keeps his right hand away from the hilt of his sword, yet the hand wanders nervously about his body, tucking, pulling, poking, and unnecessarily adjusting his accoutrements for the hundredth time. He says, "with *deep* regret I see we do not understand one another, My Lord."

In a subdued voice Rudolf says, "would you have me melt down my dinner plate? The treasure from my chapel? The frames from my paintings? Would you have me pay your soldiers in art, Hidalgo?"

The Spaniard's expression goes from angry to smug, he almost scoffs. "That is not my concern... that is *your* decision to make, Your Majesty... although I am certain you jest."

"It's *not* a jest that he will send you all packing tomorrow, and without a pfennig in your pocket, you cowardly pack of Spanish dogs!" Trautson flings this insult at the officer and shakes his fist in his face.

Soranzo closes his eyes with the effort it takes to control himself.

Not a moment too soon, Atlas responds to a knock on the door, and immediately opens it to admit the Spanish ambassador, Don Guillen de San Clemente.

Don Guillen is a man of rare intelligence and grace. He is especially valuable to his master, the King of Spain, as a spokesman who can communicate well, cleverly, subtly, with excellent and intuitive understanding. He has served Spanish interests in

Vienna and Prague as long as Arcimboldo has served the Habsburg Emperors, and although the two men serve different masters, they are good and trusted friends. The dark eyed and sallow skinned Spaniard bows to the Emperor but does not take the time to greet the other very tense and angry men in the room. "Forgive me, Your Majesty, it was difficult for me to get across the Stone Bridge, I have come as quickly as possible."

Rudolf squints his eyes and clenches his jaws in repressed rage and anxiety. He points to the bag of gold coins on his desk, "you refuse my payment and you let my city burn." He clears his throat so he may speak with more control. "Ambassador, can you offer an explanation that is less insulting than this man's?" He waves his hand dismissively at the *Maestre de Campo*.

Soranzo begins to speak in his defense but San Clemente stops him by raising his hand. He speaks to Rudolf, "Your Majesty, this misunderstanding is tragic, but let us not make things worse, we will certainly find a solution. The *Maestre de Campo* has been following his orders, do not hold him accountable."

"And what are *your* orders, Ambassador?"

"Naturally, to serve the interests of Habsburg dominion, my King, and the true religion. The prosperity of this Empire is my specific concern and mission, to be able to serve you, My Lord, is to also serve my King, Philip II." The elegant Spaniard has a hypnotic voice and beautiful elocution in any language. They speak Spanish now; this is by Rudolf's preference, he always speaks Spanish formally, he has been taught it is the language of superior nobility; however the Emperor prefers German on more informal and scientific occasions.

"Don Guillen, do not play courtier with me, my city is burning, and the troops given to me by my uncle Philip to keep the peace do just the opposite. You quibble about Jewish gold... at a time like this? Does this serve my interests, sir?"

"Your Majesty, this is easily resolved, have patience." San Clemente points to the bag of gold coins, "as champions of the true and most Catholic faith we are forbidden to touch Jewish gold; have no doubt we are sincere and not quibbling. And yet, we are all men of the world here, are we not? There is always a way. It surprises me you have not thought of it before...I speak of the good brothers at the Clementium, the Jesuits are always your best friend, My Lord, although sometimes you do not believe it, I assure you, it is the case. Now, let us give this tainted gold to the good brothers, and it is as certain as *mutatis mutandis* that they will resolve the hesitancy of the Tercio's officers and soldiers. It is easily done, and immediately done, My Lord. Good Catholics everywhere will be overjoyed to know you have such faith and trust in our Jesuit friends, that you allow them to help you with this impasse." San Clemente fixes Rudolf with a smile of good will and supreme confidence.

Marshall Trautson slaps his hand to his forehead and exhales loudly with frustration, "God's blood, we are led by the nose. We can use the Household Guard and the Hartschire knights to restore order in the city, Sire, we do not need these men! Do not allow the Jesuits to control this situation, I beg you!" Rudolf ignores him, and the Marshall turns and strides to the window behind the Emperor to join Baron Schwartzenau who stands with arms folded, scowling at the Spaniards.

All eyes are on the Emperor to see what he will do. Rudolf does not reply and does not look the Spanish ambassador in the face; his eyes slowly, thoughtfully, scan the room, and the pause in conversation lingers on. In stifling silence, the Emperor slowly appraises the other men and objects in his office one by one until his gaze falls on Arcimboldo. He finally speaks, "you have blood on your hands, sir."

Arcimboldo is momentarily startled, then he realizes what the Emperor says is literally true. He self-consciously rubs the back and side of his left hand. He answers quietly and respectfully, "it belongs to Master Bardi. He was injured in the... head."

"Mmm. And his Epiphany parade decorations?"

"Gone, My Lord. I'm afraid they are all gone. And there are hundreds-"

"Gone? What do you mean?"

"Destroyed, My Lord. Completely."

Rudolf slumps back and seems to shrink in defeat. Arcimboldo casts a quick glance around the room. Each man, on both sides of the issue, has tightly pursed lips and downcast eyes. They avoid looking directly at the Emperor, but each is thinking the same thing – if only Rudolf would take governance as seriously as he takes art. Arcimboldo also knows when it is time to speak and when not to.

Eventually, with a deep breath followed by a long sigh, the Emperor pushes the bag of gold coins several inches in San Clemente's direction. He then turns his attention to the cogs, wheels, springs, and other clock making pieces that are strewn across his desk. This is one of his favorite occupations, tinkering with mechanical clockworks. He appears to have forgotten the room is full of very tense men waiting for him to lead them to a solution.

San Clemente seizes the bag of gold, he says, "wisdom itself, Your Majesty! You always see directly to the heart of the matter. The *Maestre de Campo* and I will immediately take this to the Jesuits, we'll make certain that your wishes are fulfilled to the letter." He bows deeply to the Emperor and begins backing toward the door. He nudges the Spanish officer who appears to awake from a dream and the man clumsily copies the actions of his countryman; the Hidalgo's eyes shoot daggers of hatred toward Baron Schwartzenau and Marshal Trautson. Before he exits, Don Guillen quickly glances at Arcimboldo, and quicker than a flash of lightning, he winks his left eye. Then he is gone.

As soon as the door is closed, Rudolf's advisors all begin protesting at once, even those who have remained mute during the long and acrimonious debate.

Colonel Choma steps forward and cries, "let my cavalry deal with this, Your Majesty, you cannot trust the Spanish!"

High Steward Dietrichtstein whines, "why give gold to the Jesuits? By God, they have cheated us!"

Marshall Trautson sputters, "the damned Jesuits and Spanish are in this together, this is outrageous! We've been manipulated!"

Baron Schwartzenau is incandescent, "this is an affront to Your Imperial dignity, Your Majesty, you must dismiss these foreigners immediately!"

Arcimboldo earnestly breaks in, "Your Majesty, I believe there is more going on here than just the Spanish and the Jesuits." He steps forward to show the Emperor the bloody broadsheet he has brought from the Old Town. As he holds it out to the Emperor he notices that there are already several copies of the troublesome broadsheet on the desk.

Rudolf waves him off, saying, "I have seen that piece of villainy, sir."

"But Master Nigrin, the printer, has explained to me and to Doctor Hagecius why he thinks this was written by a Frenchman."

There is a chorus of appropriate gasps and comments from the advisors: "The French again!" "I knew it!" "This is the Holy League's doing!" "Those sneaky bastards!" "They're *all* in it together!"

There is a knock, the door opens and Atlas leans in. He signals to the Emperor by placing two fingers of his right hand on his forehead and then on his heart. The Emperor nods and stands. The door opens fully and Katharina Strada enters. She curtsies to Rudolf, and he nods to her in return. She immediately crosses the office to the door to the Emperor's bed chamber; she turns to the group of staring men, curtsies to them politely, and then enters the bed chamber, closing the door behind her.

Rudolf stands straighter, smoothes his doublet and strokes his beard. He says, "gentlemen, we are finished. Please leave me now, we will speak again later. I wish to speak with Master Arcimboldus alone, you will stay, sir." The tired and frustrated advisors bow and back toward the door. The Emperor adds, "not you Vilem, you may stay as well." For the first time, Arcimboldo notices Count Vilem Rozmberk sitting in a chair in a dark corner of the room, the Count has not spoken a word all this time.

Fifty-two year old Count Vilem Rozmberk is the most important man in the Czech lands of Bohemia. He holds titles of High Burgrave and High Treasurer. His extensive and fertile personal property to the south of Prague is larger than many German Duchies and Principalities. Vilem raises armies to fight the Turk. He develops his ancestral lands according to the latest scientific methods of agriculture, forestry, mineralogy, and social organization. He is admired and respected across Europe, and was even offered the Crown of Poland in 1575. Vilem refused the offer out of deference and respect for Rudolf, knowing the Emperor was also interested in claiming Poland. He peacefully and contentedly rules his lands from his capital at Cesky Krumlov and is allowed to issue his own currency – gold coins with his picture on them and his personal motto: *Festina Lente.* Fortunately for the Habsburgs, the Rozmberks are absolutely and unshakably loyal to the Holy Roman Empire; fortunately for Rudolf, Vilem is a supportive and enthusiastic personal friend, as well as extremely interested in all the same things, namely: Humanist learning, religious tolerance, art, science, and, of course, alchemy.

Rudolf seats himself at his desk once more and says to Arcimboldo, "sit, sit. You are otherwise unhurt from your adventures today? Vilem, join us."

Arcimboldo seats himself where he has a view of one of his own paintings, in fact it is the very first painting done in the style which has made him famous. It is a portrait of Rudolf's Imperial historian and librarian, Hugo Blotius. Just as Titian and Tintoretto filled their portraits of the Stradas, father and son, with messages about the personalities of those men, Arcimboldo's portrait attempts to tell a story about the librarian's personality and character. But Arcimboldo's pictorial style in conveying that wider and deeper message is far, far different than that used by the Venetian painters. It is far, far different from any style seen before in Europe; it is most likely the first time such a thing has been seen in the entire World. Arcimboldo created this astonishing visual experiment in 1562, it was received with such great success, and it so profoundly affected the artist's intellect and career, that his life was never the same afterwards.

This portrait of Hugo Blotius shows a bust high view of the librarian standing in front of a dark blue curtain. The drooping beard and moustache, and floppy shapeless cap are characteristic of the dry and pedantic old scholar. However, after several seconds of closer inspection, one notices that the portrait is made up of images of books and manuscripts... and nothing else! They lean and tilt, they are open and closed, with projecting and drooping bookmarks and varied textures, bindings, and covers... nevertheless, visually, infallibly, they assemble themselves as a portrait, a man, an old man, a librarian, Hugo Blotius himself! Undoubtedly, it is amazing. Whether it is viewed as a curiosity, or a deeper message to be read by the informed and initiated, it is amazing – and continues to be seen as such.

As Count Rozmberk pulls his chair over to the Emperor's desk, Arcimboldo says, "may I say, My Lord, that I scarcely know whether I'm hurt or not, such has been the extraordinary tumult of action these past hours. It's a day unlike any other I have experienced!"

Rozmberk laughs politely, and smiles a friendly greeting at Arcimboldo as he sits. Arcimboldo returns the smile and nods in greeting. Rudolf appears to relax for the first time, he does not smile but says pleasantly, "what else should we expect, my friends? Today *is* unlike any other. After tonight... tomorrow the World will be a different place... we will be different men." He gazes wistfully into the distance. The men now speak in German.

"Certainly, My Lord, certainly. Yet, I'm compelled to say, the destruction I witnessed in Old Town was shocking. Many, many have died. Many of your subjects will *have no* tomorrow." Arcimboldo says this very earnestly.

Looking away, Rudolf mumbles distractedly, "how can one be a gentle ruler to a fractious people?"

Balding and white bearded, Vilem Rozmberk leans forward with concern on his face, "mmm, tut tut tut, for that to have happened on this day, a day we've all looked forward to for so long, that is truly a sad and untimely coincidence."

"Perhaps not a coincidence, perhaps the World around us, the Heavens above us, can sense what we are about to do. Perhaps the World around us reels with anticipation and excitement, just as we do. Perhaps it prepares itself for a new age." Rudolf stares into space in an almost mystical way.

Arcimboldo swallows a worried sigh. The Count says, "if it *is* preparing itself, Rudolfus, let us hope it is all for the confounding of the French and your Spanish relatives." He laughs at his own wit, but the laughter is not shared by either of the other men in the room.

Rudolf's eyes have come back into focus. "Maestro Arcimboldus, I have a favor to ask. Our special guests have had a very bad impression of this city; I wish to impress them, as far as it is possible to impress a Florentine and a Frenchwoman. I'd like you to give them a tour of our Wunderkabinet; I understand Christina Valois is unusually interested in clever mechanical devices and astronomical instruments; we'll show her Prague is as modern, cultured, and scientific as Paris. The Tuscan Grand Duke is surfeited with art, but he may want to see our curios, coins, weapons and medals; I will leave it to you to decide, he is your countryman, you will get along well. They are at Mass I believe, or have been. I will have the Archbishop bring them to you, where will you be for the next several hours?"

"I will be delighted, My Lord. I'll wait in my rooms in the Palace."

"Excellent. Entertain them for an hour or two. I will send the Chamberlain to fetch them when I am ready to escort them to the Summer Palace for our banquet."

Rozmberk says, "may I join them, Rudolfus? I heard you received the Durer painting, I cannot wait to see it... my mouth waters."

"The blue bird wing in still with Ottavio Strada, I have not had a chance to see it myself, but you may do as you please." Rudolf leans forward, excited, "Vilem, a far grander sight than that single Durer is waiting for you. You have not seen the finished Cosmos room; I wish I could be there when you do. It is extraordinary beyond description. Arcimboldus has done something that no other artist who has ever lived has even dreamed of, let alone attempted." To Arcimboldo he says, "it is your supreme accomplishment and invention, sir, I honor you, and I intend to reward you most liberally... most liberally."

"Such praise is reward itself, My Lord, but surely Masters Bartolomeus and Mont deserve equal praise. Indeed, the Nolan and the Englishman, Doctor Dee, have been instrumental as well. This could never have been accomplished by one man alone. If Your Majesty had not gathered the resources together our ideas could never have attained substance. If I may say, My Lord, you are the canvas upon which we paint our dreams."

"You will all be rewarded, more than you can imagine. You will be raised high. You will not be disappointed." With that, Rudolf opens a drawer in his desk and removes a small bag of what sounds to be coins; he tosses it across the desk to Arcimboldo. The artist thinks he is being given an immediate bonus, and he prepares himself to politely and gratefully protest. Fortunately, he does not speak before the Emperor continues, "the Nolan has guided our efforts with great skill and intelligence, and I will say... inspiration. Give him those three-hundred thalers before we begin tonight. And before you send him back to Wittenberg tomorrow, give him my most profound thanks. I anticipate being distracted, most likely unable to do this myself, you will do it for me, sir."

"I believe he intends to remain here in Prague, Your Majesty, he has expressed something of the kind."

"Out of the question. Do not entertain that thought for a moment. He will return to Wittenberg at the first opportunity."

Arcimboldo forces an agreeable and pleasant look onto his face. Inside his head, his thoughts whirl around, thinking of how poorly the Nolan will take being dismissed like this, knowing how much he expects to continue his connection to the room and the Emperor's experiment. He knows quite well that Bruno considers this *his* experiment as well. Were the bag of coins twice the size, the Nolan would throw it back in his face. Yes, Bruno will in fact definitely throw this back into his face. That will be the least of it; the scene will be most unpredictably unpleasant. Arcimboldo almost shudders with the thought.

"I see you are moved by my generosity toward your friend. Tell him more will come his way. This is only the beginning of my gratitude." The Emperor looks very pleased with himself.

Count Rozmberk reaches out and touches Arcimboldo lightly on the arm, "Arcimboldus, I'm dying of curiosity, what of the homunculus?"

Rudolf echoes the thought, "oh yes! How could I have forgotten? Have you seen Rabbi Loew? Will he provide the Golem?"

Arcimboldo bows slightly to the Emperor, "I have seen Maisel and the Rabbi. The book is ours. But the Golem... no. I have not secured the Golem. I'm most profoundly sorry, My Lord. Rabbi Loew would not even speak of it."

Rudolf is sobered. He sits back with a frown, thinking. "He is jealous. That is understandable. The man can see behind things, he can feel the current of event, of portent. Yes, he is jealous. He said nothing?"

"He refused to speak of it."

Rozmberk says, "ah well, Rudolfus, it matters not. After tonight you can create your own Golem, an army of them!"

Rudolf brightens, "of course! An army of them, yes. Now, Arcimboldus, I will begin to reward you too. I will surprise you. When we conclude our experiment, when we change the World, when Prague becomes the center of the Universe, the New Rome... our lives, all things, will be very different. After tonight, I give you leave to return to your beloved Milan. Yes, at last I agree. You may return home."

Arcimboldo is dumbstruck. He can hardly grasp the meaning of what the Emperor has just told him, let alone express his feelings. Milan! Family, home, grandchildren, old age, he will die and be buried in Italy, in the land of his fathers! He rises and quickly moves behind Rudolf's desk, he falls to one knee (far less gracefully than he would have even five years ago, he must hold on to the desk to steady himself), he grasps the Emperor's hand with unprecedented familiarity, he kisses the Imperial ring. Almost in tears he says, "My Lord, My Emperor, I am your servant until death. I'm as grateful as the night shrouded Earth is for the morning Sun."

Count Rozmberk watches and chuckles with pure delight at the two men. The enormous lace ruff he wears bobs up and down, it makes his stout body appear to have no neck at all. He says, "wonderful, wonderful! Lord God, bring us all such happiness and gratitude for your blessings!"

Rudolf is smiling! A tight but genuine smile. "But you must finish my Vertumnus. You may send it to me. You will do that, won't you?"

"Without doubt, without question! It will be more than you can imagine. It will be filled with my joy. It will be my finest painting!"

He stands, wondering if he should excuse himself now. Rudolf says, "sit, sit. We are not finished yet." Rudolf pauses, and busily begins arranging and tidying his desk. He distractedly pours wine from a greenish glass beaker but does not drink or even touch the cup, nor does he offer any to his guests. The painted enamel decoration on the beaker illustrates Rudolf's emblem, 'ADSIT', an acrostic of the Emperor's personal motto. Above ADSIT an eagle flies up to the sky holding a laurel wreath in its talons. Arcimboldo sits and waits, almost unable to focus his thoughts on the present moment. The Count is silent as well. As the seconds can be heard to tick away on the group of animated and cleverly designed clocks on the Emperor's desk it becomes apparent that the next subject Rudolf intends to discuss will contain far less welcome news.

Finally, stony faced once again, the Emperor looks up and says, "Chancellor Curtius is unwell. I have heard he is unable to rise from his bed. He will not be able to assist us tonight. We are short one person for our experiment."

Arcimboldo is relieved; this is not as bad as he anticipated. "That is a shame for the Chancellor, I'm very sorry to hear it. But we will not be short, surely Doctor Hagecius or George Erasmus Schwartzenau can stand in his place, they'll be there anyway. Even Hans Mont might serve, if you approve, My Lord."

Rudolf does not look either Arcimboldo or Rozmberk in the face. "I believe I will invite Katharina Strada to take his place."

Arcimboldo stammers, "wwwhat?" Even the permanent look of contentedness and aplomb on Count Rozmberk's face disappears into confusion.

"She has expressed a desire to be a part of our activities. I believe this is foreordained, she will join us. You will tell the others."

"My Lord..."

"You don't intend to dispute this do you?"

"Nnnooo..."

"I did not think so."

"It is just... she is a woman!"

"Exactly! *Her* point exactly! We intend to represent the Cosmos, don't we? All things in the Cosmos? Certainly it was an oversight on our part, on the Nolan's part, not to include womankind, however I forgive him, perhaps it is his Dominican education, I do not hold it against him. She is astute, you see? Don't forget she is the daughter and granddaughter of educated and subtle men. I protested myself, I assure you, for a long time I wouldn't hear of it. But after some time what she said made sense, indeed I see her reasoning and it is sound, intelligent, informed. Now, I believe it makes perfect sense."

"Rudolfus, what will the others say?"

"Vilem, surely you are mistaken if you think I care."

"But, she carries your child! This is dangerous, this is not a party, this is..."

"Exactly again! She carries my child! How could it not have occurred to me how appropriate this is... more than that, necessary, it is a powerful embellishment. We will have womankind, a female, and not just any female, a pregnant female! We complete an important part of the Cosmos; we represent reproduction, fecundity, birth, we will have an unborn child with us. *My* unborn child. My child, *my son,* will witness his father's elevation to the pinnacle of human Civilization and achievement."

"I believe you decided on this long before now."

"Not true. Actually, not true. I resisted for a long time, even after agreeing with her interpretation, I resisted. I admit, through fear. But now, with Curtius' illness, I see it is Heavenly ordained. I do not resist, I welcome it. It is right. It is in perfect keeping with all we intend to do, all *I* intend to do...and all I intend for my *son* to do."

"My friend, although I protest, I am impressed, the girl has courage, *you* have courage to-"

"She *is* courageous. She is a lioness. My son will be exceptional."

Arcimboldo says carefully, "My Lord, I understand you, and yet I must urge you to reconsider, this is-"

"Arcimboldus, you will not debate this with me, will you? There is no point, my mind is made up."

"Please, My Lord, I will not debate. I just wish to leave this one thought with you. I'll be brief, be good enough to hear me out."

Rudolf strokes his beard, looks toward the door to his bed chamber. He narrows his eyes and frowns, but he says, "you may continue, but be brief."

"Please consider how often alchemists become ill from the strange and potent chemicals they transmutate, and the vile odors and smoke. You subject Katharina and your unborn child to these powerful and pernicious substances. I only say this because-"

Rudolf holds up his hand to stop him, but Arcimboldo can see that the Emperor's mind is troubled by what he has just heard. The Emperor stands, "I understand now that you do not try to change my mind, but your concern is for my son and his mother. For that thought I thank you. But I feel

Heaven has brought me to this point and will protect me *and* my son from harm. I am resolved."

Count Rozmberk lays his hand on Arcimboldo's arm to keep him from speaking again. Rudolf walks toward the door to his bed chamber. He says, "gentlemen, I will leave you now. We will meet again this evening, I bid you good afternoon. We have had a very productive conversation. Oh, and Arcimboldus, Count Rozmberk will give you the *bad* news."

Arcimboldo looks at the Count with bewilderment as Rudolf enters his bedroom and closes the door. It opens again immediately, Rudolf sticks his head out, "and the Leonardo, sir?"

Arcimboldo bows to avoid looking Rudolf in the eyes, "it is as you have ordered, My Lord. All will be ready... as you have ordered."

The door to the Emperor's bed chamber shuts quietly; it is followed by the clicking sound of a lock being turned.

"Bad news, My Lord Rozmberk? Can it possibly be *worse* than this?"

Rozmberk's frank and patrician face has returned to its uniform complacency. He smiles good naturedly at Arcimboldo, "I admit that I am as surprised as you are about Katharina. And yet, don't you think, there is a valid logic there, I cannot fault it. Unless, as you have said, it proves to be unhealthy for the child. I cannot tell what the right thing to do is, and since it's not my decision anyway, I will accept it. Our rewards if we succeed are incalculable."

"I know you have just married, would you expose Polyxena to-"

"No, not for a second. But, Arcimboldus, you have known the man as long as I have, which is to say all his life, why gnaw on this bone? He will have his way should the Apostle Paul himself dispute the issue.

Let it go. And it is not *just* Rudolf but the man's Mistress that pushes this, an even *more* irresistible force. Rejoice, you have what you desire most, do you not? Rudolf and Katharina must accept the consequence of their decision, any opinion of yours at this point is needless meddling."

"Meddling with the Emperor's plans has never been a successful venture, I grant you that. But to explain my concern, Vilem, I admit to you confidentially that I don't argue only for the Emperor's sake or even Katharina's sake... I take the part of Jacopo, Katharina's grandfather. I can't help putting myself in his place. He's been like a brother to me. If he were to hear of this... Madonna! It would be the end of him."

"I see, I see. Yes, Jacopo Strada. I remember him well, I'm very fond of the man. He has taken this affair badly, I understand."

"I can't tell you to what degree! Her connection to the Emperor has gone far towards breaking the old man's spirit. He disapproves to the very *last* degree... and so he stays in Vienna. Sadly, we'll never see him in Prague again. It has made much trouble between Jacopo and Ottavio as well. You will keep this to yourself I trust, My Lord."

"Of course, my friend." The wise and good hearted Count absent-mindedly passes a pink and bloated hand across his face, stroking beard and moustache. He sighs, "yes, this is the state of the World: what is happiness for one is tragedy for another."

Arcimboldo stands, "My Lord, may I ask you to walk with me to my rooms, there is a very important matter I must attend to there."

"Of course." Agreeably, the Count rises as well and they walk toward the Emperor's outer chamber. Next to the door, and permanently enframed within the wall, is a large allegorical picture painted by

Bartolomeus Spranger. The Triumph of Wisdom. The canvas shows an almost life-size Katharina Strada sword in hand as Athena, goddess of wisdom, treading down ignorance, which is a dark and hulking creature with the ears of an ass. Emerging from the darkness in *chiaroscuro* style, and surrounding the nearly nude and provocatively posed goddess, are Bellona and the nine Muses; the most prominently displayed (and also inspired by the lovely Katharina) are Urania holding her celestial globe, and Geometria with compasses and book.

As he opens the door, Arcimboldo says, "and so, My Lord, the *bad* news?"

"I will tell you in a moment."

In the outer chamber, Atlas and Rudolf's valet, Nelle, play cards on the central table. Wolfgang Furboch, Secretary of the Privy Council, waits along with the downcast German couple. The others have gone. Rozmberk informs them all that the Emperor has retired to rest, and will be receiving no further visitors that day.

Once alone with the Count in the dark wood and tapestry lined hallway of the Royal Palace, Arcimboldo repeats his question, "the bad news, My Lord?"

Rozmberk clears his throat and expels a long sigh, "it seems that the English alchemists have failed to produce enough of the White Tincture, and just barely enough of the Red Tincture."

Arcimboldo stops in place; he throws both fists up in the air about a foot apart, *"gli faremo un culo cosi...mi sono rotto il cazzo!"* Now he shakes his fists in anger. "Pardon me, My Lord, pardon me. The confusion of this day would try the patience of a saint. How is this simply bad news and not disaster for us all?"

"Doctor Dee has explained that there is enough Tincture for a transformation, just not the transformation we had planned."

"I see. Well... not really. What exactly does that mean?"

Rozmberk looks over both shoulders to be sure they are alone. He lowers his voice to a very confidential level, "well, we had planned at first to transform iron into gold. When Dee and the Nolan discovered how much Tincture would be needed, as you know, we changed our plans to transform *silver* into gold; silver being much closer to a perfect substance than iron is, therefore easier to purify and convert. Yesterday, at my Castle of Trebon, where we have been working, Kelly, that strange man, accidently knocked over the beaker of White Tincture, there is very little left. There is just enough left to do a backwards transformation."

"I'm lost, what do you mean *backwards*?"

"Dee and Kelly say they cannot transform silver to gold tonight, but they are confident they can transform *gold* to *silver*. It's much easier, it requires far less Tincture."

"*Gold* into *silver*?"

"Exactly so, yes."

"Gold into silver! Jesu! How is it that the Emperor isn't a raging madman? How does he call this just bad news? I would expect him to skin them alive... if he can get to them before Giordano Bruno does!"

"I admit, the Emperor has been admirably philosophical about this. But consider a moment, although our Emperor is constantly in need of money, what is it he seeks tonight? He dreams of transforming *himself*. It is the transformation of the man who is *performing* the alchemy that Rudolf seeks. He is primarily concerned with transforming himself into a Being that can penetrate the secrets and strictures of the Natural World. The Master of all Secrets and all Causes."

Arcimboldo's pinched and pained expression lightens, "ah, yes, Vilem, I see, of course you are right, this is much more than making gold for the Emperor, he wishes to remake himself. I understand. In this, he and the Nolan are very similar."

"If we can prove our method tonight, we know that at our leisure we can transform silver, iron, who knows – perhaps *butter*, into gold. Our Emperor above *all* longs to be the man, the one man in the World, the one man in History, who can do this."

"But... the Emperor still has trust in the Englishmen? I must admit that I suspect they play a very dangerous game-"

"If they play a game with us it will be the last thing they do in this World... *and* the next one." The two men begin walking again.

"Do you trust them?"

"I trust Doctor Dee implicitly. He is a giant of intellect and learning. He would not pursue such a devious path intentionally."

"And Dee's scryer, Kelly, what of him?"

"Are you familiar with this popular new word 'enigma'? This man is that. Enigma."

"How so? He does what Dee tells him to, does he not?"

"Yes and no. Sometimes he does. Often they quarrel. His ability to see within Dee's crystal is amazing indeed. And I must tell you, you will be discreet I'm sure, Kelly pursues Dee's young wife. Her name is Jane. It is an embarrassment to watch. But the good Doctor is blissfully unaware."

"*Holy* Mother of God."

"Another thing, the man has no ears."

"Ears? Do I hear you correctly, he has no *ears*?"

The Count reaches around his ruff to tug his fleshy earlobe, "neither one of them. Yesterday I happened to be looking in his direction when a gust of wind blew back his hair. You know how he wears it, yes? No ears."

"You astonish me. But he hears, he answers, he speaks..."

"Oh yes, he hears. It appears his ears have been *cut* off!"

"Madonna! Stranger and stranger." Arcimboldo sighs thoughtfully. "Vilem, when you are my age-"

"I am your age."

"You are a few years shy. At a certain point in life one yearns for simplicity, calmness, security...a certain predictability. One so easily feels...tired, and forgive me, that is poorly expressed, but perhaps you understand me. The siren call of adventure and excitement becomes muted, hoarse, reduced to a mere whisper. I fear I reach that point in my life. Frankly, today is the first time I have realized it."

"Do you refer to your return to Italy...and family?"

"Mmm, perhaps that is part of it."

"I know of a tranquil sense of fulfillment when a long held desire is finally achieved, is that what that you're anticipating?"

"It's a feeling that I'm not accustomed to. *Some* feelings strike all the chords of the heart at once, but language is forced to keep to one thought at a time... I find that I lack the proper words and references...an unusual admission coming from me, you'll agree with *that* I'm sure." He laughs lightly, self deprecatingly, and his listener smiles politely. "Ah well, here we are. Vilem, will you come in for a cup of wine?"

"I am a bit dry, I thank you, sir."

The men enter Arcimboldo's room. Immediately Rozmberk's sharp eyes notice Leonardo's painting of St.

John the Baptist through the open door to the artist's painting studio. He walks toward it, "weren't we going to use this in the Summer Palace tonight?"

Arcimboldo is pouring two cups of wine from an engraved rock crystal ewer. The ewer's dramatic silver-gilt handle is a beautiful rendering of Narcissus, bending over, contemplating himself in the vessel's contents. "Oh yes, we still *are* using it. I need to make some changes. Water with your wine?"

"Never touch the stuff."

Arcimboldo adds no water to the Count's wine, and brings him a small faience cup glazed in white and blue. The two men touch glasses and toast.

"Salve."

"Salve. Did you say you're *changing* this painting? A Leonardo?"

"Did you not hear? The Nolan convinced the Emperor that this St. John should be turned into a Bacchus."

The Count cannot repress a short bark of amazed laughter. "You're serious? By Mercury! You're going to paint over a Leonardo?"

Arcimboldo feels he must defend this idea, if he begins complaining he will never be able to bring himself to do it. "We need to change it just a bit, I'll be subtle. This message of transformation can be very powerful. It won't take long to do, but I must begin immediately."

Rozmberk looks at him as if he still thinks this might be a joke. He shakes his head wonderingly, "well, I should leave you to it." He says that, but stays, perhaps to see if Arcimboldo is in earnest after all.

The painter begins to gather the materials he will use. Silvius has left terre verte and raw umber, ground and ready. Arcimboldo uses a knife to mix what he will use with walnut oil on a porcelain plate. He will also need carbon black, and very small amounts of

Naples yellow and yellow ocher. He must begin before he loses his nerve. The gray light of a snowy January afternoon needs strengthening, Arcimboldo lights several lamps and candelabra in his room and studio. "You may stay if you like, pardon my back, Count, but I must begin now." He sits at his easel.

More to himself than to Arcimboldo, the Count whispers "by Mercury!" He finishes his wine. "Well, I believe I will seek out Ottavio Strada."

"Not a word now, you will be careful?"

"I only wish to see the Durer. I thank you for the refreshment. And Arcimboldus, my friend, I should congratulate you quite heartily, I know how you've longed to return to Italy... but how we will miss you here!"

"I'm still trying to convince myself it's really true! By the way, Count, a thought strikes me, where are the Englishmen?"

"They were escorted to the Summer Palace."

"They are alone there with Bruno?"

"I understand the young sculptor is with them."

"That poor lad. I recommend you join them at the first opportunity. Giordano Bruno and Edward Kelly locked up together with the greatest collection of art the World has seen... the thought boggles the mind! God speed, Count."

"God save you, my friend. Don't get up, I'll see myself out."

As he mixes raw umber and carbon black on his palette with a squirrel hair brush, Arcimboldo thinks of Leonardo's motto: *hostinato rigore*. He scans the canvas in front of him with that same *hostinato rigore*, determined severity, in his eyes. It is the look of a master, it misses nothing, spares nothing; no detail, however small or insignificant, may escape; no distraction, no other consideration may turn aside the creative purpose. It is a moment akin to birth; the image that has grown within the Mind is ready to emerge into the World as tangible reality. The brush hovers over the slender cross John holds carelessly his left hand. Arcimboldo sucks in his cheeks and purses his lips, frown lines deepen on his forehead, and his eyes turn steely blue with intensity. With a soft crunch the bristles meet the canvas, pigment covers pigment, he has begun.

As he works on the painting, Arcimboldo notices Leonardo's fingerprints, and even the marks of the ball of his hand, where the ingenious Maestro has dabbed and modeled his freshly applied oil paint. This was a trademark of Leonardo's, especially in his early paintings in Florence; a technique mocked by a few, remarked on by many, and imitated only by the very daring. Arcimboldo himself does not use his hands to touch his paintings directly, although the technique is undoubtedly effective; he does, however, apply a secret personal touch to all his paintings: he uses hair from his own head along with squirrel and horse hair in his brushes. Hairs will often fall out of a brush and become invisibly embedded in the wet paint. It is often impossible to tell when this happens; so it becomes an interesting mystery, perhaps divinely inspired, perhaps pure accident. Arcimboldo finds it deeply interesting (and slightly amusing) to know that a part of him lives on within his paintings, unknown to all.

The Christian cross has disappeared, now it has become a tall staff of rough wood. Arcimboldo loads umber on a rounded brush, then drags one side of the brush through yellow ochre, with this he quickly paints the necessary pinecone on top of the staff; the contrasting colors create highlight and shadow in the same stroke.

Next, the artist paints a scanty black fabric over the Baptist's nudity, barely covering waist and thigh, dropping away into shadow. He roughly mixes Naples yellow, yellow ochre, and umber into a streaky, uneven, tawny color. With a knife he carefully scrapes away most of the black paint he has just put down; then, with a narrow, flat brush, and with long strokes, he pulls the tawny pigment along the scraped off areas, creating a semblance of draped and folded fabric. Arcimboldo uses a small pointed brush and very liquid color to draw the details and spots that make this a leopard skin, characteristic of Bacchus, the riotous, frenzied, unpredictable God of wine and mirth.

At last, with beads of perspiration forming on his brow, he studies the beautiful face of St. John. The Baptist's mouth is slightly open – is he about to breath in or breath out...is he about to speak? Are these delicate lips those of a 'he' at all? Far too beautiful to be a man, the soft *sfumato* blending of color and light on the skin creates a face with all the subtlety of absolute realism. Arcimboldo asks himself, why has Leonardo painted the uncompromising and severe Baptist with such a soft, sensitive, feminine face? It is a choice and a Humanist message that is so indirect as to be indecipherable.

Arcimboldo removes his wool skull cap, loosens his collar and unbuttons his doublet. The face stares back at him relentlessly. He mixes Naples yellow with carbon black on his palette, creating a muted and natural olive green. Using this, terre verte, and small amounts of umber, he paints the wreath that crowns Bacchus' head. Arcimboldo makes this wreath as subtle and unnoticeable as he can; he overpaints as little as possible the long, beautiful, curly rings of hair that graced the Baptist's noble head – it is no longer the head of a saint, but a figure far more ancient; more ancient than the Greek, Dionysus; this has become a

God as old as Man's love of drunkenness and revelry. Now, this figure, this Bacchus, points back to the shadowy darkness behind him, suggestive of the impenetrably dark beginnings of Time itself, the Mystery of the World before Creation.

He has done all he intends to do and is satisfied with his work. As he always does at this point, when finished with a painting, Arcimboldo spends long minutes sweeping the canvas with his eyes, up and down, left and right, around in circles, following the dynamic movement created by shapes, colors, light, and suggested action. At the same time, he thinks of what may happen this evening, what mysteries he may penetrate, what secrets he may learn. If Leonardo could speak to him, perhaps through the beautiful mouth of St. John-Bacchus, what would he say? How would he feel about this transformation? Arcimboldo distinctly hears a delicate female voice speak right behind him, "delightful! Fascinating! Is that Bacchus, sir?"

Arcimboldo whirls around in confused astonishment. His small cups of walnut oil and naphtha spill all over his lap and the floor; wildly and instinctively he tries to hide the painting he has been working on. He cries out, "Jesus, Mary and Joseph! What? How..."

The three people standing behind him recoil in surprise and embarrassment. They are: the old and frail Archbishop, Martin Medek, and two elegantly dressed and accoutered women. The Archbishop stammers, "I beg your pardon, sir! The door was open so we took the liberty of entering."

"I beg *your* pardons! My God, but you startled me! Please forgive my disarray." Arcimboldo can feel the scarlet blush that must paint his face.

The tall, blonde woman, so sumptuously dressed that she can only be Christina of Lorraine, speaks behind her hand in a stage whisper to her companion, Arcimboldo understands perfectly well, she says, "ha, ha, and *this* is supposed to be the most cultured man in Prague? I knew we should have gone to Munich!"

With a look of acute embarrassment, Christina's companion whispers back urgently, *"Madame, s'il vous plait garder votre voix, vers le bas... il peut vous entendre!"*

Doing his best to ignore the Princess' amusement, rallying his sense of dignity, Arcimboldo speaks precisely and fluidly in French, "I have expected you, forgive me for being so distracted, it is inexcusable! I am embarrassed beyond words, mesdames."

The Archbishop, as embarrassed as Arcimboldo, rushes forward with introductions, "My Lord Arcimboldus, may I present Her Highness, Christina of Lorraine, and her companion, the Marchioness, wife of the Marquis d'Olivan. Mesdames, I introduce you to Lord Josephus Arcimboldus, chief Court painter and Master of masques, festivals, pageants, and Court entertainments." Arcimboldo bows deeply once again, and his courtesy is accepted by nods from the women.

The smell of naphtha has become very strong, trickles of it still drip from Arcimboldo's lap. Christina wrinkles her nose and frowns; she holds a scented handkerchief to her mouth and coughs gently. The Marchioness says very considerately, "those of us without creative genius cannot imagine what it takes to produce such beauty, sir, I'm sure the Princess forgives you as I do. Your extraordinary painting has mesmerized us all, I'm sure, it is *so* alike the style of Leonardo da Vinci that I marvel! May I ask again if it is Bacchus you portray?"

"Madame, you are well informed indeed, it *is* Bacchus, I am impressed. I must also confess that it is not my work... entirely... it's by the divine Maestro Leonardo, after all. I only... repair it here and there, slight damage, very, very slight. I'm finished now and eager to be of service to you." Yet another bow.

Christina coughs again less gently, she says, "oh yes, we know da Vinci's work well, my relative, Francois le Premiere, collected the man as well as his artwork." She chuckles in appreciation of her own wit.

Arcimboldo tries to smile brightly, although, as an Italian, he finds her comment slightly distasteful. She refers to the elegant chateau in Blois the French King gave to Leonardo to lure him to France, it worked so well that the Florentine artist spent his remaining years there, never returning to Italy again. Using Leonardo's full name intentionally he replies, "indeed, Your Highness, your illustrious ancestor was very generous to Maestro Leonardo di ser Piero da Vinci, your country is privileged to own so many of his finest works."

In a lovely voice (Arcimboldo wonders, *where* does that accent come from?), the Marchioness d'Olivan says, "My Lord, we have intruded. Forgive us our impatience, we're eager to explore the many Wonders we've heard you possess in this fine castle. Your Highness, Archbishop, shall we wait outside while Maestro Arcimboldus finishes his important business?"

"You are very kind, Madame, I *am* finished, and I will only take a moment to make myself presentable." Courtiers must bow often, no matter how stiff and sore the back may be.

The Archbishop is grateful to escape this awkward introduction, and the Princess is eager to escape the smell of naphtha; the three visitors exit his rooms, careful to close the door fully behind them. With a constant stream of fiery Italian oaths flowing under his breath, Arcimboldo rushes to clean and redress himself. When he passes a mirror and glances at himself he nearly chokes in embarrassment; he looks like a mad man, his hair has gone in all directions after the removal of his skull cap, his lace neck whisk and doublet hang about him, making him look like a comical stage character, there is paint on his face and hands, and of course, he radiates the noxious smell of naphtha. They must think him eccentric to the point of lunacy.

Now, resplendent in peacock blue and gold, smelling perhaps too strongly of orange oil and aqua mirabilis (but better than naphtha), Arcimboldo collects his thoughts as he stands patiently at his urinal. He remembers the letters he has not had a chance to read and his incised ruby. Rubies have been known since antiquity to be particularly lucky. A master engraver has created a delicate little picture on Arcimboldo's one inch gem stone; Fortune is portrayed as a beautiful nude woman, blindfolded, balancing with one foot on a large ball, she holds a cornucopia under each arm. Fortune is lovely, therefore desired by all; she is blind because she does not favor one over another; she balances on a ball because she is unstable and always shifting and changing; from her cornucopias fall the riches and honors of the World. Engraved on the back of Arcimboldo's ruby is a motto: *Quisque Suae Fortunatus Faber* – 'each man forges his own Fortune'; a very wise warning. He feels sure that the good fortune contained in this artfully carved gem has been overwhelmed by the hurricano of unexpected events this Epiphany Day.

He collects both letters and ruby from his soiled clothing and tucks them into a secure inner pocket. Discovering the bag of coins for Giordano Bruno, he secrets this in a hidden pocket inside his cloak. He pauses for one small cup of wine, no water. Well, perhaps a cup and a half...all right, two cups.

Refreshed, clean, fortified, and as confident as will power and wine can make him, Arcimboldo exits into the hallway to greet again his foreign visitors.

Archbishop Medek listens in apparent fascination as the Valois Princess describes the opulent repository created in the heart of Paris for Christ's Crown of Thorns, brought back from the Holy Land at the end of the Seventh Crusade. "Oh, it is the thing I love most about being in Paris, visiting the royal chapel of Sainte-Chapelle, it is just like being inside a piece of jewelry! The colors surround you *everywhere*, it is simply a *cage* of stained glass! Oh, yes, I prefer it to Chartres or Notre Dame. It feels as though a goldsmith has built a reliquary large enough to house an entire Church. The colors! The light! *Mon Dieu, cette une vertu merveilleuse!*"

Smiling as he closes his door, Arcimboldo says, "beautifully described, Your Highness!"

"Have you seen Sainte-Chapelle, sir?"

"I have not, but now I feel as though I had." And a bow. "A very joyous Epiphany Day to you all."

"And to you," they all reply.

To the Archbishop he says, "and the Grand Duke? His party? Will they accompany us?"

"The Grand Duke de Medici, and the gentlemen, say they prefer the hunt to the Emperor's galleries."

"The hunt?"

The Archbishop clears his throat uncomfortably, "yes, they join Colonel Choma and his knights, they hunt... Protestants... in Old Town. Quite eager they were too to join the sport."

Arcimboldo is disturbed, "but I thought... we just... eh... never mind." He turns to the ladies, "now, is it jewelry or goldsmiths' work you would like to see this afternoon, mesdames?"

"Paris is full of jewelry and art, My Lord. But we have been told that there are scientific machines here that are simply without rival." Christina adds with a note of caution, "as long as we do not stray *too* far from sensible Catholic philosophy..."

Her sentence trails off, and Arcimboldo cannot help but wonder exactly *what* they've been told concerning the sensible Catholic philosophy of Rudolf's Court. He can guess, however.

In rather inelegant French, the elderly Archbishop Medek stammers defensively, "in this modern day and age, bold men of learning may test the limits of knowledge, My Lady, but our Catholic philosophy is as pure as your own, I assure you."

The Marchioness adds earnestly, "there *is* sense in what the Archbishop says, how can *any* philosophy be tested for correctness without contrasting it to other ideas and-"

The Princess cuts in, "that is for the Church to do, surely."

Smiling with as much urbane confidence as he can muster, Arcimboldo replies, "Emperor Rudolf believes that artists and philosophers can engage in that practice as well, and that all together we may please God by revealing His Divine truth, and benefit Mankind by identifying falsehood."

With a mischievous twinkle in her hazel-green eyes, and looking up at the ceiling, Marchioness d'Olivan thoughtfully says, "if I'm not mistaken, Plato says in the Republic that it is not wrong, nay, it is necessary to admit that either the whole World is deceived or at least the greater part of it. How can we pretend otherwise? We know that there are at least three religions, those of Christ, Moses, and Mohammed; either they are *all* false, and thus the *whole* World is deceived, or at least two of them are, and thus the greater part of Mankind is led astray. God has made a World in which what is *false* is at least as common as what is *true*."

With admiration in his voice and eyes, Arcimboldo says, "well said, Madame! Plato! You are remarkably well read."

"I must do something with my time, sir, since I cannot hunt day in and day out as my husband does. Indeed, I would not hunt even if I were a man."

Arcimboldo laughs, and Christina says, "the Marchioness is proud of her independent mind, although some would use the word *heretical*. Still, I love her dearly. It's just the *English* in her, she cannot help it." And she kisses her lovely friend on her alabaster cheek. Arcimboldo thinks, so that's the accent, English, charming! Smiling, Christina goes on to tease the Archbishop. "Now see what you've done, Samantha, you've made the Archbishop distinctly uneasy!"

Truly, that perfectly describes the look on the Archbishop's face. He blushes to complete his discomfort as all three look at him. "I... I believe I must return to my duties. Pardon me, mesdames, Monsieur, I'm sure I will see you at Mass tomorrow morning. Good day to you."

The silver silk of the French Princess' gown is embellished with vertical strips of pearls, and it makes a liquid swishing sound as she walks; the watery rhythm is occasionally punctuated by little clicking sounds as the pearls knock together. Arcimboldo imagines pebbles bouncing and sliding along the rocky bed of a swiftly moving stream. The Marchioness wears a golden-yellow gown with a coral-red bodice; she wears her pearls in a net on her head to hold back her auburn hair. Her lovely, one could say, lilting, voice asks the artist question after question as they walk through Prague's labyrinthine Royal Palace towards the Emperor's Wunderkabinet. "I am curious, My Lord, what is it exactly that the children were doing in the streets this morning? The singing, the star on a stick? The Archbishop told me it was a German and Czech custom to do these things on Epiphany Day."

"Ah, he is correct. It is a custom that I would have had you see on a happier day than today. But I'm glad you did see some of it. The children pretend to be the Wise Men, come searching for the infant Jesus. They follow the star... that star on the stick which the leader carries, it represents, of course, that Heavenly apparition that served as guide for those Magi traveling from the East. On Epiphanies past, every Christian home in the city has been visited and blessed by these happy children. In my long experience here, it has always been a joyous occasion. Today has been a sad exception."

"*C'est malheureux.*"

"The children bless the people's homes? Charming!"

"You have perhaps seen them doing it. They write the blessing above each door in chalk."

"Oh! That's a blessing? Upon my soul, I imagined it to be a sinister message. Something to do with the riotous violence your citizens engage in today."

"Not *my* citizens, madame, I am Italian." Arcimboldo clears his throat and quickly continues. "But you will think the message charming as well, did you see it closely? It is the blessing of the Magi. It reads thusly: 15 † C † M † B † 87. Obviously, the numbers correspond to the calendar year, 1587; the crosses stand for Christ; and the letters have a double significance: C, M, and B are the first letters of the names of the Three Magi: Caspar, Melchior, and Balthasar; but also are an acronym for a Latin blessing, *Christus mansionem benedicat,* which means-"

"May Christ bless this house."

"Just so."

"Charming indeed."

"We will go down these stairs, after you, Mesdames."

"Have you been to Florence, Princess?" Arcimboldo enquires.

"I haven't, but we have so many paintings by Florentine artists in France that I know many parts of the city. I'm looking forward to making comparisons: the Campanile di Giotto, the Duomo, the doors of the Baptistery, the Ponte Vecchio."

"Who is your favorite Florentine painter, is it Leonardo?"

"No, my family owns several Peruginos, and I cannot help being partial to him. I grew up with his Christ in the Garden with His Apostles, and his Saint John and Mary Magdalene. They remind me of my childhood. But alas, Mary Magdalene is sadly faded and seems to get worse every year."

"That would be the black he used, madame. Black is dramatic, but a difficult color. Burned ivory is better than smoke black, charcoal, burned paper, or lamp black, but still is too acidic. Black pigment made from burning is dangerously unstable; it causes the colors around it to deteriorate and fade, especially with tempera. Frescos are the most easily damaged of all by the acidity of burned black pigments. Giulio Romano's panels in Santa Maria dell'Anima are excellent works, they could not be more skillfully done, brushwork and invention that would be world famous if they had not faded from too much black, even though Romano mixed his black in oils and varnished the finished paintings."

The Marchioness says admiringly, "painting is like magic!"

"No, madame, painting is science. *Creativity* is like magic."

They pass by the closed door to Ottavio Strada's rooms and turn left at the end of the hallway, descend several more shallow steps, coming at last to a formidable and securely locked door. This sturdy barrier is flanked by two Imperial Household Guards who straighten to attention. Above the door, in a lozenge, a quote from Petrarch is painted in gold – *undique fulgentes auro speciesque Deorum, et formae heroum stabant atque acta priorum.* Immediately, the Marchioness translates, "everywhere, glittering with gold, stood the figures of the Gods and heroes, and the deeds of the forefathers."

Arcimboldo says to the soldiers in German, "open, please." To his guests he speaks French, "the rooms of the Emperor's Wunderkabinet are through here."

Passing through the door, they enter a long hallway with doors on one side only. The wall opposite to the doors is lined with a sinuously patterned fabric of pale green and spinach green above a dark wooden wainscoting. Along this vegetable-green wall hang a series of large paintings done by Bartolomeus Spranger, a series illustrating stories from Ovid's *Metamorphoses* and *Ars Amatoria;* grandiose images of Venus and Mars, Venus and Adonis, Venus and Vulcan, Vulcan and Maia, Mercury and Psyche, Jupiter and Europa, Ulysses and Circe, even Salmacis and Hermaphroditus. The predominating colors are the ivory and pale pink flesh tones of the mostly nude figures, glowing in light as they emerge from shadowy dark brown or black backgrounds; however, in marvelous contrast, the scraps of clothing and accessories of the gods and heroes are accented with vibrant colors: shades of orange, bottle green, sulfur yellow, acid pink, and brittle, icy blue. The figures are, of course, almost entirely modeled on Hans Mont and Katharina Strada.

Arcimboldo explains, "these rooms on your right contain the Emperor's collections. Books, coins, antiquities, paintings, arms and armor, *naturalia, artificiosa,* and *mechanica.*"

"What's in this first room, My Lord?" The Marchioness speaks in a hushed yet excited tone. She steps to the first door, lays her hand on the door handle and looks questioningly at Arcimboldo.

"You may." He smiles and nods. "It is the room of coins, medals and medallions. The Emperor's father, Maximillion, was very interested in numismatics. Most of the coins here are from his collection."

The Marchioness d'Olivan opens the door and the three look inside. It is a vaulted space, long and narrow like a hallway, and, as are the other rooms, dimly lit by lamps that are continuously kept burning (the Emperor may visit unexpectedly at any time of the day or night). They see that windowed cabinets line the walls. Near the door, a splendid cabinet in the shape of a pyramid displays items of particular beauty and rarity. A large desk in the center of the room holds books and manuscripts on numismatics, several small statues, magnifying lenses, and tools for die stamping, burnishing, and polishing. This is where Rudolf sits to contemplate the collection.

Arcimboldo cautions them, "we have just a short time, mesdames, the room of *mechanica* holds the instruments and devices you are interested in. It is at the end of the hall."

The Marchioness says with enthusiasm, "I would love to see it all! May I visit again tomorrow?"

The artist bows, "I'm at your service, madame, and I have no doubt the Emperor will accommodate you. This way please." But he thinks, with some regret, *who knows what tomorrow may bring to this castle in*

*Prague?* The women follow him down the hallway in total silence, and Arcimboldo cannot help feeling pride as he senses, *they are already impressed!*

Christina of Lorraine pauses and then stops by one of Spranger's exuberant paintings. She says thoughtfully, "that figure of Venus looks familiar to me."

"I wasn't aware that any of Master Bartolomeus' paintings had been sent to France, Madame. Perhaps you've seen a print? The Haarlem engraver, Hendrik Goltzius has produced many fine engravings from Bartolomeus' designs."

"No, not from a print or a painting. I believe I passed her in the hallway earlier today."

"Ah."

"Oh, yes, Christina, you are certainly right. I remember her as well."

"Well... that would not surprise me." Arcimboldo goes on haltingly. "It is true that this is Master Bartolomeus' favorite model... um, *obviously*, I should say. She is the daughter of Ottavio Strada, the granddaughter of Jacopo Strada. A most beautiful young woman."

"*Mm hmm*. Strada. I have heard of her... have we not, Samantha? The Emperor's whore." Cristina says tartly.

"I would prefer not to use that word, My Lady. But certainly she inspires both artist and Emperor." He squirms inwardly; thinking of his dear old friend, Jacopo Strada, who sits alone in his palazzetto in Vienna, imagining conversations such as the one Arcimboldo is having right now, about his granddaughter and his good family name.

Apparently, the French Princess believes herself to be quite droll as she comments, "I begin to understand why Rudolf has not married, although all

Europe wonders, watches, and holds its breath; I see Isabella of Spain is neither on the Emperor's mind *nor* on his walls."

From as far back as 1568, the Emperor has been unofficially engaged to his Spanish cousin, Isabella, known as the Infanta. Isabella is the daughter of Rudolf's uncle, King Philip II, and Rudolf's older sister, Anna, Philip's fourth wife. Obviously, the Habsburgs believe in keeping all of their property within the family, permanently; their marriages have created a tangle of relationships that are the talk (gossip and entertainment) of European Courts. This marriage, once confidently expected, has been revived and shelved repeatedly as Rudolf's relationships with his family have declined, emotionally, politically, diplomatically, spiritually... on all fronts. Currently, the confusing situation in Poland is the official excuse for suspension of marriage talks, but shrewd observers, such as the Spanish ambassador, San Clemente, are not fooled; as the years go by, Rudolf edges further and further away from predictability and normalcy. The only predictable thing about Rudolf is that he will never move another inch closer to putting himself under the scrutiny of his Habsburg relatives. There is no dowry or inheritance, no matter how large, that can attract his attention to the proposal.

The Marchioness whispers something in the Princess' ear, and Christina says in a conciliatory manner, "Lord Arcimboldus, perhaps I seem harsh towards our host, your Emperor. You are a man of some sensitivity and understanding, I will share something with you." She shows him a medallion she wears around her neck; it is a gold mounted crystal, carved and painted in enamel; it pictures a broken lance, with the motto *'lacrymae hinc, hinc dolor'*, – from this comes my tears and my sorrow. "This is the emblem of my grandmother, Catherine de'Medici, Queen of France. I am her favorite, sir, and I share her pain."

"Her pain? She is renowned, a legend throughout the World. The most powerful woman in France."

"She is renowned and powerful, yet she is a woman, with a woman's heart." The three stand close together, the Wunderkabinet momentarily forgotten. Christina of Lorraine speaks in complete frankness. "My grandmother was married at the age of fourteen to Henry II of France. She gave her Lord three sons, yet by the time he was nineteen Henry had excluded her from all affairs of State, Court, and bed chamber. He showered gifts and honors upon his mistress, Diane de Poitiers. In June, 1559, as you may remember, my grandmother's eldest daughter, my aunt, Elisabeth, God rest her soul, was married to the King of Spain. The celebration in Paris was the most elaborate the city had ever seen: festivities, balls, masques, and five days of jousting. My grandmother's husband, King Henry II, insisted on competing in the jousting tournament, and to publically humiliate my grandmother he wore the colors of Diane de Poitiers, black and white. Henry defeated the Duc de Guise and Duc de Nemours, but in his third competition, the young Comte de Montgomery knocked him half out of the saddle. That prideful, stubborn man, King Henry, forced the terrified Comte to ride against him again. This time, Montgomery's lance shattered into the King's face. Henry fell from the saddle, his face pouring blood, with an enormous splinter of Montgomery's lance sticking out of his eye and head." With a look of extreme sympathy, the Marchioness takes the Princess' hand. Clearly unfinished with her story, Christina continues, "my grandmother Catherine, Diane de Poitiers, Prince

Francis, and half the Court all fainted on the spot. The doctors removed the splinter, and for ten days my grandmother stayed by her husband's bedside while he slowly lost sight, sound, and reason, and finally, his life. She has worn mourning black ever since, and she has taken this as her emblem." Christina holds up the medallion of the broken lance. "I am wary...very wary of the fickleness, selfishness, and unkindness of men, particularly that of Princes. I apologize if I have unkindly insulted your Emperor Rudolf, and I ask you to forgive me." The Marchioness consoles her dear friend by putting an arm around her shoulders and patting her arm comfortingly.

Arcimboldo hastily bows, "Princess, I am now sensible of your family's pain. I am moved beyond words by your story. There is nothing to forgive. Let me attempt to distract you by showing you our modest collection of scientific and practical machines."

He is glad to see the melancholy moment pass quickly, with a gentle smile Christina says, "you are too modest, sir, we have heard otherwise about your collection."

The Marchioness adds animatedly, "it is understood that the most accurate astronomical and mathematical instruments in Europe come from your workshops here in Prague. Do not tell us we are wrong!"

Laughing, "no, you are not, and what is certainly the case, I would have to say, they are the most beautiful as well. You shall see. This way, mesdames."

"It is fortunate that you do not count on seeing our room of *naturalia*. It ordinarily holds the Emperor's collection of minerals, animals and plants, skeletons, shells, eggs, fossils, and other strange curiosities of the Natural World; but that room is being... rearranged and reformed. The collection is sadly depleted and scattered at the moment, perhaps another time you will have an opportunity to appreciate it. This door here, next to *naturalia*, is a compendium of *artificiosa*, that is, Natural objects that have been changed, crafted, or embellished by human skill and ingenuity. However, it also is somewhat short of its usual exhaustive perfection at this time... my apologies, we have been moving some things around. And now *here*, at last, *this* room, mesdames, is our gallery of mechanical and scientific devices, it surely will interest you greatly." Arcimboldo opens the door, "please enter."

'Interest' would be too weak a word to describe the look in the eyes of the two women as they survey the long room. Arcimboldo moves about trimming and adjusting wicks and lighting additional lamps, and gradually the illumination in the room increases. At first, it may seem they have wandered into the wrong gallery, the contents of the space appear to be more the work of goldsmith, jeweler, and lapidary; such is the sparkle and glint of gems and gem-like colors, and such is the rich gleaming of metallic textures and elaborately modeled shapes. Arcimboldo watches the French noblewomen as they stand side by side, shoulder to shoulder; the Princess looks to the left and the Marchioness looks to the right. To the artist they seem emblems of the Moon and the Sun. The Princess: with blond hair, blue eyes and milky skin, clad in silver accented with the iridescence of pearl. The Marchioness: with auburn hair, dressed in gold and red, wears a choker of gold set with rubies. He thinks that even by their personalities they resemble the Moon and the Sun. Arcimboldo studies them in this moment, when they are wonderfully distracted, they have dropped their masks and all pretense, all posturing. These two young women, in their early twenties, may perhaps never look as beautiful as they do now. This is a scene that should be painted and preserved. Or, it may be, that this beauty is impossible to preserve, uncapturable; once painted, however skillfully, no matter how rich the palette, the Mystery of the moment will transform into something different, something that is sadly unable to *truly* convey what the artist has felt.

"Emperor Rudolf has attracted the finest astronomers, geometricians, and mathematicians, not to mention the instrument makers themselves. And it is not only Rudolf, but Count Rozmberk, whom you will meet this evening, that encourages these inventive geniuses. The Count's silver mines at Jachymov, and the Emperor's at Kutna Hora are worked according to the latest scientific techniques. The Count has constructed the most astonishing fish ponds on his property. The results are more than astonishing, he can feed hundreds where before there was just a handful of poor, hungry peasants. That gilt-copper clinometer you hold, for example, Marchioness, is not just art-"

"Oh, yes it is!"

"Not just art," he continues smiling, "but a most accurate device, accurate to six inches. It was recently used by the Imperial surveyor, Matous Ornys, to calculate the path of a tunnel under Letna Hill up to the Emperor's pond in the Royal Game Preserve."

"How does it work, sir?"

"It determines horizontal positions, and measures the incline of a plane and angles, much the same as a theodolite. It may also serve as a shadow quadrant to determine the geometry of tangent and subtangent."

"I have no idea what you've just said, can you show me?"

Arcimboldo and Christina laugh. Arcimboldo takes the device, shaped like two sides of an equilateral triangle connected by several elegant arcs. "Well, for example, this pendulum attached to the central hinge acts as an indicating hand, you slide it along one side here, you see, and it will give you distances. Do you see the very small numbers engraved along here?"

"Impossibly small, I can barely read them! But, I must tell you, what I love most is the engraved plant motif running along the edges. Why, I would never use this in the dirt, it is beautiful!"

Again, they are amused. Arcimboldo says, "the engraver, Erasmus Habermel, is the finest in Europe. He has built many devices for the Emperor. Look at his work here, this torquetum, this equatorial ring-dial, this beautiful sextant-"

"I thought that was a music stand! I say again, far too elegant to be used outside. Why have they made them so beautiful?"

"It is a sign of respect for the knowledge they convey, madame. These devices unlock secrets of the Natural World unknown to the ancients... unknown even to the last generation!"

"I see." The Marchioness murmurs as she drifts along the cabinets and shelves, lightly running her hand across random objects.

"These are the most beautiful globes I have ever seen. Such detail! There is nothing like it at Fontainebleau!" Christina of Lorraine has discovered the collection of marvelous spheres mapping the Earth and Heavenly bodies.

"This globe was not made in Prague, but purchased by the Emperor from Willem Janszoon Blaeu of Amsterdam. But *this* celestial globe was made right here in the castle, in the workshop Johann Reinhold; the moon moves along this arc here, and this little statue at the top serves as a sun dial. And *this* one may *appear* to be a globe, but it is actually a clock. Look closely, the two hemispheres are connected by this bayonet mount, and they turn just so. It shows the constellations as they pass along this equatorial grid, do you see the major stars and constellations are labeled? It will revolve once every twenty-four hours. This flattened ring around here is a calendar, it is marked into 365 days and shows months, days of the week, and important Christian holy days. Look, here is Epiphany Day. It also chimes on every hour."

"The colors are magnificent." The Marchioness spins a globe of the world.

"Brass, gilt, silver, and iron painted with enamel. Assembled with the discriminating taste of a true artist."

"Oh, Christina, my word! What is that you have discovered?"

The French Princess has wandered farther down the room, and has moved a brass lamp closer to the armillary spheres she is examining.

"Wheels within wheels, and they all turn... how can a man's hands make such things? It is a marvel."

Arcimboldo says, "those devices have always fascinated me. I'm jealous that I don't have the skills to craft something like that with my own hands. Even the shadows they cast can stimulate the imagination. My imagination at least..." He is thinking about the Cosmos he has created in the Summer Palace. It waits patiently for him. And in just a few hours...

"I must confess, sir, if I were a man I would be an astronomer. I can think of nothing as interesting as capturing the movements of the Planets and Stars. It almost seems heretical to look so closely over God's shoulder."

"Look at this Planetarium here, Princess, different color gems line the path of each planet. I must admit that I do not know exactly how it works, but is it not splendid?"

"My Lord," the Marchioness calls to him, "what are on these shelves?"

"More sextants, scales, many different kinds of compasses... here is a reduction compass I have used myself; protractors, sun dials... this is a measuring instrument for firing a cannon."

"It looks like a miniature catapult."

"It does."

"What is this?"

"Ah. I would have been surprised if you had known. Have you ever heard of a *syringe*?"

"*Syringe*? Never."

"It's used by a doctor. This one is made of ivory. You see, it unscrews, and fluid goes in here. Then you press down this handle, it is called a *piston*, a French word you may note, and the fluid comes out here, out of this long hollow tube."

"To what purpose?"

"That the doctor may apply a curative solution to the eyes, ears, or nose."

"Of a human?"

"Certainly."

The Marchioness looks appalled. "I will most certainly *not* go to see a doctor while I'm here in Prague! And I hope I never see one of those dreadful things again. Why, it makes me shiver to think about it. Christina, dear, did you hear that? *Syringe*. Upon my soul!"

"I have never seen so many clocks together in one place before. The sound is very restful. I'm inspired to have a room made full of clocks for prayer and contemplation. Shhh, Samantha, listen to them tick. Do you not adore it?"

"To be honest, My Lady, it makes be nervous. It reminds me of whispering going on behind my back. One clock is fine, but all this chattering... what can they all be saying to one another?"

"You are fanciful, my dear. Have I not read a phrase – *the clockworks of the Universe*? That is what the sound makes me think of. God is in His Heaven, and all is well."

"My Ladies, the Emperor is particularly fond of clocks and clockwork mechanisms. He has helped to craft many of these elegant objects with his own hands. He believes that all things animate have a kind of life to them, that creating such a thing is akin to giving life to the inanimate."

The Marchioness d'Olivan purses her lips and rolls her eyes; she appears to be searching her mind for something to say to contradict this.

"Marchioness, do you see that object on the desk over there?"

"This?"

"No, next to that, the spider."

"I had hoped that was *not* what you meant. A large metal spider, even studded with gem stones, can only be thought clever and interesting by a man. I'm sure I will dream of it tonight."

"Touch that emerald on its back."

"Must I?"

"You will not be disappointed."

Christina of Lorraine walks to the desk and touches the emerald on the spider's back. There is a whirring noise, then the spider jerks its body upward and begins to slowly crawl across the desk. Both women are startled and hastily step back. The Marchioness lets out a little shriek and clutches her companion's arm. "Holy Virgin! My Lord, you are wicked! I'm *sure* I will dream of this tonight!" She crosses herself twice.

Fighting back a smile, Arcimboldo says, "I beg your pardon, I couldn't resist." He walks to the desk and turns a foot high statue around to face them. It is a jeweled and enameled figure of St. Jerome; a fawning golden lion raises a paw to the saint. "Now, madame, do you trust me enough to press the thorn in the lion's paw?"

The Marchioness presses the thorn and quickly draws back her hand. The whirring noise begins and St. Jerome turns his head from side to side, he raises his hand and beats his breast with a small rock. "Ah! Delightful!"

Arcimboldo moves around the large desk to a magnificently detailed golden galleon about two feet high. He moves the ship to a corner of the desk and clears a path in front of it. "Now, mesdames, I will lift this anchor." The clockwork whirring begins, and the galleon slowly begins to roll across the desk, propelled by hidden wheels. The trumpeters that line the deck of the ship raise their instruments; a miniature organ hidden within the golden hull pipes a fanfare tune. The women laugh and clap their hands. Arcimboldo says, "I'm not sure if it's loaded with powder…"

"Powder, sir?" The Marchioness backs away.

When the fanfare ends, the tiny golden cannons protruding through the gun ports along the sides of the galleon fire in sequence with little popping sounds, and smoke rises from the guns. The women clap again, "Bravo, Maestro!"

"Quick, quick, lower the anchor before it runs off the desk!"

The four sails of the galleon are crafted to billow out as if caught by the wind. The Marchioness closely studies the elegant paintings on the sails, scenes of nautical mythology. While she does this, Arcimboldo opens a large drawer in the desk to display an assortment of clock making tools and mechanisms. Christina of Lorraine is very interested in the internal workings of the Emperor's clever automatons. Arcimboldo explains, "this is called a mainspring, and this is what provides the power to move all the other mechanisms. Look how thin and strong the metal is, it must be crafted by a master. The spring goes inside a barrel, like this one, and a chain is wrapped around it. The chain is connected to this cone shaped devise, it's called a *fusee,* this regulates the power going to the *verge escapement,* these notched wheels here, they will smoothly drive-"

"Oh, I must have this!" The Marchioness interrupts him.

"Eh?"

"This splendid boat. I must have it. I will make my husband buy it from the Emperor!"

Arcimboldo smiles, "I regret, Madame, to tell you that will be impossible. The Emperor only buys, he never sells... never. Do you see the golden flags with Habsburg insignia, the two-headed eagles? This was made for Rudolf specifically. He is a collector without compare in Europe, perhaps the entire World."

The Marchioness pouts, "do you not think I can persuade him?"

"I am as certain of it as I am of anything, madame. But you may commission one like it from the maker, Hans Schlottheim, his workshop is here in Prague."

Christina has discovered a small clock decorated with ivory and pearls, "I am very attracted to pearls, their subtle colors are sublime. Does this object do anything clever, sir?"

Before he can speak, the Marchioness interrupts again, "that is *lovely,* Christina, and you know I love *ivory,* it can be carved so delicately, may I see it?"

Arcimboldo's voice is full of enthusiasm, he also is very fond of carved ivory, "oh, then you should see the ivory in the gallery next door, among the *artificiosa*, we have works that will stun you with their beauty! There is an ivory ball a foot in diameter perforated with dozens of hexagonal holes, through them you can see a perfectly carved rearing horse in the center of the ball. *E perfetto... stupendo!*" His hands have been busily forming shapes to illustrate what he is describing; then remembering himself, he says apologetically, "um, *Princess*, I beg your pardon, that clock is beautiful, but there is no special automation to it."

"I *must* see the ivory, Arcimboldus, can we do that now?" The Marchioness is ardent, "Christina, you've seen enough machines by now, haven't you?"

Arcimboldo looks at Christina, "Princess? There are many things made of pearl there as well. Also, large bezoar stones, are you familiar with them?"

"Yes, they remind me of a gigantic pearl. We have very few in France. I believe I would enjoy seeing your *artificiosa*, as you call it."

As they walk toward the door they hear the sound of loud voices, seemingly arguing voices. There is a knock on the door as they approach. Arcimboldo opens it to discover a pinched and ill-favored man with long, oily hair to his shoulders and a stringy beard and moustache. An Imperial halberdier stands nervously behind the man. The soldier says in German, "I'm sorry, My Lord, he insisted. He says he is with Her Highness of Lorraine."

In a disagreeable, whining voice the man speaks over the soldier, and ignores Arcimboldo; to the Princess he says, "the Cardinal, your brother, is waiting for you, madame. He has *been* waiting, you are late. You must come immediately."

The women look at each other and wrinkle their noses. Distantly, Christina says, "I have forgotten the time. I will come presently, tell the Duc."

The man looks at the room behind Arcimboldo and the two women, seeing it is filled with clocks. "I *see*, you have forgotten the time. You must come with me. Immediately. It is the wish of the Duc."

The women exchange whispers and Christina of Lorraine nods politely to Arcimboldo, "I expect to see you this evening at the banquet, My Lord. Yes?"

Arcimboldo bows, "of course, Princess."

Christina brushes past the man without a look or a word and walks down the hallway. The Frenchman now fixes his beady eyes on the Marchioness. "Your husband awaits you, Marchioness, you must come as well."

The Marchioness looks back at the man with contempt, "I will come shortly, you may tell my husband so."

"But-"

"You may tell my husband so, I say. I will be escorted by Lord Arcimboldus, we have matters to discuss. You may go."

The man frowns and fumes, he opens his mouth to speak and closes it again. He twists his stringy moustache. Christina has stopped half way down the hallway, she calls back, "well, sir, will you escort me? Or am I to find my own way back?"

The Frenchman scrutinizes Arcimboldo up and down, then, with a last disagreeable look, he rushes off to join the Princess.

Arcimboldo turns to the Marchioness, "who is that extraordinary creature?"

"A *most* unpleasant man. Crude, quarrelsome, and uncouth, with the manners of a Barbary ape. He is a toady to Cardinal Guise. He is not even French, do not be offended, but I believe he is a countryman of yours. Why he and that loathsome Spaniard have been allowed to join our embassy I cannot imagine… unless they have been forced on the Duc by the Holy League."

"The Holy League! What is his name?"

"His name is Signore Fabrizio Mordente."

"Fabrizio Mordente!"

Arcimboldo has many questions for the Marchioness concerning Mordente and the Holy League, but he must be circumspect. While he considers what may be discussed, the Marchioness looks at him suspiciously, "you are surprised? What is this man to you, My Lord?"

"It's just that I have heard of him through… an associate."

"Hmm. Apparently, he is mathematical."

"Yes, it is just such an association."

"One would not take him for an intelligent man."

"Does skill in mathematics make one an intelligent man, Marchioness?"

"If I understand you correctly, my answer is *no* indeed. I believe intelligence is a far more complicated thing."

"Yes, you do understand, that is my thinking as well, you make a most sensible distinction."

"I take that as a complement. There is far more knowledge than sensibility in the World, and that imbalance grows greater every day. I would much rather be sensible." She smiles agreeably.

He returns the smile and nods, "madame, I consider you to be intelligent *and* sensible."

Arcimboldo holds open the door of the *mechanica* gallery, and they exit into the hallway. He says, "it seems it is after the seventeenth hour, Marchioness, do you have time to examine the ivory in our room of *artificiosa*?"

"Unfortunately, I don't. But tomorrow I'll spend all day in these galleries. You have promised to be my guide, have you not?" Her eyes widen with a look of hopeful expectation that he is loath to disappoint.

"Of course."

"And *your* paintings, Arcimboldus, when may I see them? The World speaks of them, but I have only seen the set in Fontainebleau. I have so many questions for you."

Modestly he replies, "the Emperor always dines while viewing my paintings of the Elements or the Seasons, tonight will be no exception, the Seasons will be in front of us. I will be happy to explain them to you, madame."

She looks delighted, "wonderful! And while we are alone you may call me Samantha."

Arcimboldo bows, "I'm honored, Samantha."

"Sa-*man*-tha."

"Pardon me, Sa-*man*-tha. It's the first time I've heard the name. It is English?"

"Yes. My father is Sir Leslie Steele. I don't expect you've heard of him either, our property is far to the north, near the Scottish border. You don't speak English by any chance?"

"Regrettably, no, madame... Samantha."

"And I may call you... Josephus, is it?"

"I much prefer Giuseppe."

"Giuseppe. I do not speak Italian. I wish I did so, so I could understand Italian songs. It is the *most* beautiful language for singing. But I prefer French for speaking, French is by far the most elegant language for *conversation*, such... mmm... fluidity *and* precision of expression."

"I have always believed that it is the abundance of vowels at the end of words and syllables that makes Italian so apt for song and poetry."

"Why... yes. That is good, you are correct."

Arcimboldo speaks German to the Imperial guards as they leave the Emperor's Wunderkabinet. He says to the Marchioness, "so, where may I escort you, madame?"

"Oh, I need to return to that enormous hall near the Cathedral where we had refreshment when we first arrived."

"Vladislav Hall?"

"Yes, that's it."

"This way then."

"I've been wondering about your name, Arcimboldus-"

"Josephus Arcimboldus is a Romanized conceit, my family name is Arcimboldo, or occasionally Arcimboldi, we use various spellings. There are even Arzimboldis. It is Italianized German."

"Oh, you are of German origin?"

"Well, the name itself is. But that was a very long time ago. Our ancestor was a German knight named Siegfried, who served Charlemagne. During a campaign, this man discovered a silver deposit deep in a forest, and for his faithful service Charlemagne rewarded him with this silver mine. As a mark of nobility Siegfried took the name *Erz im Wald*, which means 'Ore in the Forest'. When his offspring moved south to Lombardy, and settled in Milan, *Erz im Wald* became Arzimbald. We have discussed the Italian fondness for vowels at the end of words, and so it became Arzimbaldi, and eventually Arcimboldo."

"So, is that the way it's pronounced in Milan? Ar-jim-*bold*-o?"

"Yes, in Italian, it's Ar-jim-*bold*-o. But here in Prague, as you've heard, I'm called Ar-*kim*-boldus."

"Fascinating."

"Like so much else in life, Samantha, it's a matter of perspective."

They have turned into yet another long hallway, and the Marchioness' eyes widen with bewilderment. "These hallways are like a maze. I would be wandering this palace for days without you to guide me. I wonder if Christina has found her way back."

"She has Signore Mordente to accompany her, I imagine they'll ask someone if they become lost." The thought of the man freely wandering through Hradcany's palaces is slightly disturbing. "It will be a long walk to Vladislav Hall, Samantha, unless we cross the courtyard, but I'm afraid it will be too cold for you if we go outside."

"Not at all, I am a child of the North Sea, I'm well used to cold weather, this is nothing to me." She makes a charming, casual gesture with her hand, as if brushing something away.

"Really? Well then, let us go down these stairs here. After you. Tell me, when did you leave England?"

"I was married to the Marquis when I was fifteen, sir."

"Ah, so young. And do you have children?"

Her posture has been confidently upright to this point, but now she arches her shoulders back with pride; her smile is radiant, showing perfect, pearly teeth, she lifts her chin and puts her right hand to her heart, "I have a daughter, Leona, she is the light of my life! My angel! She is six now. I miss her *terribly*. Her hair and eyes are the same color as mine, I'm so glad! I know I should not admit this, but I had prayed for it." Her auburn hair is held to her head by a net of pearls, but from her neck it spills down her back in a cascade of elegantly woven coils. She proudly reaches back to touch her hair to be sure he has noticed it. "She is an angel, but *so* headstrong sometimes... like me, yes, just like I was at that age. And you, sir, I believe you are not married?" She watches him closely.

"No, my studies, my work, my travels... most of all my responsibilities at the Court of the Holy Roman Emperor, have not left me the time. Although, I admit, I do have a son." Without intending to, his hand pats the pocket holding Benedetto's letter; yes, it's still there.

"Tell me about him, Giuseppe."

"His name is Benedetto, and he will be thirty-seven this year-"

"Goodness! Thirty-seven! If I am not being too bold, how old are you, sir?"

With a sigh (and really, how foolish, why should he sigh?) he says, "I am sixty, madame."

"*Samantha.*" She stops, and very frankly and thoroughly studies his face, "why... you do not look it." She begins walking again. "Go on, Giuseppe, tell me about Benedetto."

So different are father and son that Arcimboldo feels he must tell the Marchioness more about his own life, in order to contrast that of the boy, indeed, the man, he has only infrequently seen, and never really understood. Arcimboldo remembers watching his own father at his craft from the earliest age. So all consuming was young Giuseppe's interest in art that he cannot even remember his age when he began to work closely beside his father, painting frescos and stained glass panels for churches in and around Milan; it feels as though he has been an artist from the moment of his birth. Arcimboldo might have happily spent the rest of his days doing exactly as his father had done, in exactly the same palaces, town halls, guild halls, churches, and monasteries, but two chance events changed the course of his life. The first was the summer he spent with the family of Bernardo Luini to avoid plague in Milan. Like Arcimboldo's family, the Luini's were artists, father and son. Bernardo was a friend and disciple of the Florentine master, Leonardo da Vinci, and when Leonardo moved to France he left several of his books of drawings with the Luinis for safekeeping. He had never returned to reclaim them, and the books of drawings had become holy objects in the Luini household. Arcimboldo had been sent into a dream world by the images he saw in Leonardo's notebooks. He studied them for hours and hours, more than anything in the world he longed to draw like that; and also, something even more difficult than drawing like Leonardo, Arcimboldo longed to understand the secret details of the Natural World with the same intensity and thoroughness.

The second event, also dictated by chance, was when Arcimboldo met Emperor Ferdinand I, Rudolf's grandfather. The painters' guild had awarded him a small commission, painting heraldic shields for Emperor Ferdinand's grand visit to Milan in 1561; surprisingly, the Emperor took an interest in the earnest painter with Humanist ideals, and invited him to the Court in Vienna. Since that time he has devotedly and without interruption served three Holy Roman Emperors.

His son, Benedetto, however, has never shown the slightest interest in art or following the craft of his forefathers, in spite of his father's international fame and success. In fact, to Arcimboldo's dismay, Benedetto has rarely shown an interest in anything other than grousing about his neighbors and fathering as many children as possible. Arcimboldo has so many grandchildren than he can't remember the exact number, let alone their names.

At this point in his tale the Marchioness laughs, she says, "you men! The intelligent and talented ones have no time for us, and the stupid ones are annoying brutes. I do not mean Benedetto, of course. But tell me, Giuseppe, does it disappoint you greatly that he is not an artist?"

"No... no, that is not as disappointing as his lack of..."

"Lack of?"

"This is hard for me to say. He lacks a sense of honor and propriety that grieves me deeply. It shames me. I feel..."

"You feel it is your fault."

"Your mind is very quick. I was not present during his childhood. I did not offer him an honorable model, or any model at all... and it is strange that I would say so to you, but I did not offer him love, or at any rate, surely not the love my father gave me."

"You are an honest man to say so."

"Indeed, it makes me feel just the opposite."

"What did he do that you feel is dishonorable? You may not tell me if you do not wish."

"He... cheated a neighbor. He forged a deed to property that did not belong to him."

"Was he caught?"

"Let's say, he was not punished. I was able to buy the property at a price that gave the neighbor a reason to forget the matter. To forget, perhaps, to forgive..."

"He is lucky he did not lose his ears."

"Ears? Did I hear you correctly? What do you mean?"

"Indeed, his ears. Such is the punishment in England, for fraud, swindling, forgery, and legal impropriety."

Arcimboldo is stunned. "A man in England would lose his ears for such an offense? How would he lose his ears?"

"They would be cut off, in a public place. A public disgrace, and a warning to all who would deal with the man hereafter."

Arcimboldo slowly repeats her words, his mouth has gone dry, "a warning to all who would deal with the man hereafter."

"But your son was very lucky. He is Italian, and he has a father that saved him from punishment. What is the punishment in Milan?"

"Prison, confiscation of property. Certainly not disfigurement. I think it is very possible that we Italians are used to cheating each other more than you English. We are passionate, but we accept certain human failings more readily than other cultures, it is our long and complicated history. But tell me, madame, what would be the penalty for an Irishman?"

"The same, certainly the same. Why do you ask?"

He shakes his head as if trying to clear his thoughts. Muttering, as if to himself, he whispers, "no ears..."

"Don't let it perplex you, sir, as I say, Benedetto is lucky to be Italian. And to have a father that *does love* him. Giuseppe, do you think you will return to Italy some day?"

Although his joyous news should be on the tip of his tongue, Arcimboldo is reluctant to tell her, something constrains him, and he answers irreverently, "if only to learn the names of my grandchildren."

A small figure comes bounding past them, a figure Arcimboldo knows very well; he says, "excuse me a moment, Marchioness." He calls out, "what ho! Silvius!"

The boy stops immediately, recognizing his master's voice. He comes trotting back and bows respectfully, "My Lord, pardon me for running in the hallways, I know you have told me many-"

The conversation proceeds in alternating phrases of German and Czech. "Well met, lad. I have two important tasks for you. Listen closely."

"Yes, sir."

"There is a painting in my studio, the one I was working on this morning. It is finished, but be very careful, the paint is wet. I want you to wrap it as I have taught you how to wrap a painting with wet paint. Do you remember?"

"I twist up the rags and place them across the corners, then I cover-"

"Yes, good. Then very, very carefully you will take it to the Summer Palace. Take it upstairs and give it to Master Spranger or Master Mont. Please, please, do not leave it with the Nolan or the Englishmen. Do you understand?"

"I'm to give it to Master Spranger or Master Mont, sir."

"Very good. If they are not there you will wait for them."

"Yes, sir."

"Then, you will return to the Summer Palace tonight at midnight. Do not knock or try the door. Wait on the steps until I come out."

"Yes, sir."

"Good. I trust you got some rest today, my boy?"

"I did, sir."

"Good. And Silvius, you *must* speak German when in the Palace. You are old enough to know that now. Do you understand?"

Silvius answers in Czech. "All right, sir, I understand."

Master and servant lock eyes for a moment. Finally Arcimboldo says, "you may go. And do not run. Silvius, remember, midnight, not a moment later... and bring some gloves and a warm hat for me when you return. Now... go."

The boy walks for several yards and then breaks into a trot. Arcimboldo turns to the Marchioness, "pardon me, madame, my servant."

The Marchioness says questioningly, "were you speaking different languages?"

Arcimboldo sighs, shrugs, and waves his hand in the air vaguely by way of answer. "This is how we live in Prague."

To take the subject off himself, he asks casually, "you had mentioned the Holy League earlier, can it really have influence over this Royal marriage?"

"There *is* no marriage yet, My Lady has barely met the Tuscan Grand Duke, it is not my impression that her family will force this upon her, and there are many other suitors."

"Yes, naturally, the Princess will be allowed some say in the matter. I can't imagine the Grand Duke being displeased though. And the dowry-"

"I may not discuss that."

"Of course, of course, I was only going to say that it *also* would be under discussion between the parties. I was wondering about the influence of the Holy League-"

"Oh, the Holy League, the Holy League... you will make me cross if you try to make me say something complementary about them. Let me pretend they do not exist."

"I beg your pardon, madame, however, I would have you know that I feel as you do."

"Then I apologize for being impatient with you. The people I travel with sing their praises continuously."

"I assure you, it is just the opposite here in Bohemia."

"I can imagine, with half the population being Protestant."

"Half the population? Can you imagine that only *one* person in ten is Catholic in this city? And those are mostly foreigners and Imperial officials."

"One person in ten? Can that be?"

"I assure you, it is the case."

"These Bohemian Protestants are the people who call themselves Utraquists?"

"Yes, now they are Utraquists; they used to be called Hussites, after Jan Hus... it is the same as the followers of Martin Luther are called Lutherans."

"Then what is this word, Utraquist?"

"Utraquist comes from the Latin, *sub utraque specie*, meaning 'in both kinds'. This is the principal difference between Utraquist and Catholic, it is what makes them Protestant."

"Both kinds of what? I'm not sure I understand."

"Utraquists demand that they must receive the Eucharist in *both* bread *and* wine. As you know, Catholics receive the Eucharist as bread only, the *body* of Christ; the wine, the *blood* of Christ, is reserved for priests only."

"The blessed wafer *and* wine? And this makes them Protestants?"

"Samantha, never doubt that such *subtle* differences can cause discord and strife. It hardly seems credible, but there it is... and it has always been this way. I believe it is not the difference itself, but how the exaggerated *perception* of difference is used to create groups of 'us' and groups of 'them'. The fearful, fanatical, and unscrupulous use such slight discrepancies, such subtle differences, to advance their own fortunes, and bludgeon those who may stand in their way." Arcimboldo sighs with melancholy.

For a moment she is at a loss for words. "Then... why are we here? Will they murder us in our sleep, Giuseppe?"

"Certainly not. You are absolutely safe." His hand casually searches his pocket for his ruby. "You are here, we are *all* here, because the Emperor chooses this as his home and his capital. The Medici and Valois come here because of the Emperor's international status."

"And why does he choose this place?"

"For several reasons – let us pause here until the portal to the courtyard is less crowded – shall I speak frankly? He chooses Prague because it is as far as possible from Habsburg relatives he cannot tolerate. He chooses Prague because it is much farther away from the violent assaults of the Sultan's armies, often they are at the gates of Vienna, as you know. He chooses Prague because it is closer to the mines that produce the metals and gems that the Emperor covets. And as long as I've said so much, I'll tell you that the Emperor views Prague as being part of his prophetic destiny. The Czech word itself, Praha, means threshold, and the Emperor is convinced he is on the threshold of greatness that will eclipse all the other Princes of Christendom."

"That is *extremely* interesting."

"At the same time the Emperor seeks greatness, he seeks to retire from the World, as did his famous ancestor, the Universal Monarch, Charles V. The greatest, richest, most powerful man in the World, ruler of an empire upon which the Sun never set. Holy Roman Emperor, King of Spain, Milan, Naples, Sicily, the Netherlands, and master of land in the New World that is larger than all of Europe; Charles *voluntarily* abdicated all his authority and power, and wearing the modest robe of a Benedictine monk, leaning on the shoulder of his young favorite, William of Orange and Nassau, he entered the Monastery of St. Yuste to end his days in meditation and prayer. You are too young to know this, but I remember well, the ceremony at the

Escorial was attended by a Christian frenzy such as a Pope has never seen."

"It is often discussed... what would Europe be like had he not abdicated and split his empire? Surely the World has never seen such an act, and never will again."

"In fact, Charles did emulate, I suspect intentionally, the action of the pagan Roman Emperor Diocletian, who split his Empire into the West, that of Rome, and the East, Byzantium. That *most* un-Christian man retired from the World to tend his vegetable gardens in Dalmatia. One may also speculate on how different History may have been had Diocletian not divided the Roman Empire."

"You are an artist *and* a philosopher, sir. I begin to understand that your Emperor is much more complicated than his critics would credit." In answer to Arcimboldo's questioning look she says, "he is called indecisive and *politique*."

"This new word *politique*, a French invention, madame, is much misused. It is too often used simply as an insult toward those whose actions one does not agree with. *Politique* really means one who seeks a solution through peaceful persuasion, compromise, and careful balance, instead of bull-headed, self-righteous forcefulness."

"Truthfully, I do not respect the intelligence of those who use that word."

"Doctor Thaddeus Hagecius, Rudolf's physician and an astute student of the human Mind, has an appropriate saying – the *egotism of the ignorant*. It allows much of the human race to feel that they have all the answers to life that they need; it forestalls questioning and critical thinking. And worse than that, it allows them to be manipulated by the cunningly unscrupulous."

Hesitatingly she mutters, "the egotism of the ignorant? How should I understand the word you use – egotism? In what sense?"

"Egotism in that, once satisfied with simple answers, many people allow themselves to feel superior to those who would continue to examine and question... not only superior, but irritated and impatient with those who would question further. It is the greatest luxury of all, the luxury of hypocrisy."

"These are deep and interesting subjects, Giuseppe. Frankly, I am not used to being spoken to in such a way by men, I have not found them to... well, respect my intelligence to such a degree. In fact, I mean to say *trust* as well as *respect*... what you say could be interpreted as an insult to the Church. You trust that I do not find you heretical."

"I do not mean to insult the Church, I attempt to understand its faults and weaknesses. But, as you say, this would amount to heresy in many places. The acceptance of questioning thought is one of the reasons I am grateful to live at this Court in this tumultuous but fascinating city."

"Your acceptance of questioning thought has not gone unnoticed, as you must know. Your Emperor is not considered to be a serious Catholic in many circles."

Arcimboldo sighs and shakes his head. "Did you know that Rudolf and his brother Ernst spent their entire childhood at the Castilian Court in Madrid? A place even more Catholic and conservative than Rome itself. As a child Rudolf watched the expulsion of both the Jews and Moriscos from Spain, and more tragic than that, he was witness to the most brutal days of the Spanish Inquisition, the mass burnings of heretics, the auto-da-fes. His uncle's Court would consider it entertainment, they would sit under canopies of gold and banquet while heretics would be burnt in front of them, dozens, scores in a day! The Emperor does not speak of this, but I am convinced he does not forget those childhood horrors, and would never visit them on his subjects here in Bohemia."

The Marchioness is appalled, her eyes narrow and her brow wrinkles at the image he paints.

"The Emperor's greatest difficulty is fending off those who would control him to their own advantage. The Pope, the King of Spain, and those destructive zealots from France, the *Holy League*. Here is the game we play in this city: the hate and mistrust between Protestant and Catholic increase every day, a cycle of violent actions always labeled 'retribution' by the perpetrators and 'provocation' by the victims; whose hate for each other seems only to be surmounted by their hate for those who would separate them and find compromise." Arcimboldo finds himself strangely carried away by a tide of emotion.

The Marchioness is as unmoving as a statue. She stares at Arcimboldo with her lovely mouth half open in anticipation of more serious revelations.

"Today's tragic riot, in which many hundreds of *Protestants* lost their lives, was created by the distribution among the public of a calumnious broadside, terrifying *nine out of ten* citizens with the warning that the Holy League is coming to Prague at the Emperor's invitation. Do you follow me?"

She answers mutely by shaking her head.

"This put you and the rest of the Emperor's *Catholic* guests in great danger. One wonders if it was intentional, the timing is certainly suspicious. Nothing would undermine the Emperor's efforts at moderation faster than an attack on foreign Catholic nobles; nothing would bring the Holy League to Prague faster than such an international scandal. And, as long as I've gone this far, I'll tell you that it is very probable that this provocative broadside was written by a *Frenchman!*"

"Surely you do not suspect…"

"*I* suspect the Holy League, the Emperor's advisors suspect *everyone*."

"Merciful St. Agnes, you have quite put me out!" She covers her mouth with her hand.

Arcimboldo strokes his beard and moustache. "I had not intended to disquiet you, madame. I've been, perhaps, too passionate. Having been witness to the slaughter this morning… I'm still not myself. Let's put this grim discussion behind us. The portal is clear now, we may proceed… I will calm you with more gentle thoughts."

-Night-

As they walk out into the chill air of the courtyard they see it has stopped snowing, patchy holes in the cloud cover show an inky black sky with a sprinkling of bright stars. Torches burn around the Cathedral and workers slowly disassemble the booths and other structures that had been set up for Epiphany celebrations.

"I'll tell you the legend of the founding of Prague, Marchioness. Are you interested?"

She nods her head but does not speak.

"Long ago, a tribe from the east was migrating west, the leader and patriarch of this tribe was named Czech. They crossed three rivers, the Oder, the Elbe, and the Vltava. After crossing the Vltava the people become restive, tired of wandering. Patriarch Czech climbed to the highest point in the landscape, he looked out over green forest and fertile meadow in every direction, uninhabited as far as the eye could see, up to the bluish mountain ranges. After three days of meditation Czech announced to his people – 'this is the land long promised, this is our new home!' The people prospered under Czech and his son Krok, however Krok died without an heir. Czech had also left behind three daughters, the eldest two were wicked sorceresses, but the youngest and most beautiful was a soothsayer, named Libussa. She could see what others could not, and the people chose her as their leader. Watch that puddle, my dear. After some time, the people demanded that they must have a man as their leader; Libussa's rule was one of compassion and compromise, and this was mistaken for weakness. She warned the people that a male ruler would demand service and tribute, but the people *would* have a man, so Libussa sent her magic white horse to find the man who should lead the tribe of Czech. The horse led Libussa and the other elders to an industrious and clever plowman named Premsyl, and he became their leader. Then, seized by a spirit, Libussa told them all to follow her. She climbed to a spot where a man was building a house, he was finishing the threshold. Libussa claimed this would be their capital and its name would be Praha, threshold. She told them to build a castle on that spot and she said 'I see a great city whose fame will reach the stars. Just as Princes and army commanders must bow their heads when they enter a house, so they will bow their heads to my city. It will be honored, noble, and respected by all the World.' We are standing on that spot right now, Samantha."

When he looks at her closely he sees this child of the North Sea is pale and shivering. He takes off his cloak and puts it around her shoulders. She is grateful and does not resist, but Arcimboldo feels as though his spine has been sliced open from neck to tail bone. He sneezes twice.

Since both of them have chattering teeth, they walk in silence across the square until they are outside St. George's Basilica. Arcimboldo points to the large and elaborate doorway passing into the building next to the Basilica. "That is the entrance to Vladislav Hall, madame."

"It's an impressive building on the inside. So large... why I cannot think of a hall so large in all of Paris."

"It's two-hundred feet long and fifty feet high. You can't tell from here, but five separate domes form the roof. You've been inside already you say? Come, I'll show you some splendid features."

"One moment, Giuseppe." She removes his cloak and hands it to him. "I am much obliged, sir."

He longs to wrap it around himself immediately, but chivalrous conduct dictates that he hold it casually over his arm while she is uncovered as well.

With a trusting smile, she says, "now tell me, sir, my hair, my dress, am I presentable?"

Arcimboldo bows, although his shivering makes it a bit jerky, "Madame, you are perfection itself."

She has been patting the pearl net that covers her lustrous hair and adjusting the folds of her shimmering yellow dress. She looks at him with a mischievous twinkle in her hazel-green eyes. "Perfection, My Lord? You are famous as a courtier... I suppose you would flatter me, call me beautiful... Venus... would you not?"

Smiling, he will rally with her. He strikes a pose, flourishes his hand, and uses an affected tone in his voice, "now, madame, a merely intelligent man would call you Venus. A *courtier* would embellish, he would say to you that *as Venus is the mother of Grace, of*

*Beauty, and of Faith, my Goddess, these Virtues descend in a similar way from her Celestial power as your-"*

She has been laughing and stops him by briefly putting a hand on his chest over his heart. It stops him indeed. He feels he has been struck by a lightning bolt. His heart, that anchorite, leaps within his chest. Suddenly, his chill is replaced by a flush. Still laughing, she tosses her head, "come, sir, I will introduce you to my husband, the Marquis." And she enters Vladislav Hall. Shuffling like a chained captive, he follows.

Vladislav Hall was built in the reign of King Vladislav Jagiello, supposedly by the architect Benedikt Rejt, but Arcimboldo cannot be fooled, the flamboyant windows (at least) are clearly the work of another unknown architect, obviously, an Italian. They enter the busy hall from the north, and it stretches away to their right and left. Far above their heads, the arched rib-vaults are unadorned except for the stone tracing of the rib-vaults themselves; these gigantic and powerful designs create a pattern that is almost floral in their sinuous, interlocking shapes. Below the massive ceiling hang five equally massive bronze chandeliers, suspended from the center of each of the five domes. Below these chandeliers throng the Catholic nobility of Bohemia and the Empire, the richest Catholic citizens of Prague, officials of the Imperial Court, and Rudolf's foreign guests. Servants dressed in Imperial livery scurry about serving refreshments to the guests who are happily, busily, in conversation. The booths and stalls that usually line the walls and do a brisk commercial business have been removed for the occasion, and the walls are now lined with tables laden with drink and seasonal delicacies; between and behind the tables, halberdiers of the Imperial Household Guard stand immobile and impassive. Arcimboldo looks up toward the western wall separating Vladislav Hall from the Imperial Chancery; Rudolf has an office on the second floor of the Chancery, and there is a window in that office covered with a black curtain that looks down on the inside of the hall. He sees the curtain is partly pulled aside; no doubt Rudolf is there now, secretly watching the activity in the hall below him. This is one of his favorite pastimes.

The Marchioness looks over her shoulder and impatiently waves Arcimboldo forward. They approach a group wearing enormous ruffs that extend almost beyond the shoulders, all the fashion in France, cut-pile velvet clothing, and expensive and elaborately decorated swords. The long, waxed, curled, and sharply pointed moustaches they wear are also fashionably French. It must be irresistible to twirl and pull on moustaches like this, Arcimboldo thinks, since most of the men are engaged in this occupation as they speak. In their midst, wearing a sickly sycophantic smile, is Fabrizio Mordente.

The group turns to greet the Marchioness, and she greets her husband with a curtsey and a small kiss on the cheek. He is a short, stocky, powerful man with dark eyes and a bad complexion. With playful exaggeration he says, "madame, where have you been? You have left me all to myself!"

"My Lord, forgive me, but I see that you are *not* all to yourself. I have had the most interesting afternoon. I have been to the Emperor's Wunderkabinet, escorted by this famous and very learned artist. May I introduce you to Maestro Gio-, Josephus Arcimboldus. Maestro, may I introduce my husband, the Marquis d'Olivan."

The Marquis nods and Arcimboldo bows. The Marquis says with a gruff but not unkind tone, "I have seen your work at Fontainebleau, sir, I do not understand it, I must tell you, but it always makes me laugh heartily!"

Arcimboldo bows again politely, he reasons that this is as close to a complement as he will get from this man. "I have been honored by your wife's company, Marquis, she is a most knowledgeable woman, with a discerning eye for beauty and art."

The Marquis snorts, "I hate to tell you what all this beauty and art costs me!" This is directed to his companions as much as Arcimboldo, and they all laugh appreciatively.

The Marchioness says, "and tomorrow, My Lord, you will accompany me, I am sure. Maestro Arcimboldus has much, much more to show us. The Emperor's collection is remarkable! It puts Fontainebleau to shame!" Several of the company scoff and shake their heads in disbelief. She continues, "you will be vastly entertained by the History, Symbolism, erudition, and rarity of their collection. Why, there must simply be acres of it! We will start early."

The Marquis' face is overcome by a look of worried discomfort, he stammers, "History? Symbolism? *Acres* you say? Well... well... we'll see, we'll see. It's very possible that I have another engagement that I'm forgetting at the moment." The Marchioness looks quickly at Arcimboldo, and her lips are twitching with a suppressed smile of amusement. The Marquis says, "Maestro... is it Lord...?"

Arcimboldo nods, "yes, Marquis, I have been ennobled by His Imperial Majesty Maximilian II."

"Lord Arcimboldus, permit me to introduce, Louis of Lorraine, Cardinal of Guise; his brother, Charles of Lorraine, Duc de Mayenne; Charles of Guise, Duc D'Aumale; Bernardino de Mendoza, Spanish Ambassador to the King of France; and Don Guillen de San Clemente, who, perhaps you know. Eh? Oh, and Signore Mordente."

Arcimboldo bows and the gentlemen bow in return, except for Mordente who is busily whispering into Bernardino de Mendoza's ear. The Spaniard is nodding, and scans Arcimboldo with a very unpleasant and critical look.

In her delightful voice, the Marchioness says, "what were you going to show me in this splendid hall, Lord Arcimboldus?"

Although he would like nothing better than to leave this group immediately, Arcimboldo puts on a show of relaxed cordiality. "Why there, to your left, Marchioness, next to that fireplace, the largest in Prague by the way; that grand gateway leads up to the street on that side of the Castle. It is a ramp called the 'Rider's Stairway', it is large enough for mounted riders to enter Vladislav Hall. This allows us to have jousting tournaments in here no matter what the weather outside."

The Marquis shows great interest in this, his face animates, "is that so? Jousting tournaments? Why, I say, that would be capital! Does Rudolf plan a jousting tournament for us? Do you know?"

"I regret to say, My Lord, he does not. Perhaps another day, when we have had more time to prepare."

The Marquis has now lost interest. The Marchioness asks, "and what are those decorations around the gateway, shields?"

"Yes, Madame, heraldic shields, every knight and ennobled family in Bohemia has their device on that wall. That one there, with the bend sinister, belongs to the knight Adam Krug."

The Marchioness begins to ask something else, but the Cardinal interrupts her, "madame, my sister is changing, and perhaps she requires your assistance. We will dine shortly I believe." The Marquis d'Olivan adds, "by Heavens, yes, madame, you must change as well. Make haste! Make haste!"

The Marchioness pats her husband's cheek, then pinches it, saying, "don't eat too much now, My Lord, we'll dine soon enough. And no more wine until dinner! Not a drop. Promise!" She curtsies and excuses herself; she is escorted by Cardinal Guise. Arcimboldo also excuses himself, "gentlemen, My Lords, as Master of Entertainment I must be about my responsibilities. I look forward to seeing you all at our banquet shortly." He bows, and practically runs for the door.

Once outside, even before he wraps himself in his cloak, he scuttles around to a sheltered and hidden corner alongside the great hall. There, in deep shadow, shivering, but with great relief, he is able to urinate. Hearing approaching footsteps, voices, and the clanking of metal weapons, he tenses, then relaxes as he realizes it is two soldiers on the same mission as himself. He cannot help overhearing their conversation.

"Did'ja see the collars on those blokes? Out to 'ere! Jesters ain't half that funny! Ha!"

"Those Frenchies 're odd ones, ain't they?"

"Did'ja see that fat lil' Frenchie an' 'is wife?"

"Which ones?"

"You know, she come flouncin' in wi' the ol' Eye-talian draggin' behind."

"Christ's corpse! She's a bit of all right, an' then some!"

"No lie there! Anyways, Red come flouncin' in, an' she goes up to this fat lil' Frenchie, an' she pats 'is cheek and kisses 'is 'ead. Right? Well, Franz leans over to me and 'e sez, lookee there Tomi, if it ain't Salomee wi' the 'ead of John the Baptist on a platter! By Christ, I nearly pissed me pants tryin' not to laugh!"

"Ha! Salomee with the 'ead of John the Baptist on a platter! Ha! By God, that Franz, I'll be damned if 'e ain't as funny as a pig in a Pope's hat!"

Arcimboldo walks away with an attempt at dignity; although the thought of the Marquis' head on a platter is admittedly amusing, his own role in the farce as the 'ol' Eye-talian' is sobering. And worse, any mention of the head of John the Baptist at this point is disturbing and unwelcome. Arcimboldo crosses himself and for good measure gives his lucky ruby a firm pinch.

Now, cloaked and feeling much more himself, he heads back toward the Palace. Arcimboldo crosses paths with the Chamberlain, Jan von Muhlhausen. Muhlhausen says, "a busy day, Arcimboldus, and no end in sight. I think I could sleep for a week."

"Oh, that sounds wonderful! I'm as tired as you are! But no rest for the wicked, eh, Jan? I'm glad to have met you, tell me what you have arranged for the promenade."

"Well, we had servants ready to carry canopies over the heads of the guests as they walked to the Summer Palace, but it looks like the snow has stopped. I may dismiss them until midnight."

"I would not. Let me advise you, instead of canopies, have all those servants carry flambeaux, they will walk alongside our guests, on either side of the walkway, it will be an impressive sight… I have just thought of it. Hmm, they'll need boots so they aren't stumbling in the snow, send them to the stables to get boots, tell them it's the Emperor's order. One more thing, get people out there sweeping snow from the walkway right now."

"I'm ahead of you there, the sweepers are at work. But the boots and the torches? We don't have much time… are you sure that's necessary?"

"It's not necessary, but very impressive, well worth the effort. The Emperor will be delighted. Try your best, will you?"

With a tired sigh, Muhlhausen says, "I will, I will. So glad I ran into you, My Lord. God speed."

"You are a champion, Lord Chamberlain! God speed to you as well!"

The unexpected diversions of this Epiphany Day have kept Arcimboldo's mind from dwelling on the alchemical experiment in the Summer Palace. This is curious, he had imagined that this day would be consumed with thoughts of the decisive and secret undertaking. Now, the actuality is so close at hand he feels surprised, his stomach knots with nervousness. *Now, Giuseppe Arcimboldo, now begins the event that has shaped your life for the past year;* so the artist tells himself as he passes through the rusticated north portal of Hradcany Castle and into the walkway that will lead him to the Summer Palace.

The hundreds of hours of work and the thousands of details involved in preparing for the experiment are recorded in Arcimboldo's Memory Palace; the gallery is nearly complete, the handful of hours and details that remain to be experienced will reveal the outcome. When he next walks this path, back the way he comes, it will all be over, and he will tread with the slow footsteps of ignominious defeat or with the joyous confidence of victory. If a victory, it will be more spectacular and famous than any battle ever fought or any discovery ever made. It's not just Arcimboldo's world that will be changed forever, the entire World will be a different place. The relationship between the Creator and His Creation will follow a new course, and Rudolf Habsburg will be the pilot.

If Rudolf's alchemical Cosmos can penetrate Heaven's secrets, how much will this change Arcimboldo and the Emperor's other assistants? Thinking of his conversation with Giordano Bruno, the artist wonders if tomorrow he will still want to return to Milan. Now it has become his own choice to make and no longer dependent upon the Emperor.

With that thought, he pauses under one of the lanterns that have been hung every twenty feet along the walkway. He takes his son's letter from his inner pocket and opens it. He reads: *'Dearest, Honored Father, I'm sure this letter finds you well and prosperous, living as you do at the Center of the World, at the Court of the Holy Roman Emperor'*. A charmingly respectful and articulate beginning. Good. He reads on, Benedetto's wife, Maria, is ill. Nothing unexpected here, this always seems to be part of the news from Milan. Benedetto's children are, as usual, teething, reading, stealing, and mending broken bones. Now, this is new, an investment with Florentine wool merchants. A good step forward. Profits expected. Good again. An additional loan to increase his investment. Hmm, suspect. And now, sadly, the expected, his son is pursued by debt collectors and he lacks the funds to comply. A confrontation with the landlord, his son quotes the landlord's argument, Arcimboldo reads: *'... how shall I believe you do not have the money to pay me? Because they are boasting through the whole market that you have lent them money. Therefore I ask you in your own interest not to appear shabby, you will not thus favor your own affairs.'* With a long sigh, knowing what's to come, Arcimboldo skips to the end of the letter, *'so a paltry amount, fifty scudi d'argento, will set me right. And when my promised profits come in I will repay you handsomely, this time I swear and promise, right now my hand lies on a statue of St. Ambrose, and God is my witness. I eagerly await your reply. Best wishes to you father, from your ever loving family, and your devoted son, Benedetto. Post script – perhaps one-hundred-fifty scudi will be a better amount, one never knows what emergencies may arise.'*

This Epiphany Day has seemed enchanted by the extraordinary and the unexpected; it had led him to believe his son's letter might have some of the same qualities. Hearing the usual and expected news from Milan has somewhat brought Arcimboldo back down to earth. Strangely, rather than feeling disgusted, he is relieved, and in fact, reassured by the calming predictability of his son's tangled affairs. It makes Arcimboldo feel that returning to Milan is the best thing to do, the safe, healthy and wholesome thing to do. He must move to the side of the walkway as far as he can to make room for a donkey pulling a small cart. He asks the servant guiding the donkey, "have you seen Cesare Ripa, do you know where he is?"

"Up ahead at the Summer Palace, My Lord. I'm delivering this to him."

To his right, Arcimboldo sees that the sgraffito façade of the Italianate Ball Games Court is brightly lit by torches, causing the deeply textured decorative surface to vibrate with shadow and light. Far up ahead, at the end of the walkway, the famous singing fountain is also lit, but unfortunately shrouded by snow and ice. This large and beautiful fountain, made from the finest bronze and bell metal, is richly adorned with motifs of foliage, mythological creatures, and ornamental faces. When the water spurts from the mascarons, the jets of water create a melodic, rhythmic sound as they fall on the bronze plate; a mellifluous 'singing' that can only be ascribed to perfect harmony between Natural magic and the skill of the artisan. These musical sounds can only be fully enjoyed if one is sitting below the level of the bronze basin. Regrettably, the Emperor's guests will not be able to enjoy this unique and delightful experience; and Arcimboldo must admit to himself that he is really only thinking of one guest, the Marchioness d'Olivan. This unusual woman has awakened something within him.

The mercurial nature of his mind has often surprised him, occasionally betrayed him, and always fascinated him; perhaps this is reflected in his paintings, his fondness for creating a mesh of separate components jostling one another, competing, fusing, seeking a unified meaning while at the same time proclaiming individuality. This contemplative walk through the Imperial gardens has led Arcimboldo deep within his heart and mind. He slows his pace further, allowing himself a few more moments of private thought – even though adventure and destiny lie literally within sight. There, behind the fountain, is the Summer Palace, bright as day, a beacon to the revelers and banqueters that will follow in his footsteps within the hour. Arcimboldo's uneasiness, beginning the night before, even before he was attacked, begins to identify itself in his consciousness.

The night before, he had felt something akin to dread, and he imagined it was the risk of losing his life in the course of the dangerous task ahead. The fear of dying had been replaced by despair that the attempt itself was a foolish endeavor, driven by the Emperor's insecurities and Giordano Bruno's superabundant egocentricity. *That* fear had been replaced by a foreboding that the unprecedented experiment would be a failure through an omission on his own part, and he would be diminished in the Emperor's eyes and the eyes of his companions. Recently he has become fearful of duplicity on the part of the Irishman, Edward Kelly. Now, Arcimboldo has a new clarity. These recent fears are minor fears, insignificant to him. His uneasiness is caused by the staggering realization that the experiment itself is no longer important to him, he does not care, certainly not in the way Rudolf and the others care. Arcimboldo has already received his reward through the work of preparation; creating the Emperor's Cosmos has exercised his creative Spirit, the skills of his eyes, hands, and brain. It has given him new insight into the inexhaustible diversity and complexity of the Natural World. There is no power or knowledge that the artist seeks so desperately that he must tear apart Nature's barriers to attain it. Preparing the Cosmos has led him to a profound respect for those barriers between the World of Man and the World of primal causes. Those barriers are what make us human, Arcimboldo believes, and he finds at this very late point, that he does not have a craving to be more than human. Simply human is perfectly enough for him. Being human is a state full of so much complexity, contradiction, and wonder that there is no need to be God as well.

On the steps up to the Summer Palace, Arcimboldo must dodge a flurry of last minute activity. Many, many soldiers of the Imperial Guard lounge under the arcade, good naturedly bantering with the servants and craftsmen who rush about with chairs, boxes, tools, planks, platters, rolls of fabric, swaths of greenery, stacks of dishes, and armfuls of candles. As Arcimboldo steps inside the Palace, it seems he has stepped *outside*, into a splendid garden. The walls and ceiling are festooned with holly, ivy, and evergreen boughs. Where they are not covered with vegetation they are decorated with colorful tapestries and painted surfaces of trompe l'oeil trickery – windows and arches looking out on lovely gardens, sublime landscapes, and enchanting grottoes. Even now, with an hour to go before guests arrive, the room is lit by hundreds of candles of every size and shape.

The stage for the pantomime play sits along the northern wall of the room; its area has been extended with forest-green curtains which (intentionally) conceal the stairway that leads up to the floor above. Cutting through the din of preparation (not overpowering but penetrating), come the unmistakable fulminations of Cesare Ripa, still at work! The man is tireless! His voice comes from behind the green curtain, and Arcimboldo looks for a way through or around the thick hanging cloth.

He finds and steps through an opening, and is spotted by his haggard looking assistant. Cesare stops what he is doing and calls out to Arcimboldo, "Too late, Giuseppe, you've just missed the sight of a lifetime... the ass has just gone upstairs!"

This causes a chorus of guffaws from the workers clustered around him, one of them cannot help but add, "by the Cross, what a sight that was! *And* he left a pile of shite on the stairs!" The man is rewarded by a cuff on the ear from Cesare, who says, "then you're the one to clean it! Get it done now, and I mean right now, by Jesu!"

Ignoring these strange comments, Arcimboldo speaks with feeling to his countryman, "Cesare, the room looks magnificent, you have done a prodigious job here!"

Cesare beams with pride, "I have made it, by the Holy Sacrament, with hardly a moment to spare. These blockheads will work behind this curtain tonight." He steps close to Arcimboldo. "You can trust them. They have been instructed. They will follow directions from you and only you."

Arcimboldo lays his hand on the man's shoulder. "You must be exhausted, my friend. Tell me what remains to be done and you may go."

Arcimboldo stops a servant carrying a tray, and looking under the covering cloth he sees, to his perfect delight, a steaming assortment of rolls and buns. Like a greedy child he grabs one, two, hesitates, then quickly replaces the cloth and nods his thanks to the frowning servant. He bends almost double to eat to avoid spilling crumbs on his ruff, then, his eyes rolling with pleasure as his hunger is placated, returns to the job at hand. He has forgotten his logbook, but Cesare has his, and they gather together with the Master of Servers, Master of Drink, Master of Candles, Master of the Play, and the Master of Music. These men are responsible for the teams that will produce tonight's banquet. They have all worked with Arcimboldo before, and the artist himself, as the Master of Entertainment, trusts them to do their jobs competently.

None of these assistants is aware of what will go on upstairs, but they know it is secret and crucially important to the Emperor. Fortunately, there are no issues or problems except for an actor who is too drunk to be allowed to perform, and the Master of the Play will take this man's place himself. The Master of Music, Phillipus de Monte will be particularly important, and so will the famous female singer from Mantua, Laura Peverara, known as *La Peperara* throughout Europe. Tonight *La Peperara* will sing *El Cant de la Sibil* during the Epiphany play. This haunting Catalan masterpiece is Rudolf's favorite piece of music and the Emperor has brought *La Peperara* here to sing it for his guests, (and as a background to his own alchemical transformation). Arcimboldo must now test to see if it can be heard in the room above when sung down here. He asks Master Phillipus to rehearse with his orchestra and *La Peperara* while he goes upstairs to listen.

On his way to the stairs Arcimboldo shakes Cesare's Ripa's hand and embraces his friend warmly.

He thanks him for brilliant work and dismisses him for the evening. The fiery but exhausted Italian seems reluctant to go, and Arcimboldo can well understand, having been in Cesare's place many times before. Cesare has created this magical world through an entire day of hard work, he is loath to leave it, he says he will just sit for a while on the stairs before he returns to the Palace. Arcimboldo expects him to try to stay for the entire evening, and smiling with understanding, leaves him sprawled there at the base of the staircase.

At the first floor landing two Imperial halberdiers come to attention. They stand just where Giordano Bruno delivered his exhortation to the Emperor, to 'think like God Himself'; this is an image that has been indelibly recorded within his Memory Palace, and it serves as a warning of what their fundamental mistake has been, an overreaching of the most dangerous kind. In German, he asks the halberdiers, "who is your Capitan tonight?"

"Capitain Morhof, my Lord."

"Where is he? You will be here throughout the night?"

"No, my Lord. We await the Capitain. He will bring new sentries with him."

Arcimboldo nods to the men, and pauses before the door; he collects his thoughts and his energy, breathes deeply, adjusts his clothing, checks again for crumbs, and knocks.

It is Count Rozmberk who opens the door. Behind him the room is very dark, the art is not lit, the fireplaces have burned low. Arcimboldo sees that there are candles burning around the alchemists' furnace in the center of the room, several men stand near it. He hears the strident tones of the Nolan, and answering, the raspy, subdued, breathless voice of the Englishman, Doctor John Dee; they speak in Latin. Rozmberk welcomes him, "Arcimboldus, this is a triumph! I feel like an unseasoned youth, I am atremble with excitement! Does the Emperor come?"

"No, My Lord. We still have some time. Is all well?"

Still smiling, Rozmberk nods, and stretches his arm and hand toward the men speaking in the depths of the room, "welcome to the School of Athens."

He refers to the famous painting by Raphael in the Apostolic Palace in Rome, labeled by the artist as *Causarum Cognitio,* but widely known as the *Disputa,* or the School of Athens. Raphael's enormous fresco shows all the greatest philosophers in history crowded around the central figures of Plato and Aristotle. Rozmberk points, of course, to our modern giants of Hermetic Philosophy, Giordano Bruno and John Dee. And, as Arcimboldo might have guessed, they are engaged in a dispute. He says to the Count, "I understand the ass is here already?"

Laughing, "that he is. The sight of him coming up the stairs was almost as unforgettable as this room!"

Arcimboldo is not relaxed enough to be amused, he merely grunts, "and he is... where?"

"There, Master Mont has him tied up by the treadmill."

"Good. We will begin immediately." Then he has a thought, he steps close to Count Rozmberk. "My Lord, purely by chance, I have spoken to an Englishwoman today. Hear this, you will be interested and amazed. Can you guess what the punishment in England is for fraud and forgery?"

The Count is mystified by what he hears and shakes his head no.

"The punishment for fraud and forgery in England is to have one's *ears* cut off... publically. And, in her own words, '*as a warning to those who would have dealings with him in the future*'. Chilling, no?"

The Count is agast. "You think... Kelly...?"

"Don't you?"

"*Der Teufel*! Have you told the Emperor?"

"I don't intend to. At this point... what could we do? But I will keep my eye on him, and, my Lord, perhaps you will assist me in this?"

"I will indeed. Good God... fraud and forgery!"

"Where is he now?"

"I'm not sure that I know."

"We will light the room. There is much still to do. But... first things first." Arcimboldo walks toward the alchemists furnace and the men around it.

"... so that God, considered absolutely, has nothing to do with us, but only as He communicates Himself by the effects of Nature, so that if He is *not* Nature itself, certainly He is the *nature* of Nature, and the *soul* of the Soul of the World... if He is not the very Soul itself!" Bruno finally must pause to breathe.

Dee's much weaker, pedantic voice takes up the argument, "He *does* communicate. The Symbol is the mysterious language of the Divine. Unless we know the names of things it is impossible to penetrate to the knowledge of the significance... except in the case of trivial images which general usage has made recognizable to everybody-"

"It is true that the stupid and senseless idolaters had no reason to laugh at the Magical and Divine worship of the Egyptians, who contemplated the Divinity in all things, and the diverse Divinities in Nature, all of which centered at last in one Deity of deities, the fountain of ideas above Nature itself."

"You refer to the absolute truths contained in Egyptian Symbols, their heiroglyphs?"

"I do."

"Consider, Nolanus, this famous passage from St. Thomas." Dee shifts from Latin to Greek. "Any truth can be manifested in *two* ways, by things or by words. Words signify things and one thing can signify another. The *Creator* of all things, however, can not only signify anything by words, but can also make one thing signify another. That is why the Scriptures contain a twofold truth. One lies in the things meant by the words used, that is the literal sense. The other in the way things become figures of other things, and in this consists the Spiritual sense."

"So do you consider a hieroglyph to be a word or a thing?"

Arcimboldo must interrupt this esoteric debate. He clears his throat and says, "Doctor Dee! A joyous Epiphany to you, sir. Well, here we are at last." He makes a short bow.

Dee bows stiffly. "My Lord Arcimboldus, joy of Epiphany to you. Yes, at last...we are here."

"You are *both* here?"

"Eh? You mean..."

"Your man, Kelly."

The frail looking English savant strokes his long, sharply pointed, and perfectly white beard thoughtfully, "Edward? Edward, I say! Where are you?" He peers around in the darkness.

"I am here, My Lord." And the man himself follows his voice into the light. Edward Kelly is dressed in a brownish suit of clothing more appropriate to a tradesman than a gentleman. His expressionless pale face does not wear beard or moustache but has gone several days without a shave. Long and stringy brown hair falls from a central parting to his shoulders. His lusterless brown eyes dart here and there and seem to miss nothing, yet never make direct contact with another's gaze. He carries Doctor Dee's famous black mirror. "I am preparing myself to speak with the spirits, My Lord."

"Maestro Arcimboldus has arrived."

Kelly and Arcimboldo exchange brief, miniscule bows. Arcimboldo examines him closely, Kelly does not look the Italian in the face, he looks down, humbly… or apparently so.

Arcimboldo says, "we will begin setting things in motion. It is better if you all stay here in the center of the room for now." He turns to Georg Erasmus Schwartzenau who has been sitting nearby, captivated (if not enlightened) by the learned discussion between Bruno and Dee. "Georg, may I ask for your assisstance once again? Would you mind helping Master Mont begin to light our Cosmos?"

"Of course, My Lord, what shall I do?"

"Master Mont will show you."

Hans Mont has joined the others around the alchemist's furnace. Arcimboldo walks to him and claps the handsome and virile young man on the shoulder. "Hans, you have been a tower of strength. Your rewards will be great. We are so near our goal. Will you begin – by the way, where is Bartolomeus?"

"He went to see his wife in the city, sir."

"He left the castle? When?"

"Oh, several hours ago, sir."

"Well… um…" Arcimboldo is slightly worried about this. "Hans, will you and Georg Erasmus begin to light everything. Begin at the top, use the ladders. The donkey is secure?"

"It is tied securely, My Lord."

"Good." He bows again to Doctor Dee, "excuse me just a moment, Doctor, I must speak privately with

Master Bruno." To Bruno he says, "Nolanus, kindly give me a moment of your time, this way, if you please."

As they walk away into the darkness, Bruno says in Italian, "You will scold me again, Giuseppe? What have I done now?"

Arcimboldo looks at him earnestly, "not a thing, my friend, not a thing. I can tell you that the Emperor is quite pleased with you, quite pleased. I do have some important news from the Emperor though, an important decision he has made." Bruno is waiting expectantly. Arcimboldo licks his lips nervously, steals a glance at the others in the distance, calculating how much they will be able to hear. "Now, Giordano, this is not my decision, please understand that from the start, and I don't say this to be tedious, but things have changed."

"Changed? Nothing can change, you know that. What do you mean?"

"Well... umm... you've seen the Leonardo? You approve?"

"Yes, it's perfect. What's changed?"

"Well... Chancellor Curtius is too ill to fulfill his role tonight, so the Emperor has chosen a replacement. The long and short of it is...he has chosen Katharina Strada, his mistress, you should know that she is the-"

"What! He invites his mistress? Why not have the ass take Curtius' part? Why not find a stray dog off the street? What can you possibly be thinking? This is-"

"Giordano, please! Keep your voice down. Let's discuss this calmly, you may find points of agreement. She is-"

"I will only agree that this is idiotic! I will leave... I will leave right now, I will not be associated with-"

"You will not leave, Giordano."

"You think not?"

"I realize you are upset, and rightfully so. You see, I do not criticize you. But you will not leave...you *may* not leave. If you leave this room, it is a certainty that the next room you see will be the Emperor's prison. He will not tolerate argument or independence from you or anyone else concerning this night's experiment. You must make the best of it, as we all must do."

Bruno is shifting from foot to foot in agitation, his gaze wildly scanning the room as if looking for escape – no doubt reflecting the actions of his brain. But he holds his peace for the moment.

"Please consider, Rudolf's mistress is *pregnant* with his child. Rudolf considers this extremely significant, and it is *overwhelmingly* important to him."

Bruno is still, he stares at Arcimboldo with full attention now. "She is pregnant?"

"Yes."

"With the Emperor's child?"

"I have said so."

Bruno closes his eyes and puts his hand to his chin, in intense inward reflection. "Mmm. Unexpected. Quite unexpected. There's precious little time for proper study of the matter... hmmm... however... it *may* be tolerable."

"See, it is not so bad."

"But this is not the way to do things. This is the very last minute. I should have been consulted. If we err here..."

Arcimboldo releases a long sigh of relief. Thank God.

"What did Doctor Dee say?"

"I have not told him yet, that is my next task."

Bruno is not complacent, but it seems he will accept the change in plans. His eyes begin to search the room again. Arcimboldo can see that the Nolan is too perturbed to receive the news about his immediate return to Wittenberg. He will keep that message until the experiment is concluded, and the three-hundred thalers for Bruno as well; it may perhaps sweeten that harsh and unwelcome message. The Nolan begins to walk left, then he strides right... what on Earth can the man be looking for? Suddenly, Bruno strides to a stand holding a large illuminated page from Cristoforo Landino's *De Anima;* he rips the parchment from its frame. Arcimboldo protests, "Giordano! What are you doing?"

"Incompetence! Error! Travesty! How much of this will I have to take before this becomes a complete farce!"

"For God's sake, what is the problem?"

"Look, is it not obvious? Landino's structural analogy of the Macrocosmus and Microcosmus...could you not even get this right?"

"Now wait, this is almost one-hundred years old... it comes from the Emperor's library, we didn't do this, it's Landino's own work. How can it be wrong?"

"Here, here, look. From Materia comes Natura, then Spiritus Mundanus, then Luna, Sol, the Planets, Stella Fixae, up to the Empyreum. Do you see? Where is Anima Mundanus?"

"And how should I know? I have no idea what you're talking about. This is Landino's own work, I say again, how can this be wrong?"

"Well, it is!" Bruno strides to the fireplace, and before Arcimboldo can stop him, he flings the parchment into the fire Hans Mont has just relit. The beautiful image of concentric circles in pale blue, gold, pink, and grey immediately catches an updraft and disappears over the flu, up the chimney.

Arcimboldo stands helpless, disbelieving what he has just seen, "Madonna! Are you mad! What have you done? By Christ, if the Emperor had seen that..." But the Nolan is no longer listening, he stalks away into the shadows, mumbling and cursing in Latin and Greek.

Arcimboldo hastily produces a scented lace handkerchief, wipes his brow and blows his nose. He feels as old as Landino's parchment at this moment. He cannot hear the slightest sound of music, perhaps they have stopped playing. Wearily he walks to the door and opens it; he hears the majestic sound of *El Cant de la Sibil*, The Song of the Sibyl, floating up the stairs. He closes the door. Silence. He opens it, music. A problem that must be resolved.

As the room becomes brighter and brighter, those who have only seen it in the dark are stupefied by the effect; Rozmberk, Dee and Kelly slowly turn in circles, looking up, down, swinging their heads right and left. Arcimboldo joins them near the central oven but he is ignored. Rozmberk gapes, his eyes move rapturously from one thing to another. Kelly is craning his neck, too distracted to notice his hair falling back. Arcimboldo can see the ugly stump of his right ear as it's exposed to the light. Dee speaks some words in English that are unknown to Arcimboldo. He looks at the artist and says in Latin, "Arcimboldus, I have argued that mathematics is the closest expression of the Divine... but in this moment of wonder, I concede to you the power of Art and Beauty, it can express things beyond all human language and experience. I can *feel* the Macrocosm around me... already! Edward, can you feel it? Can you sense the Spirit world?"

Arcimboldo hurriedly says, "you are gracious, Doctor Dee. May I distract you for a moment, I have a communication from the Emperor concerning this evening."

Dee composes himself, clasps his hands at his chest and focuses his intelligent gaze on Arcimboldo.

"Good Doctor, you know Chancellor Curtius well, I must tell you he is too ill to join us tonight. The

Emperor has chosen a replacement. Ahem... he has chosen Katharina Strada as-"

"Katharina Strada!" This comes from the usually taciturn Irishman.

"Ahem... yes, he chooses her above all others for this reason... and I must insist you be discreet with this knowledge, Katharina carries the Emperor's child."

"Katharina Strada is pregnant by the Emperor?"

"She is. And although it's a secret we are privileged to share, I can tell you that the Emperor is enormously proud. This decision of the Emperor's, and Katharina herself, are not to be taken lightly. I trust you don't feel it's unacceptable for our experiment?"

"*Very* interesting." Kelly speaks with something approaching enthusiasm.

Dee removes his black skull cap and runs a thin pale hand over his bald scalp, he opens his mouth, closes it, considers, and finally says, "an extraordinary improvement to this Cosmos. We could not have planned a more significant addition. Auspicious. Monumentally auspicious. I hope the Emperor will allow me to cast a horoscope at the soonest occasion."

Arcimboldo hopes Bruno has heard the Englishman's words in whatever corner he is sulking in. Feeling relieved, he says so, and tells his compatriots he will return shortly. He must go downstairs to see what can be done about the music.

As Arcimboldo reaches the base of the staircase, he sees Cesare Ripa is curled up sound asleep on the bottom step. Cesare's crew are playing cards and listening to the music, which is coming from the other side of the stage. He halts *La Peperara* and Phillipus de Monte's small orchestra, which consists of two cornetti, viol da gamba and bass viol da gamba, cittern, tabor, lute, sackbut and viol. He says, "beautiful as always Master Phillipus, and Signorina, bellissima! There is one detail we must work out. We cannot hear you upstairs."

*La Peperara* protests, "ah, no, Signore! You didn't tell me I would have to sing loud enough to be heard through walls! A curtain is bad enough! Madonna! This is not right. What would you have me do, destroy my voice for-"

"No, no, Signorina, not for all the world, your voice is a treasure. We will find a better place for you. You may relax, have a cup of wine..." he looks sternly at the musicians, "a *small* cup of wine. Master Phillipus, come with me, if you please."

Arcimboldo and the Master of Music stand in the middle of the room facing the stage; this is the area where the Emperor's guests will dance. To his right are the doorways to the dining room and a grand fireplace, to his left the doorway out to the gardens and another large fireplace. The chimneys of these fireplaces continue up to the floor above, and serve the fireplaces there as well. Arcimboldo knows from experience the sound will carry up these chimneys. "Phillipus, we can't hear a single note of your music upstairs, we will have to move you to a better spot. I'm thinking of placing you close to a fireplace, I believe the sound will carry better."

"What, stand in front of the fire? Arcimboldus-"

"No, listen, my friend, we will have the fire put out...of course. We will use this fireplace." He points to his left. The fireplace on the right is the one that has eaten Landino's parchment, he will avoid that one, he shudders with the memory. "You will have the servants put out the fire in this one, against the outside wall. Arrange your orchestra as close as you can in front of it, yes? You understand?"

Phillipus nods, he is not reluctant at all. He will be a part of the festivities and not hidden behind the curtain.

"Send a man upstairs and knock when you are ready again." Arcimboldo shakes his finger at the Master of Music, "and don't let the musicians drink too much!"

Upstairs once again, Arcimboldo takes a moment to marvel at the diversity of the hundreds of objects displayed throughout the Cosmos room. He stands before a series of tempera portraits by Octavius van Veen of Roman Emperors: Tiberius, Nero, Caligula, Galba, Vitellius, and Vespasian. To his right are watercolors of freshwater fish from the Danube: brown trout, whitefin gudgeon, and spined loach. To his left is a sketch on parchment of a wild European polecat and a domesticated ferret, and their prey: voles, rats, mice, and marmots.

He turns his attention to the live humans in the room. Hans Mont is placing the final few candles inside their glass bowls. Rozmberk wanders as if in a dream. Dee and Bruno are once again in deep conversation. Kelly fondles a golden statue from India, obviously a demon, with four arms, holding an hour-glass, a conch shell, a snake, and fire. The figure perches on one foot as if dancing, and appears to have a third eye in the middle of its forehead. This is a very Symbolic, and possibly, very dangerous object. Rudolf takes a great risk possessing this rare and un-Christian entity; nevertheless, he owns numerous strange and Symbolic statues, porcelains, ivories, and gemstones from India, Persia, China, Africa and the New World, all representative of the diversity of culture and religion across the globe.

Arcimboldo would like nothing better than to pause and admire his completed handiwork for much longer, however, time is now pressing upon him, he must keep in motion. "Gentlemen, my Lord Rozmberk, please stand near the alchemists' oven, we are about to untie the ass! Georg, move that ladder back. Hans, your assistance, if you please."

Against the eastern wall of the room, away from the racks, shelves, stands, and the giant wheels, a grey and black donkey is calmly standing near a treadmill. Arcimboldo and Hans Mont struggle to coax and pull the reluctant animal onto the treadmill and tie it in place. Mont hangs a basket of apples and carrots in front of the treadmill just out of reach of the animal's mouth; he snaps a carrot in half, gives half to the eager and hungry donkey and drops the other half into the basket. As reliable as clockwork (or perhaps more so) the animal follows its instincts, and the treadmill begins grinding away. The old Italian nimbly hops around his contraption with a beaker of oil and a wooden mallet, greasing gears and wheels, tapping and adjusting here and there. When he is satisfied he calls out, "here we go! Clear the wheels! Hans, engage the gear."

A clunk is followed by a rasping chatter; the treadmill slows considerably, and then the animal, machine, and sound stop altogether. A pause. Hans smacks the ass on the rump to start the stubborn creature moving again, another half carrot fuels its enthusiasm; the treadmill picks up speed and shortly afterward a muffled grinding sound is heard throughout the room. The twelve foot wheels that hold hundreds of pieces of artwork on their fronts and backs slowly, slowly, slowly start revolving. There is a collective gasp from the group of men around the central oven as they see the six giant wheels surrounding them begin to sweep around. "Hans!

Grease that axel... again... enough! Loosen the brake all the way. Now, don't touch a thing!" There is crash as a tripod stand is knocked over by a slowing revolving wheel, Arcimboldo quickly rushes to the spot and sets it up correctly. Another stand must be moved six inches. He snatches another one out of the way of a ponderous wheel in the nick of time. Arcimboldo's eyes, hands, and attention are everywhere at once; he has no time to marvel at his own cleverness, however he feels a flush of excitement as he sees his scheme working just as he imagined... no, this is truly beyond imagination!

The Count has fallen onto his knees, tears in his eyes, and whispers a prayer in Latin – *"Celi Regina me protege queso ruina"*, meaning 'Queen of Heaven, protect me, I beseech thee, from harm'. John Dee clutches Edward Kelly's arm and shoulder, and, for once, the Irishman is too distracted to shrug him off. Young Georg Erasmus Schwartzenau laughs delightedly and childishly claps his hands. Giordano Bruno stands as though turned to stone, his hands raised palms out, as though either to defend himself or to bestow a benediction. Although it is cold in the room, Arcimboldo is perspiring; he stands back and watches; where is the flaw? where is the problem? where is the imperfection? My God! There are none... it is incredible, it is magnificent, it is perfection!

He has forgotten to put out the fire in the westernmost fireplace. As he attends to this he shouts, "stay where you are! Mind the wheels! Hans, a little more brake now, just the smallest amount... and so! Just so, right there, hold now!" And at this point, Arcimboldo hears music, The Song of the Sibyl, emanating from the large marble fireplace. The sackbut and cornetti are loudest; *La Peperara's* voice has somewhat less than its usual crystal clarity, yet it can be heard. Arcimboldo's confidence is lifted by this test, the various components are coming together very well; he has satisfactorily combined sight, sound, and movement; the incense burners will not need to be tested, that element is a certainty that will be ready when the actual need arises. It is time now to light the alchemists' oven. As Arcimboldo calls to Hans Mont to halt the donkey and brake the wheels, there is a knock on the door. Upon opening the door he sees one of Cesare's workers, trying to peer beyond Arcimboldo as he says, "as you wanted, the musicians are at it again, My Lord."

"Yes, I know, tell them we can hear them, all is well, they may stop now." He quickly shuts the door on the fellow's astonished face, then opens it again with the admonition, "tell Master Phillipus to keep the musicians away from the wine... tell him I said so, it is on *his* head!"

Arcimboldo's sixty year old legs and his aching back must have a rest. He asks Hans to bring him a stool and he sits near the oven. Count Rozmberk is wiping his face with a large handkerchief; he does not speak but grasps Arcimboldo's hand and shakes it vigorously. The Nolan is looking at him with an expression of respect that he has never seen on his friend's face before. Arcimboldo speaks to the Dee and Kelly in Latin, "gentlemen, would you be so kind as to start the alchemical fire in the oven, I believe you have experience with this?"

"Not oven, My Lord, *athenor*. We are men of science, we must be meticulously correct."

"Very well, athenor."

The alchemist's athenor, or oven, that has been built in the center of the room, is a circular structure of brick, approximately four feet high. It is artistically patterned with spiraling layers of rowlock laid bricks;

interspersed along the layers are small windows plugged with cast iron doors. These small doors have been stamped with Hebrew letters, astrological signs, and alchemical images. The presence of these metal doors allows the alchemist to control the airflow and the heat within the structure. As Kelly inserts wood and sets it aflame, Dee explains to Arcimboldo, "we begin with cedar, which is an excellent starter. You will see many sparks, but do not be alarmed, when the cedar is well lit Edward will use beech and oak, which are far more difficult to light but burn much hotter and do not spark." The cedar creates a delightful odor around them. Dee continues, "now, there are certain times when we will require more smoke, and then we will use larch."

Kelly examines the baskets of wood provided, "there's no larch wood, Doctor. Is this spruce?" He asks Arcimboldo.

"It is. We couldn't find larch, but I believe you said spruce would do well, yes?"

"There are many more sparks and less heat with spruce, but it will serve, yes."

"Master Kelly, as chief alchemist, you will keep the fire as you see fit. Where would you like Master Mont to leave the baskets of wood?"

"Mmm, right there. And I will need a small table for my other tools and books."

"Yes, we will have stands for the books." Arcimboldo calls to Hans Mont, "Hans! Would you come here, I want you to assist Master Kelly with his setting up." He stands and arches backward with his hand in the small of his back. He breathes deeply, and attempts to chase away his fatigue and stiffness. "Also, Hans, set up the tripods at the cardinal directions and place my paintings, you know the correct placement. I will go downstairs to see about Bartolomeus, I'll return before dinner begins. Gentlemen... good luck to us all." He asks Count Rozmberk, "will you await the Emperor downstairs, my Lord?"

As if it is a difficult decision to make, the Count says, "um... well, I suppose I must." With many glances over his shoulder, he follows Arcimboldo out of the Cosmos.

Downstairs, activity has all but ceased. The actors are costumed and waiting behind the curtain. Servants line the walls ready for command. Arcimboldo's assistants stand near the door, and the Italian joins them. The Master of Servers says, "the Emperor's valet has just come to tell us the procession has left the castle, they will be here soon." Arcimboldo nods in acknowledgement. He is struck with a sudden realization: this is the last time he will play this role – a role he has played countless times during his adult life, overseer of royal pageantry, marshal of tournaments, coronations and jousts, principal provider of noble pleasures and delights. He commands, "Master Marco, assemble a basket of bread, cheese, olives, water, and wine, and have someone deliver it to the room upstairs. Do this as soon as possible. Now, let's open the doors fully and stoke up the fire. Gentlemen, be attentive and we will have success. Master Phillipus, you may begin now with a pavane, play loudly. When all the guests have entered you will play a courante, but softly. You will cease when the Emperor speaks, look to my signal, I will let you know." To the Master of Drink he says, "Master Martin, when the Emperor finishes speaking you'll have your men begin serving... wait until he is fully seated before anyone stirs. Very well."

Giuseppe Arcimboldo and Vilem Rozmberk stand on the steps of the Summer Palace looking west through the Imperial gardens. The sky above has cleared of clouds, and a moonless but star laden

Bohemian night graces the Emperor's Epiphany feast. Behind the artist and the Count, the Imperial Guard have taken places all along the walls of the Summer Palace; an imposing display, with seven foot halberds at perfect attention, morions gleaming in the torchlight, and long military cloaks hanging in sculptured folds. In the distance, Arcimboldo can see a double line of flickering lights snaking along the walkway, the Chamberlain has been as good as his word and marshaled servants with torches to flank the royal entourage.

"Here they come." Arcimboldo sticks his head back through the door and calls out, "Master Phillipus, have your cornetti stand here by the door. Play loudly."

The Count's thoughts are still in the room upstairs. "Arcimboldus, how much *is* there exactly in your Cosmos?"

"Exactly?"

"Have you really gathered an image of every living thing?"

"Everything that grows in the ground, walks, crawls, flies, or swims in Europe; everything that is known in Pliny, Dioscorides, Servetus, Mattioli, and Villaneuve. Plus many novel creatures and plants from Africa, Asia, and the New World." Arcimboldo momentarily closes his eyes and scans his Memory Palace. "They are contained in one-thousand one-hundred and ninety-six illustrated images."

"By Apollo! One-thousand one-hundred-"

"Of course, that does not include statuettes, object d'art, cosmological diagrams, and transformative artificiosa-"

They hear the sound of horses approaching, and Arcimboldo is both surprised and relieved to see Bartolomeus Spranger riding behind one of the mounted soldiers. The men dismount, and a group of elegantly dressed Hartschire calvary officers bound up the steps. Arcimboldo asks, "Captain Morhof?"

An officer strikes his arm across his chest by way of salute and bows smartly, "My Lord. We are late, beg pardon." To his subordinate officers he says, "take your positions."

"Captain, I am Arcimboldus. Joy of Epiphany to you, sir. Do you understand I am to command the sentries upstairs on the first floor?"

"I have been instructed so, My Lord. I will place them in a moment."

"You will be here in the Palace all night?"

"All night, my Lord."

"Very good. We will speak again shortly."

With concern, Arcimboldo sees Bartolomeus Spranger stagger up the stairs. He is disheveled and smudged with soot. His face is grim. "Bartolomeus, how is it with you, sir? Your wife and family are safe? Your house, your property?"

"Arcimboldus! Such madness! Those Spanish bastards!" The Dutch artist shouts this even though Count Rozmberk and many soldiers stand nearby listening curiously.

Arcimboldo's heart sinks as he pulls his friend to the side. Quietly but urgently he asks, "Sancta Maria, what has happened?"

Spranger takes a deep breath and attempts to smooth his wild hair; he has lost his cap, his ruff is tattered and blackened, his hands are filthy. "My wife is safe, praise God, and I believe my house will survive as well. But the madness of the Tercio's soldiers is diabolical!"

"What? Tell me!" Arcimboldo seeks to hold eye contact with his distracted friend by grabbing his shoulders and bringing his face to within several inches; he can smell the sourness of panic and fury on

Spranger's breath. Count Rozmberk, with growing curiosity, edges closer to listen to Spranger's report.

"The soldiers, on the command of their officers, prevent Catholic homeowners from putting out the fires until the blaze has spread to all their Protestant neighbors! The frantic families must watch their homes burn! And Protestants, both innocent *and* guilty, must stand by while their homes *also* ignite and burn. The soldiers keep them from putting out the fires with curses and blows!"

"My God!" Arcimboldo is riveted with horror.

"The tactics of the Duke of Alva! They treat Prague like they do to the occupied cities of Holland! Shame! Shame!" This is from Count Rozmberk who stands by, agog at the news. He refers to the Iron Duke, the man the King of Spain has tasked with subduing the Protestants in the rebellious provinces of the Netherlands. The officers of the Prague Tercio are all veterans of that horrible conflict.

"Yes, there is no doubt where the Spanish officers have learned their lessons. Barbaric! Cruel beyond belief! The city is ready to explode!"

"Does the Emperor know this?"

"How should I know, for Christ's sake?"

"Bartolomeus, go upstairs, clean and compose yourself. Drink some wine. Think yourself lucky, your family is safe. We will discuss this with Rudolf when the time is appropriate. We can do nothing right now. Go upstairs."

Arcimboldo looks for a tall man in Imperial livery who stands nearby in the snow; he motions to this man to come closer. "Master Tomas Rackerby? You may begin the fireworks now."

Unfortunately, because of the snow, only one in ten of the prepared rockets actually works. Ordinarily, this would set Arcimboldo fuming, however, he hardly notices, his mind is far away. When he sees the Emperor leading the procession several hundred feet away, he quickly reenters the Summer Palace and walks to the dais set up against the south wall, facing the stage and dance floor. Three chairs sit on this platform. The tallest and most regal chair has the Imperial scepter resting on it. Arcimboldo takes the scepter and returns to the steps outside.

  The Emperor walks with the Tuscan Grand Duke and the French Duc d'Aumale. He is dressed in a formidable armor breastplate of red gold patterned with the Habsburg double-headed eagle in blackened silver. The red gold pauldrons on his shoulders are sculpted as snarling lion heads. A fillet of gold rests on his head, and a magnificent black and white ermine cloak trails behind him. The Emperor's bodyguard and the servants carrying flambeaux split off to the right and left as he mounts the steps to the Summer Palace. Arcimboldo steps forward, bows very low, and with both hands he raises the scepter for the Emperor to take. Rudolf grasps the scepter, turns and flourishes it as if to marshal his guests, he then passes into the Summer Palace. Some chatting pleasantly, some looking around with wonder, some huffing and puffing from the long walk, the Emperor's forty-odd guests follow him inside.

  The Emperor of the Holy Roman Empire stands alone on the dais in the Summer Palace. His guests stand before him on the dance floor, looking up at him expectantly. Arcimboldo motions to the Master of Music, patting his hand downward, and the music softens. Rudolf holds his Imperial scepter casually in his left hand; he steps forward with his right leg and raises his right hand elegantly before him. Arcimboldo now holds his palm toward Master Phillipus and pushes forward, the music stops abruptly. The

Emperor speaks in the impeccable and formal Castilian he was taught from the time he was a child, "The Holy Roman Empire welcomes you to Prague, to Hradcany Castle, and to our Feast of the Epiphany. Honored guests, join us in this evening of festivity and entertainment. We are privileged to see our esteemed cousins, the Grand Duke of Tuscany, Ferdinando de Medici, and the Princess of France, Christina of Lorraine, in our company; please join us." The Duc d'Aumale and Cardinal Guise escort Christina to the dais. Ferdinando is accompanied by his brother, Cardinal Giovanni de Medici, and Vincenzo Gonzaga, Duke of Mantua.

Rudolf may be melancholy, secretive, and insecure, but when he is called on to speak publically one would never know it. He is articulate, loud and clear, and accompanies his words with graceful gestures. His years of training at the royal court in Madrid have not been wasted on him. The Emperor concludes, "honored guests, tonight we celebrate the announcement of the coming of our Saviour, Jesus Christ, to the Gentile World; and the visitation, adoration, and obeisance of those three Kings, the Three Magi, the Three Wise Men. Lords and Ladies, please, join us in a dance!" Arcimboldo points to Master Phillipus and the orchestra strikes up a lively courante. Rudolf sits in his central seat and motions to Ferdinando and Christina to join him on either side. Servants begin to circulate with trays of glasses. The guests mill about, laughing, talking, and some begin to dance. The evening's entertainment has begun.

Arcimboldo surveys his realm, as it were, and all is well. The Summer Palace is beautiful, the guests are happy, and Rudolf... well, Rudolf appears to watch the dancing, but Arcimboldo, who knows him well, sees that he has withdrawn into his own mind and imagination. Christina of Lorraine and the Grand Duke talk over and around him as though he is not there. The two Cardinals, de Medici and Guise, stand behind Rudolf's chair in solemn conversation. Vincenzo Gonzaga and the Duc d'Aumale listen with interest to Ferdinando as he describes his capital city, the heart and soul of his kingdom, Florence, to Christina. The Princess had earlier reminded Arcimboldo of the Moon, now, there is no doubt she is the Sun. She wears a gold silk gown resplendent with seed pearls and intricately embroidered patterns. Her blonde hair is wound about in a complicated design and interwoven with golden ribbons. Her earrings and necklace appear to be honey-colored topaz fixed in heavy gold settings. She is magnificent, and Ferdinando can hardly take his eyes off her.

Arcimboldo spares a moment to search the room for the Marchioness d'Olivan. He sees she is dancing, currently forming graceful poses with the Duc de Mayenne. Her dress is made of blood-orange silk interwoven with threads of green; each movement reveals another shimmering shade or combination of the two colors. From her waist, the skirt blossoms out in the most modern bell-shaped Farthingale style. Her puffed sleeves are slashed and reveal a deep, golden-green underlayer of silk. For jewelry she wears tourmaline, garnets, and orange sapphires accented with brilliant emeralds; her hazel-green eyes now shine emerald-like as well.

Arcimboldo notices Doctor Hagecius in conversation with a rich German burgher and Herr Wolfgang Furboch, Secretary of the Privy Council. As the Master of Entertainment approaches, he hears them speaking in German.

"Ist's bis Dreikönigs kein Winter, kommt keiner dahinter."

"Well, that doesn't apply this year," answers the Doctor. The others laugh and nod. They are exchanging *Bauernregel*, rhyming sayings, known as 'farmer's rules'. Secretary Furboch has just said, 'if there hasn't been any Winter (weather) until Epiphany, none is coming afterward.'

Arcimboldo snatches an elegant crystal vessel off a passing servant's tray. Holding his glass of golden liquid high, he quotes, *"Dreikönigsabend hell und klar, verspricht ein gutes Weinjahr,"* meaning: 'if the eve of Epiphany is bright and clear, it foretells a very good wine year'. The others laugh and nod again, saying, "good! Good, My Lord!" They all toast and drink.

To Hagecius, Arcimboldo says, "Doctor, have you met the French Princess yet? You'll get along with her splendidly, she's quite interested in astronomy and Celestial phenomena."

"Truly?"

"Shall I introduce you?"

"I'd be delighted! Gentlemen, excuse me."

They begin to cross the room, but Arcimboldo pulls Doctor Hagecius off to one side. "Thaddeus, tell me this, you know Dee and Kelly, you let them use that house of yours in Old Town when they lived here in Prague... do you trust Edward Kelly?"

"I'm not going to meet the Princess?"

"Yes, of course! You jest I see. But tell me, I'm in earnest, can the man be trusted?"

"There's trust... and then there's *trust*. The man is gifted. Perhaps he's a channel for spirits... I cannot say, but certainly he has a gift for seeing beyond what is obvious. I appreciate his talents, but is this a measure of trust? No, it has nothing to do with trust. A man may be a scoundrel and still be gifted. I am fascinated by-"

"Can we trust him in our endeavor? Can the Emperor trust him?"

"I must say again, and I see you *are* in earnest, trust is not the issue. We can *use* him. The Emperor can *use* him. There is no one like him that I know of...so what would you have me say? He is not a priest or a money lender, he is a skryer, a seer. I will whisper this in your ear... *a necromancer... a conjurer... an alchemist*! Without a doubt, he is necessary to the Emperor's plans. If he shows he cannot be trusted in certain essential ways, if he is merely a cozener...he will pay dearly."

"A cozener...yes, that's exactly what worries me. Ahem...you know he has no ears?"

"I do, yes."

"How did this happen?"

"He forged deeds to properties in Lancaster, England. Many years ago. Does this make him less gifted as an alchemist?"

Arcimboldo wipes his forehead with a handkerchief. "No... yes. Look, I understand what you're saying, although, had I known this earlier, I may have come to a less sanguine conclusion than you have, dear friend. However, I understand what you say. Let us move forward. A second topic before we accost the Princess. Have you heard about Curtius, and his replacement?"

Hagecius looks more concerned than he did about Kelly, he twists his head right and left and briefly massages his neck, "*another* philosophical conundrum you present me with. On the one hand, it *is* delightfully appropriate for our conception of a complete Cosmos. On the other hand, a grave health risk for woman and child. I am irresolute as to what I should tell the Emperor... therefore I tell him exactly what he wants to hear."

"Strange. That is Vilem's conclusion exactly."

"Ah ha! Not yours though, I take it?"

"I no longer know what to think. This all comes at the last moment, there's hardly time for sober reflection." Arcimboldo shakes his head and touches the ruby in his pocket. "Come, Doctor, you are sure to be warmly received by the Princess."

Having played several dance tunes, Master Phillipus now has *La Peperara* sing a song made popular just last year, *La Mantovana*. Putting the orchestra among the audience has proved to be an advantageous adjustment. *La Peperara* is captivating; her hands speak as volubly as her mouth. As she sings, she continuously forms shapes with her hands and arms, gracefully, imaginatively, accenting her songs. One minute she appears to be holding a large ball, the next minute she is caressing a lover, now she balances something in her hand, now she flings it away. She sings, "*fuggi, fuggi, fuggi da questo cielo; fuggi, fuggi, dolente cor!*" With her raised arms and hands she perfectly mimics a person about to flee in terror.

Arcimboldo and Hagecius approach the dais. Arcimboldo nods a greeting to Atlas, who stands unobtrusively off to the side, but always within sight of the Emperor. Rudolf appears to be studying the architecture of the ceiling. Speaking in French, Ferdinando is telling Christina, "she sang this at the Accademia in Florence last year, it was a sensation, it has been copied continuously since then."

"I have heard of your Accademia. You Florentines love Plato, don't you?"

Ferdinando looks over his shoulder quickly at the two Cardinals, he leans forward confidentially, "it is Neo-Platonism that is taught at the Accademia, madame. My ancestor, Cosimo de Medici, allowed that immortal genius, Marsilio Ficino, to establish the

Accademia to study the lost knowledge of the ancients. It is an adornment to our venerable city that I am supremely proud of."

Rudolf notices Arcimboldo and Hagecius standing in front of them, his eyes and attention come back into focus, "My Lord Ferdinando, here is another famous son of Italy, may I introduce Lord Josephus Arcimboldus." Arcimboldo bows respectfully.

The Grand Duke nods toward Arcimboldo, and genially responds, "we have never met, but we *have* corresponded, have we not, Maestro? I must admit to you, Your Majesty, I have often tried to lure him away from you and this city, but his loyalty to you is steadfast."

All laugh pleasantly, except, of course, Rudolf, who merely says, "mmm hmmm."

Arcimboldo smiles engagingly, "I am glad you enjoy, Signorina Peverara, My Lords, My Lady."

"She is the Muse herself!"

"Ah, Euterpe, the Muse of music! Yes, you are right, she is the very thing!"

Arcimboldo clears his throat and looks toward Rudolf, but the Emperor stares into space, lost in thought. The Italian will introduce Hagecius himself. "Your Highnesses, may I present Doctor Thaddeus Hagecius, famous in his own right as astronomer, mathematician, and physician. No astrological prognostication may be printed in Prague without the approval of the good Doctor here."

Christina exclaims, "our greatest astronomer! I am very pleased to meet you, sir. Your study of the Stella Nova in Cassiopeia led me to my fondest passion!"

Hagecius blushes and cranes his neck nervously, "tut, tut, tut... that was back in 1572, madame."

Ferdinando looks cautiously back and forth between Christina and Hagecius. "And that passion is...?"

"Why, astronomy, My Lord."

"Oh, I see..." spoken with relief, "and you refer to the Constellation of Cassiopeia?"

"Naturally! Oh, to discover a new star! If only I had been older when that phenomenon happened! How did you find it?"

Warming to his favorite subject, Hagecius begins, "well, I was observing Cassiopeia, that area known as the 'bending of the flank', and right above those stars Flexura and Ilia..."

Arcimboldo bows and backs away, leaving the group around the dais in astronomical conversation.

A minor commotion is going on near the stage, an evergreen bough has accidently caught fire, not an uncommon occurrence, but the Master of Candles and his assistants are dealing with it in a satisfactory manner. Arcimboldo knows he should circulate among his assistants before he goes upstairs again. Beginning with the Master of Candles, Arcimboldo commends the man for his prompt response to the accident; he suggests it is time to burn some pleasant and subtle incense, such as styrax with cedar, to mask the burning smell. He visits the Master of Music and commends *La Peperara*, telling her she has found great favor with their Highnesses. He instructs Master Phillipus, "beginning in about ten minutes, you will pick up the pace, play some saltarellos, and make the last number before dinner a lavolta. I will advise you as to the timing. When the guests are called to table you will stop playing. Look to me, I will stand in that doorway, I will signal you when to begin again, and tonight we have something special planned, when I signal you, you will immediately play a hunting fanfare.

This is understood? Very good. Then, during the meal, you will play some toccatas and ricercar... alternate with madrigals; our guests are very sophisticated, you may be as modern as you like."

Arcimboldo wanders into the adjacent dining room seeking the Master of Servers. This large room has been similarly decorated as an indoor garden. The dining tables form a squared off U shape, with the central bar furthest away from the entry doors; Rudolf and his favored guests will sit along one side of this table. The two flanking tables are set with chairs on both sides. The tables are covered in the whitest imaginable Flemish lace, and the crystal, silver, and gold table settings gleam in the dazzling candle light. Affixed to the entry wall, facing the Emperor and his most important guests, are four paintings, Arcimboldo's paintings, the series known as the Four Seasons. Several private conversations are taking place in the relative quiet of this room; among them are the Spanish ambassadors, Don Guillen de San Clemente and Bernardino de Mendoza.

The Master of Servers is found here with his staff, waiting instructions; Arcimboldo tells this man, "Master Marco, you may send men now to get the boar and the fish, we will eat in about half an hour. Who will serve the boar to the Emperor?"

"I will do that myself, My Lord."

"You have the bow and arrow?"

"It is behind the Emperor's chair."

"Very good. Look to me for a signal before you open the boar, I will be in that doorway."

Arcimboldo approaches the two Spaniards. He bows respectfully, it is returned by Don Guillen; Mendoza offers him the barest suggestion of a nod. The surly look on the man's waxen face somehow becomes worse, he looks as though he has a very bad taste in his mouth, "I will return to the dance, Don Guillen. Until dinner then." And the man stalks off.

Arcimboldo comments to San Clemente, "I believe that man dislikes me. Strange! I have never seen him before in my life."

Don Guillen sighs, "be very careful of him, Giuseppe, he knows you have Giordano Bruno here...somewhere."

Arcimboldo tries to keep his surprise from showing in his face. "Well... and would that be any business of his?"

"Rudolf has promised both the Pope and the King of Spain to banish that heretic from the Empire... and the English alchemists as well. And yet..."

"Don Guillen, that is the Emperor's business, and no matter what he may have promised Sixtus or Philip, it is his business *alone*. In spite of the shameful way your King manipulates the Emperor and the citizens of Prague, Rudolf is still sovereign ruler of this Empire. Who he invites into his capital is his prerogative *entirely*. Certainly it is not the business of the Spanish ambassador to France! And I hope, my friend, you will not try to make it your business either."

San Clemente does not answer, so Arcimboldo adds, "or do you?"

Finally, reluctantly, the ambassador answers, "why would you even ask that, my friend? You know full well that we are alike, you and I, we simply do what we are told. And if we have a clever idea of our own, we make sure we allow someone above us to take credit for it. Why question things when we really do not wish to know the answer? Why torture ourselves over unpleasant things we cannot change? We serve the most powerful men in the World, and we have for most of our lives. We are, you and I, when all is said and done, merely servants... we are pawns in a much, much larger game that is not ours to win or lose."

"Well, I thank you for your frankness. Let *me* be honest with *you* – I assure you, Don Guillen, as a friend, what the Emperor does... *tomorrow*... has nothing to do with the Pope or your King." Arcimboldo lies. "It is a harmless diversion, you know his strange conceits and fancies. There is nothing in the least for you to worry about."

"Hmm. Well... I will leave you with a warning, because you are my friend, and I dislike that man Mendoza probably as much as you do. He is exceedingly dangerous. He has resources far beyond his diplomatic status. He is Philip's agent in France for the King's interventionist foreign policy, he is the agent and paymaster for the Holy League, and his agenda does not stop at the French borders."

Arcimboldo now looks every bit as surprised as he feels. "This is... I cannot say..."

"King Philip sends money, through Mendoza, directly to the Guise faction to fund the League. He encourages them to try, through popular riots, assassinations, and the spreading of false information, to undercut any moderate parties in France that offer a policy of rapprochement and compromise with the Protestants." San Clemente nervously peers over Arcimboldo's shoulder into the next room. He leans forward and speaks quietly and quickly. "Moreover, Mendoza views Rudolf as no better than a heretic, he would have you all rooted out and crushed like an infection. So I repeat, be very, very careful, and counsel your masters to be likewise. We have spoken too long. Until later, Giuseppe."

Arcimboldo wipes perspiration off his brow even though he feels chilled. He tries to calm himself and refocus on those mundane things that are his responsibility. He cannot be seen, at this point, running to Rudolf, or Trautson, or Dietrichstein, or any of the other ministers. He does intend, however, to find Capitan Morhof immediately. He hurries through the door to the dancing room. *La Peperara* is singing the lively and very popular canzonetta, *Zefiro Torna*, written by the young Milanese, Claudio Monteverdi, Court musician to the Duke of Mantua.

"*Pardonnez-moi, Monsieur... vous ne dancez pas?*"

Arcimboldo hears this French spoken with a charming lilt, and knows immediately who it is. He tries to wipe away the somber and anxious expression he knows he wears on his face, and turning, says, "Marchioness, it is delightful to see you again! Your dress is beautifully harmonious, it reminds me of a persimmon tree on a fine Autumn morning."

"And just my dress, sir?"

"You are beautifully harmonious from head to toe!"

"You will not dance with me?"

"Madame, the passing years have stolen my grace on the dance floor. You have my regrets and apologies." Arcimboldo bows gallantly. "Even more, I regret that I cannot spend time in conversation. There are important details needing my attention."

Petulantly she says, "but you have promised to explain your paintings! I see they are in the other room, just as you said they would be. Speaking of fruit, Monsieur, I find your painting of Summer to be my favorite."

"Madame, my greatest wish would be to do that right now. But, alas, the consequences would be most unpleasant. Again, forgive me for being burdened with responsibilities in the midst of this gaiety. I promise absolutely that we will speak of the paintings as soon as dinner is completed. My promise!" Arcimboldo holds his hand to his heart and smiles as charmingly as circumstance allows.

After the briefest of pauses, during which she purses her lips, the Marchioness answers, "*very well*. It is a promise. I will be patient." And she whirls around and merges again into the crowd of revelers.

Arcimboldo steps outside into the bracing air and walks along the arcaded porch. Although Chancellor Curtius is ill, the Emperor and Marshal Trautson must realize who Mendoza is, their intelligence network is formidable; there is no need for him to be involved, and yet his anxiety for Bruno's safety, his own safety – that of all the Emperor's secret group, is great. He stops to ask a soldier in German, "do you know where Captain Morhof is?"

By way of answer, the halberdier points down the arcade to several officers shelling nuts and tossing the husks out into the garden. Arcimboldo walks to the men, "Captain, do you have time now to accompany me upstairs?"

Captain Morhof stuffs the remains of his snack into a pocket and smacks his hands clean. "Of course, My Lord."

Arcimboldo notices both Ambassador Mendoza and the Marchioness watching him as he reenters with the officer. He does not speak again until he has passed behind the green curtain. "Captain, it's going to be imperative that we keep all curious persons from passing beyond that curtain, and especially, we must keep anyone from coming upstairs. The Emperor considers this of the highest importance. That's why these men loiter here. They have been instructed."

"I understand, My Lord."

"I will instruct the sentries in your presence so we have no confusion as to their duties."

Cesare Ripa is gone, Arcimboldo is glad, this event has become complicated enough. He stops and holds up a hand to halt the Captain as well. He notices a man in a red gold breastplate with lion faced pauldrons on his shoulders sitting among Cesare's crew; he is watching them play cards while he eats a large sausage. The man has his back to Arcimboldo, so he doesn't notice the Italian coming up behind him. Arcimboldo snorts in frustration, and brusquely slaps the sausage out of his hand. "I have told you, you lout, that you must *eat less*! By Saint Christopher, we'll never get you out of that armor!"

The man turns indignantly; in truth, the armor looks painfully tight on his stout frame. There are snickers from the others sitting with him. His mouth is too full of sausage to protest, so Arcimboldo continues quickly in Czech, "keep your damned mask on, your mouth shut, and your eyes open! You have the easiest job in Prague, and if you can't do it properly you'll be on your way to the silver mines in Kutna Hora by morning! And that goes for the rest of you too; mouths shut, eyes open!"

This man in armor is the Emperor's double, Valentin Soucek; he has been enlisted to play Rudolf's role in the coming pantomime play of the visitation of the Three Magi. He must convince the guests that the Emperor is on stage or waiting behind the stage while, in reality, Rudolf will be upstairs transforming himself into an alchemist *par excellence*. Arcimboldo's patience is stretched rather thin and he glares at the group of men. "You know what this man does here," he puts his hand on Soucek's shoulder, "you have been chosen for discretion, if not intelligence, so look to it, your job is crucial to the Emperor's plans, do not disappoint him! You will keep Master Soucek here, in careful disguise, for the duration of the evening. Do not speak to anyone; with the exception of myself, this officer, and the Emperor; do not let anyone other than the actors behind this curtain, *especially* if they are speaking French or Spanish. Consider these instructions as coming from the Emperor's mouth itself. You can choose to be either rewarded for your compliance, or punished for your foolishness."

One man raises his hand and Arcimboldo impatiently nods at him, he says, "My Lord... com-pli-ance? Is that some kind of tool? 'Cuz I didn't bring-"

"Just do the job we've asked you to do. Do your job. Do you understand?"

The man nods with comprehension. Arcimboldo gives Soucek a last stern look, and climbs the stairs with an amused Captain Morhof at his side.

At the top of the stairs, with Captain Morhof listening closely, Arcimboldo counsels the sentries on the importance of security and secrecy. No one is to be allowed to knock on the door unless they are accompanied by either Arcimboldo or the Emperor himself. There are no exceptions whatsoever. He dismisses the Captain who salutes and begins down the stairs, but Arcimboldo calls him back, "Captain Morhof, there is a man downstairs with the French, he is the Spanish Ambassador to France. He must be watched at all times; if he leaves the building he is to be followed. I will tell Marshall Trautson I have tasked you with this, and you will report to the Marshall at the end of the evening. I thank you, sir, joy of Epiphany to you."

Captain Morhof salutes again and descends the stairs. Arcimboldo knocks and is admitted by Georg Erasmus Scwartzenau.

"Thank you, Georg. Your father is downstairs, you'll see him soon. Have you had a chance to eat something?"

"Why yes, My Lord, we have just finished." In a lowered voice he confidentially tells Arcimboldo, "that alchemist, Kelly, was not pleased to be fed bread and cheese, he claims it makes him feel he's in prison!"

"Indeed! Prison! Well, perhaps he knows well whereof he speaks. Do not be concerned... but, look here, Georg, I will ask you another favor, help me keep an eye on the man, to be honest with you, I wouldn't give a white groshen for his trustworthiness. If he acts strangely do not hesitate to let me know." Arcimboldo squeezes the young man's arm in friendly gratitude. "And Georg, can you tell me where you fellows have left the urinal?"

Arcimboldo has assembled his comrades around the alchemist's oven, which is radiating pleasant warmth. A white circle has been drawn on the floor around the furnace, and a golden pentangle twenty feet in diameter has been drawn around the circle; this pentangle is in turn circumscribed by another circle, this one drawn in silver. Within this larger circle, at the exact points of east, west, north, and south, four remarkable paintings rest on easels. This is Arcimboldo's series of paintings known as 'The Elements'; they portray Earth, Fire, Water, and Air.

Feeling tired and humorless, and no doubt looking it as well, Arcimboldo addresses the assembled group, "gentlemen – our banquet is about to begin, it will be followed shortly after by the Epiphany play. The Emperor will join us at that point and the transformation can begin. Starting immediately, you may begin your process of alchemy and Hermetic science. Is there anything else you require?"

"The gold."

"The Emperor will bring that with him when he comes, Master Kelly. Will you need it before then?"

"I suppose not."

"Anything else?"

"Will he bring Katharina Strada with him as well?"

"Giordano…" Is this sarcasm? Arcimboldo looks at the Nolan closely, he can't tell. "Frankly, I don't know when she'll join us, I'll have to find out. Do you have a particular concern?" As soon as he's said this, Arcimboldo thinks it's the wrong question to be asking Bruno, but the Nolan does not pursue the matter.

Hans Mont asks, "when should I start the wheels turning again, My Lord?"

"As soon as the Emperor is here and ready, let's not exhaust the donkey. Make sure all the candles and lamps will last for the next several hours, this will be your last chance to change them." He looks at Doctor Dee, "Doctor, I think you and the Nolan can change now, do you know where your costumes are? No? I'll show you." He leads the two men to the east wall near the treadmill and opens a low cassone to reveal a stack of long robes, crowns, hats, and other accessories.

It has been customary among Christian artists to portray the Three Magi as representing those three known parts of the Earth at the time of Christ. Balthasar is commonly portrayed as a young African king. Giordano Bruno will play this part, and Arcimboldo shows him the cloak of animal skins, lion, cheetah and zebra, that he will wear. This will be accessorized with a tall traveler's staff, shell necklace, and a zebra patterned hat inserted into a crown. Bruno's eyes light up like a child's. He mumbles, "yes, yes, perfect. Let me have them, I know what to do."

John Dee will take the part of old Caspar; he represents Asia and the East. He will wear a rare and valuable robe that has come from China over the route known as the Silk Road. The long robe is yellow with red trim and patterned with rampant dragons. Dee also carries a traveler's staff, and wears a necklace of foreign coins. Arcimboldo is in the act of helping Dee try on his pointed silk hat, tasseled at the top and trimmed with a golden fillet, when he winces and grabs the small of his back. The Doctor asks, "is it your back, sir? You are in pain?"

"Ahhh... it is nothing, it will pass. Old age, I'm afraid, is a relentless foe."

"What age are you, Arcimboldus?"

(Twice in one day?) "I am sixty this year, Doctor."

"1527! The same year as myself! We are of an age. It was a portentous year, the year Charles V sacked Rome, the year of the Battle of Tarcal, the year Niccolo Machiavelli-"

"The sacking of Rome by a *Habsburg* Emperor is *not* a popular subject in this Court, Doctor."

"Ah, yes. But for your back... what do you take for the pain?"

"Why, nothing. Rest. I avoid certain movements, certain foods. I drink far less red wine than I used to. Golden Hungarian Tokaji is much kinder to my constitution. I have just had a glass downstairs."

"Have you tried herbs?"

"I prefer not to ingest herbal potions, they are too unreliable."

"No, not to ingest, to breathe."

"What do you mean?"

"Edward has introduced me to the inhalation of smoke from the hemp plant. I find it relaxing, and often it sooths muscle pain. You must try it. Edward will burn some during our ceremony."

The room is now scented with an unpleasant metallic smell, it comes from the still where Kelly prepares *Sal alkali*. This substance, also known as the *alkahest,* is a solution of potash in alcohol; it is a powerful liquid which dissolves many substances. The alchemist will mix this with olive oil to create 'sweet oil'. Arcimboldo brings Kelly his costume. As *chief* alchemist, Kelly wears a long leather apron and leather gloves, over this he will wear as costume a black cloak embroidered with astrological Symbols and a tall pointed hat with Symbols of the Sun and Moon on it. Arcimboldo places these items on a table near the oven, where Kelly has laid out an array of glass beakers, alembics, cucurbits, and retorts. There are also several old and much used books on and around the table, among them Arcimboldo recognizes the *Sefer Yetzira,* the *Picatrix,* the *Codex Argenteus,* and the *Corpus Hermeticum.* Kelly has propped open in front of him Raymond Llull's *Ars Magna* and *Liber Chaos* – the Book of Chaos.

Bartolomeus Spranger stands by, watching. He has washed, brushed his hair, and removed his tattered ruff, however his eyes are dull and unfocused, and his face is expressionless. Arcimboldo would like to rouse the man's spirits. "Bartolomeus, may I ask you to help me with something? Will you come with me?"

"Your enthusiasm has greatly diminished, my friend."

"I have noticed that myself, Arcimboldus. I can't forget those things I saw in the city today."

"I also saw things today I had never seen before, terrible things. They haunt me as well."

"I wish I could say *I* had never seen them before! They bring back vivid memories of the sack of Antwerp, my family lost their house... everything... and now, once again, even *five-hundred* leagues from Madrid, a Spanish Tercio terrorizes civilians in the name of the true religion; those bastards! I thought I had left all that behind me."

"But Bartolomeus, that was two years ago, you were right here, in Prague."

"I don't mean 1585, I mean the sack *eleven* years ago, the first sacking of the town, the one that destroyed the *most* important things, the spirit and resourcefulness of the citizens."

"Ah, the mutiny of Sancho d'Avila."

"Everyone blames d'Avila and the Tercio, but why were they there in the first place? They were sent by the King of Spain to *force* the people to be better Christians! The kind of Christians His Most Catholic Majesty decided they should be, and if not, to suffer for it!"

"Shhh, Bartolomeus, calm, calm."

But again, the Dutchman's passions have been stirred. "D'Avila's soldiers had been fighting with no pay and no rest for months. What would you expect... they were mad dogs! They burned everything they could not carry away. They paid themselves with the wealth of Antwerp... the richest, most beautiful city in Holland."

"A tragedy, to be certain. Your family's house...?"

"My family..." tears form in Spranger's eyes, and he squeezes them shut. "That was when I left for Italy. I'll never go back, not as long as the Spanish are there."

"There's no need, Bartolomeus, no need. The Emperor loves you well. Prague loves you. This is your home now." Arcimboldo is desperately searching his brain for something to distract his friend. "Listen, perhaps this is the wrong moment, but I will tell you something astonishing to distract you, this is something immense – Rudolf gave me permission to return to Italy. It's hard to believe, is it not? I think it's easier for me to believe we will penetrate Heaven's secrets tonight than the fact I'm actually free to live in

Milan again! After forty years! I believe I will go as soon as I can. Of course, I'll miss you, my friend."

This finally makes Spranger look the Italian in the eye, "when did he do that, today?"

"Yes."

Unconvincingly, Spranger says, "I'm happy for you, Maestro. I am. Perhaps I will go with you."

Arcimboldo looks skeptical, "will the Emperor give you permission so easily?"

Spranger shrugs. They stand near the door, and sympathetic as Arcimboldo is, he must keep to his busy schedule. "Look here, do what you can to cheer yourself. Contemplate our *successful* experiment. Rudolf and Prague, all of us, will be impervious to manipulation by the Pope and the King of Spain. Does that not excite you?"

"I see it does not excite *you*."

Arcimboldo is taken aback, is he so transparent? He stammers, "I'm tired, it's been a long, long, strange day. I believe I'm too old for so much excitement." He tries to rally his friend by punching him lightly in the chest and forcing a laugh as he says, "but rouse yourself! Drink another glass of wine. And do this for me: I have finished the Leonardo, God and the Maestro forgive me, set it up here by the door, it must be the first thing the Emperor sees when he enters. We will begin our great experiment in an hour, you will see, we will change the World and the course of History!"

As Arcimboldo descends the stairs he thinks: *'this is it, one hour, one meal... is it possible, after all this time, can it be so close?'*

At the base of the stairs, Cesare's crew plays cards with Valentin Soucek, who is properly masked (and apparently losing every hand). They have been joined behind the curtain by the Master of the Play and his actors. The actors have begun to assemble the props and backgrounds that will be used in the first act. In response to Arcimboldo's inquisitive look, the Master of the Play assures him, "all is well, My Lord. We will be ready at your command."

"Bene. Perfetto. It will not be long."

One of Cesare's crew has approached; he stands by, obviously waiting to say something. Arcimboldo nods to the man.

"One of 'em tried to slip through, M'Lord. We set 'er straight. No comin' behind the curtain, M'Lady, we sez."

"What, who... a lady?"

"Sure 'nuf. A right looker too, pardon my sayin' so, M'Lord."

"Wearing orange? Red hair? Speaking French?"

"Right you are, sir. That be the one."

"Mm hmm. Very good. Stay vigilant."

"Pardon, M'Lord?"

"You did well. Thank you."

Stepping past the green curtain, Arcimboldo enters a different world, a glittering, fragrant, jovial realm of aristocratic pleasure. Christina of Lorraine and Ferdinando de Medici are dancing, as are the Marquis and Marchioness d'Olivan. Rudolf sits with High Steward Dietrichstein and his wife Marguerite of Cordona. Arcimboldo will cross the room to join them.

During Rudolf's childhood at the Court of his uncle Philip, Adam Dietrichstein served as Ambassador to Spain from the Holy Roman Empire. The Emperor Maximilian had also appointed Dietrichstein to be tutor and mentor to his sons Rudolf and Ernst while they were in Spain. Nowadays, much to Rudolf's annoyance, there are times the High Steward seems to think he may still treat the Emperor as a young man in need of governance and mature advice. Nevertheless, Rudolf has always kept the man close by and in a position of importance and authority. At the moment, Dietrichstein is doing all the talking, but he talks to himself, Rudolf is obviously a thousand miles away, and the High Steward's kindly Spanish wife, Marguerite, is deaf as a post.

Arcimboldo approaches and bows. He clears his throat and tries to speak with a degree of seriousness he hopes will get the Emperor's attention. "My Lady, Your Imperial Majesty, My Lord High Steward, our banquet will be ready momentarily, I'm about to have the last dance played. But first, I must interrupt you with something I feel is quite important." Arcimboldo looks over his shoulder to be certain they have privacy, then plunges on with lowered but urgent voice. "Forgive me for involving myself in something that is none of my business, but Don Guillen has confided to me that Mendoza, the Spanish Ambassador, knows Giordano Bruno is here. Worse than that, Mendoza is the agent, paymaster, and commandant of the Holy League!"

The High Steward's eyebrows shoot up in surprise and alarm. Rudolf fixes Arcimboldo with a very stern look. "We know the man is a villain, yes. Is there anything else?"

"Well...I have taken the liberty, and forgive me if you disapprove... I have taken the liberty of asking Captain Morhof to have the man watched and followed. I have asked him to report to Marshall Trautson-"

"Who will report to me, My Lord?"

Turning in surprise, Arcimboldo sees the Marshall now stands directly behind him. "Oh, I did not notice you. I've just told His Majesty what Don Guillen has confided to me." Trautson grits his teeth at the mention of the Spanish Ambassador. "Don Guillen says this Bernardino de Mendoza is much more than Ambassador, he's a highly placed agent of the Holy

League, and he suspects we are hiding Giordano Bruno."

Trautson can be volatile, "*Die Beiden kann ich nicht aushalten!* And who's reporting what, when?"

"I've asked Captain Morhof to follow the man and report to you at the end of the evening."

"Hmmph! A prudent thought, Arcimboldus. Your Majesty, will you permit me to at least detain this man?"

"I will not, Marshall, you may keep watch on him, as you know very well we are doing *already*. That is enough."

Trautson exhales with frustration. "And why, Sire, may I ask, do you allow *Der Scheisskerl* to dance around free as a lark in our castle?"

"Tomorrow things may be different. We will see. Keep him away from my plans for tonight, and tomorrow we will see." Rudolf stands. "Arcimboldus, I am hungry, one more dance you say? Fine, then we will eat. I will prepare myself."

Arcimboldo steps close to Rudolf to speak in his ear, but the Emperor pulls away, and gives him a cautious look. With an apologetic look on his face Arcimboldo whispers, "Katharina? When can we expect...?"

Rudolf curtly nods, "yes, Atlas is seeing to that now."

Arcimboldo notices with surprise that Atlas is no longer in sight. This is very rare; usually the Emperor will not move a step unless his bodyguard is right behind him. It shows to what degree Rudolf values Katharina and what she carries within her.

The wild boar has arrived and secretly awaits its revelation. The orchestra plays its last dance tune, a lavolta. This lively dance begins as a galliard, and involves the group of dancers forming two facing lines, then, with a change of music and tempo, the dancers partner up and move apart. The complicated forms and positions that follow involve an unusual amount of hopping about and touching between the man and woman; some feel it is too risqué, but it's very popular and enjoyed at every cosmopolitan European Court.

Arcimboldo has given the word to his men guarding the stairway to expect Atlas and Katharina. He now stands at the main door into the banquet hall; he will help guests find their seats if they cannot find their name on the chart posted in the front of the tables. He watches the dancers energetically completing the last few frenzied moments of the lavolta. He notices Ottavio Strada and his wife, Annamarie, hurriedly enter the Summer Palace...surprisingly late. The Stradas are creatures of the Court and are usually among the first to arrive and the last to leave. Ottavio searches the room with a serious look on his face, and when he discovers Arcimboldo he dodges and weaves his way across the dance floor, leaving his wife standing by herself. Arcimboldo greets him, "Ottavio, I thought you would not make it, but you have arrived exactly on time for supper. But... is there something wrong?"

Without a smile, Ottavio steps close to Arcimboldo and speaks in a low and earnest voice, "My Lord, have you seen Katharina? I have not been able to find her all day. She cannot be with Rudolf, he is *here*... have you seen her, do you know where she might be?"

Arcimboldo must bite his tongue to hold back his first answer. He smiles a false smile, "why... I'm sure I have no idea where she is right now. But do not worry so, I'm sure she is well."

"How can you be sure, did you not tell me you yourself were attacked last night?"

Arcimboldo quickly looks to see if anyone is standing near enough to hear their conversation. "Calm, Ottavio, calm. That was all about the Nolan,

Katharina has nothing to do with that. Do not fret so. If you cannot find her tomorrow morning, I swear, I'll join you in your search. Perhaps she is unwell. Be calm."

"If she were unwell would she not come to her parents? I will ask the Doctors."

"You may do that, but there may be other perfectly logical reasons that don't occur to us right at this moment. Above all, my friend, *calm* yourself. I can tell you that I have a very, very strong feeling that all is well."

Ottavio nods and rushes off. Arcimboldo is irritated with himself that he couldn't offer more reassurance to the poor man.

The dance finally ends with a flourish, and the sound of music is replaced with chatter and laughter. Breathing hard and fanning themselves from exertion on the dance floor, Rudolf's guests begin filtering into the resplendent hall where they will dine. The guests are mostly men, and mostly dressed in black, as is usually the case at the Emperor's Court, but this makes the colorful and expensive attire of the women stand out beautifully. Count Rozmberk's new wife, Polyxena, wears a jewel encrusted, high-necked, surcoat gown of violet taffeta silk that must be worth as much as a coach and four horses.

Amidst the delegation from France that has accompanied Christina of Lorraine is the Emperor's Ambassador to the French King, Ogier Ghiselin de Busbecq. The sixty-six year old Ambassador totters into the banquet hall arm and arm with Doctor Hagecius. Arcimboldo is delighted to see the old man, and in the French style, they hug and kiss on the cheek in greeting.

"Ghiselin, I'm so glad you could make the journey, I hadn't realized you were here as well! What have you brought us?"

"Myself and nothing more, Giuseppe, my dear friend. I'm too old to travel and collect any more." Ten years ago he would have used the words 'my *dearest* friend', (occasionally, such subtle and miniscule deviations are powerful reminders of the inexorable passing of time). Busbecq is famous as a collector and antiquarian. While Ambassador to the Ottoman Emperor, Suleiman the Magnificent, in the 1550s and '60s he discovered many intriguing antiquities: manuscripts, coins, and curios. Among the works he has sent back to Prague is a copy of the *Res Gestae Divi Augusti*, a detailed historical account of the Roman Emperor Augustus' life and accomplishments; such information has been lost to European scholars for a thousand years, and fuels modern historians' appetite for understanding and reevaluating our past. The best known of Busbecq's discoveries is a sixth century compendium of medicinal herbs by Dioscorides, *De Materia Medica*; Busbecq convinced Emperor Ferdinand to purchase this rare and expensive manuscript as a gift for his daughter, and it has become a valuable addition to the Habsburg library in the Wuderkabinet. While in Constantinople, Busbecq fell in love with a colorful Asian flower known as the tulip. He sent bulbs to friends all over Europe, and Busbecq's Flemish friend, Charles de l'Ecluse, has even adapted the plant to live in Holland's challengingly cool weather.

Arcimboldo exclaims, "what do you mean, 'too old'? You have traveled here! And certainly you look like a young man compared to this hoary old Doctor here!"

Hagecius pretends to protest, but the three friends laugh heartily together. They have known each other for decades.

"I wanted to see Vienna one last time. I will go there tomorrow. I will stay with Jacopo until Spring."

Arcimboldo embraces the old Ambassador once again and says in his ear, "we must talk, I have much to tell you. It is wonderful to see you, Ghiselin."

Arcimboldo breaks away to greet the next couple coming through the doorway, he bows gracefully to the Marquis and Marchioness d'Olivan as they enter and politely indicates where they should sit. The Marchioness nods coolly, but doesn't speak.

Christina of Lorraine and Ferdinando de Medici will again have places of honor on either side of the Emperor in the center of the main table. The Marchioness d'Olivan sits several places to Christina's left among the guests who are French, Spanish, clerics, or ultra-Catholic Bohemian aristocrats. To the Emperor's right sits the Tuscan embassy, Imperial ministers and their spouses, Rudolf's favorites at Court, and, among them, the few Protestants who dare to attend this event. One of these, Peter Vok Rozmberk, Vilem's younger brother, must be on his best behavior; Arcimboldo will keep an eye on how much the impetuous young nobleman has to drink. Arcimboldo's place is at the very end of the table to Rudolf's right, nearest a door. This is not because of his status; he is in great demand because of his cultured and articulate conversation and interesting accomplishments, however he must be able to get up and move around at a moment's notice to facilitate his duties as Master of Entertainment.

As he waits for the guests to be seated, he sees Atlas enter the Summer Palace with another person who is concealed completely in a hooded brown cloak, they quickly pass behind the curtain; Katharina Strada has arrived. When all the guests have been seated, Rudolf rises and cordially welcomes his guests once more to his Summer Palace and his Epiphany banquet. Diplomatically, he invites the French Cardinal Guise to rise and grace the gathering with a prayer. With delight on his fat, pale, and pious face, the Cardinal rises and begins to speak. The long, extremely boring, and sanctimonious homily that follows gives Arcimboldo a chance to hand Rudolf the golden bow and arrow he will use momentarily, and then position himself back in the doorway where he can see Master Phillipus de Monte.

When the Cardinal finally sits, Arcimboldo has servants carry in the enormous roasted wild boar on a waist high platform, and they place it several feet from the Emperor. The size of the animal and its wicked tusks and bristles are impressive. The Master of Servers stands nearby, holding a string and watching for his cue. Rudolf raises the golden bow and arrow which gets the attention of everyone in the room. He says, "honored guests, perhaps you know that this Palace was built in the midst of Our Imperial Game Preserve; it is the richest hunting forest in Bohemia. *This* boar was caught practically on Our doorstep!" This elicits a murmur from his audience. "Let me show you the excellence of Our Bohemian game!" With this, he cocks the bow and lets fly with the golden arrow; and as the arrow strikes the boar, the Master of Servers pulls the cord he holds, and the huge carcass opens up; a cascade of meat tumbles out: suckling pigs, rabbits, geese, partridges, quail, larks, linnets, game hens, sausages and sweetbreads of all kinds. Arcimboldo points to the Master of Music and the 'killing of the boar' is accompanied by a hunting fanfare from the orchestra in the adjoining room, and the applause and delighted exclamations of surprise from those at table. Smiling young men bearing drink, fruit, cheeses, and of course, platters and platters of meat, begin serving the tables.

Arcimboldo sits at the end of the right hand table, across from the third wife of the Moravian nobleman Karel Zerotin, and they discuss food. As Klara Zerotin daintily eats a pigeon, she explains how she cooks her husband's favorite dish, pigeon tart. "One must temper the meat with verjuice after pulling it off the spit, that is the secret, *then* I stuff the open tart with prunes, herbs, and the meat. Are those meatballs on your plate, My Lord?"

"In Italian we would call them *polpette di polpe di lucio cotte,* they are meatballs made from spit-roasted pike, madame, usually one of my favorites, but my appetite is weak tonight." Arcimboldo sips from his crystal glass, he drinks only water.

"Surely that is too heavy for you then. You need something light. What I make for Karel when his appetite is off is capon's breast, stuffed with cheese and herbs, very lightly cooked in safflower broth. Isn't that right dear?"

"Mmm mmm." Karel Zerotin is a very large man and a very large eater. He is also one of the most widely traveled men in Bohemia. When he has finally swallowed he says, "oh, but nothing compared to your capons Florentine style, Klara! I brought the recipe back from Florence myself. Tell the Italian how you cook them, my angel."

"Well, I crush almonds in a mill for making mustard, and then I soak them in two parts capon broth and one part grape verjuice. For one pound of almonds I add four ounces of sugar and a little ginger soaked in rose water. I mix this with the grease of the roasted capon, six ounces of starch, and another dash of rose water. When this sauce is ready, I slice the roasted capon on a plate and pour the sauce over it, and then cover it all with sugar and cinnamon."

While she has been talking, Arcimboldo's gaze (and attention) has drifted to those sitting around the banquet hall. The Emperor is being earnestly talked to by the Cardinals, the Nuncio, and the Spaniolated Bohemian Count Lobkovic; they are trying to persuade him to *only* appoint Catholics to the Privy Council, as an unambiguous declaration of his intolerance of Protestants. Rudolf is supremely indifferent to this colloquy, and his heavily lidded eyes restlessly roam around the room. The Emperor's other guests, however, are happily enjoying the delicious food, and the room hums with lively conversation.

Several places to Arcimboldo's left, Ogier Ghislain de Busbecq is telling librarian Blotius about a book he has just received from Cologne, an interesting story by a man named Speiss about a German scholar named Faust who sells his soul to the devil in return for unlimited knowledge.

Christina of Lorrain must raise her voice to be heard by Doctor Hagecius; she asks him for his opinion on the astronomical phenomenon known as the Fiery Trigon, which is due to begin in 1588. The alignment of Jupiter and Saturn with the fire signs of the zodiac has not happened for eight-hundred years, and many are predicting the end of the World.

Naturally, Arcimboldo glances often at the Spanish Ambassador to France; but strangely, he finds his attention repeatedly slides over to the man sitting next to Mendoza. This man's resemblance to the artist Albrecht Durer is uncanny, and Arcimboldo is thinking of a particular painting, Durer's self portrait, painted when the German artist was thirty. It has been on public display in the Town Hall of the city of Nuremburg since 1528. Arcimboldo considers the painting a masterpiece, a subtle work of genius. With great sensitivity it portrays: a handsome and confident man in the prime of life; a long, serious, and asymmetric face, with ringlets of brown hair falling freely to the shoulders; sensual but unsmiling mouth framed by a scanty beard and drooping moustache; a prominently veined and well modeled hand with extremely long fingers; large and sensitive eyes – but unlike Durer's portrait that looks directly and challengingly at the viewer, this man's eyes rarely look up, they stay calmly, almost shyly on his plate. When he does look up he has the gaze of a mystic, soulful, appearing to see miles beyond what he is looking at. He eats slowly, deliberately, and abstemiously. He even resembles Durer's painting in the clothing he wears: a fur lined Hungarian jacket with long and bunched sleeves, with no ruff or collar adornment at all, not a glimmer of jewelry or frivolity. Dressed as he is, he cannot be French or Spanish. Occasionally Mendoza will address him, and he modestly replies with a shake or nod of the head. Arcimboldo's curiosity is too great, he must find out who this man is.

The artist ends his conversation with Madame Zerotin by giving her a polite smile and a nod of appreciation for her lessons in cooking. He turns to his left and addresses the Augsburg banker, Hans Fugger von der Lilie, "Herr Fugger, tell me, sir, if you had to guess, what nationality would that man be who sits next to the Spanish Ambassador to France?"

With his mouth half full, the German answers immediately, "I don't have to guess Arcimboldus, I know the man is Hungarian. Count Mihaly Cseszneky de Milvany, famous hero of Var-" he swallows, "Varpalota. Pardon me. Now, alas, he is impoverished, he sells his services to the highest bidder. An unhappy man." Fugger studies the Hungarian Count for a moment as he wipes perspiration off his pink face. "Yes, unhappy. One of the *Vitezi Rend.*"

"Ah ha." Arcimboldo knows of the *Vitezi Rend,* which means 'Order of Valiants' in Hungarian. These are Hungarian knights and nobility who have lost their lands and castles to the Turks; all they have left is hollow pride in what they have lost and implacable hatred for those who have stolen their ancestral birthright. The *Vitezi Rend* are ferocious and ruthless warriors who fight without concern for their own lives or welfare (or that of their comrades who fight alongside them); they slake their hatred by fiendishly barbaric treatment of those Turks who are unlucky enough to be taken alive. It is whispered that the souvenirs they collect on the battlefield have nothing to do with weapons or jewelry. They are greatly feared by Turk and European alike. Arcimboldo muses, "*Vitezi Rend*... you would not suspect it by looking at him. I have never heard of Varpalota, what is that?"

"Cseszneky was chief lieutenant to Gyorgy Thury during the defense of Varpalota Castle. Five-hundred Hungarians against eight-thousand Turks under Arslan Pasha. They held out, almost to the last man, until Count Salm's relief troops arrived. Then, the heroes of Varpalota helped Salm to reconquer Veszprem and Tata. Count Cseszneky's exploits are legendary." Herr Fugger leans toward Arcimboldo and puts his hand next to his mouth to keep private what he says, he whispers, "they say he has killed over a thousand men... with his own hands!"

"That cannot be!" Arcimboldo reappraises, "I say again, you would not suspect it by looking at him."

Fugger laughs shrewdly and winks, "well, it reads well in the *Zeitungen*! Ha ha! Is the pike not to your liking, sir? I have not tried it yet." Arcimboldo knows the *Zeitungen*, the Emperor receives it every month. One might describe it as a letter of news. It is a strange idea, but perhaps it will catch on; the Fuggers publish a brief journal of current happenings from around Europe: important deaths and births, battles won and lost, ships sunk and ships come into port, coronations, riots, bankruptcies, the price of metals and grain, the value of various currencies, notable meteorological and astronomical events. They send these letters to prominent institutions, men, and families. It must help the Fugger's money lending business; they are among the richest families in Europe.

Arcimboldo excuses himself; he is being summoned to arbitrate an artistic dispute between Vicenzo Gonzaga and Cardinal Guise. The Duke has been bragging about the painting by Simone Peterzano he has just purchased for his palace in Mantua. The Cardinal dismissively describes the painting of Solomon, King of Jerusalem, as "a naked man surrounded by a ridiculous garden! If he *is* Solomon, where are his kingly robes, where is the Temple, where is the Queen of Sheba, where is the Judgment? And Peterzano paints any kind of tree or bush he feels like, it is a horticultural fantasy! I have seen it; a palm tree next to a rose bush, a cedar next to an olive... it has no religious meaning at all, other than the artist's *arbitrary* title. *Solomon*... pshaw!"

Gonzaga looks to Arcimboldo; who smiles and says to the Cardinal, "I know this painting, Your Excellence, the man in the picture *is* Solomon and the garden represents *Ecclesiastes*. Pardon me for presuming to quote the Hebrew Bible to you, but may I remind you of the words – 'I was exalted like a cedar of Lebanon and as a cypress tree on the mountains of Hermon. I was exalted like a palm tree on the seashore, and as rose plants in Jericho, and as a fair olive tree in the plain'. Such is the story the artist tells."

"Bravissimo, Arcimboldus!" The Duke claps his hands. The Cardinal looks less than pleased. Proudly, Gonzaga tells Arcimboldo, "I have told Simone to paint me another with the same colors... any invention that will please him provided that it contain neither hypocrisies, stigmata, or nails."

Rudolf has taken an interest in this conversation, he says, "the Cardinal objects to my paintings of Venus. He says they are unfit for public display because they do not convey a Christian message. I could not remember how you described this to me. Tell our guests what you have told me about Venus."

"It is once again a Symbolic interpretation, Your Excellence. Venus is not simply a pagan goddess, she is a Symbol of certain qualities, she stands for Humanitas which, in turn, embraces Love and Charity, Dignity and Magnanimity, Liberality and Magnificence, Comeliness and Modesty, Charm and Splendor... surely these are all proper Christian qualities and a Virtuous message."

Rudolf repeats, "love and charity, comeliness and modesty, charm and dignity... yes... you see?"

Christina says, "I see, yes, I see."

Arcimboldo has been hearing muffled shouts coming from outside, and he excuses himself... escaping the scornful stares of the Cardinal and the other French aristocrats.

Passing across the empty dance floor, he asks the orchestra to play louder. Outside on the steps the shouts are louder, and they are in French. Out in the garden, two very large soldiers of the Imperial Guard hold a squirming man by the shoulders, they lift him almost off the ground and the man's feet kick and scrabble in the snow. Captain Morhof surveys the scene and Arcimboldo joins him. The man is shouting, "this is a diplomatic outrage! Release me! Call the Duc d'Aumale immediately! Call Ambassador Mendoza!" It is Fabrizio Mordente who squirms and shouts.

Captain Morhof explains to Arcimboldo, "we caught this man and another trying to scale the balcony at the back of the Palace, My Lord."

Arcimboldo speaks to Mordente in Italian, "foolish of you, Mordente. What are you looking for upstairs?"

"I don't have to tell you anything, heretic! If you know what's good for you, you'll let me go this instant!"

Arcimboldo asks the Captain in German, "you said two men, where is the other?"

"He fell, My Lord, he is unconscious. Are they thieves? What shall I do with this rogue?"

"We shall let Chancellor Curtius decide when he is feeling well again. Until then... the Emperor's prison will be the best place. Or perhaps we should let Marshall Trautson decide... hmm... no, I cannot be that cruel. Prison tonight, then we will see." To Mordente he says, "you are lucky you only go to the Emperor's jail this evening. Others can decide what to do with you in the morning."

Mordente shouts in French, "Help! Mendoza! Help! Help!"

Arcimboldo quickly says to the Captain, "take him away this instant."

"You heretical bastards! You'll pay dearly for this! There will be *war* in the morning!"

As Mordente is being dragged away struggling and kicking, Arcimboldo calls after him in Italian, "in the morning, there will only be hilarity at your exploits, Mordente, you foolish man! Joy of Epiphany to you, Signore, sleep well."

Arcimboldo feels relief as he reenters the Summer Palace; one of his headaches has been dealt with, for the moment. Ambassador Mendoza is crossing the dance floor followed by the Hungarian knight. Cseszneky walks with the same economy of movement he eats with, and Arcimboldo notices he is armed with a new type of sword the Hungarians have copied from the Turks; it's slightly curved, they call it a *szabla* or saber. Mendoza looks at Arcimboldo with uncertainty, obviously he hates having to speak to the Italian at all. He asks tersely, "did I hear my name being called?"

"Did you Ambassador? I'm sure that I did not."

Mendoza scowls, "what's going on outside?"

Arcimboldo walks past the two men saying, "you are free to look for yourself. Do not miss the rest of your meal, Ambassador."

When Arcimboldo returns to the banquet table, the conversation has turned to a discussion of Virtue. He hears the Marchioness quoting Aristotle to Count Rozmberk, "when Aristotle was asked what he had acquired from philosophy, he answered, *'what you do from hope of reward, and shun from fear of punishment, I do from the love of and the nobility of Virtue, and shun from hatred of vice.'* So the philosopher does not need to be punished by Hell or tempted by-"

Papal Nuncio Germanico Malaspina protests, "Marchioness!"

Cardinal Guise says severely, "you are misled by the honeyed words of pagan rhetoric, madame, philosophy alone is not enough. Men are rewarded and punished by God's will alone."

Count Rozmberk asks, "but why are some rewarded or punished accidentally?"

"Who says it is accidental, Count, do you claim God's will can be *accidental*?"

"But where is the Divine justice in undeserved punishments?"

"Undeserved punishment can teach a person a lesson in proper behavior far more effectively than your philosophy."

Count Rozmberk's brother, Peter Vok, can be heard scoffing, even though his mouth is hidden behind his wine glass.

Cardinal Guise speaks with passion, "I see the true Catholic religion downtrodden by the enemies of God's will, Christ's kingdom neglected and the realm of the Antichrist growing, the pious followers of pure orthodox doctrine oppressed, and impious, arrogant men raised up, men who have fled God's word, degenerates for the most part, to whom all virtuous living is abhorrent!"

Nuncio Malaspina, who is tasked by the Pope with the unenviable job of returning Bohemia to the Catholic faith, takes up the Cardinal's thought, "certainly, these men violate our faith, murder the faithful, trespass against law and justice, break underfoot our traditional habits and customs," he looks directly at Rudolf, "yet all is tolerated, not only with equanimity but with a false sense of security and all manner of foolish hopes!"

Rudolf turns in his chair so his back is to the man; he crosses his legs and studies his fingernails as if he hasn't heard a thing.

Vratislav Pernstein, a rich and important Catholic nobleman who understands the difficult situation in Prague and Bohemia, speaks in an attempt to be moderate, "I cannot take it amiss that the Protestants should be zealous and watchful of their affairs, but I know it to be a great necessity that we follow their example and do the same. And that we Catholics, although we are only a small handful, consider how to present our case, so that our Catholic religion should not be further reduced and oppressed... with the virtuous desire that all of us in this kingdom may be able to live together in love and harmony."

Peter Vok replies to this intemperately, "that it has come to such a reduction in the number of Catholics in this kingdom is the result of the righteous judgment and wrath of the Lord God for our sins and wickedness, and in my opinion, hiccup, it is the Catholics and not the Evangelicals who are to blame."

Cardinal Guise says tiredly, "babble falling on deaf ears."

Malaspina spits out, "empty rhetoric... if not blasphemy!"

Count Rozmberk, while glancing nervously at his brother, tries to calm this passionate debate, "what seems empty rhetoric to one may be reasonable truth to another. It is a question of perspective."

Arcimboldo says, "I believe that the *master* of rhetoric *paints* the truth while speaking. One must distinguish between rhetoric and sophistry. The Marchioness does well to quote such a master of rhetoric as Aristotle. When I was young I was told that truth rests with things that can be taught and beauty stems from images meant to delight – but I have discovered that these things rest one upon another, and the one can enhance the other."

Bernardino de Mendoza, who has rejoined the dinner party, says darkly, "this means that, and that means this, bah, why these words sound as though they might have been spoken by that disgraced Dominican, *Giordano Bruno*." And he looks significantly at Arcimboldo, who is unsure of how to reply. Arcimboldo looks at the Ambassador with an expression that God created for a particular purpose. It is the look a carp gives a fisherman whose hook he has just spotted, or the look a squirrel gives to the barking, leaping dog at the base of the tree; there is no doubt that God created this facial expression for Adam in the moment he noticed Eve fondling the brightest, shiniest apple on the tree. Mendoza continues, his voice bitter with sarcasm, "*wherever* Bruno is, he is probably with those vile English *spies* and necromancers. I congratulate the Emperor for banishing them so *effectively* from his realm." He picks up his glass and holds it high, "I toast to the confounding of the English Queen and all her rabble, a pox on them, damn their souls to Hell!"

Although many join the Spanish Ambassador, the Tuscan side of the banquet tables merely look puzzled and nervous. Rudolf acts as though he sits alone in an empty and silent room. At the mention of Queen Elizabeth, the Duc d'Aumale pretends to cough behind his hand, but can be heard to exclaim, "Jezebel!" The Marquis d'Olivan, flushed with wine, emits a loud belch that forms the word "STRUMPET", and laughs at his own wit. He is joined by all the French and Spanish. The Florentines turn away in embarrassment. The Marchioness calmly strokes her husband's cheek and whispers in his ear. The florid smirk is wiped off his face to be replaced by an ashen dread. His shoulders slump, he looks down and studies his empty plate as if it is the most interesting thing in the world.

Without betraying the slightest hint of embarrassment, and skillfully clearing the tension in the room, the Marchioness says to Arcimboldo, "Maestro Arcimboldus, I have been admiring your paintings all evening. Just now, looking at your painting of Flora, or is it Spring? I am reminded of the words of Desiderius Erasmus in his *Convivium Religiosum*, may I quote?" She does not pause for answer, but of course Arcimboldo is delighted by the distraction, he bows as she continues. "*Our delight is doubled when we see the opposition of painted flower and living flower. The latter fills us with amazement at the artifice of Nature while the former astonishes us with the skills of the artist. Both together fill us with amazement at the Lord's unfailing miraculous and kind generosity, for He has given us all these things to use.*"

There is some applause, led by Christina of Lorraine; even her brother, Cardinal Guise, smiles with pleasure. The Duke of Mantua exclaims, "brava, Marchioness!" With supreme aplomb, the Marchioness stands and bows theatrically; when she rises, she tosses her head back to settle her magnificent auburn hair in place. The men in the room are riveted with admiration. She sweeps around the tables toward the paintings hanging on the front wall, speaking to Arcimboldo as if they are the only two in the room. "I have so many questions for you about your style, Maestro, but I must ask, "how do you decide what goes where?"

Arcimboldo thinks: here is elegance worthy of the most accomplished courtier, an instinctive nobility; a manner so far superior to vulgar charms that it is obvious it stems, not from training or personal pride, but from a profound *indifference* to everything that is vulgar. How this instinctive manner has developed in a woman from the nether regions of that barely civilized nation to the far west is puzzling and fascinating to the Italian.

The Marchioness pauses in front of Arcimboldo's painting of Summer, a lovely and colorful portrait of a man made entirely of fruit and vegetables. These objects have been arranged together with a skill and creative genius that is so novel that it stands alone in European art. The picture contains: ruby red cherries and green grapes, quinces, plums, mulberries, hazelnuts, brown and yellow pears, a melon, a lemon, an artichoke, a dark wild cherry for an eye, a blushing ripe peach for a cheek, ears of corn and wheat, bulbs of garlic, onions, peapods, eggplants, various color squashes, including a long and twisted zucchini for a nose. Braided and woven wheat spikes make a golden jacket. And braided into the high golden collar is the artist's signature, 'Arcimboldo'.

The Marchioness has asked him to explain how he composes his paintings, and although he has been asked this many times before, he pauses to compose an answer that must condense a subject that is complicated, vague, and protracted.

"Madame, in the beginning stages, the process is, I must admit, much more like dreaming than it is craftsman-like work." There is a snort (perhaps of derision?) from someone at one of the tables behind him. "Associations form in my mind according to words, pronunciations, Symbolic meanings, similarities in shape, color or texture-"

She lays her hand on his arm to stop him. "Please explain that more."

"Well, for example, look here. We say an 'ear' of corn, so I have placed the corn here, where the ear would be. Melons and gourds have always been Symbolically associated with knowledge, and the large rounded shape of this melon makes it perfect for this part of the skull. The word in Italian for cheek is '*guancia*', and so this fruit, pronounced '*arancia*', serves as a suitable representation for this part of the face because of the rhyming sound. A peach goes right here because the color is a perfect match. And down here, as you know, this part of the wheat is not eaten, so it is not used as part of the *body*; but the straw may be used for the figure's *clothing*."

"I see, it is complicated. And do you lay them all out in front of you when you have decided?"

"I will paint one thing at a time, I don't lay it out *all* together, but occasionally, one or two things against another...and I find that stimulates new ideas."

"You never refer to an overall image, a sketch perhaps?"

"I do, but that image is here." Arcimboldo points to his head. "I arrange the components of my paintings here, and I am guided by that image."

"You're able to keep it all in your head?" Her curiosity is apparent by the intelligent sparkle in her eyes, and how closely she watches the words forming in his mouth as he speaks them.

"I've trained myself in a Memory system, and it's a very *visual* system. Have you heard of Signore Giulio Camillo, or his famous Memory Theater in Venice? No? He was a teacher of eloquence and logic in San Vito, a friend of that immortal genius, Titian. I learned my system from him. I can compose my ideas and hold my images together in something I think of as a *Memory Palace*, a limitless storehouse with many rooms. It's very much like a picture gallery in my Mind."

Her eyes dance about. "You raise as many questions as you answer, Maestro. I am tempted to divert to your *Memory Palace*, as you call it, but I will try to stick to my course. Tell me what the overall meaning of the painting is."

"The overall meaning is a Symbolic representation of the Natural World as it is in Summer. A time of abundance and ripe colors. All of these natural gifts of the Earth come together during the Summer months for the sustenance and pleasure of Humans; and so, in a Symbolically similar way, all of these separate images I have painted come together in this painting as a person, a Human." Arcimboldo takes several steps to his left. He notices that he has drawn a small crowd of guests who listen to his descriptions; Rudolf, the French Princess, and the Tuscan Grand Duke are among them. This is a subject that has finally gotten the Emperor's attention; this is something he never gets tired of hearing and discussing. Many people are still eating; the French and Spanish clique huddle together at their table, drinking and gossiping. Arcimboldo points to his painting of Spring. "Here is the time of year for new growth, blossoming, bright colors that rest on the shoulders of luxuriant greenery.

In the Spring, flowers delight the eyes of Humans, as, I hope, these painted images delight the eyes of those who view this picture."

"The rosebud lips are particularly charming, My Lord."

Does she realize her own lips are as lovely as rosebuds, he wonders? "All together this series of paintings represents the Natural World that Humans live in and are part of; Humanity being the highest and most complete part of the Natural World, the part closest to the Spirit of the Creator. These pictures also represent the wonderful gifts of God that we live amidst. The Seasons are a reminder of the inexorable continuity of the Universe."

Christina of Lorraine asks, "where is animal life, Maestro Arcimboldus?"

Rudolf answers before Arcimboldo can. "He has done another set of paintings in the same style, representing the Elements." Now, the Emperor is inspired and articulate. This subject is what interests him. "His painting called Earth contains an extraordinary assortment of animal life; Water represents life in the seas, lakes, and rivers; Air represents life in the air, creatures of the wing. They are beautiful. When I look at them I think I can almost imagine how God views his Microcosm – he sees all his creations at once."

"My paintings of the Seasons represent *inanimate* life, Princess, things helplessly dependent on the changing times of the year. *Animate* beings, while still greatly influenced by the Seasons, are significantly more independent."

"I have tried to convince Arcimboldus to do a series of paintings on higher forms of animate life."

"True, Your Majesty, but I find it more difficult to understand the exact Nature and relationships of animate life. It's much-"

Rudolf interjects, "the animation is often hidden. Consider a running stag, is the animation on the outside, because the animal moves? Or is it on the inside, beneath the skin? The propulsion of the muscles, the beating of the heart, the pumping of the lungs." Rudolf pulls an impressive silver watch out of a pocket and holds it in his hand. "This object can be said to have life, it moves by its own impetus, and where is that life, on the outside with its moving hands, or beneath the skin, so to speak, the spring, gears, and wheels that drive it? I believe all things that have motion have a kind of life!"

Arcimboldo looks nervously at the Cardinals and the Papal Nuncio, who have stopped their conversation to stare at Rudolf, and listen carefully to his enthusiastic (and unorthodox) dialog. "The Emperor is deeply philosophical. But, Princess, you can see how difficult it may be to define what is animate in the World around us. In my paintings of the Elements I choose a representative selection of well known creatures of the land, sea, and sky."

"I regret we cannot show you these paintings this evening, but I will send a servant for something that will interest you greatly." The Emperor steps away to speak with a servant.

The Marchioness says, "oh, I must see those. You *will* show them to me tomorrow, won't you?"

Arcimboldo simply bows. He continues, "in addition to what these paintings represent, there is an aspect that involves the person who is looking at them, the act of *viewing*. I must admit that as the creator I find it fascinating to observe the observer; to study how people absorb the messages within my creations. These paintings may be said to engage the viewer in *four* dimensions."

"Four dimensions? I don't understand that at all."

"Look here. Stand closely in front of this painting of Spring." He dares to gently take the Marchioness by the shoulders and position her in front of the picture. "What you see are flowers, they have height and width, as does the picture frame itself. These are *two* dimensions. But now, what else does this painting offer you? You must step backward, little by little, step by step; and as you go, you see, it is no longer a group of individual flowers, it has become a face. At this point, midway, it is magically both things: flowers and face, and here at this distance, it is simply a portrait of a woman. This *distance*, where it becomes something other than what it started as, is the *third* dimension. And we may say there is a *fourth* dimension, in that there is a certain amount of *time* it takes to move from one point to another. So a measure of time may be added to those measures of distance and size. The diligent viewer may contemplate these four aspects of understanding and appreciating the messages of this painting. Do you see?"

The Marchioness nods mutely with eyes wide open in wonder. The Grand Duke says, "extraordinary, unbelievable. You *must* come to Florence, Maestro. If only for a month. I will discuss it with the Emperor."

The Marquis d'Olivan has joined the group, from the look on his face it is not from enjoyment of the subject under conversation. In a slightly slurred voice he says, "that painting of Winter is mostly an old dead tree, is that part of your Natural World?"

"Of course, Marquis. Every life must come to an end sometime. Winter is unfortunately a common time for that. Death is necessary for the renewal of life. I am suddenly reminded of a beautiful Italian song. It begins:

*O come t'inganni*
*se pensi che gl'anni*

*non hann' da finire,*
*bisogna morire.*
*La morte crudele*
*a tutti è infedele,*
*ogn'uno svergogna,*
*morire bisogna.*
*È pur O pazzia*
*O gran frenesia,*
*par dirsi menzogna,*
*morire bisogna."*

Ferdinando smiles and says, "ah ha! *Bisogna morire!*" But the Marquis says, "I don't speak Italian."

"I realize that, My Lord. The words and the rhymes are *so* much more elegant in Italian, but I will translate:
Oh how wrong you are
to think that the years
will never end.
We all must die.
Cruel Death
is unfaithful to all,
and shames everyone.
Die we must.
And yet, Oh madness
Oh ravings,
it seems like lying to oneself.
Die we must."

The Marquis puffs out his cheeks and says, "well, that's a pleasant thought! I find this painting grotesque."

The Marchioness frowns, but Arcimboldo answers brightly, "yes, exactly, you are right! That is the point. Life is often grotesque... naturally so. Beautiful, *then* grotesque. And sometimes, both at once. I am not alone in painting what is grotesque, I admit I learned this from the drawings of the Florentine, Leonardo da Vinci. He was fascinated by the naturally grotesque as well as by the naturally beautiful. I explore the sensations that move the human heart and Mind. What do we feel when we are shocked, surprised, disquieted? We are stimulated, we are moved, we are transformed. We are surprised and delighted – and *transformed* when confronted with the new and unexpected, as well as with the grotesque."

The Marquis has had enough. He grunts and shambles off, back to his seat at table.

Looking closely at the paintings, Ferdinando says, "your details are perfectly realistic, Signore. You observe closely."

"The close scrutiny of common objects has led me to fascinating observations of detail and nuance; it is a never-ending revelation of life's complexity. In fact, it has led me to discoveries in fields other than painting."

"How do you mean?"

"I have discovered that there is a mathematical similarity between color and music according to Pythagorean principles. I have been able to demonstrate this with my Harpsichord of Light."

"Oh! Can we see that? What in the world can that *be*?"

As he speaks, Arcimboldo gracefully extends his hand to usher the guests away from the paintings and back to their tables. "I can't show you this evening, I apologize. I'll attempt to describe it to you though. Please sit and finish your meals."

While the Emperor's guests are reseating themselves, Arcimboldo finds the Master of Servers. "Marco, you have done very well, I commend you. We're almost at an end here; I'd like you to send men to fetch the desserts from the kitchen, and you may dismiss

Master Paulus and his staff on my authority, there will be nothing else tonight."

The Master of Servers bows. "Will we serve it in here, My Lord?"

"You will. Place it where you put the boar. And while you are waiting for the dessert, you may begin setting up chairs for the play. Send to the Chamberlain, have him prepare his team to escort the guests back to the castle. A word of caution, should the Emperor's guests be looking for him, or me, or any other noble who may not be present, you will have nothing to say. When the play is over you will close this Palace, send the guests away, and answer no questions... at all... about anything. Is that clear?"

The Master looks at Arcimboldo with curiosity, but says, "yes, My Lord."

"Perfectly clear?"

"Yes, perfectly, My Lord."

"Very good. Once again, you have done well. I thank you."

The Master of Entertainment walks to the table where the Emperor's most important guests are seated. He is feeling fatigued but he must press ahead. The Emperor is nowhere to be seen, and this is slightly disconcerting. Arcimboldo bows to the Grand Duke of Tuscany and the Duke of Mantua, "I see you are finished, My Lords, your dessert will come soon. Will you allow me to sit here? I'm not as young as I used to be, I begin to tire at this time of night." Arcimboldo moves a salt cellar to the side. The marvelous vessel is carved out of a single large piece of rock crystal in the shape of a boat; it's engraved with acanthus leaves, and is embellished with gold, silver-gilt, gilded copper, and enamel. It rolls to the side on carved crystal wheels. With a small sigh of relief, Arcimboldo perches on the edge of the table in front of them, and the Italian noblemen graciously indicate their approval. He speaks to them and also to the guests nearby, including the Princess of Lorraine, the Marchioness and her husband, Cardinal Guise, and the Duc de Mayenne. "Shall I entertain you with a curious mathematical discovery that inspired me to create a Harpsichord of Light?"

"Please do, Maestro!"

"As you might possibly know, the Natural magic of music can be described in mathematical terms. I refer to the curious fact that octaves progress at the uniform rate of one being double that of the one before it; and we find this is true by plucking a string at different points along its length. This was first discovered and described by Pythagoras. Notes an octave apart will have a ratio of two to one, and this is what the ear finds pleasing. It occurred to me that if music has this natural and constant mathematical progression of two to one there may be other applications of this principle in the Natural World. And for me, what is most interesting is how the Natural World is sensed and understood through the *eyes*. I used this technique with colors."

"But how could you do that with colors?"

"I will explain. I made eight squares of pure white, and then I covered each succeeding square with twice as much yellow as the one before it until I reached pure yellow. Then, I did this using five colors that naturally follow each other, and shaded them by regular steps of two to one: so beginning with pure white, white is shaded by yellow, yellow by green, green with blue, blue with purple, and purple with red." Now that he is engaged on his subject, Arcimboldo's blue eyes sparkle and dart about the room searching for the correct words to explain what is in his Mind. His hands and fingers sketch out shapes and nuances in the air. "When I had made this chart of shaded colors, which I found very pleasing, I wondered how I could select different colors in the same way different notes are selected by a musical instrument – fluidly and randomly."

The number of guests listening to Arcimboldo is decreasing, (and perhaps there is a mathematical correlation here, related to how complicated his story becomes, but that is another secret of the Natural World).

"I constructed a harpsichord type of device containing glass vessels, each filled with a single colored liquid according to the color chart I have just described. I inserted lanterns into this harpsichord so that they would project their brilliance through the thirty glass jars."

Those who have been able to follow him now show signs of being fascinated.

"With the help of a maker of harpsichords, I devised a system so that each key on my harpsichord opens a door that allows a particular color, let's call it a note of colored light, to shine forth. This keyboard matches that of a normal musical harpsichord; and I discovered that I could play musical compositions following standard musical notation, and instead of producing sounds, different color lights would be revealed and projected from this device, which I call a Harpsichord of Light. Do you understand my explanation? When I play in unison with another harpsichord of *sound*, the effect is miraculous!"

Arcimboldo can see that he has lost many in the room, but those he guessed would have the patience and intelligence to follow him, namely the Grand Duke and the Duke of Mantua, Christina of Lorraine, and of course the Marchioness, are astounded. Hans Fugger and Doctor Hagecius have wandered close by and stand listening with extreme interest. The mathematically inclined French Princess claps her hands and exclaims, "oh, you *must* show me, you *must*! Will you build one for me, My Lord?" The Italian Dukes are enthusiastic as well.

Arcimboldo throws up his hands and says, "God willing, I will demonstrate this for you tomorrow." Seeing that neither Rudolf nor dessert have arrived, Arcimboldo takes a deep breath and says, "shall I also share with you the mathematical secrets of geometry that have allowed me to build something I call a Perspective Lute?" But he is spared this tedious recitation by the Emperor who bustles back into the room carrying one of Arcimboldo's paintings in his own hands. The name of this painting is The Man in the Basket.

The Emperor proudly says, "Now, look here at this picture he has painted for me." He holds up what looks to be an ordinary still life picture of fruit in a wicker basket. It is painted absolutely true to life in its detail, colors, shadings and shadows. He holds it up over his head for all to see, and there is a respectful silence, no one is sure why the Emperor is excited about this basket of fruit. Then, in an instant, Rudolf spins the picture around, and upside down the picture has become a portrait of a man wearing a hat! Grapes for curly hair, peaches for cheeks, melon for chin, etc., and the basket makes a wicker hat. There are gasps and cries of, "turn it again, and again, now the other way again!" Cardinal de Medici is surprised by this visual trickery to the point of crossing himself several times. Even the Marquis, in spite of his drunken dullness, is open-mouthed with amazement, this is something he can appreciate!

Arcimboldo is not as appreciative of this attention to his creative inventions as he used to be. He has begun to feel like Petrus Gonzalez, a famous but unfortunate man known as 'the wolf boy of the Canary Islands'. Doctor Hagecius has explained that Gonzalez suffers from a condition known as *hypertrichosis universalis*; that is, the poor man has thick hair like a dog over his entire body including his face. Gonzalez was 'gifted' by Spain to the King of France, and since then has been traded back and forth among European Courts as a remarkable curiosity; dressed according to the fancy of his 'owner' and paraded at entertainments, often subject to the cruelest and most unthinking comments by his 'admirers'. Gonzalez has been allowed to marry, and regrettably, his children exhibit the same hirsute condition as their father.

Arcimboldo is spared having to further entertain the Emperor's guests by the arrival of dessert. This culinary masterpiece created by Imperial Chef Paulus now draws the guest's gasps of surprise and exclamations of compliment. The large tray the Master of Servers has set down in the middle of the room has two sugar trees several feet high. The trunk, boughs, and twigs are made of gingerbread. The leaves and perching birds are made of colorful spun sugar. In addition, the gingerbread structures cascade with Italian sweetmeats of all kinds.

With a handful of candied chestnuts, Arcimboldo returns to his place at the end of the right hand table, but his seat has been taken by Anna of Hradec, who speaks with Klara Zerotin and another woman he does not know. Arcimboldo motions for her to stay seated and finds a chair on the other side of Herr Fugger, who seems to have an entire aviary on his plate. The German says apologetically to Arcimboldo, "gingerbread! I can never get enough of it!" Arcimboldo listens to the women gossip about beauty products.

"Just feel my face! Go on. You see? I use this softener every night. I will tell you how to make it. Half an ounce of deer marrow, and another half of heron fat;

one ounce of bitter almond oil and two ounces of poppy oil; as much ground sheep skull as would fit into an egg, and the same amount of kid tallow; and as much turpentine as would fit into a walnut shell. I put all these things into a glass vessel, and put this into a pot of boiling water, be very careful not to get any water into your potion. When it has all melted, wash it well in rose water, and you may store it in a sealed container. It will last a month! You simply *must* try it!"

"You must write that down for me. Do you write, dear? Splendid! Now I will tell you what *I* use. White beans and shelled black chick peas, corn cockles and white radish seeds..."

Sitting among the French and Spanish guests, because of his Spanish wife, High Steward Dietrichstein has drunk himself into a stupor. His head rests on the table pillowed by his arms. Ambassador San Clemente appears to be stoically tolerating a scolding by the perpetually angry Bernardino de Mendoza. Arcimboldo notices that the Hungarian Count Cseszneky is as calm and abstemious as ever. He rarely touches his wine glass and then sips sparingly. His pale face and quiet behavior stand out amidst the florid complexions and loud voices of the men around him. Arcimboldo would think this man an artist; how strange to be told he is a dangerous mercenary.

Arcimboldo is being summoned by the Emperor. Rudolf says to him congenially, "Arcimboldus, We would have you sing the madrigal written by your Milanese friend, Comanini. The Marchioness is charmed by your paintings, and she would hear the song he has written about you."

The Princess chimes in, "oh, do, sir! You have so many talents it is hard to keep track!"

Arcimboldo bows in confusion. Not this too! But can he refuse? Trying not to sigh with impatience he says, "but... I'm afraid I am not in voice this evening. You will not enjoy it."

"Nonsense," the Emperor says peremptorily, "it is brief. We do not expect you to be *La Peperara*, entertain us with the song."

There is nothing else to be done about it, he must comply. He quickly goes to the orchestra and borrows a twelve string lute. He returns, sits on the edge of the table near the Marchioness, and begins to tune the instrument.

The Marquis says, "that's out of tune, are you sure you can play?"

Patiently, Arcimboldo explains, "it is *scordatura* style, Marquis. It makes it easier for me to play and sing to."

"What is scoredturda?"

Patronizingly, Ferdinando de Medici tells the Marquis, "*Scordatura*, Marquis, the style is *modern...* and *Italian*. It's probable that you have not learned of it yet where you live. It is *intentionally* mistuned, for the effect. Go on Arcimboldus, let us hear Comanini's madrigal!"

Arcimboldo explains to the French guests, "my dear friend, the poet, Gregorio Comanini, has written this poem about my painting of Spring, which may also be called Flora, the goddess of springtime and flowers. He has made a madrigal of it... the song is not meant to be profound, but I hope you will enjoy it."

He clears his throat; he is an agile lute player, when his fingers aren't stiff. His voice lacks the flexibility and depth it once had. In a light and almost fragile voice he sings:

"Am I Flora, or am I flowers?
If I be flowers, how then can Flora
Have a smiling face? And if I be Flora,

How can Flora be only flowers?
Ah! I am not flowers, nor am I Flora,
Yet Flora I am, and flowers.
A thousand flowers, a single Flora,
Living flowers, a living Flora.
But if flowers make Flora, and Flora flowers,
Do you know how the flowers into Flora
The wise painter changed, and Flora into flowers?"

There is applause and laughter and congratulations, with certain predictable exceptions. Arcimboldo bows and smiles; he returns to his table, he must drink some wine and water to sooth his strained throat. He is thinking: yes, whatever the outcome tonight, he will return to Milan as soon as he is able. He has grown too old for these games.

Atlas enters the room and quickly moves to the Emperor. The Ethiopian's hand goes to the table upon which he makes several signs and gestures. Rudolf nods and rises from his seat; he glances significantly at Arcimboldo. It is finally time to begin the play. As Atlas quietly leaves the room, Arcimboldo notices that the Hungarian has finally come to life. He looks at Atlas with incredible hostility. Is it the color of the Ethiopian's skin? Does the Hungarian imagine him to be a Turk? No doubt he has seen thousands of them... and killed many of those. Cseszneky looks at Atlas as one lion would look at another over a piece of fresh meat. Arcimboldo is glad Atlas does not notice. Truly, this man is dangerous indeed!

While the rest of the guests are coming to the realization that the Emperor has concluded his meal, Arcimboldo quickly exits the room. He sees the Master of Servers has set up chairs for all the Emperor's guests facing the stage. Good. Going behind the curtain, Arcimboldo calls to the Master of the Play, "it is time. Be ready."

He informs the Master of Music that the Emperor will shortly lead his guests out of the banquet hall for the night's last entertainment, the Epiphany play. *La Peperara* is ready. The orchestra is ready. Arcimboldo asks for one final ritornello to be played while the guests are being seated. At this point, the Italian feels it will be prudent to step outside for a moment. He joins Count Rozmberk in the garden.

As the men stand shivering side by side, urinating in the snow, Arcimboldo says, "what a day! I thought I had this day carefully *planned*, but from beginning to end it's been full of unexpected events! It's like a rosary!"

"A rosary? How do you mean?"

"One thing after another!"

The Count laughs and readjusts his clothing. He waits for Arcimboldo to finish.

"Vilem, this is none of my business, but I am concerned about leaving your brother alone with those Frenchmen…"

"You are right, but don't worry, I've just had my servants escort Peter back to our Palace. He's so drunk he could not even argue." The Count sighs with disappointment.

"That's well done, My Lord. I have not told you, but that Ambassador Mendoza is with the Holy League… he *is* the Holy League in France, he's Philip's paymaster and watchdog; and he's immeasurably hostile to all of us who do not fit his image of perfect Catholics."

"I know this, Baron Schwartzenau informed me; that's why I wanted Peter Vok away from all of them as quickly as possible."

"Captain Morhof caught two more of the French spies, including Mordente, trying to climb up to the first floor of the Sumer Palace."

"No! Mordente?"

"Yes. The good Captain has sent the miscreant to the Emperor's prison. We'll leave him there for a while to contemplate his sins."

"Ha!"

"What a time for all this to happen! All we needed was one more day... one more night!"

"Things that are difficult are often the most rewarding."

"Then our rewards are close at hand. We will begin the play momentarily. You will go upstairs with the Emperor?"

"I will, yes. You'll be last, I assume."

"It must be so. Do this for me, tell Hans to start the wheels moving. Make sure everyone is out of the way. Do you mind doing this for me?"

"I will do it, never fear. Well then, I'm freezing out here, I'll leave you to it."

"Yes. I should just be another moment. I thank you, My Lord."

When Arcimboldo reenters the Summer palace he sees Rudolf stands in front of the stage looking around expectantly, looking for him no doubt. The Emperor is flushed and looks very nervous. Arcimboldo bows to him and says, "Your Imperial Majesty, shall I begin the play?"

"By all means."

Arcimboldo speaks much more loudly than necessary, wanting to be heard by as many as possible, "come backstage, Sire, I will help you into your costume."

Once the two men are backstage, they see Doctor Hagecius, Baron Schwartzenau, and Count Rozmberk are already there waiting. The Emperor goes up to Valentin Soucek. He looks the man up and down and says, "Hmm. Mm hmm." To Arcimboldo he says, "do not be long." Escorted by the Baron, the Doctor, and the Count, the Emperor climbs the stairs toward his destiny.

The Master of Entertainment speaks to the Master of the Play, "I will remind you, when the play is over you will keep all your people here, out of sight, until all the guests have left. When you leave, take Valentin with you, but first, take that damned armor off of him. Yes? One thing more, I have forgotten to ask Marco, so do this for me please: the High Steward has fallen asleep at table, again, if he is still asleep at the end of the play and Madame Dietrichstein has left with everyone else, wake him please. I'm much obliged to you... and the High Steward will be as well. Now, you know how this works, when I say, 'let the play begin', you raise the curtain. At that point it's up to you. Good luck!"

Arcimboldo walks through the curtain and stands in front of the stage. He raises his hands and the room hushes, all eyes are on him expectantly.

"Welcome honored guests! Tonight, we are especially gratified to have the Emperor himself playing the role of one of the Three Magi. Our pantomime is in five parts. The first part will be the Journey of the Magi, the wise kings follow the Star that leads them toward Bethlehem. The second part will be their Meeting with Herod, where they tell him that a King of the Jews has been born. The third part will be the Dream of the Magi, where it is vouchsafed that this is the long awaited birth of the Messiah. The fourth part will be the Procession of the Magi, the kings approach the

Nativity scene. Our final part will be the Adoration of the Magi, where they present the King of the World with the gifts of frankincense, myrrh, and gold." Arcimboldo extends his arms, palms upwards, toward the audience, as thought he presents *them* with these valuable gifts. Then, he gracefully sweeps his right arm toward the orchestra on his right. "Signorina Preverara will sing The Song of the Sybil to accompany our Epiphany reenactment. Honored guests, let us go back to that cold January night in Judea, one-thousand five-hundred eighty-seven years ago. In the name of the Holy Roman Empire, His Majesty wishes you all a joyous Epiphany! Let the play begin!"

There is applause as the curtain rises to reveal a painted background of dusty sand dunes and camels; the Three Kings sit around a fire. Three loud and penetrating strikes on the triangle brings the room to silence, and then the orchestra begins the Song of the Sybil.

As he backs away, Arcimboldo scans the room one final time; he seeks the Marchioness... one final look. He regrets not being able to say farewell to her in any way more tangible than this last look. He ducks around the curtain and heads up the stairs.

Arcimboldo studies the grotesque face around the door as he waits for it to be opened. If that enormous mouth could talk, what secrets it could tell about what takes place inside! Georg Erasmus Schwartzenau opens the door and Arcimboldo enters; as he expects, the first thing he sees is Leonardo's St. John-Bacchus several feet from the door, staring directly into his eyes. Bacchus points over his shoulder to the glittering Cosmos behind him, truly a cave of wonders! Arcimboldo walks carefully toward the group gathered near the alchemists' oven. The closer he gets the worse the smell becomes. Kelly is busily at work around the oven, the *athanor*. "Georg, would you ask Hans to burn incense? Thank you."

Arcimboldo notices Atlas standing by a rack of objects from the nethermost regions of the World. The Ethiopian holds an ivory carving of an African chief's head and strokes it gently. The grave and noble ivory figure wears a helmet in the shape of a bird's head with a beak that arcs down over his forehead, and around the chief's neck is a necklace of large, pointed animal teeth. The ivory is skillfully carved with broad nose, deep set eyes, high cheek bones, large and resolute lips; Atlas' face is as noble and ageless as the exquisite ivory he holds. Arcimboldo knows this man to be harder than an anvil – made so by his tribulations, he knows him to be impervious to the hammering of fate and circumstance. Yet he sees there is moisture in the Ethiopian's eyes and tears on his cheeks as he studies the object he holds. When Atlas looks up and sees Arcimboldo watching him, he looks away, turns his back, and hastily replaces the ivory head.

Arcimboldo pauses a moment to let one of the wheels sweep by him before he walks forward. He watches dozens of illustrations of Alpine plants and insects rotate closer and closer, and then pass by with a soft whoosh, his face is fanned by the breeze, and on the reverse side of the wheel, painstakingly displayed, are animals of the African and Arabian deserts; he sees an illustration he painted himself, a white leopard leaps upon the back of a wild eyed Arabian stallion while gazelles and oryx scatter in terror.

Conversation among the waiting participants is dominated by the Nolan and John Dee, it seems as though they have not paused in their disputation for a moment during all the time Arcimboldo has been away. This time, their learned debate is about Bruno's most controversial and heretical theory, something he calls Cosmic pluralism. "But your mathematics matter not, Doctor, I don't care if *one* is prime or not, if *two* is prime or not, if *three* is prime or not... all I care about is that there are more Stars in the Heavens than primes in the earth." With logic led forward by Copernican discoveries of a heliocentric Universe, Bruno claims that there *must* be an infinite number of Suns; each Star in the night sky must be a Sun orbited by Worlds such as the Earth, and those Worlds inhabited by multitudes of God's creations. Just as the Nature of the Creator knows no limits, so the Macrocosm has none, and stretches away into infinity and eternity.

When Bruno sees Arcimboldo, he breaks off, "now we are all here. We may begin. Magister Kelly, are you ready?"
"The seventh stage, cibation, is complete. The *aqua fortis* is ready." Kelly points to a metal pot known as an aludel, it sits over the fire. In the pot, a rod of copper, encrusted with hair-like silver crystals emerges from a steaming milky-yellow liquid. This liquid is nitric acid, *aqua fortis*, and is the source of the noxious odor in the room. Kelly's usually dull expression has now transformed into the most lively look of intelligence and mindfulness. "We must have the gold to begin the digestion, ceration, and dulcification."
"Arcimboldus, do you have the gold?"
"I understood the Emperor was bringing the gold... where is he?"
"He's costuming himself as Melchior. Ah, here he is!"

Rudolf now approaches with a bearing of regal pride that exceeds anything Arcimboldo has seen before, although he has watched the Emperor receive many crowns and royal titles, beginning at the age of twenty-two, with his coronation at Regensburg as King of the Romans, and culminating just two years ago in Vienna, with his investiture into the Order of the Golden Fleece. Flanked by Baron Schwartzenau and Count Rozmberk, the Emperor nobly strides forward, head high, eyes fixed on some distant glory, hands holding scepter and orb. Over his Imperial Habsburg armor, he wears a purple cloak fastened at the throat with a delicate chain of rubies and gold. On his head he wears the crown of Melchior, the third Wise Man, the middle-aged King of Europe. Giordano Bruno beckons the Emperor forward to stand in his place of preeminence, in front of the alchemist's oven, and opposite Edward Kelly, who manipulates the tools of transformation. Bruno, as Balthasar, King of Africa, stands to Rudolf's left; and he summons John Dee, as Caspar, King of Asia, to come stand to the Emperor's right. The alchemist and Three Magi are now in place within the pentagram.

Bruno calls to the noblemen, "Count, you stand over there, and Baron, you there." They take their places at the two points of the pentagram behind Kelly, facing the three kings. "Arcimboldus, you stand back there, and where is your companion? Bartolomeus, you stand there." The two artists take their places at the points of the pentagram behind Rudolf. "Katharina Strada, where are you, come forward."

Katharina and Doctor Hagecius come forward from a distance. The woman would approach the Emperor, but Hagecius restrains her, he points to the remaining point of the pentagram, directly in back of Kelly and facing Rudolf. This is to be her place, and the Doctor shows her exactly where to stand; he is there to monitor the well being of the Emperor, and now, his mistress and unborn child as well. Hagecius takes a large handkerchief out of his robe and hands it to

Katharina, motioning to her to put it over her mouth and nose and to breathe through it, then he steps back, outside the circle of transmutation, to watch the proceedings. Bruno looks to Arcimboldo and snaps his fingers. Arcimboldo, in turn, calls to Hans Mont. "Hans, bring us the tapers, then you must watch the treadmill, keep it slow and steady."

Hans Mont brings five tall wax tapers, such as those used for Church processions. He lights them and delivers one to each of those standing at a point of the pentagram. Georg Erasmus Schwartzenau stands not far behind his father, agoggle with awe and expectation. Arcimboldo sees Atlas standing far off, outside the rotating wheels of art, a look of great uncertainty and fear on his face.

Bruno says to Kelly, "Magister, begin the ritual."

"Before I do, we must settle the gold to a process of inbibation and inceration. Give it to me."

Rudolf hands the Imperial orb and scepter to John Dee. He reaches around his neck and pulls a massy gold chain out from under his armor. It is the badge and chain awarded to him in solemn ceremony, the highest rank of knighthood in Europe, certification of his membership in the Order of the Golden Fleece. He passes this to Bruno who passes it on to Edward Kelly. Approvingly, Bruno says, "a creative and auspicious choice, Your Majesty."

Unimpressed, Kelly asks, "is this all?"

"What? You need more?"

"More would be better."

Rudolf motions to Count Rozmberk, who, reluctantly, and with a pained expression on his face, removes his own badge and chain of the Order of Golden Fleece from around his neck and passes it to Kelly.

Kelly sets all this gold into an alembic, which he places onto a pan of hot sand; this in turn gets set onto the fire. The alchemist increases the heat by opening two of the metal doors in the athanor. Carefully he pours enough *aqua fortis* over the gold to cover it. A slight hiss can be heard coming from the alembic. He says, "now I am ready to begin."

The Order of the Golden Fleece is the most prestigious order of chivalry known. Membership is exclusively Catholic, and limited to fifty individuals. It was initiated in 1430 by Philip III, Duke of Burgundy, and the current master of the order, known as the King of Arms, is Rudolf's uncle, Ferdinand of Tyrol. In 1585, in the course of two days of grand and effusive ceremonies, Rudolf, his brother Ernst, Archduke Charles of Styria, Vilem Rozmberk, and Linhart von Harrach were invested as Knights of the Order, and solemnly presented with gold chains of membership.

The badge itself is in the form of a golden sheepskin, and it represents that Golden Fleece stolen from the kingdom of Colchis by the Greek hero Jason and his Argonauts. It hangs from a chain, or collar, made of flattened links of gold in the shape of a B, signifying the kingdom of Burgundy. Engraved on the front of the central link is the motto *'Pretium Laborum Non Vile'*, (No Mean Reward for Labors), and on the back, Philip's motto, *'Non Aliud'* (I will have no other).

The chains and badges belonging to Rudolf and Rozmberk are now softening and liquefying in *aqua fortis* as Edward Kelly searches among his books and manuscripts for the proper words to begin the alchemical experiment. He finds what he is looking for and raises his head to be sure he has the attention of all around him; then, with his finger on the page, and his dark eyes searching the faces of those staring back at him, he says, "many books have been written on the art of alchemy, which, by the multiplicity of their allegories, riddles, and parables, bewilder and confound all earnest students. The cause of this confusion is the vast number and variety of names and methods, which all signify and set forth one and the same thing, the conversion of elements, and how through the predominance of one element the substance of metals is generated. For this reason I have resolved to loosen and untie all the difficult knots of the ancient Sages. Your Majesty, I will show you the affinity and homogeneity of metals, procreated in the bowels of the earth, their sympathies and antipathies according to the purity and impurity of Sulfur and Mercury, and that as metals consist of Sulfur and Mercury they can furnish us with the Prima Materia, the coalescence of chaos."

After this impressive and solemn preamble, Kelly returns his attention to the manuscript before him; he licks his lips and reads from where his finger lies. *"This alchemical art is given by Divine inspiration, and as a secret revealed from above. We implore God's help for every part of our work, the small as well as the great, for He alone has the power to give or withhold this knowledge from whomsoever He will. No one taketh this honor to himself, but God alone can enlighten the eyes and lift the cloud of Natural mysteries, so that albeit you cannot understand the simplest things without Him, yet you will apprehend the most difficult arcana if He give you light."*

Kelly pauses. He shifts to another manuscript, checks the gold liquefying in the *aqua fortis*, clears his throat, and continues. "All sages agree that the knowledge of this art of *chymia* was first imparted to Adam by the Holy Spirit, and passed from him to the Thrice-great Hermes, Hermes Trismegistus, preeminent magician of Egypt, who has passed down these things in his book, the Hermetica. And so it is written, *'whoever would imitate Nature in any particular operation must first be sure that he has the same matter, and, secondly, that this particular substance is acted on in a way similar to Nature. For Nature rejoices in natural method, and like purifies like'*. We will use Nature's own methods to effect our transformations, and convert the elements... for in this work Art assists Nature and Nature assists Art."

The alchemist puts the manuscripts aside and lifts a large, dusty and crumbling tome, sets it in front of him and searches within it. The large room is silent except for: the occasional coughing of those irritated by the powerful smell and smoke coming from the alchemists' athenor; the subtle rumbling and whooshing of the rotating wheels of art; the squeaking and grinding of the treadmill; and the angelic music of the Song of the Sibyl, which floats up the chimney but sounds like it drifts down from heaven itself.

"You shall understand the power of Mercury by these words of the Persian, Avicenna, who writes, *'Quicksilver is cold and humid, and of it, or with it, God has created all metals. It is aerial, and becomes volatile by the action of fire, but when it has withstood the fire a little time, it accomplishes great marvels, and is itself a living Spirit of unexampled potency. It enters and penetrates all bodies, passes through them, and is their ferment. It is then the White and the Red Elixir, and is an everlasting water, the water of life. It is the wanton serpent that conceives of its own seed, and brings forth on the same day. With its poison it destroys all things. It is volatile, but the wise make it to abide the fire, and then it transmutes as it has been transmuted, and tinges as it has been tinged, and coagulates as it has been coagulated. Therefore is the generation of Quicksilver to be preferred before all minerals; it is found in all ores, and has its sign within all. Quicksilver is that which saves metals from combustion and renders them fusible. It is the White Tincture which enters into the most intimate union with metals, because of its own nature, mingles with them indissolubly in all their smallest parts, and being homogenous naturally adheres to them.'* My Lords, through many hours of great labor we have created the Red and White Tinctures." Kelly slowly and carefully bends and lifts two long necked glass vessels known as a 'bolt's heads'. There is a small amount of red and white liquids in the vessels. He cautiously sets the bolt's heads on the edge of the brick oven. Taking a glass rod, he pokes the impure, liquefying gold, and shifts the pan to the center of the athanor's flame. The alchemist pauses to sip from a small cup before continuing.

He consults another book, "Albertus Magnus and Roger Bacon speak of the quintessence of aether, and agree on this, there are four elements: air, water, fire, and earth, with their four qualities, dry, moist, hot, and cold. Two are active, air and fire, and two are passive, water and earth. Two are light, and two heavy. Contradictory qualities are united only by means of a third. Hot and dry are not contradictory, and therefore form the element of air, cold and dry are not contradictory and become earth... nor are cold and moist, which constitute water. But hot and cold are united only by a medium, such as dry, as otherwise they would destroy each other. Moist and dry, on the other hand, are united and separated by constriction and humectation, simple generation and natural transmutation by the scientific operation of the elements. For those elements which conquer cold generate that which is hot..."

Arcimboldo's mind wanders, and his attention turns to his four paintings, the Elements, which stand within the pentagram at the four cardinal points of the compass. Of all the work he has done, Earth and Water are his favorites. The artist relives, within his Memory Palace, the creative labors that went into these splendid paintings. He remembers how many months it took to decide which animals of the land and sea he would use, and how long it took to find sources to paint from, how difficult it was to finish before the carcasses became too rotted to use. With a smile, he remembers how long his studio smelled like an abattoir, and how people would avoid passing anywhere near his rooms because of the horrible smell of corruption. Discovering the intimate details in the appearances of these animals was a supremely interesting and rewarding experience, and the results are beautiful as well as philosophically significant.

He looks at the most difficult composite head he ever attempted, the Element of Fire, a head made from objects associated with fire. It is composed of fire making tools, candles, lamps, burning embers, chunks of sulfur, slow match, firearms, a cannon, and of course, flame itself, forming a head of magnificently wild orange hair.

Looking beyond the painting of Fire, Arcimboldo sees Doctor Hagecius approach Katharina Strada, holding a cloth that is apparently soaking wet. The Doctor motions for her to put this over her face and breathe through it. Unfortunately, the harsh smell in the room is made worse by the fact that all the windows and doors have been blocked. The alchemist makes things even worse by choosing to put a pinch of asafetida on the fire... the stands of incense Arcimboldo prepared in advance are unable to sweeten the odors of alchemy. He hopes these smells are not filtering down the chimney from which The Song of the Sibyl rises.

The Song of the Sibyl that *La Peperara* sings is the newest Spanish version. There are older versions in Latin and Provencal, but Rudolf (and Arcimboldo) prefer the beauty of the Catalan words and accompaniment. The Song of the Sibyl alternates solemn, sometimes martial, orchestral passages with acapella song, sung by the talented Mantuan singer with a mysterious and emotional intensity. The words are by Anselm Turmeda, who translated into Catalan the *Judicii Signum*, the Book of the Final Judgment; which is based on St. Augustine's City of God. The haunting words Arcimboldo hears *La Peperara* sing are:

> *On the Day of Judgment, he will be spared who has done service.*
>
> *Jesus Christ, King of the Universe, man and true eternal God, from Heaven will come to judge, and to everyone will give what is fair.*
>
> *Great fire from the heaven will come down; seas, fountains and rivers, all will burn. Fish will scream loudly and in horror, losing their natural delights.*
>
> *Before the Judgment the Antichrist will come and will give suffering to everyone, and will make himself be served like God, and who does not obey he will make die.*
>
> *His reign will be very short; in these times under his power will die martyrs, all at once, like those two saints, Elijah and Enoch.*
>
> *The Sun will lose its light, showing itself dark and veiled, the Moon will give no light and the whole world will be sorrow.*

*To the evil ones God will say very sourly: go, damned, into the torment! Go into the eternal fire with your prince of Hell!*

*To the good he will say: my children, come! Lucky ones, you possess the kingdom I have kept for you ever since the World was created!*

*Oh humble Virgin! May you who have given birth to Child Jesus pray to your son so He will want to keep us from Hell!*

Arcimboldo is roused from his reverie. He notices the men around the alchemist's fire are moving back and away, speaking calmly among themselves. Kelly is pulling off his leather gloves and wiping perspiration from his brow. He says, "now, we must wait to allow the gold to cool. You will have some time, gentlemen, My Lords... while I bathe and clean the gold in sweet oil. Arcimboldus, would you have your man bring me the bucket of snow... and another cup of wine?"

Arcimboldo brings a cup of wine for Edward Kelly as well as one for the Emperor, who sits with Katharina, and stares into space with a mystical, unreadable look on his face. He absentmindedly accepts the cup Arcimboldo offers him, without a word of thanks; he holds it in his hand and does not drink. The Baron and Count stand nearby and include Rudolf in their conversation, but the Emperor does not comment, his thoughts are far away.

Katharina stands and says to Arcimboldo, "My Lord, Uncle Giuseppe, I have not told you how beautiful this room is. It's like being in a dream. I wish my grandfather were here to see it. He would be so proud of you."

At the thought of Jacopo Strada being here, seeing his granddaughter in such a situation, Arcimboldo is speechless, unable to reply immediately to this kindly intentioned compliment. He pats her cheek and tries to smile politely. Fortunately, he is interrupted as Doctor John Dee joins the group. "My Lords, I envy your possession of the *Sefer Yetzira*, if only I had the means to buy it from you!"

"What Doctor, more books! You have six cases as it is. How can you manage the difficulty of traveling as you do with so many books?"

"My good Count, who can have enough books? Before I left England I had the largest library in the land. I could not bear to leave some behind, and those I have brought with me are too few, and as precious to me as my family. I travel with five-hundred books."

"Five-hundred! Good Lord!"

"These few are indispensible to me... actually, I lie, I no longer have five-hundred, alas, I have had to sell many to finance our travels. In that way, they have come in very handy. Better than gold." A rare expression which may simulate a smile comes across the Doctor's face. "After all, what highwayman wishes to carry away a crate of heavy books, eh?"

Arcimboldo asks him, "would you care for a cup of wine?" And when Dee shakes his head no, "did you have a chance to eat something earlier, good Doctor?"

"No, sir. I only eat one meal a day on Saturdays."

"Why so?"

"When my son, Rowland, was a year and a half old, in 1584, he woke up one morning with the sweat, he was extremely sick by noon, and by thirteen on the clock was ready to give up the ghost. He lay as if dead, his eyes set and sunk in his head. I made a vow that if the Lord could foresee him to be his true servant, and would grant him life, and confirm his health against this danger, I would, during the rest of my life, eat but one meal on Saturdays."

"And you keep your bargain? Well done, Doctor, well done. Water perhaps?"

"I would be greatly appreciative, sir."

Arcimboldo intends to speak with Doctor Hagecius about the well being of Katharina Strada, but as he returns with a cup of water for Doctor Dee, the alchemist recalls them to their places; he is ready to progress.

Caspar, Balthasar, and Melchior are again in place before the alchemist's fire, and there are three alembics resting in a pan of sand being heated by the blaze. Kelly has opened another volume of alchemical lore. The man seems to have grown physically larger as well as more assertive; his voice is one of authority, confidence, and wisdom. "Gold and silver have a common first matter in Mercury. Rosinus says, *'from Mercury, the living water, we obtain earth, a homogenous dead body composed of two natures, that of the Sun and that of the Moon. I, the Sun, am hot and dry, and thou, the Moon, art cold and moist, when we are wedded together in a closed chamber, I will gently steal away they Soul'*. Astratus says, *'whoever would attain the Truth, let him take the humor of the Sun and the Spirit of the Moon'*. The Turba Philosophorum says, *'in my sister, the Moon, grows your wisdom, and not in any other of my servants, says the Lord Sun. I am like seed sown in good and pure soil, which sprouts and grows and multiplies. I, the Sun, give to thee, the Moon, my beauty, the light of the Sun. And the Moon says to the Sun, thou hast need of me as the cock has need of the hen, and I need thou operation, which is perfect in morals, the father of lights, a great and mighty Lord, hot and dry, and I am the waxing Moon, cold and moist, but*

*I receive thy nature by our union.'* So now we reach the grand Arcanum. Gold and silver must be in the Tincture, and also the ferment of the Spirit. This is our goal, the twelfth and final stage of alchemy, called 'projection'. " Kelly gradually pours a red liquid into the vessel that contains the gold that once graced the necks of the Emperor and Count Rozmberk, and sets it over the fire once again.

Arcimboldo is distracted from Kelly's alchemy by a tug on his arm. Hans Mont, with a worried look on his face, coughs out, "My Lord, the fireplace is smoking."

"What? Can you tell why? Does it come from below?"

"It appears to come from *above*, I believe it is blocked, My Lord."

Arcimboldo cannot see the western fireplace from where he stands. He takes several steps in that direction. He is stopped by a booming voice, "stay where you are! Do not leave the pentagram, for the love of God!" Kelly has noticed him, he would have assumed the man to be far too busy.

Arcimboldo calls out, "I will return immediately, the fireplace is smoking."

"I say stay where you are! Do not interrupt this process! Go back to your place, Arcimboldus!" Imperiously, Kelly points at the spot where Arcimboldo is supposed to be standing.

Now, Rudolf turns and looks at Arcimboldo with great annoyance on his face, and the Italian reluctantly returns. He says to Mont, "if it does not stop, you must put out the fire. Do you understand?"

"I do. I will." Mont trots off into the glittering splendor of the Cosmos, nimbly dodging candelabra, tripods, stands, and the slowly rotating wheels.

With a stern look, Kelly continues. "The gold has been bathed in the Tincture. What will happen next may be understood by the parable of Bernard, who says, *'the Sun, on entering the bath, first of all puts off his golden robe. For what the eagle is among birds, the lion among beasts, the salmon among fishes, the Sun among planets, such is gold to other metals. For gold is made out of the substance of the most subtle living Mercury, and out of pure red, fixed, self-cleansed Sulfur, which tinges and contains in itself the soul which is called the form of gold, and by some sages, the Ferment of Philosophers. This soul of gold, with its heat digests and tinges its substance, and imparts to it its form, so that through its mediation the day begins to dawn'*. To corrupt the gold, to dissolve and volatize it while still preserving its form is our great object, as it is also our grand labor. When the putrefaction of the gold is sufficient we will notice a black color and a fetid smell. Your Majesty, it is time for you to put on apron and gloves."

Arcimboldo thinks, how much more fetid can it possibly get? He looks up and to his dismay sees smoke obscuring the ceiling; the twinkling stars, represented by hundreds of painstakingly placed mirrors, are invisible. The tops of the wheels create eddies in the smoke as they rotate, these smoke clouds elegantly swirl, and give Arcimboldo the uneasy impression of a gathering storm – and a premonition of tragedy.

Kelly has taken up the black mirror, Doctor Dee's famous magic mirror, made of jet black obsidian brought back from the New World. The ship's captain that sold the stone to Dee told the Doctor that it had been taken from a temple of a people called Aztecs. The obsidian had been part of a sacrificial stone, where the Aztecs tear the hearts from their victims. This stone had been drenched in the blood of thousands of sacrifices to pagan gods; it possesses untold magical powers. Dee has had it polished and made into a mirror, a black mirror, wherein his skryer, Edward Kelly, speaks to the angel, Uriel, in the language of Adam. Now, Kelly raises a small bowl of burning herbs to his face and inhales deeply. He sets the bowl down and studies his reflection in the black mirror, and mutters in an unknown language to whatever he sees within.

The alchemist intones, "we have made the conjunction of metals, gold, mercury, and sulfur. Now, our second conjunction, that of body, soul, and spirit – and out of these three we must make one. For as the soul is the bond of the spirit, so the body must also join itself to the soul. The alchemist who will successfully transmutate matter must also transmutate himself. His upper soul must be resurrected in a manner parallel with that of Christ. He must descend deep into the inner mysteries of his soul, as Christ descended into Hell, and return with renewed energies in a resurrected form bearing the mysteries of the upper Trinity. This is true transmutation."

As Arcimboldo watches it seems that Kelly is growing larger, taller. He looks more closely, no, the alchemist is not growing taller, he is slowly rising up off the ground! Now his feet are almost at the level of the athenor. Arcimboldo holds his breath, rather, he forgets to breathe; the alchemist hangs in the air, his feet dangle six feet off the ground. Can this be? Arcimboldo closes his eyes and shakes his head, and then he looks again. Kelly stands at the athenor, continuing to mumble in his strange language, he is not six feet in the air.

But several seconds later, he begins to slowly rise again. Higher and higher. Arcimboldo gasps in fright; he takes a deep breath, and tightly closes his eyes for several seconds. He looks... and Kelly stands solidly on the ground. The Italian's heart is beating faster, and then still faster when, once again, he sees Kelly rise up into the air. When he is ten feet off the ground, Kelly begins to slowly rotate, at the same pace as the rotating wheels around him; now, Kelly has four arms and they twist and writhe like snakes; he holds fire in one hand, a conch shell in another, a snake and an hourglass in the other two. Madonna! What can this mean? Can no one else see this? Arcimboldo quickly glances to his right, at Bartolomeus Spranger. The Dutchman is watching, but without awe or panic.

Fearing what he will see, Arcimboldo returns his attention to the alchemist, who, of course, is in place on the ground, continuing to whisper into the black mirror. The artist stares, not daring to blink or breathe. Kelly remains attached to the earth. With every passing second, Arcimboldo's heart, lungs, and mind regain a small amount of composure. Perhaps this foul miasma has played tricks on his consciousness. He is still shaken, but distracted from his thoughts of Kelly when he hears his name called in a loud whisper.

Hans Mont returns to Arcimboldo's side, face and hands blackened with soot. "I have put out the fire, sir, but the fire in the room below continues to burn. The smoke is considerable, the donkey is becoming disturbed. What should I do?"

"Fan the animal to clear the air around him. Put out all the incense burners. Let me know if the smoke coming out of the fireplace becomes worse." In this moment, Arcimboldo has a vivid recollection of Bruno pitching Landino's parchment into that fireplace. He watched it fly up over the flu and disappear. By

Heavens, it has not burned; it's become stuck in the chimney, that is what blocks the exit of the smoke! The smoke will soon be noticed by the people in the room downstairs as their fireplace also backs up. Sancta Madonna, the Nolan himself has brought this disaster down on all their heads!

With the fire of genius in his eyes, the alchemist scans his audience, "there is *no* philosopher, alchemist, or Natural scientist who is able to transmutate their body, soul, and spirit in the required way. It is beyond the Nature and capability of common man." Kelly points to Rudolf and grandly claims, "but here, among us, is a man who is to other men what gold is among metals. He is pure, unique, chosen by God to serve His special and unknowable purposes. This man and only this man may bring our labors to a successful conclusion. Rudolf Habsburg, Emperor, philosopher, scientist, and alchemist, prepare your Mind and body. Rudolf Habsburg, you have created this Cosmos, you are King Melchior, you bring the gift of knowledge to Mankind. Find in yourself that unique power which will allow you to transcend the capabilities of Human Nature, you must become like God to be able to change the form and substance of matter itself."

There is much coughing in the room now, and everyone except for Rudolf and Kelly are worriedly looking up at the smoke being fanned by the great wheels. It is impossible to see the topmost illustrations on them; the creatures of the air have become concealed by smoke. Arcimboldo can hear that the music coming from below has ceased. The Song of the Sibyl has been replaced by indistinct shouts of alarm, among which can be distinctly heard the word 'fire'. Doctor Hagecius enters the pentagram, pointing upward, but is brusquely ordered back by Kelly. The alchemist pours the White Tincture into the vessel containing the gold, and it begins smoking and sputtering immediately. He uses metal tongs to slide the pan holding the alembic across the athanor so it is within reach of Rudolf. Kelly passes a metal hammer across to Bruno, who hands it to the Emperor.

The wheels have been slowing and moving irregularly, and now they halt with a jerk. Arcimboldo can hear several things falling to the ground. The ass begins a panicked braying, and can be heard kicking and struggling to escape the treadmill. Hagecius pulls Katharina Strada away from her place on the pentagram and away from the athanor, back into the recesses of the room.

Rudolf says urgently, "go on. Go on!"

Seemingly aware now that all is not well, Kelly nervously continues, "Mercury never dies, except with its brother and sister. When Mercury mortifies the matter of the Sun and the Moon, there remains a matter like ashes. Now, you may-"

He is interrupted by shouts outside the door to the room, followed by a pounding on the door. Rudolf is the only one not distracted, he commands, "continue!"

Kelly pauses, but Bruno and Dee urge him forward. Doctor Dee rasps, "keep going, Edward, don't stop. The projection must go forward."

Uncertainly, with one eye on the door behind Rudolf, Kelly goes on, "Xiphilinus and the rest of the philosophers agree in this... um... where is it? Here, *'as you can have no red color where the substance has not first been white, so the black cannot become gold unless it first be white. In like manner, the Rosary says that nothing can become gold that has not first been silver. He who knows how to convert gold into silver, also knows how to convert silver into gold. Gold, to become silver, must first be corrupted and made black. Heat, acting on moisture, causes blackening; then, acting on dryness, especially if it be continued carefully and unceasingly, there is developed a true whiteness'.* Break the alembic, Your Majesty."

Rudolf takes the hammer in hand, leans forward, and hits the glass vessel. It cracks but does not break. On the second try, Rudolf smashes the alembic; the hissing fluids and gelatinous metal gush out into the sand.

The pounding on the door has ceased. The smoke is not increasing; apparently they have extinguished the fire downstairs. However, the room is still full of an intensely noxious odor. Even Kelly is coughing now. He says, "you must say the words, the powerful spell of transmutation. You must project change onto the metal. Hold the pan over the fire, use the handles... Nolanus, help him."

Bruno helps the Emperor grasp the pan of sand and semi-liquefied, white hot metal by its short handles, and Rudolf holds it over the heat. Arcimboldo and Spranger have left their places at the points of the pentagram, and stand behind Rudolf, Bruno, and Dee, the Three Magi, watching.

Kelly consults the black mirror, and then drops it; he seems lost in amazement mingled with fear, with dismay he says something to Doctor Dee in English. Arcimboldo asks, "what did he tell you?"

"He says he can feel it, something is here."

Suddenly, the door to the room is struck by a splintering crash, followed by another, and another. There are shouts from outside of, "Emperor! Your Majesty! Let us in! Open the door!"

Rudolf shouts, "do not let them in! Atlas, keep them out!" The Ethiopian, Hans Mont, and Georg Erasmus begin to drag a large metal shelf in front of the door as the splintering crashes continue. Georg Erasmus shrieks, "they are breaking down the door!"

Now, Rudolf hysterically screams at Kelly, "go on! What are the words?"

"Eh? Um... the words... Hermes Trismegistus gives us the word of power, used by the Egyptians, the Basilideans, to call their God, Abraxas. Um... if you conjure him, do not look in his eyes; he is a demon with the body of a man, the head of a lion, and snakes as limbs. The mystic word derives from his name, Abraxas..." Kelly casts more asafetida onto the fire, crosses himself, and makes a sign with his fingers to ward off evil.

"The words! What are the words?"

"The mystical word to call Abraxas is..." and he whispers, "abracadabra." He is drowned out by the halberds pounding and splintering the door.

"What? What? Again, I couldn't hear you!"

"Abracadabra!" And with this Kelly turns and runs back into the shadows of the room.

Hans Mont calls to Spranger, "Bartolomeus, help us move these in front of the door, they're almost through!"

Rudolf mumbles over and over, "abracadabra," as he stares into the glowing hot pan of sand and metal. His eyes are starting from their sockets; his face is dripping with perspiration and beginning to turn purple. The horsehide gloves he wears are smoking with the heat. The Emperor's arms are trembling, and he is supported by Bruno and Dee at his elbows, although they draw their faces back as far as they can from the intense heat. Doctor Hagecius comes to the Emperor's side, he pushes Dee away. He says, "Your Majesty... Rudolfus... you must stop this. Put that down and come away."

With spittle and foam flying from his mouth, the Emperor bellows, "don't touch me! Get away, leave me! I will do this! I must do this! God help me. God! Help me!" The gloves he wears have caught fire and are burning on his hands. The Doctor does not leave his side, but does not protest again. He lifts a corner of his gown and swats at the flames on the Emperor's hands to put out the fire.

Forcing down his horror, Arcimboldo pleads, "Your Majesty, your hands! It's not worth it, they'll be through the door any second now! You must face them calmly. You must control yourself. Think of your dignity, think of your responsibilities to this kingdom. For God's sake, I beg you, drop that pan!"

Rudolf does not answer, but, sobbing, jaws trembling, turns to Arcimboldo with an inarticulate snarl. At that moment, the door flies off its hinges with a crash. They are through! It will be seconds before they are around the barriers that have been put in the way. Georg Erasmus draws his sword, Hans Mont draws a short poniard, Atlas grabs a five foot tall candelabra and wields it like a club, they stand in the path of the intruders. Rudolf collapses against the brick furnace and falls to the ground, unconscious; the pan of sand and metal falls to the ground. Hagecius and Arcimboldo struggle to pull off the burning gloves. Baron Schwartzenau and Count Rozmberk draw their swords and advance to protect their liege Lord. Dee stands paralyzed. Bruno is tearing off his costume as he runs away to hide in the furthest shadows of the room.

With shouts of, "to the Emperor, save the Emperor!" several Imperial Guards rush around the barrier and come face to face with Mont, Georg Erasmus, and Atlas, who also shout, "save the Emperor!" The soldiers stop short, stunned by what they see and uncertain as to what they should do next. One of them drops to his knees, clasps his hands together, and begins praying. Mendoza and Cseszneky push past them, followed by the French and Italian Dukes and Marshall Trautson, all have drawn their swords. Mendoza roars, "heretics! Holy Mother of Jesus! Heretics!"

The Hungarian Count slides past Mendoza. With his saber he swats the sword from the hand of Georg Erasmus, and with a return blow, slices the youth across the chest. In a single side step, as though he is dancing, and with lightning speed, he stabs Hans Mont in the face; the two young men reel away clutching their wounds. Like a greyhound he bounds toward the giant Ethiopian. Atlas extends the metal candelabra to keep him away. Now, with movements honed on the battlefield, the Hungarian ducks and spins; as his back is turned to Atlas, the hand not holding a sword appears with a wickedly curved, short blade, and seemingly using eyes in the back of his head, Cseszneky sweeps that blade around in a backhanded swipe, and neatly slices off Atlas' hand at the wrist. Before hand and candelabra can fall to the floor, Cseszneky completes his turn, rises onto the tips of his toes, and brings his sword down on the Ethiopian's forehead in a terrible blow, slicing down to the bottom jaw. Without a pause, continuing his movement, he kicks the staggering giant in the chest, sending him crashing backwards, dead before he hits the ground. He steps over Atlas' corpse and advances on the Baron and Count.

Count Rozmberk wisely throws his sword onto the ground, but the Baron, enraged, flings himself at the Hungarian who easily parries the Baron's first blow and brings his saber against Schwartzenau's neck. Rozmberk cries, "hold! Hold, for God's sake hold!"

Marshall Trautson echoes, "hold your hand! Don't touch him!"

In this pause, each man in the room finds that he is panting with terror and passion... except for Count Cseszneky, whose breath and expression are as calm as when he sat at supper. All the other men realize that this violent man is death itself, it is suicide to face him in combat.

With triumph in his voice, Mendoza says, "there is no need to kill them all now, these sorcerers will burn. You are all under arrest by the Holy Mother Church. Surrender yourselves now, and give up that arch heretic, Giordano Bruno!"

Arcimboldo, who stands and stares in disbelief, hears the sound of running footsteps behind him, and then a female grunt of exertion; a beautifully modeled glass statuette of a unicorn comes sailing past his shoulder, thrown at the Hungarian by Katharina Strada. Without turning to look, Cseszneky's sword flicks to the side and strikes the hurtling object, which shatters. The head and horn of the unicorn continue on course, or have been deflected by the sword, either way, the horn buries itself in the Hungarian's neck, stopping only when it drives in to the unicorn's head. Slowly, Count Cseszneky turns to look at Katharina, and (ghastly!) for the first time all evening he smiles. He raises a hand to his neck and pulls the glass free; in that moment a jet of blood spurts from his neck, powerful enough to knock over a painted canvas of Russian forest wolves attacking a stag, twelve feet away. The smile fades to a look of surprise and then disbelief, his mouth opens and blood pours forth, then the eyes dim, the knees buckle, and the warrior falls. He lies twitching on the ground next to Atlas.

"*Diablos heretica!*" Mendoza howls with outrage and leaps toward the girl, leading with the sharp point of his Spanish rapier. Arcimboldo does not think, he instinctively steps to the side and places himself between Mendoza's rapier and Katharina. The rapier stops at Arcimboldo's throat, the Italian can feel a trickle of blood passing down his chest. Mendoza hisses, "I prefer to burn you, Italian, stand aside and live a little longer."

"I can believe you would kill a girl, even a pregnant girl, but know this, Spaniard, she carries the Emperor's child. If you harm her even the King of Spain will not save you from the Emperor's wrath. You would be killing a *Habsburg*, Philip's nephew's child. Since you do not care for any life but your own, do this to save yourself." Arcimboldo stares at the rapier in front of his face. The damascened steel of the blade is a beautiful shade of blue, and the artist is astonished to find himself remembering the blue of the bird's wing in Durer's painting, in this, possibly the last moment of his life.

Mendoza's face contorts into an unaccustomed expression of confusion and uncertainty. "*Cobardes...*" He pauses, then the malignant fire rekindles in his eyes, then uncertainty returns. He sways back and lowers his sword, he spits out, "there will be time enough to see if this is true. You are all arrested by the Roman Inquisition for witchcraft, alchemy, and consorting with arch heretics."

A voice behind Mendoza speaks in perfect Spanish, "who is arrested?"

The Spanish Ambassador to France turns to face High Steward Dietrichstein, who has entered, followed by Captain Morhof and a score of Rudolf's Trabante Guards. Confidently, Mendoza answers, "these men and this woman have been practicing witchcraft and alchemy. They are heretics. Along with Nuncio Malaspina here, I arrest them in the name of the Pope. I will take them all to Rome."

Surveying the scene, the High Steward says, "you would arrest the Emperor in his own castle?" He motions to soldiers, "for God's sake help the Doctor with the Emperor." Facing Mendoza again, he says with speech slightly slurred with drink, but with more decisiveness and backbone than Arcimboldo thought him to possess, "you are, I believe, an Ambassador to the King of *France*, here as a guest, who are you to arrest anyone?"

Trautson exclaims, "you *will* not arrest the Emperor, by God!"

Mendoza's façade begins to crack as he realizes that in his anger he may have overplayed his hand, he stammers, "the *Nuncio* arrests them in the name of the Inquisition. I assist him in a righteous and Christian act."

Dietrichstein turns to an extremely pale and nervous Papal Nuncio. "Nuncio, do you take it upon yourself to arrest Bohemian noblemen, the Emperor's mistress, and artists of the Imperial Court? Am I to believe my ears, you intend to arrest the Holy Roman Emperor for witchcraft?" Malaspina suddenly sees the way this situation will play out. He has to live here in Prague, at this Court, among these people. He looks down, fidgets, and does not answer.

Mendoza protests, "all right then, not the Emperor... I have been hasty, that is not necessary. But that Englishman is a notorious spy and necromancer! That woman has killed the Hungarian Count! Giordano Bruno is wanted by the Roman Inquisition, he is here somewhere! What madness is this? Do your Christian duty!"

Dietrichstein is amazed and impressed, he looks at Katharina and then at the body of Count Cseszneky. With awe in his voice he asks, "by St. George, *she* killed the famous Count Cseszneky? No, you cannot be serious, Ambassador. But I do not see Giordano Bruno.

I see art, quite a bit of art, and an alchemists' oven. Prague is a very scientific place, as an outsider you lack the sophistication to realize this."

Mendoza glares at the High Steward and bites his tongue.

"But I do not see witches or witchcraft. I do see Baron Schwartzenau's son has been attacked and injured. I see the Emperor's favorite servant and personal bodyguard has been slain. I see a favored Court sculptor has been... will he live? That is good. Who has done *these* things? Can you tell me I am wrong, Ambassador, can you answer these questions?"

Quietly, the Nuncio, the French, and the Italian Dukes back out of the room.

Mendoza knows this will not turn out as he has foreseen. Smoldering with frustration, he mutely points to the body of the Hungarian.

The High Steward nods, "then I am glad he is dead, because when the Emperor recovers he will certainly expect that to be the case."

Hagecius says, "Lord High Steward, the Emperor will be fine, he is unconscious, he must be moved to his quarters. Katharina should go with him." Hagecius points to Mendoza, "that man almost killed her, if it had not been for Arcimboldus she would be dead too."

The High Steward nods again with concern on his face. He asks Baron Schwartzenau who, weeping, cradles his son, "how is young Georg Erasmus, Baron?"

"He will live. But he must see a Doctor."

Bartolomeus Spranger, who supports the head of the writhing Hans Mont, says, "Hans has had an eye put out, High Steward, he must see a Doctor as well, as soon as possible." Spranger looks at the Spanish Ambassador with extreme hatred.

Dietrichstein motions to soldiers to assist, and the Doctor, Spranger, and the Baron help to carry the wounded from the room. Katharina pauses before walking out, she squeezes Arcimboldo's arm, and, as she used to do when she was a child, stands on tiptoe and kisses him on the forehead. He smiles back at her and squeezes her hands. Trautson will escort her to the Emperor's bedside. Arcimboldo gingerly explores the puncture wound at his throat. He holds his handkerchief to it.

Mendoza also looks like he will leave the room, but the High Steward says, "not so fast, Ambassador. Perhaps an arrest *does* have to be made. Is this true, you threatened to kill the Emperor's mistress?" he points to Arcimboldo, "and this nobleman here as well?"

Looking shocked, Mendoza says, "now, wait..."

"You are not in Spain, you are not even in France. You have forgotten where you are. A grave mistake, sir. Arresting and attacking Habsburgs is a dangerous endeavor, I marvel at your audacity. Now, I will tell you this: if I arrest you, when the Emperor recovers and finds you have almost killed his unborn child... you will not live to see the sunset of that day."

Mendoza's face turns ashen. His hands begin to shake.

"Of course, when you return to Spain, the Emperor's uncle may have difficulty forgiving you as well, but you will have more luck there, so to be charitable and merciful – are you acquainted with those qualities, sir? As I say, to be charitable and merciful, I will allow you to leave. I suggest you leave this city before the Emperor hears the news."

Looking beaten and humiliated Mendoza makes for the doorway.

"More good advice, Ambassador, in the way of mercy and charity – it would be best if you left tonight, and change your clothes, sir. Someone has stirred the passions of the populace! A foreigner's life will not be worth a white groschen if he is spotted riding alone in the city. And a Spanish Catholic? Well, you best leave as quietly and as quickly as you are able. If you wait until daylight you will be in serious danger. Is this not good advice? Mark it well."

"I do not ride alone, the French escort..."

"I do not allow you to accompany them, sir. After your crimes, your reckless folly, you endanger any party you ride with. You will go alone, and tonight. Immediately, in fact."

"The Tercio will protect me, you cannot treat me like this!"

"The Tercio is confined to barracks. Their officers are arrested and sit in the Emperor's prison. But if you insist on joining them it will not be a difficult thing to arrange."

Too afraid to bluster with anger, the Spaniard stumbles from the room.

"Captain Morhof, see the man on his way. Brook no argument."

Arcimboldo bows to the High Steward. "Masterfully done, My Lord. You have saved the day."

"You see, Arcimboldus, I have had to enter this room tonight after all! St. Bernard, what an odor!" The High Steward wrinkles his nose and fans his face. "But I do not enjoy this. I see the building is not on fire after all? I'm glad of that. Tell me, what do you think the Emperor would have me do with all this art. By God there is a lot of it!"

"Guard the room, seal the door... we will see what happens tomorrow. And poor Atlas... see his body is properly treated."

"Did Katharina really...?"

"She did. Incredibly, she did. She avenged the Ethiopian."

"That would have been worth seeing, by the Cross! You must retell it in perfect detail at some later time, over *several* glasses of wine."

Count Rozmberk joins them and shakes the High Steward's hand. "Well played, Adam. You gave that man almost as much as he deserves. I trust you will look the other way as I take the Englishmen back to Trebon?"

"I cannot imagine why you chose this night for your occult adventures, Vilem, but please, clean up the nasty bits left over. Take them away as quickly as you can. And where is this Bruno fellow? Can you get rid of him as well?"

"I will. And tonight. I thank you, My Lord."

"And will someone please tell me what that noise is? Have you conjured up the devil himself?"

Arcimboldo points to the eastern wall, "there is an ass out there somewhere... have someone take him downstairs again, if you will, My Lord."

Wearily, with a tired sigh, the High Steward motions to soldiers to explore this strange situation. He yawns. "Arcimboldus, this is a story I am looking forward to hearing... several times, I think. But my bed and my wife await me. Now, do you have any other surprises for us? No? The air in here is very disagreeable... I will say goodnight then. Till tomorrow. Vilem, good night to you."

Old John Dee sits on the ground, overwhelmed by the night's conclusion. He calls, "Edward, oh, Edward. Where are you now? You must come, we are spared." Like mice from their holes, Bruno and Kelly come forward into the light. Dee says, "Edward, we will leave with the Count, gather our books and accessories."

Arcimboldo's servant, Silvius, has been peering, goggle eyed, around the trampled barriers. He approaches, as does Giordano Bruno. Bruno looks abashed; he is reluctant to meet his countryman's eyes. Arcimboldo removes the purse of three-hundred thalers and hands it to the Nolan. Bruno is open mouthed with surprise. Arcimboldo says to him, "this is from the Emperor in gratitude for your services. You will leave with Count Rozmberk, now. And Giordano, you *do* realize why the room filled with smoke?"

Bruno looks mystified, "what are you talking about?"

"The painting, the parchment, the one you so cavalierly threw into the fire... it clogged the chimney."

"Oh, so you're blaming it all on me, as usual, Giuseppe?"

"Well, did you or did you not do that?"

Bruno answers evasively, "you must be mistaken, I don't know what you're talking about." And he turns his back on Arcimboldo and follows the Count and the Englishmen out of the room.

Arcimboldo shakes his head sadly. As he watches the men walk out, he notices that sticking out of a large bulge in the back of Edward Kelly's pants are two sinuous golden arms, one holding an hourglass and the other holding a conch shell. Arcimboldo does nothing, says nothing. He is thinking about how quickly he can be ready to leave for Milan.

His servant stares up at him, "I am glad you are well, sir."

Arcimboldo pats Silvius on the head, "I thank you lad. I need to sleep now, I'm all out. Meet me early in the morning. I want you to help me pack."

"Pack, sir?"

"Yes, I am going on a long journey." And he follows the others out of the room.

Slowly, he descends the stairs. He wonders if he will be able to recall all of the day's events accurately to enter into his Memory Palace. He also wonders if he will be able to leave before the Emperor changes his mind. He is considering exactly what his most important possessions are when his name is called.

"Master Arcimboldus!"

"Yes, Silvius?"

The boy is excited, impassioned, he comes bounding down the stairs. "My Lord, you did it. After all, you did it!"

"Did what? What are you talking about, boy?"

"Sir, I found this on the floor just now, next to the alchemist's oven! Look, what can this be, sir, but gold! You made gold after all!"

Arcimboldo takes the warm and misshapen lump of yellow metal wrapped in a rag from the boy. He examines it and hefts it thoughtfully in his hand. To Silvius' astonishment he puts it back in the boy's hand and turns away. The Italian sighs, and continues down the stairs; dejectedly, sadly, over his shoulder he says, "yes, I see, gold. After all... it's just gold. Only... gold."

Printed by Amazon Italia Logistica S.r.l.
Torrazza Piemonte (TO), Italy